THE
SEVENTH
SLEEPER

Books by Rodman Philbrick

Slow Dancer
Brothers and Sinners

J.D. Hawkins Mystery Series
Shadow Kills
Ice for the Eskimo
Paint it Black
Walk On the Water

T.D. Stash Mystery Series
The Neon Flamingo
The Crystal Blue Persuasion
Tough Enough

THE SEVENTH SLEEPER

Rodman Philbrick

SPEAKING VOLUMES, LLC

NAPLES, FLORIDA

2012

The Seventh Sleeper

Copyright © 1991 by Rodman Philbrick

Originally published under the name William R. Dantz

ISBN 978-1-61232-855-3

To

Lynn Harnett

"I observe the physician with the same diligence
as he the disease."
—John Donne

PRELUDE

"Come not between the dragon and his wrath."

—Shakespeare

CHAPTER ONE

Coral Gables, Florida
September 21

No matter what Carlos did, the palm trees kept dying. Colonel Calavera, away on business, had left instructions that the blighted trees be replaced. And so Carlos had arranged to have the old, wilting coconut palms ripped from the ground; new trees, a supposedly hardier variety of Royal Jamaican, had arrived on flatbed trucks, their root balls wrapped in wet burlap. The cure to the problem, Carlos had assumed, as a portable crane lowered the new palms into freshly excavated holes.

But within a few days yellowed fronds began to litter the estate lawns and the heart-shaped pool. At night the falling fronds sounded like rain. In the morning they lay all over the yard, scattered by the hot breeze.

Carlos stalked away in disgust.

"There is a *malhechor* here," he said. "An evil spirit. That is the only explanation."

The colonel had hired him directly from the Homestead work farm, where Carlos had been serving a short term for assault. A small matter of defending his honor. The judge, who spoke Spanish, had suggested that six months of enforced agriculture would improve his quick temper. What did the judge know? For that matter what did the colonel know about gardening, or blights? Did he understand that there were things a man could not control?

Anger flooded into Carlos. He shook his earth-stained fists at the turf, the pool, the big hacienda with the white-tiled roof. "The ground here is cursed!" he shouted. "There is nothing a man can do!"

Dr. Vidoc, reclining in a chair by the pool, looked up from his book and laughed.

"Hey, Carlos? Try planting a coconut," he said. "Wait a few years."

Carlos scowled at him.

Emile Vidoc, the colonel's associate, had been a guest of the estate for some time now, staying in the cabana. A tall man, very long in the limbs, he was totally hairless, gleaming with oil, naked except for black bikini briefs and black-framed sunglasses that reflected an intensely blue sky. Vidoc was an Anglo, and not to be trusted.

"You know nothing about trees," Carlos said uneasily.

Dr. Vidoc shrugged. "I know about people," he said.

Carlos found he didn't care to face the dark glasses, or the glittering eyes that lurked behind them. He turned his back and walked away.

"You know the solution?" Dr. Vidoc called after him. "Pave the place over. Airbrush it tropical green and install plastic palm trees!"

Carlos muttered a curse and went to fetch a long-handled pool skimmer. Returning, he noticed a rental van parked near the cabana. A delivery of some sort. Curiosity aroused, he made sure Vidoc was still by the pool and then detoured to check out the van. It would please him to steal something from the doctor.

He tried the rear door. Locked. The driver's door. Locked, of course. Carlos pressed his face to the tinted glass, shielding his eyes from the glare of the reflected sky.

Shapes inside there, hard to make out. Wrapped bales, a cache of weapons? Whatever, it would have to wait. He would return after dark with the appropriate tools—his skills were not limited to tending palm trees.

The first thing Carlos noticed when he returned to the pool area was that Dr. Vidoc was not in his recliner.

Behind him a voice said, "You forgot this."

He turned and saw Vidoc with the long-handled pool skimmer.

"You know what they say?" Vidoc said, a thin smile tightening his lips.

"No, *señor*."

"They say curiosity killed the cat."

Carlos was not familiar with the saying.

"In the van, Carlos. See anything interesting?"

Before Carlos could reply, Dr. Vidoc lunged, slamming the skimmer handle into his chest. Astonished by the sudden attack, Carlos fell backward into the pool. He could not swim.

He kicked, desperate to keep his head above water, fighting the panic that clawed like a bird at his throat. Every time he got within reach of the edge, the doctor shoved him back, using the long handle.

"The pool is only six feet deep," Vidoc taunted. "All you have to do, grow an inch."

Carlos was strong, determined to live. Several times the doctor pushed him under, and each time he kicked up again. He choked, inhaling heavily chlorinated water, and suddenly the strength ebbed from his limbs and he imagined that he was flying underwater. See how easily he soared in this swirl of light, hearing the sonorous chime of the underwater bells.

All you have to do, his brain told him, *is open your mouth and breathe*. . . .

• • •

When the splashing had subsided, the doctor wandered over to the nearest palm tree and gathered up a few of the dead fronds. He carried the fronds back to the edge of the pool and tossed them in.

"Water wings," he said.

Then Dr. Vidoc returned to his lounge chair and began another diligent application of tanning oil. You had to be careful in Florida. The sun was a real killer.

CHAPTER TWO

Night on the Calle Ocho, in the heart of Little Havana. Heberto knew he was sick, maybe dying. It was no longer possible to ignore the pain that seared up from his left wrist, or the heaviness in his chest, or the cold knot of fear in his belly. When his vision began to blur, he managed to pull the doctor's rental van over to the curb and shut off the motor.

"I will use the telephone," he announced, gasping. "Someone else will come to drive you."

Talking was useless. The men in the back of the van did not hear, did not respond. They lay as if dead, eyes open, staring into the darkness. Or not staring. Could they see? Heberto had wondered. The unnatural stillness of those eyes frightened him almost as much as the pain in his chest.

In his sixty years he had never seen anything quite like it, not even among the dead.

"Mother of God, help me," he whispered, shoving the door open. *Santa Maria, hear my prayer, heal this heart before it kills me.*

Crawling down from the seat, he stumbled and fell to his knees. The sidewalk was crowded with revelers even at this late hour, but no one offered to help him. They looked quickly away, mistaking him for a drunk.

Heberto managed to stagger a few yards to a restaurant door where he rested, trying to get his breath. Useless. There was no way to untighten the vise that seemed to press against his heart.

Through the glass he could see a pay phone illuminated by an overhead light. He had to get to the phone, arrange for a new driver, and then call an ambulance for himself. Dr. Vidoc would be angry, but what could he do?

The door seemed massive. Heberto managed to pry it open and slip inside. A fist seemed to clench inside his chest. The phone became an icon, blurred and distant. He was reaching out to touch it when a great blinding warmth came up from the floor.

Heberto Raimez fell into it and then felt nothing.

Outside, in the van, seven pairs of eyes stared up into the darkness.

PART ONE

INCUBATION

"Shakespeare had it wrong. Sleep is not a dream.
It is a period of incubation."
—EMILE VIDOC, M.D.

CHAPTER ONE

Friday, September 29

She was late. Would the man from Missing Persons still be waiting? Sara hurried into the air-conditioned lobby and was relieved to see Valdez leaning against the wall, sipping from a small paper cup of Cuban coffee. He smiled and nodded.

"Morning, Dr. Copley," he said, offering his hand.

"I'm sorry, Detective," she said. "I'm still learning my way around Miami. They told me at the office that Cypress Medical Center was a ten-minute drive and it's taken me what, half an hour?"

Valdez waved away her apology.

"Like I said, probably a false alarm. I saw a slight resemblance, so I called."

They'd met only once before, when Sara had first arrived from Boston and filed the original missing-person report for Kurt Palmer, who had gone south to visit an old army buddy and then seemingly vanished into the sprawl of Miami. Nervous about contacting the police, Sara's initial impression of Lee Valdez was of cool, intelligent eyes the color of varnished teak. The Metro-Dade detective was a quiet type, at ease in silence, not inclined to judge her. She'd been grateful for that. Now she noticed that he had a strong, almost hawkish nose, a deeply cleft chin, and a faintly pockmarked complexion. Dark where she was light, and whip thin. Since the initial interview Sara had phoned the detective several times to check up on the case. There hadn't been any progress until now.

"You think you've located Dave?" Sara said. Dave was the army buddy—Kurt hadn't mentioned any last name.

Valdez shrugged. He had removed a creased snapshot from his pocket—a photo she had supplied. Kurt and Dave in a jungle scene, she'd never even known what country. Both young men in combat fatigues and grinning fiercely, almost defiantly, as if the camera had been a weapon aimed at their hearts. A slice of the life Kurt Palmer had never wanted to share with her. Seeing it again made her feel anxious.

"Could be him," Valdez was saying, tapping the snapshot. "Worth checking out. This way, Dr. Copley. They'll want to see some I.D."

He walked her to the reception desk. Sara showed her Dade County Public Health Department credentials and was issued a visiting physician's pass.

When she looked up, Valdez was holding the elevator. In a hurry, but polite about it.

"So how is he?" she asked as the doors slid shut.

The detective stared at the floor indicator, hands in his pockets. She could see the butt of the gun he carried at his waist. "Not so good. The victim is in a coma. Or maybe it's not a coma, they're not really sure."

"Victim?"

"Robbed," he explained. "Left for dead."

The intensive-care unit was reserved for the victims of severe cerebral damage. The chilling silence was interrupted only by the faint chorus of respirators clicking in subdued agony. Sara knew that in this stark place, death was as close as a blinking alarm light or the suddenly flat line on a monitor screen.

She followed Detective Valdez to the last curtained bed in the row. He handed her the photograph and stepped back. She glanced at the image she knew only as "Dave"—an image burned into her brain over the last few months—and then looked at the brown-haired Caucasian male lying unconscious in the bed. He was thirty or so, solidly built and deeply tanned, but both the weight and the tan were fading rapidly. His closed eyes were darkly bruised, and a small contusion showed on his left temple area. There were needle marks—tracks—on the inside of his left arm. Both hands were bandaged. He had been fitted with an intravenous dextrose drip but did not, apparently, require a respirator.

Sara studied his face. It was blank, empty.

"Can you make him?"

She shrugged. "The picture is at least five years old. He's aged a lot, but it could be him. Can you check his fingerprints with the military?"

"They've been erased."

Sara was startled.

"Erased?"

Valdez grimaced. "Check under the bandages."

She unwrapped the hand bandages, saw fresh scar tissue obliterating the fingertips.

"That's an acid burn," Valdez explained. "Sometimes we get a felon who's desperate not to be tied to a particular crime, he'll try that. Usually enough grows back after a few months so we get at least a partial whorl. Enough for expert testimony."

"You think this man is a criminal?"

"That's one theory. Or maybe somebody wanted to make it hard to identify him."

It was a sobering thought. That the man who might be Kurt's only contact in Miami was involved in some sort of criminal activity.

"How about dental records?" Sara suggested.

"I had a cast sent to a forensic odontologist at Military Records," Valdez said, "but it could take months to get a matchup. They're swamped, just like we are. Missing persons is a growth industry," he added with a slight smile.

Sara glanced at the snapshot again and shook her head.

"I just can't be sure," she said. "I never met him. All I know is his picture."

"And what your boyfriend said about him," Valdez reminded her. "That he was a surfer. You said Kurt called him 'Surfer Dave.'"

Sara nodded, distracted by something she had just noticed. The sleeper had a waxy skin tone, and his lips had a slight cast of cyanosis, as if he'd been poisoned.

Instinctively she grasped his wrist and checked his pulse.

"My God," she said, and then checked it again.

His heart rate was unusually, if not impossibly, slow. Less than thirty beats per minute. Slower than a deep-coma victim.

The sleeper, whatever his real name, was barely alive.

CHAPTER TWO

The thing Luto liked best about Miami International Airport, wild things happened there. Theft, rape, murder, sometimes all three to the same victim if the timing was right. Whenever he had the chance, Luto liked to cruise the terminals, check out the scene, maybe see if he could get something going. His airport outfit included a light nylon windbreaker to cover his Cuban prison tattoos, designer sunglasses, and running shoes because you never knew, sometimes the smart thing to do was run like a bastard.

The incoming flight he was supposed to meet had been delayed, so Luto decided what the hell, he'd get in a little practice. Play a little *seguir y vigilar*, his shadow game. He spotted a big American blonde and followed her.

Maybe she'd feel the urge, get lost on her way to the ladies' room. Be in need of directions. 'Scuze me, can I be of assistance?

He trailed the *rubia* until she ran into the arms of a large Anglo male, could have been a football player, he was that large. Luto, small and cocky, veered away, not really disappointed. He was here on the colonel's business, no time for recreational activities.

When he finally got to the international terminal, it turned out the flight *hadn't* been delayed. The two recruits he was supposed to pick up had been snared by a security guard.

They looked frightened and confused. Big dark eyes, nervous smiles.

"I guess these boys never been in a big airport," the guard said to Luto. "After they cleared Customs, the little one tried to urinate behind a water fountain."

"Hey, fuck," Luto said. "I doubt they ever been on an airplane before."

The two boys were brothers, Jorge and Fernando, recruited by Colonel Calavera on his last sweep through the Bolivian war zone. When Luto addressed them in Spanish, they both began talking at once. Couple of dumb peasant farmers with maybe a little Indian blood, had that take-me-to-our-leader look a lot of the recruits had, they first got off the plane from La Paz.

Luto smirked and adjusted his designer shades.

"Relax, *amigos*," he said. "I got transportation, you can ride in the back if you promise not to piss on the floor."

When the two boys were safely installed in the Coral Gables motel he managed for the colonel, Luto reported by phone.

"Couple of live ones," he said. "That makes six in the last week. Back up to platoon strength."

"I'll notify Vidoc," the colonel replied. "He wants to examine all the replacements."

Mention of the doctor made Luto uneasy. He tried to change the subject. "These *campesinos* stink up the rooms, I'll have to repaint."

"Open a window," the colonel advised. "And, Luto? Wait for the doctor."

CHAPTER THREE

"**I**'ve never seen anything like it," Sara said to Valdez. "He shouldn't be alive."

She hurried back to the nurses' station, asked to see the sleeper's physician of record.

"Dr. Harding is the chief of medicine," the nurse said with an air of importance. "He's very busy."

"So am I. This will only take a few minutes."

When Dr. Richard Harding finally responded to the summons, he entered the ICU like a general taking the battlefield. The nurses straightened up, busied themselves. Harding's martial bearing was accentuated by severe, steel-rimmed glasses and thick white hair cropped close to his skull. He was carrying a clipboard and let it bump against his thigh as he walked, a kind of swagger stick. Sara knew the type, overbearing and self-important.

"Public Health?" he said, peering at her pass. "What interest does the Health Department have in this charity case?"

Sara was not particularly surprised by Harding's reaction; many private-sector physicians had a low opinion of public-health medicine. As a consequence, the positions were often hard to staff. Dade County had been lacking a staff epidemiologist for more than two years when Sara agreed to take the job.

Dr. Harding riffled the pages on the clipboard impatiently. "Well, you needn't worry about infectious disease in this case. All appropriate tests have been administered."

As Sara explained that she wasn't present in an official capacity, but had been called in to make a possible identification of the coma patient, Dr. Harding visibly relaxed.

"A somewhat interesting case," he commented. "Quite unusual. Not an ordinary coma at all. Respiration is the lowest I've ever seen—at a glance he could easily be mistaken for dead. Extremely slow heartbeat, but blood pressure is not dangerously low. At the moment his condition is stable."

"Have you made a diagnosis?" Sara asked.

"See for yourself," he said, handing her the clipboard. "Undetermined neurological trauma due to a drug overdose."

"Narcotics?"

He shrugged. "There are recent needle marks on the arms—typical abuser tracks. We found traces of alkaloid toxins in the blood workups, but not enough so we can say exactly what he injected."

Dr. Harding moved to the bedside and thumbed open one of the sleeper's eyelids. Clicking on a penlight, he checked dilation. "I'm inclined to think he was exposed to some exotic designer drug—these new underground labs are very inventive. God knows what they were cooking up, but this poor devil got his brain fried—and his fingers burned."

"What sort of treatment are you recommending?"

Harding's eyeglasses glinted as he turned. "Treatment? This is a charity case, Dr. Copley. Once the patient's condition has been thoroughly evaluated—and we're *very* thorough here—he'll be transferred to another facility."

Sara was flipping through the workup, scanning test results and trying to decipher the scrawls of various specialists who had consulted on the case. "CAT scans and EEG reveal no obvious brain damage," she noted. "The persistent alpha pattern seems to indicate he's deeply asleep."

Harding chuckled, shook his head.

"You could say that. So deeply asleep he's feeling no pain."

"Pardon me?"

"Observe," he said, lifting the sheet and exposing the sleeper's feet. Extracting a large surgical needle from his breast pocket, he jabbed at the sleeper's bare toes, drawing a small, gemlike bead of blood.

There was no reaction. Not even an involuntary flinch.

CHAPTER FOUR

Dr. Vidoc sat by the pool, under the shade of an umbrella, reading *A Midsummer Night's Dream*. The blighted palm trees had been removed, the fallen fronds raked up and taken away. Rather than hire another gardener to replace the troublesome Carlos, the colonel had contracted with a lawn-care service.

"How chance the roses there do fade so fast?"

That twit Lysander, Vidoc thought, a lamebrain right from Act 1, Scene 1. No wonder Hermia kept bursting into tears, a geek like that wanting to copulate with her.

It was peaceful here by the pool, now that the police had come and gone—the drowning of Carlos was clearly accidental, the detectives had agreed, the poor man had fallen in while attempting to fish out the fallen palm fronds. The doctor had been good enough to administer CPR, but, alas, the victim had expired.

"His folly . . . is no fault of mine."

Leave it to Hermia to get right to the point. And as usual with the Bard, there were applications in the present reality.

Emile Vidoc had discovered Shakespeare in prep school, the same year he had discovered himself, as it were. His drama teacher had suggested further readings in psychology, as a way to explain the motivations of Macbeth's character, and so young Emile had stumbled on a medical text that explained what it was to be a superior being.

It was a revelation, one of those key moments that shape a life.

Sociopathic personalities, the text had read, *result from a rare and as yet unexplained dysfunction of the normal conscience. A sociopath is one who feels himself to be apart from human society, and is incapable of feeling guilt or having sympathy for the emotional needs of others. An intelligent sociopath may learn to mimic normal emotional reactions and thus disguise himself.*

The text went on to explain that sociopaths were divided into several categories or types. One in particular had special meaning for Emile Vidoc: *Narcissistic Personality Disorder is characterized by the tendency to exploit others and to crave adulation. There is a profound inability to understand other people's needs. Highly intelligent NPDs may believe themselves to have a godlike power and hold "normal" people in great disdain.*

Twelve-year-old Emile had been thrilled to recognize himself in print. Although convinced of his own superiority, he had never been able to understand the bizarre emotional displays of the beings who called themselves "normal." They cried, they laughed, they acted stupidly and often not in their own best interests.

It was as if everyone else was reading from a script that was hidden from him alone. As a result, young Emile often made mistakes, saying or doing things that made normals regard him as "strange" or even "stupid."

The psychology text had made it all clear, if you were clever enough to read between the lines: Normals suffered from a genetic flaw called conscience. Afraid of superior beings, normals invented demeaning names like "sociopath" and "narcissistic."

The knowledge that he was different, that unlike normals he was *not* flawed, set Emile free.

Learn to mimic the "correct" response and he could roam through normal society, taking what he wanted, avoiding detection.

Theater was a big help. In prep school and later in college he had learned to play roles, speak lines. How to wear the mask of the normal. And in this the Bard was the great master. A reaction for every occasion. All emotions explained.

Emile Vidoc never went anywhere without his annotated Shakespeare. It was his guide to human behavior, his bible.

Vidoc was deep into *A Midsummer Night's Dream*, Act II, the part with spotted snakes with double tongue, when Colonel Calavera arrived in his chauffeur-driven Mercedes limousine, fat wheels hissing on the gravel.

"Emile! Good news. Two more recruits arrived today!"

Vidoc put on the smile mask. "Ah," he said. "New blood. That *is* good news."

The colonel went into the main house, and again the pool area was quiet. Vidoc savored Lysander's best line: *"less than an ace, man, for he is dead, he is nothing."*

It applied to so many normals. Carlos, the new recruits, and maybe, when the task was complete, the colonel himself.

CHAPTER FIVE

The lady was a stunner. Long, slender legs, blond hair, eyes that seemed to pick up color from the environment. Light gray, maybe, but right now they looked almost tropical green.

"Coffee?" Valdez suggested. "I got a couple questions, won't take long."

Dr. Copley glanced at her watch, then smiled and said she would make time.

Valdez walked her to a nearby bodega. They sat at a table on the sidewalk, in the shade of a pink canvas awning, drinking cups of strong, syrupy Cuban coffee and nibbling *churros*, a pastry so sweet it always made his teeth hurt.

It was nice, sitting there eating sweets with this lovely woman, so nice Valdez almost hated to spoil it with questions.

"Your boyfriend," he said, "did he ever mention that Dave had a special interest in Cuban culture? Any Cuban friends or associates?"

"He never said. Why do you ask?"

"Because our John Doe was found on the Calle Ocho. Eighth Street, in the heart of Little Havana."

"Are there drug labs in Little Havana?"

"There are drug labs everywhere. But on the Calle Ocho they'd be run by Cubans. And frequented by Cubans."

Dr. Copley thought about it. A very thoughtful person, Valdez observed, but inside she was hiding something. This boyfriend, he decided, he'd done more than just walk out on her. Something had happened there, something she was keeping back.

"I got the impression Dave was the only person he knew in

Florida," she said. "That was part of the attraction, I think—going to visit this buddy who had a place in the sun."

"A surfer, right?"

"It was just a nickname. Surfer Dave."

Valdez opened his wallet and withdrew a lime-green business card. "This was found on the victim. In his left back pocket."

The doctor studied the card.

HANG TUFF SURF & DIVE SHOP
Golden Beach

"I called," Valdez told her. "No answer. Maybe they're out catching a wave. Ring any bells for you?"

The doctor shook her head. "Sorry."

"How about the drug connection? Was Kurt Palmer into drugs?"

"I don't think so."

Valdez looked skeptical.

"I know that sounds strange, but I really can't be sure. The Kurt Palmer who showed up after he got out of the army, he was, well, a very different person from the boy I knew in high school."

"In what way different?"

There she was, hesitating again. What was there about this guy that made her so nervous? What had she been holding back?

"He'd had this dream of being a writer," she said. "I think he originally went into the army so he'd have something interesting to write about. And when he came back he seemed very excited about this screenplay he'd been working on. I got the impression it was some kind of action film based on his experiences in the military. He acted very secretive, like he was afraid I might give away his plot. But nothing came of it."

"He never sold the screenplay?"

"He never wrote it," Sara said. "Just before he left he admitted he'd never written a word."

"There's something else bothering you," Valdez said, thinking, Go for it, take a chance. "Was he ever by any chance violent? Threatening?"

There, he'd scored. Her expression was one of shock, puzzlement.

"How on earth did you know that?" she said.

"Nothing magical," he said. "Just police work. I managed to

get a look at Kurt Palmer's army file. He was given a medical discharge for 'combat stress syndrome.' Violent or self-destructive behavior is fairly common for those guys. They tend to act out. So what exactly happened?"

Dr. Copley started to speak, stopped herself.

"It would help me to know who I'm looking for," he said gently. "What his behavior might be."

She nodded unhappily.

"There was an incident, I guess you'd call it. He'd been staying with me for about three months—supposedly writing while I was away at the hospital. Things had been . . . uneasy, I guess you'd say. We weren't the same people we'd been in high school, neither of us. Ten years is a long time. I didn't know what was wrong with Kurt—he never told me about the medical discharge—but I knew *something* was wrong, and one night I got up the nerve and suggested maybe he needed to seek counseling. And that it would, um, be better for both of us if he moved on."

"What was his reaction?" Valdez asked. "Did he lose his temper? Freak out?"

"Not at first," she said. "He seemed to take it amazingly well. Agreed that he had to do something to 'get himself together.' I went to work at the lab—we were in the middle of an important project, or anyhow I thought it was important at the time—and then, hours later, Kurt came storming in. Screaming that I was like all the others, out to get him. He just went kind of *berserk*, throwing equipment around, breaking glass. Acting totally crazed."

"What did you do?"

Dr. Copley closed her eyes, massaged her temples. "What could I do? I called the police. They took him into custody. And then when I went down to bail him out, he seemed very calm. Not angry at all, certainly not crazy. Made like what had happened was a joke."

"But it wasn't a joke."

"No," she admitted. "It was real. *Too* real. I was terrified."

"And after you bailed him out, that's when he decided to come down here to Miami?"

She nodded. "He left that night. I drove him to the airport."

"I hope you don't blame yourself," Valdez said. "The U.S. Army couldn't handle this guy, it's no wonder you couldn't help him all by yourself."

"That should make it easier, I guess. But it doesn't. I'd just like to find him, make sure he's okay. I owe him that much."

Valdez drained his coffee and stood up.

"I'll be in touch," he said. "You think of anything that might help, give me a call."

On the way back to her office Sara got lost again. The detailed street map didn't seem to help. It was something about Miami. Even when you knew where you were going, the city found a way to lose you.

CHAPTER SIX

The motel room was a marvel. Jorge and Nando had already discovered the bathroom, with its huge curtained stall for urinating and the plentiful spray of water that washed it away. Beds so soft and pliant no man could ever sleep in them. Bureau drawers lined with brightly colored paper. Of even more interest was the television. Nando, switching the channels, had discovered cartoons dubbed in the hard, rapid-fire Spanish they already recognized as distinctly Cuban.

Jorge was fifteen. Nando was a year younger. In their small mountain village the two brothers were considered men, and expected to behave as such. Farmers with no experience of fighting, they had been recruited by Colonel Calavera, following a spectacular slide show that had been projected on the only clean white sheet in the village. The brothers had thrilled to the images of young men dressed in crisp uniforms—paramilitary forces engaged in the long-running civil war in the lowlands. The monthly pay allotment was rumored to be more than a tenant farmer could make in a season, although the colonel had not wanted to demean himself by discussing money. He would, he promised, fly new recruits to the fabled land of Miami, where they would be trained in a special camp and given new boots and, of course, weapons. Shiny new guns.

When Luto entered, the brothers were crouched in front of the television, watching repeats of Morton Downey, Jr. They did not need to understand the language to appreciate Downey's artifice, his anger. When Morton Downey, Jr., scowled, they scowled; when he showed his teeth, they showed their teeth.

"Hey, *amigos*? Pay attention," Luto said. He had been chewing cherry bubble gum, and his tongue was fluorescent pink. "A very important man, a friend of the colonel, is here to see you."

Emile Vidoc came into the room, ducking his head under the door frame. Looming, he seemed that tall. He had dressed for the occasion, wearing combat fatigues and carrying an army-issue briefcase.

"He is a doctor," Luto explained. "He will examine you, to see what kind of soldier you will make."

The brothers, understanding only that the tall, hairless one was an important friend of the famous colonel, stood at attention.

"They are very small," Vidoc commented in English.

"Small but tough," Luto said.

"We'll see."

The doctor opened his briefcase, removed a sphygmomanometer, a stethoscope, a thin digital-weight scale, and a syringe. The physical examination was at best rudimentary. The two boys were weighed—a new experience for both of them. The doctor scratched figures into a small notebook. Nando giggled when the cool stethoscope monitored his heartbeat. Jorge had a difficult time understanding that he should not flex his muscles when the blood-pressure cuff was on—he thought his strength was being measured.

"Now we'll see how tough they are," Vidoc said, displaying the large syringe.

"*Sean valientes,*" Luto said to them sternly, chewing his gum. "Have courage, *amigos.*"

The brothers were brave. They did not flinch when the doctor poked his big needle into their scrawny arms, withdrawing a generous sampling of blood.

"They'll be fine, so long as they don't fight the needle," Vidoc said. "Just out of curiosity, how much did they cost?"

Luto chuckled. "I heard it was seventy-five dollars for the pair. Fifty to the village chief. Twenty-five to their mother."

When the doctor smiled, the two brothers, so brave in the face of the needle, had to look away. Jorge muttered a word and kept his eyes averted.

"What did he say?" Vidoc asked.

"*El Tigre,*" Luto said uneasily. "That's slang for 'Jaguar.'"

Dr. Vidoc smiled again, showing the whiteness of his teeth.

* * *

Outside, in the little gravel courtyard behind the motel, Dr. Vidoc advised Luto on matters of diet.

"Feed them meat. Plenty of starches. Potatoes or those plantains you Cubans like. They're nothing but skin and bones."

"Not a lot of food where they come from," Luto pointed out.

"Or where they're going," Vidoc said. "But for now, see that they have plenty to eat."

Luto, ordinarily not a talkative man, was nervous in the doctor's presence. And when he was nervous, he tended to babble. "Too bad about Heberto," he said.

Right away he knew it was the wrong thing to say.

"The stupid fool," Vidoc said, biting each word. "No one told me he had a heart condition. He should not have been driving."

"He did not wish to appear weak," Luto said.

"We lost seven of my best volunteers," Vidoc said. "Men selected from hundreds at the clinic. All of them proven, combat ready. All because the project was entrusted to an old man with a bad heart."

"Heberto was loyal," Luto said.

"A dead man isn't loyal," Vidoc said.

He started to leave, his long loping stride skidding on the gravel. He turned back, pointing at Luto.

"Remember what I said about the new units. Fatten them up."

CHAPTER SEVEN

Sara carried the stack of postcards out to the balcony. She shuffled them like playing cards, dealing them out, not reading them right away. Messages from Kurt.

The ocean was glassy calm that evening. Silent flashes of lightning reflected from somewhere over the horizon. The apartment she now called home was an air-conditioned tower with two hundred feet of frontage on Miami Beach—one foot for each unit. Directly to the north was that gaudy rhinestone of a resort hotel, the Fontainebleau, with its monogrammed swimming pool. There were old Jews with prayer shawls on the boardwalk, and punked-up kids on roller skates.

Sara was getting used to Miami Beach. She was almost ready to like the place, for all its touristy quirks. Like the hotel shadows that flowed over the beach in the early afternoon, or the gridlock of daytime traffic on the concrete tunnel of Collins Avenue. Still, you could smell the salty air, watch the sun rise out of the sea. And at night you could walk the sands for miles and rarely encounter another human being.

The apartment had been leased sight unseen before she left Boston, under the mistaken assumption that Miami Beach was the waterfront part of Miami. Unaware they were two separate and distinct cities separated by Biscayne Bay. Miami, she soon discovered, was a sprawling, largely Hispanic urban center with a thriving port of its own. The Beach, linked to the bigger city by a few causeways, was a toothlike row of old hotels and new condo towers rising from a narrow spit of trucked-in sand. A mirage in the mangroves, a cruise ship of a place that had somehow never left the harbor.

The postcards.

Hi gorgeous I made it.

That one, the first, showed the silhouette of a palm tree with the sunset glitter of Biscayne Boulevard in the background. It had seemed to radiate a sense of hope when she first saw it, as if maybe, just maybe, they still had a chance.

That was all changed by the postcards that followed.

Kurt Palmer had come into Sara's life when she was seventeen. The golden boy of Lowell High, or that was how he'd seemed to her then. Handsome, confident, a popular football star, not the kind of boy to be interested in a wrong-side-of-the-tracks girl like Sara Copley, whose mother worked crazy shifts as a licensed practical nurse to support them both. Her father, a boozer and itinerant handyman, had left for parts unknown when Sara was an infant. With mother and daughter just a paycheck away from disaster, Sara had focused all of her adolescent energies on her studies—being a good student wasn't enough, she had to be the best. Sara was a grind, a bookworm, resolute in her determination. Cheerleaders, boyfriends, parties, that was another world—until Kurt asked her to help him study for a difficult chemistry exam.

She hadn't at first realized he was making a pass. Why would he choose her when he could have had any girl in the school? Any yet from the beginning he made her feel special. Gradually she'd come to understand that she and the golden boy had a lot in common. He, too, came from a broken family, lived always on the verge of poverty, had never really felt he belonged with the "in" crowd, although his athletic ability made him popular. They began to date, became "serious," and in the last year of high school made plans for a life together.

Kurt was rich with ideas.

"You'll be a doctor," he'd urged her. "Not just any doctor, all they care about are cars and condos, you'll be the kind of doctor who changes the world. Maybe you'll discover a cure for cancer, something like that. And I'm going to be a writer. I'll write great books, and that will change the world, too. Maybe we'll *both* win a Nobel Prize. It's going to be great, Sara, just you wait."

It was typical kid stuff, she now realized, adolescent fantasy, but at the time it had seemed heart-achingly real. She would go off to college on her scholarship, Kurt would do a hitch in the army, finance his education that way, and eventually they would make a life together.

At first he'd been dutiful about keeping in touch. Then, after six months, the letters and phone calls had gradually petered out. When he failed to reply to her last two or three letters, Sara had assumed there was someone else.

Caught up in the grueling schedule of pre-med courses, Sara got over the heartbreak by renewing her academic concentration. Bear down, get through it. Kurt Palmer and the hurt of losing him faded.

Ten years went by, and then one day, out of the blue, he'd wandered into the Mass General epidemiology lab wearing a grin that melted her heart all over again.

"You made it," he'd said, touching the name tag on her lab coat. SARA COPLEY, M.D. "Next thing, we'll have to get you that Nobel Prize."

On the outside he was the same old Kurt, a romantic boy full of intoxicating ideas. But inside something had gone terribly wrong. The gentle dreamer had become the prey of violent mood swings. He suffered from nightmares that woke him screaming. And there was nothing she could do to help him. Every time she raised the subject, he responded in a spasm of anger, trying to change the subject.

"You're selling out," he'd told her. "You're becoming part of the problem. Doctors are supposed to help people, not poison lab rats for some big drug company."

"The research is important," she'd insisted. "We're learning how to control the spread of disease. That's what epidemiology is all about."

His reaction had been withering.

"You can fool them, Sara, but you can't fool me. You *want* to be part of the machine, the big research complex. You want the rewards, the status, the cars and the condos, all of it."

"Kurt, I'm driving a five-year-old Plymouth."

"It'll come, Sara. Big salary, grants, a piece of the research pie. They'll offer you the moon, Sara, and you won't be able to say no."

In the heat of argument she'd thought, Why not? She'd labored long and hard, her own mother had died of overwork and the lifelong stress of poverty, why *shouldn't* Sara Copley get the perks?

One argument had led to another, with Kurt demanding some part of her she was just not able to give, until the final confrontation had taken place. Sara demanding that he seek counseling, that he move out—and Kurt responding, hours later, in a full-blown rage that would nearly destroy her lab.

Later, while being bailed out of the Charles Street Jail, he tried to make it all a joke. "You're Dr. Jekyll," he'd said. "I'm Mr. Hyde. Come find me."

Two weeks later that first hopeful postcard had arrived from Miami.

Sara dealt out the second postcard. Three bikinied girls riding huge surfboards on a puny-looking wave. *Surfer Dave sends his best*, Kurt had written. *Strictly margaritaville* . . .

A whole month passed before "Moon Over Miami" made it to Boston. There was no message, just the letter *K* followed by an exclamation mark. From the postmark Sara figured the card had been in transit for three weeks.

The cards that followed came at irregular intervals and were equally enigmatic and frustrating. Some with a message like *Wish I was here, love K.*—that one drove her crazy, what did it mean?— others with just his signature. The last card, a flock of flamingos rising over a racetrack, was blank.

In a way the frightening blankness of that final postcard was what had made her decide to take the position with the Dade County Public Health Department. Her colleagues at Mass General had been stunned. Why would Sara, after years of training for medical research, take a job that amounted to social work? To her colleagues she explained nothing. What right did they have to question her decisions? Pampered and privileged, what did they know about her life?

And it wasn't just because Kurt was somewhere in Miami, she told herself. It was because the people of Dade County really *needed* an epidemiologist, whereas a prestige facility like Mass General could replace her easily. The Boston area was crawling with overqualified physicians.

And of course they *did* need her in Dade County. The first six weeks on the job had been a total immersion in all the administrative details her predecessor, gone for two years, had been unable to complete. Programs that had never been evaluated. Population/disease data that needed to be entered into the new computer system. Funds that had been appropriated but never utilized for mobile diagnostic clinics, community outreach.

There was enough work for six doctors, but she was beginning to get a handle on it, starting to get a feel for the job and the city, for the way county government worked, for the ways it didn't. Steering an underpaid, overworked staff, begging pro bono work from the huge for-profit Miami medical establishment, that was part of it. Another role was setting up ghetto clinics to treat people who had never seen a doctor, let alone the inside of a hospital. Making medicine *work*, that was her vocation now.

Somewhere in there she'd found time to place an ad in the *Miami Herald*, asking Kurt Palmer to reply to a P.O. box. When that failed to produce a response, she went to the Missing Persons Unit of the Metro-Dade Police.

Detective Sergeant Lee Valdez had made her feel at ease about filing the report. It had sounded so lame, admitting that she had no last-known address for Kurt, no real clue as to where he'd been. Detective Valdez had been patient, although hardly optimistic.

"If he does turn up, it'll probably be because you bump into him on the street, not because *we* locate him. All we can really do is process information, match up prints and photographs. I'll enter his name in the computer, and if he happens to be arrested, it'll eventually turn up in our files. We'll circulate the picture you supplied—but we've got so many, our officers can't be expected to remember each face."

Later he had informed her, rather delicately, that the most effective means of locating missing persons was to find a match with unidentified bodies, of which there was no shortage in South Florida.

"I'll request that the U.S. Army supply copies of Mr. Palmer's fingerprints. Some of the bodies that turn up can be identified by prints, others cannot."

Valdez had not gone into the details, but Sara could well imagine why such means were not always effective, what with the tropical heat and the proximity of swamp and drainage canals as convenient body dumps. It was a grim reminder that "missing" often meant deceased.

If the worst had happened, she had to know. When she first arrived in Miami, Sara believed she could feel Kurt alive somewhere in the city. She kept expecting to spot him on the street, exactly as Valdez had suggested. Lately she wasn't so sure. And today, seeing a coma victim who might be Kurt's friend Surfer Dave, today she'd had a feeling of great emptiness. For the first time it seemed distinctly possible that the golden boy himself was dead. Or worse than dead.

As darkness fell, a sea breeze stirred the postcards. Sara let the wind move them around. All she could do was wait. Maybe give Detective Valdez another call—if he didn't call first.

CHAPTER EIGHT

Breakfast was black coffee and a bagel that was borderline stale. Sara carried the tray out to her little balcony and checked out the beach scene. Eight o'clock on a Saturday morning, and the sunbathers were already dutifully taking up positions. Along the blue horizon sportfishing boats were parading off to deep water, in search of the Gulf Stream. Another day in paradise, the mantra of South Florida.

Sara pushed the bagel aside, sipped her coffee, and watched a Fontainebleau guest make a fool of himself on a rented windsurfer. The guy kept slipping from the board, crashing into the water. Eventually he gave up and just paddled around, looking up at the sky as if he expected the wind to come straight down and find him.

Surfer Dave. Detective Valdez had said it might be weeks before the dental identification came through. Weeks before they could be sure it really was Kurt's army buddy lying unconscious in that bed. Would the sleeper survive that long? Sara wondered.

She was on her way to the refrigerator for a glass of juice when she remembered Detective Valdez telling her about the business card found in the sleeper's pocket. A cutesy name. The Hang Tuff Surf Shop. Where was it, Golden Beach? Valdez had called, got no answer. Would he bother to check it out in person? Sara had the impression that routine inquiries were handled over the phone, or through computer files.

It being a beautiful day, Sara decided a ride up the coast was in order. She could at least determine if the Hang Tuff Surf Shop was still in business. Relay the information to the detective, let him take it from there.

No big deal, Sara told herself as she went to the telephone book to look up the street address.

Just a drive by, just a look.

Traffic heading north along the beach was slow, made slower by lights that were hopelessly out of sequence. After passing the glitz of Bal Harbour, with its new malls and condo swarms, there was a gradual devolution as the neon chic of Collins Avenue reverted to the potholed remnant of Route A1A. The glass towers that resembled giant ice-cube trays gave way to stuccoed two-story motels that lined the ocean edge like discarded pieces from an old Monopoly game.

Time travel, Sara thought. Drive a few miles and regress to another era.

The Hang Tuff Surf & Dive Shop was located on the ground floor of the Palm Court Motel, a relic of the fifties resort boom. Had the look of a place that would contain small damp rooms with big sagging mattresses and more than a trace of gritty beach sand in the shower stalls. The cinder blocks were starting to show through the dull pink stucco, and the flat roof had been patched so many times the tar had dripped over the edge and run down like icing on a stale wedding cake.

Sara had pulled into the parking lot. The place existed, why not check it out? There were a few brightly colored surfboards in a rack outside. The door was open, and she could just make out a figure inside, lounging behind a counter.

What could it hurt?

She locked her car, walked into the shop. The man behind the counter was lean and balding, with a sun-ravaged complexion. His watery, yellow-flecked eyes had followed her in from the car. A thin gold hoop dangled from his left earlobe. Beach-boy handsome once upon a time, Sara decided. The time had long since passed—you couldn't help noticing the pink spot on the tip of his nose where a skin cancer had recently been removed.

"Hank," he said, offering a limp hand. "What can we do ya?"

Sara opened her purse, removed the snapshot of Kurt and his buddy Dave. "I'm looking for a man," she said. That set Hank to grinning. Not lewd exactly, but interested.

"That a fact?" he said.

"Actually I think I may have found him," she said, feeling

herself blush slightly. "He's in a hospital, unconscious, and I'm trying to identify him."

Hank glanced at the snapshot. "Army guys, huh?"

"This man on the left had one of your business cards in his pocket. Maybe he was a customer. We think his first name is Dave."

Hank squinted. The name meant something to him, Sara was sure of that.

"Please look," she said. "This is important."

The ride up to the surf shop had been a game, something to do on a rare day off, but now her heart was pounding. Hank studied the snapshot. Sara could see another pink cancer spot on his balding skull.

"Shit, it could be," he said, looking up. "How old is this picture?"

"At least five years," she said.

"David Melborn," he said. "Worked here. Dave was my main man on the beach. Until one day he never showed up."

Nerves made a cold fist in her stomach. She'd never been so close to locating Kurt Palmer. "How about the other man in the snapshot," she said. "Does he look familiar?"

Hank studied, shook his head. "Can't say he does."

Sara closed her eyes, took a deep breath. It had been too much to hope for, that Kurt would be known here.

"You say Dave's in the hospital?"

"Cypress Medical Center," she said. "It would be helpful if you could identify him in person. Just so we're sure."

Hank was immediately uneasy with the idea.

"I'm tied up here," he said. "Real busy."

"He may be dying," Sara said. "It's important we find out what happened to him. It's possible he overdosed on drugs. We don't know what kind. A positive I.D. is essential."

Silence. Hank pushed the snapshot away and folded his arms. "You a cop?" he said finally.

Sara shook her head. "A doctor. With the Public Health Department."

"Show me some I.D., lady, or get out of here."

Sara opened her wallet, showed him her PHD card and a driver's license. He seemed satisfied but in no mood to cooperate.

"I don't know about any drugs," he said. "Dave just worked the beach. Keeping an eye on the rental stuff. These kids, they walk off with a nine-hundred-dollar Windsurfer, it ruins my day. Hell, it ruins my month."

Sara nodded. "Did he live here in the motel?"

That got a laugh out of Hank. "The fabulous Palm Court? Not on what I paid him, he didn't. You want the truth, Doc? I barely knew Dave. He did the beach thing for me, he got paid at the end of the day. Cash. I never even knew where he lived."

"Come on, Hank. He worked for you."

The proprietor was insistent. "You new to the area? Hey, I thought so. Look, the way it is around here, with the type of dude who'll work for thirty bucks a day, you don't push for an address. Dude might be living out of his car, no need to embarrass him."

Sara frowned. "You had the impression David Melborn was homeless?"

"My impression was, he was a private dude," Hank said, exasperated. "If he wanted me to know where he lived, he'd have mentioned it. Maybe he *did* tell some of the rats. Go ask 'em."

"Rats?"

"Kids. Beach rats."

The shoreline along Golden Beach had been eroded by a recent tropical storm. Thousands of tons of sand had been swept away in a few hours. Now placid, the blue-green waters lapped against a crumbling embankment. Where water met shore, a group of young, golden-brown bodies lay on towels and beached surfboards, as if left behind by the storm, or waiting for it to resume.

Sara kicked off her sandals and began to clamber down the steep embankment. When soft ground gave way, she rode the slow-moving avalanche, sitting on her bottom. She stood up laughing, shaking sand from the cuffs of her shorts, and several of the kids looked her way.

Cool eyes blinking in the hot sun. So young, she thought, so knowing.

"It's dangerous here," Sara said.

"Not if you know what you're doing," said a bored-looking adolescent boy.

Better try one of the girls, Sara decided, and focused on a small brown-haired girl who was sitting apart from the main group. A wannabee who wasn't, quite. Sara plopped down in the slightly damp sand a few yards away, not so close as to be threatening.

"Nice day," Sara said. The surf rats stared at her.

The brown-haired girl nodded shyly, rocking on her skinny, bikinied hips, willing enough to concede that it was, indeed, a nice day.

"The man who runs the surf shop said you guys might be able to help me."

"Old Hank the Shank?" the bored-looking boy responded.

Sara took the snapshop out of her purse and handed it to the girl. "The guy with the short brown hair, does that look like Dave Melborn?"

"I guess."

The boy moved languidly from his surfboard, crouching behind the girl.

"Ditzy Dave," he scoffed.

He shuffled back to his board and hunched down, an expression of smug satisfaction distorting an otherwise pleasant face.

"Did you know him?" Sara asked.

The girl nodded. "He hung out for a while, then later he worked, sort of. Keeping track of the rental boards. Lugging the stuff back inside when the shop closed up. Stuff like that."

Stuff like that. As Sara gently probed, a sketch of David Melborn slowly emerged. A quiet loner who had sought to attach himself to a much younger group, originally by paying the boys to give him Windsurfing lessons. Later, as they began to accept or at least tolerate his presence, he'd supplied beer, a case at a time. That generosity had ceased when he became a Hang Tuff employee.

"Old Hank was worried about the underage thing. Like we'd rat him out to the cops, right?" the boy said scornfully. "Dave was weird, but I guess he was okay, for an older dude."

"Weird?" Sara asked.

The girl was shaking her head. "He's not weird. Not really. Just, you know, kind of . . . lonesome."

The boy barked a laugh. "Yeah, right. Lonesome. Horny is more like it. Tried to get in your pants, didn't he, Charlene?"

The girl, Charlene, shook her head. Brown bangs flew up, exposing a sun-freckled forehead. "He never," she said, blushing. "Not really."

"Yeah, right."

The boy shoved his board into the water, pushing it ahead with his knees as he waded in after it. It was glassy calm, with no discernible surf. A few of the others followed, making a show of sleek entry.

Sara smiled at Charlene and was rewarded with a fleeting grin in return. "You know him pretty good, huh?" Sara said.

The girl shrugged and examined her toes. "A little. He talked to me sometimes. How come you're asking?"

"Dave has been hospitalized. We're trying to help him."

"What are you, his nurse?"

"I'm a doctor. One of several doctors interested in his case."

"But you knew him before, right?" the girl said, defensive.

"No, Charlene. I didn't know who he was for sure until a few minutes ago."

The girl scrunched up her nose, making a face. "I thought maybe you were his real girlfriend or something."

Real girlfriend. So whatever had happened between Charlene and David Melborn hadn't been quite real, as far as she was concerned. Or maybe as far as Surfer Dave had been concerned.

"Charlene, I think you can help me help Dave. Would you do that?"

"Sure. If I can."

"He's in a sort of coma, with neurological damage. His nervous system is all screwed up. It looks like he may have been exposed to a dangerous drug, we don't know what kind."

Charlene was shaking her head, staring at her pink-painted toenails. "Dave never even smoked dope."

"So he never took drugs?"

"Well," the girl said, hesitating. "Just his regular medicine."

"What kind of medicine, Charlene?"

"The kind from a doctor."

"You mean a prescription drug?" Sara said.

Charlene nodded, hugging her knees. "You could tell from the bottle."

"He ever say what the medicine was for?"

Another headshake. "Whatever it was, he said it meant he couldn't drink. Sometimes he'd sip a little beer, but that was it."

"Charlene? This is really important. It's possible that what happened to Dave is the result of an allergic reaction. Maybe a mistake at the drugstore. We have to find that bottle of pills, and check out any other kind of medicine he was taking."

The girl's expression was concerned, fearful.

"Where does he live, Charlene?" Sara said.

The girl's eyes shifted away. She was back to studying her toes. The way her shoulders hunched, Sara knew she was getting ready to lie.

"He never said."

"You never went to his home? He never invited you?"

The girl fidgeted, hugging her knees. After a while, in a voice smaller than a smear of cheap lipstick, she said, "There's a problem."

"I can handle problems," Sara assured her. "That's part of my job."

"I mean like against the law."

"Please," Sara said. "It could save a life."

CHAPTER NINE

The summons came while he was in the shower, covered with depilatory cream. He stepped out of the tiled stall and picked up the phone.

"The colonel requests that you join him for breakfast in the courtyard," a voice said.

Vidoc grunted, hung up the phone, got back into the shower. He rinsed away the depilatory, and with it the body hair that he found so offensive. Hair was filthy, a jungle of microbes. After the shower he stood under a heat lamp until his body was dry, then anointed his skin with a sterile ointment.

Total body cleanliness was not, as some normals believed, a fetish. It was a way of life. Soon enough he would be in a place where he had absolute control of his personal environment. Where he had control of everything.

Until then he would just have to be patient. No more lashing out at the normals. It wasn't safe.

Dr. Vidoc arrived at the courtyard wearing a black silk robe and Birkenstock sandals. The robe was cinched samurai-tight, emphasizing his long, ectomorphic slenderness.

"Good morning, Colonel."

"Emile, welcome."

They dined under a white canvas awning. The meal consisted of mango, fried bread, black beans, and strong coffee. A soldier's breakfast. Colonel Calavera began by raising a machete. It caught a glint of morning sunlight before arcing downward. Newly sharpened, the blade split the mango cleanly, leaving a thin, perfect groove in the plastic cutting board.

"A surgeon could use one of these, yes?" the colonel said, carefully daubing beads of moisture from the blade.

"A butcher might," Vidoc replied with a shrug. He found the colonel tedious, especially at meals, all that macho posturing.

"On the battlefield all surgeons are butchers. It is necessary, that quickness."

"You know best," Vidoc said, feigning deference.

The colonel, his host and benefactor, was a dull, venal man who had made a fortune out of training peasants to fight wars they did not comprehend. He would have made, Vidoc decided, a perfectly adequate Nazi of the lesser ranks, or a flunky under Stalin.

But what the colonel lacked in imagination, he more than made up for in money, connections, political influence. Hence the unpleasant necessity of helping to keep his *machismo* fully inflated.

"You like mango, Doctor?"

"Yes, of course."

"Then you must try it," he urged.

Vidoc made his face smile. It was an actor's trick he had learned many years before. Amazing what you could get away with, if you paid attention to the details. A raised eyebrow, a certain gesture, it was not necessary to feel the emotion so long as you projected it correctly. Normals believed what they saw; they rarely glimpsed beneath the mask.

To please the colonel, he made a show of lifting the spoon to his lips. The faintly acid fecundity of the fruit was nauseating. He hated mango. It was unclean.

The colonel, surveying the pleasing elegance of the courtyard, sighed deeply. "It is good to be back," he said. "Conditions in the paramilitary camps are very bad. The men are discouraged."

His latest endeavor was a power struggle between factions of Bolivian landowners, all of whom were intent on controlling the vast coca crop. The conflict had dragged on, depleting the forces on both sides, necessitating the importation of mercenary advisers. The colonel, who'd been without a good money war since Nicaragua, had been only too happy to offer his services.

"The spring offensive was a failure," he said, and launched into the details of the prolonged engagement.

Vidoc let him drone on, tuning most of it out. He wasn't interested in the details of yet another ugly little war. All that mattered was that someone—the colonel, the CIA, the Bolivians—

provide the financing for his project. If the combat demonstration was successful, money would no longer be a problem. Never again would he be forced to play supplicant to a cretin like the colonel. Sanctuary had a price, and he knew it to the penny.

"It was not just the bad weather," the colonel was saying. "The men have become discouraged. Lately they are finding ways to avoid action. Any excuse will do. The rain, the heat, the malaria."

Vidoc fiddled with the mango spoon. He had not yet swallowed the sliver of fruit. He allowed himself to picture the place called Castillo. Built into the remote mountains of Paraguay by a drug lord, since deceased in a car-bomb explosion, it now lay vacant. A high-tech fortress, forged of steel and inert plastics, self-contained and virtually impregnable. Best of all, the square miles of the estate include a village population of primitive Indians. Whoever owned Castillo owned the normals who lived there, which raised all sorts of interesting possibilities—living experiments in the Vidoc method, for instance.

For now Castillo was a place Vidoc went to in his head. Soon enough he would go there in the flesh, and make it his own.

The colonel was still blathering on about the conflict.

"Courage is all up here," he said, tapping his head. "A man has to believe he can win before he will risk his life. That is where you come in, Doctor. If your theory is correct, it could turn the war around."

"My method is no longer theoretical," said Vidoc, focusing his dark, expressionless eyes on the colonel. "It is a fact. Fear works, provided the controls are in place."

"As you say," the colonel conceded.

"The proof was in your possession."

The colonel shrugged elaborately. "A tragedy. Heberto was a trusted friend."

"My best units are missing, lost," Vidoc pointed out. "It was a stupid risk, using him. The whole project was jeopardized."

"Sometimes the unexpected happens. You have to adjust."

Vidoc made himself nod. It would not do to antagonize the colonel. Not before funding was in place.

"You have examined the replacements," the colonel said. "Are they satisfactory?"

"They'll do," Vidoc admitted.

"The paramilitary commanders arrive next week. Can we proceed with the demonstration on schedule?"

"I'll be ready."

The colonel grinned. Vidoc happened to know that his teeth, beautifully shaped and installed by a Los Angeles celebrity dentist, had cost the equivalent of a new Porsche.

"Come now, Doctor. You insult me if you don't try the mango."

Vidoc forced himself to swallow a small sliver of the fruit. In the privacy of his cabana he would disgorge it.

"What are you thinking, Doctor? You look *preocupado*. Very pensive."

"It's nothing, Colonel. A small detail."

Actually he was thinking that a spoon capable of gutting a mango could as easily be used to pluck out a human eye.

CHAPTER TEN

Valdez, alerted by her phone call, got out of his unmarked cruiser, shaking his head. "Hey, Dick Tracy," he said with a grin. "Nice work."

Following Charlene's directions, Sara had located the site of an abandoned condo project less than a mile from the surf shop. Large, sun-faded signs announced AQUATIC LIFESTYLES! LUXURY LIVING FOR LESS! The waterway was tinged brown here, mud churned up by boats speeding for Haulover Cut and the open sea.

The detective seemed genuinely enthusiastic about her discovery. "With a last name confirmed, I can plug into his military records, maybe get a line on him that way," he said.

"You're not mad?"

He looked surprised. "Why should I be mad?"

"I thought you might think I was interfering in police business."

"Hey, you tracked the guy down, found out where he lived, right? I don't call that interfering. Now where is this trailer located?"

"I'm not sure," Sara said. "The girl said it was hidden from view."

"Probably a construction trailer," he said. "Let's look around."

The real estate kiosk had been left open to the weather. A few sales brochures were glued to the splintered plywood, bleached white by the sun. None of the condo towers had been completed, or occupied, and mangrove roots had taken hold near the water's edge, seeking, with thin green shoots, to reclaim the landscape.

Bleak, Sara thought, even in sunlight it was a bleak, empty place.

"Charlene said he moved in without permission. That he never turned on the lights without covering the windows."

"You'd make a good detective, Dr. Copley."

"I got lucky, that's all. And please call me Sara."

"You make your own luck," he said, as if that settled it.

They found the trailer in the cavern of an unfinished parking garage. Pools of milky-gray water had collected where the drains were blocked by debris. Black plastic trash bags had been torn open by small claws, the reeking contents strewn. All the dim heat of the day seemed to have collected there under the thick concrete beams. Sara could feel the sweat running freely down her back, under her arms.

"The smell," she said, picking her way around a puddle.

"Just garbage," Valdez said, as if it could have been worse, much worse.

There was a stenciled sign on the little round-edged trailer.

PROPERTY OF MIDAS CONSTRUCTORS

Valdez tried the door. It was locked.

"Do you need a search warrant?" Sara asked.

"I need a pry bar."

He found a length of rusty steel re-bar, hefted it, and pried away the padlock and hasp. He stepped back as a pong of heat and stink wafted from the inside.

Sara was a little surprised to find that she was frightened by the prospect of entering the trailer. Of what she might find inside.

Valdez, sensing her hesitancy, said, "Let me check it out."

He ducked inside while Sara stood on the corrugated steel step and waited, squinting at the low slant of light that penetrated the gloom.

This is silly, she told herself, there's nothing to be afraid of here. But when Valdez touched her on the shoulder, she jumped.

"Hey, it's okay. Nobody home. Just a few rotten vegetables in the sink."

The air inside was hot and stale. Her eyes watered. Expecting a mess, the chaos of an unordered life, Sara was surprised by the tidiness of the interior. The single room had been organized by a methodical mind. A sofa bed was fitted with a clean white sheet, the corners neatly tucked under. Precisely folded clothing was arranged on an open shelf. A collection of self-help paperbacks, alphabetized by author, occupied another narrow shelf. A few cooking implements, all clean, were within reach of a single hot plate.

Even the rotting vegetables, collapsing into goo in the tiny sink, had a kind of precision about them. Sara revised her opinion of David Melborn. The troubled drifter who bought beer for kids and attempted the seduction of young brown-haired girls was not, at least, a dirty old man. Nor was there any evidence of sexual kinkiness. The only photograph, prominently displayed over the small bookshelf, was Melborn perched on a Windsurfer, looking drenched but happy.

"Know what I see?" Valdez said. "I see a guy who's trying to get his life back together. Recently divorced, maybe, or a boozer who's on the wagon. These shoes, for instance." He picked up a pair of gleaming black shoes. "Spit-polished, just like in the army. And it's not like he was wearing them to the beach."

The heat and the sweet organic stench made it hard to concentrate. "Charlene said he was taking medication. Let's try to find the bottle," Sara suggested.

In the tight tin box of the toilet stall Valdez found a medicine cabinet containing a dozen or so pill bottles. Sara took inventory.

"Vitamin supplements, aspirin. An unopened bottle of Valium. Elavil." She sighed. "All perfectly ordinary."

"Elavil?"

"Helps relieve depression."

Valdez peered at the prescription label. "Maybe he can help us," he said.

Sara looked at him expectantly.

Valdez shook the pill bottle. "E. Vidoc. The doctor who prescribed this stuff. I'll bet you dinner his first name is Edward."

The pill bottle was a lead, a possibility, but the real discovery was lying under the sofa bed. Sara noticed it on her way out. She got down on her hands and knees, retrieving a tightly rolled sleeping bag.

Holding it, her eyes filled with tears.

"Hey, take it easy," Valdez said. "Maybe the guy intended to go camping."

"This is Kurt's sleeping bag," she said. "He had it with him when he left."

CHAPTER ELEVEN

Lee Valdez sat in his Cherry Grove backyard, nursing a beer as he watched the sky fade.

Rain coming, he could feel it.

The Grove, a sixties project of modest bungalows, had neither cherries nor a grove. It was a thoroughly middle-class development with no particular ethnic affiliation, which was just the way Valdez liked it. The kind of safe, American place he'd yearned for as a kid, in the squalor of the Calle Ocho tenements.

He closed his eyes and pictured Sara Copley. Those long legs, the bright, intelligent look in her eyes. It was amazing the way she had checked out the surf shop on her own, got a location from some kid at the beach. Kids probably would have taken off at the sight of a real detective. Showed a streak of independence that could be trouble in the future, though. He would have to keep a close eye on her. A civilian could get in big trouble nosing around certain parts of Miami. Hell, *everywhere* in Miami.

When the phone rang, he half-expected it to be Sara, telling him she'd cracked the case. It was Derrick Clancy, the young patrolman who'd found Surfer Dave unconscious in the street.

"Detective Valdez? You gave me your number, told me to call if I heard anything about that John Doe we found on the Calle Ocho. Remember?"

"Sure I do. What have you got?"

"This is kind of weird, sir. I think I've got another one. Right in the same area, too."

* * *

It was just starting to rain when Valdez backed out of his driveway. Grape-sized pellets detonated against the windshield, rattled the car roof as he cruised the expressway, looking for the exit to Eighth Street and Little Havana. For a few minutes it was like driving underwater. Then, as abruptly as it began, the deluge stopped. Valdez enjoyed a rainstorm, provided it was brief. For an hour or so the city would look clean and new. He liked the way it shined, especially at night, renewed and bright, like an enormous tropical toy.

Officer Clancy, despite the Irish name, was African-American, a migrant from upstate New York. His patrol car was parked, lights flashing, outside a little Cuban grocery. The headlights illuminated an alley beside the store.

Clancy grinned. He had the cocky confidence of a patrolman who'd never been burned, who expected to do well on the exams.

"You sure you wanna catch this, Detective?"

Valdez shook hands. "I appreciate the call. You the one who found him?"

"Nope. That honor goes to the owner here, a Señor Morales. He called in, I responded."

Valdez nodded. "You called for EMS?"

Clancy indicated that an ambulance was on the way.

"Great," Valdez said. "Could you stand by out there, make sure they don't move the victim until I've had a chance to interview Morales? Get somebody to take a few pictures, if possible."

The bodega owner was waiting inside the store. A portly middle-aged grocer with thinning gray hair and sad brown eyes.

"I take it upon myself," he said. "I give him cash from my own pocket."

Valdez got out his spiral-bound notebook.

"From the beginning, please. Your full name?"

"Rolando Garcia Matero Morales. I am called Rolly. This is my store."

"Did you find the victim, Rolly?"

Morales sighed heavily. "What happened, I buy him. I think I am doing the right thing, now I am not so sure. Policeman, detectives, where does it end?"

"You *bought* the victim? Please explain."

"This Marielito, I don't know his name, he comes into this place, very drunk. Or maybe high on drugs, how do I know? He comes to beg for money. So of course I show him my gun."

"Of course," Valdez said. Bodega owners were perhaps the best-armed merchants in Miami. Many kept shotguns beneath the counter. Fuck with a bodega, you might get blown right out the door. "Go on."

"This scum comes in, he says to me, I have an Americano to sell. Like you, Detective, I am confused by this. An Americano to sell? What does this mean? And why does he come into my store? I tell you, he was a *peligroso loco*, a lunatic. He thinks he can sell this unconscious Americano he has found. A hospital will buy him, he tells me, they will have use for his organs. His heart and liver, for transplants. You crazy, mon, I tell him, you need brain transplant. 'Give me ten dollars,' he says. 'For ten dollars he is yours. Then you can sell him to the hospital and make a great profit.' What could I do?"

"What did you do, Rolly?"

The grocer sighed, rolled his eyes. "Like a fool, I give him the ten dollars and he gives me the Americano."

The victim was lying in a child's red wagon in the alley beside the bodega. An American Flyer wagon, Valdez noted, which seemed weirdly appropriate. Caucasian male, dark hair, aged about thirty. His legs and arms were splayed over the sides, touching the wet ground. Needle tracks on the right arm. His torso and feet were bare, but his lower body was clothed in tattered blue jeans, damp from the rain. Pulse was barely there, but Valdez was convinced he was alive. As much as the other sleeper had been alive.

"The crazy Marielito was pulling him around in that little wagon," the grocer said. "All he give him to eat was some water, from a spoon. Drip it in his mouth, I don't even know if he swallow. I think the man is dying."

The EMS team arrived.

As the gurney was being unloaded, Valdez knelt down and quickly checked the victim's hands. No surprise, the fingertips were covered with new scar tissue. An acid burn, just like Surfer Dave.

Valdez gave the grocer ten dollars.

"You did the right thing," he said. "Any idea where I can find this crazy Marielito?"

"Sure thing," the grocer said. "He's right over there, standing in the crowd."

When he pointed, the suspect took off, a scrawny, long-haired guy running in big, loping strides.

Valdez chased him, thinking, You're mine, Mr. American Flyer. Mine.

When the rain broke, Sara ran to shut the sliding glass door to the balcony. The sea had turned white, boiling in the downpour. A gust of wind made the glass shudder, and her hands were slick with moisture.

Back in the little kitchen she poured herself a glass of white wine and carried it to the couch. She had been reading a medical reference on neurological disorders. Specifically the coma state. What she found there wasn't encouraging. So-called designer drugs, compounds cooked up in illicit labs, had been known to mimic the effects of a wide range of disorders. Parkinson's disease, for instance. In many cases the damage was irreversible. Victims had suffered paralysis, respiratory failure, a whole range of symptoms. Treatment depended on the individual case—it was such a recent problem that there was no standard literature on the subject.

If Kurt had been exposed to the same drug as David Melborn . . . but she didn't know if that was true. The fact that Kurt had been staying with Dave, or at least had visited (the sleeping bag proved that) didn't mean he had suffered the same fate. Did it?

But if Kurt Palmer wasn't similarly incapacitated, where was he? Wouldn't he have been looking for his friend? Checked the hospitals? At the very least left a note on the trailer, or inquired at the surf shop?

Sara closed her eyes. A trained scientist, she had never quite given up on the idea of instinct. Was Kurt still out there? She couldn't feel him. She couldn't feel anything.

When she got up to refill her wineglass, the rain had stopped.

CHAPTER TWELVE

He went by the street name Cacahuette. Peanut. A refugee of the Mariel boatlift, he was a career criminal. And from the marks on his scrawny, tattooed arms, a drug addict as well.

"So I found this Americano and gave him to the grocer. I rescue the man. So what?"

Peanut stirred nervously in his chair, ignoring the tape recorder on the table. His attention was focused on the one-way mirror. Peanut had black shoulder-length hair that gleamed with oil, a much-broken nose, an undercut chin, and no teeth. An ugly specimen and, Valdez was certain, an habitual liar.

"You sold him to Señor Morales, Peanut. For ten dollars."

Peanut was shaking his head, making jittery signs of denial with his hands. "No way, man. No way. The fat grocer, I ask him for money and he gives it to me. So what? Is that a crime? Where is the crime here?"

Valdez didn't care one way or another about this sleazeball. If they found a way to indict him, fine. If not, he'd soon enough be arrested for the next crime, or the one after that. Right now all he wanted from Peanut was a location, where exactly the sleeper had been found. To that end, Valdez had obtained use of a Detective Division interrogation room. The idea was to impress Peanut with the severity of his situation. Maybe the tape recorder or the one-way mirror would make him feel important enough to tell the truth for once, or at least give himself away.

"Where did you find the Americano?"

Peanut shrugged elaborately, watching his reflection in the mirror. Valdez knew the routine. Peanut was attempting to convey the impression that he was a hard case, not easily intimidated by a mere cop. The stalemate went on for thirty minutes, with Valdez prying, wheedling, threatening, all to no avail.

"The Americano is very sick," Valdez said, exasperated enough to try the sympathy angle. When that had no effect, he countered with, "If he dies, you could be charged with accessory to murder."

Peanut scoffed, played with his hair. He was unimpressed by idle threats. In his world murder was not a very severe crime.

"Speak to me, Peanut," the weary detective sighed, "or I'll tell everyone you're my snitch."

Valdez saw the flinch, knew he had scored: By a process of elimination he had found a way to jerk the Marielito's chain. The realization made him smile.

"I'll have you charged with solicitation," he threatened. "I'll make sure the word goes out on the street that you're a *maricón* selling yourself to fags for heroin. Then everyone will believe you're my snitch."

Peanut glared at him. "Fuck your mother," he said.

It was the worst of insults. Killing words.

Valdez grinned even more.

"Where did you find the Americano?" he demanded.

Peanut named the place, a salvage yard located no more than five blocks from where the first sleeper had been recovered.

"They got the van in there, man. Stripped it down good. Had nice new tires, ten bucks each."

A tingle of alertness went through Valdez. Salvage yard? Van?

"What kind of van?" he asked in a conspiratorial tone. Exuding the impression that he and the suspect were pals, street buddies.

"Alamo Rental," Peanut said. He giggled; it was a surprisingly feminine sound, *tee-hee-hee*. "That was the bumper sticker until somebody, he took off the bumper."

"Are you saying you found the Americano inside a rental van?"

"Sure, him and the others just lying in the back," Peanut said impatiently. He seemed to have lost track of what he had revealed, what he hadn't.

Valdez took a deep breath, eased it out.

"What others?" he asked, feigning a casualness he did not feel.

Peanut snorted, disgusted at the detective's obvious ignorance of the situation.

"The undead, man. The other undead ones. I only took just one. That's all would fit in the little red wagon."

Clancy was waiting in his cruiser outside the salvage yard when Valdez arrived. The detective got out with Peanut handcuffed to his wrist. The Marielito had protested vigorously about being cuffed, at one point threatening to bite (not much of a threat considering his toothless condition), but Valdez had no intention of giving chase again. One footrace per evening was plenty.

"Are we going to need a warrant to go in there?" Clancy wanted to know.

"We have a report that several impaired individuals may be inside," Valdez said. "It would be a dereliction of duty to risk lives by waiting for a warrant, right, Peanut?"

The Marielito shook the cuffs and swore in gutter Spanish.

"I help you, man, and this is what I get!" he protested.

"What'd he say?" Clancy asked.

"He said there are more sleepers in that yard, and we better get them out right away."

"That's what I thought he said," Clancy said, grinning. "You want to go in now, or wait for EMS?"

"I'm tired," Valdez said. "Let's get this over with. Old Peanut here is a pathological liar. He could be making this up."

Valdez didn't think so, though: Peanut didn't have that much imagination.

The salvage yard was small and decrepit, the size of a house lot, enclosed by a cinder-block wall that was topped with barbed wire. Valdez knew the place had once been used as a chop shop for stolen cars; from the outside at least it now looked to be out of business.

"How did you get in there?" he asked the Marielito.

"Take off these bracelets, I show you."

Valdez sighed. "I guess I'll have to go over the top, drag you through the barbed wire."

Peanut led them around the corner to an iron gate in the cinder-block wall. A heavy chain secured the gate. Valdez swore—he didn't have any chain cutters.

"Relax, dude," Peanut said in a parody of English. In Spanish he added, "Man who used to own this yard, he lost the key to the padlock, so all he do, the stupid fool, he just wrap the chain around."

"Where is the owner now?"

Peanut shrugged, looked away. "They say he in jail."

Officer Clancy unwrapped the chain and pushed the creaky gate open. He unclipped the flashlight from his belt and unholstered his sidearm. Flashlight in the left hand, gun in the right, with the safety off. Readiness posture by the book, Valdez noted.

"They got a dog in here?" Clancy wanted to know. "I bet they got a dog."

With Valdez translating, Peanut insisted that there was no dog, or that there had been a dog and it died; it was hard to tell what he was saying. Valdez shook him by the wrists, demanding that he get his story straight.

"Somebody poison that crazy junkyard dog," Peanut finally admitted. "Wasn't me, I swear," he added, without much conviction.

The salvage yard was cluttered with heavily rusted auto parts; mostly axles, torn-apart transmissions, and stacks of truck tires. The only structure was a creaky shed roof with a chainfall. Under it was a cannibalized delivery van with the rear axle pulled.

"Is that the rental vehicle?" Valdez asked.

Peanut nodded. Valdez jerked him along to the van. The lock on the rear door had been chiseled off. Valdez yanked the door open.

Inside the van someone screamed, *"¡No disparen! No disparen!"*

Officer Clancy held his fire as requested. His flashlight beam revealed a rail-thin Cuban kneeling on a wretched mattress with his hands up. He stank of fruit-flavored alcohol and vomit.

"Whatta ya know," Clancy said. "This one isn't asleep. Musta been the cheap wine woke him up."

The drunk was babbling incoherently. It became clear that he knew and feared Peanut, that despite evidence to the contrary—the cuffs, Clancy's uniform, Valdez's detective shield—he was convinced they were killers Peanut had hired to collect a debt or exact revenge for some unspecified affront.

Peanut, of course, encouraged this ego-enhancing scenario.

"Pig fucker!" he swore at the cowering drunk. "Eater of turds! Where did you put the undead ones? They belong to me, cocksucker!"

Valdez had had enough. He jerked Peanut to the ground and placed the business end of his 9-mm pistol against the scrawny Marielito's nose.

"You will shut up, now," he warned. "Not one word. Silence. Nod if you understand."

Peanut nodded. Valdez jerked him back to his feet.

"Let's get out of here," he said to Clancy. "I can't wait to get this little scumbag off my wrist."

It was Clancy who heard it first.

A kind of low humming, accompanied by a feral scratching noise. The sounds seemed to originate behind a pile of sheet-metal fenders. The dirt underfoot was muddy with spilled crankcase oil and rain puddles. Mud adhered in clumps to Valdez's shoes as he dragged Peanut behind the pile, following the beam of Clancy's flashlight.

He saw small red eyes. Lots of small red eyes.

"Oh fuck," Clancy said in a high-pitched voice. "Rats. I *hate* rats."

There were, indeed, rats. Most of the rodents exploded away, frightened by the flashlight. A few of the bolder specimens refused to abandon their feast until Clancy kicked at a fender.

"Holy Mother of God," Valdez whispered.

The rats had been feeding on human flesh.

There were five bodies sprawled in the oily mud. Blending in, hard to see until you really looked. Dragged from the van and just dumped, Valdez assumed. What kind of human beings would do this?

The flashlight beam trembled. Most of the rodents had congregated around one mud-caked victim lying flat on his back, arms sprawled out.

Valdez thought—hoped—the man was dead.

But the humming noise continued.

"I think he's alive," Clancy said in disbelief.

They knelt in the mud next to the rigid body. The eyes were open, Valdez noted, staring fixedly up into the night sky. Most of his left ear was gone, and bone glistened where the soft parts of his cheek had been gnawed away by the small, furtive teeth of the feeding rodents.

The humming came from between tightly clenched teeth.

"The poor bastard," Valdez said. "He's trying to scream."

CHAPTER THIRTEEN

"The situation is temporary," the nurse told her. "Monday all of these, ah, special cases are to be transferred to Experimental Medicine."

"Is Dr. Harding here?" Sara asked.

Valdez's call had awakened her from a sound sleep. She was aware that she looked a mess, and didn't care.

The nurse shook her head. "Dr. Harding is assisting in surgery."

"I need to see them."

The nurse hesitated, examining Sara's pass. "I really should check with Dr. Harding. He'll be out in an hour or so."

"Just a look. It's important to me."

The detective had told her that none of the victims resembled Kurt Palmer, but she had to be sure. She had to see for herself.

"I'm sorry if this sounds rude, Dr. Copley, but the chief of medicine makes the rules. He was very clear on enforcing staff-only access to these particular patients."

The nurse finally agreed to let her in "just for a peek" when Sara promised not to interfere with any ongoing treatment.

The ICU was crowded with personnel. Several harried-looking nurses and a young, baby-faced trauma specialist. A hyper type, he seemed unaware of Dr. Harding's "staff-only" rules, and was perfectly willing to let Sara inspect the victims.

"This is a new twist," he said, sounding almost pleased. "We get multiple gunshots, slice and dice, car wrecks, but this is my first mass rodent attack."

Sara checked out the sleepers. Four new victims were being

treated, bandaged, hooked up to IV and life-monitoring equipment. All of them looked as blank and lifeless as David Melborn. And none of them was Kurt Palmer.

"This is it?" Sara asked. "I was told that five victims had been recovered."

The physician was nodding. "Harding's in there with a surgeon," he said. "These four aren't too badly bitten, maybe lose a few toes, but the fifth guy had his face pretty well chewed off."

"Where's the surgery?"

"Down one," he said. "But you can't go in there."

Sara turned and headed out of the unit. "All I want is a look."

Lee Valdez squinted through the bug-flecked windshield, looking for street signs as he drove slowly through Coral Gables. Conceived as a fantasy residence for wealthy Americans, the Miami suburb was now a vast landscaped fortress, a fiefdom for the rich Hispanics who had displaced the original inhabitants. Bordered by canals, patroled by private security forces, Coral Gables was the plump underbelly of Miami, haven for the entrepreneurs, bankers, politicians, and drug czars.

He was not looking for a drug dealer's estate, however, but for Cresido Arms, an apartment complex. The address of the man who'd signed the rental agreement found in the van's glove compartment.

Almost midnight. That was good. Roust a suspect from deep sleep and he tended to babble. Such a man might inadvertently tell the truth about where he happened to be on a certain night, how he happened to leave five helpless human beings to be nibbled by rats.

The curved entrance to Cresido Arms was landscaped with coconut palms illuminated by spotlights submerged in the Bermuda grass. It was a nice postcard effect, and Valdez couldn't even guess how much luxury apartments went for in this part of the city. He left his car running, located unit one, and leaned on the doorbell. He was pleased to hear it pealing loudly inside the apartment.

Wake up you fuck, talk to me.

There was no response. After he got bored with the doorbell, Valdez began to use his fists. Still no response. Valdez went to a window, hooked his hands around the wrought-iron security bars and began to rattle them.

The door to an adjacent unit opened. A little old lady came out on the steps, dressed in a pink nightgown. She had bluish hair, and she aimed an Uzi submachine gun at Valdez.

He held himself still.

"Detective Valdez," he said, hoping she could see the badge hanging out of his breast pocket. "Metro-Dade Police."

The Uzi remained firmly aimed at his abdomen.

"It's the middle of the night," the old lady said in precise, formal Spanish. "What do you want here?"

"I need to ask Heberto Raimez a few questions. I was trying to wake him."

The old lady said, "Then you're trying to wake the dead, Mr. Policeman. Heberto died last week."

"What?" His hands slowly slipped from the wrought-iron bars.

"His heart killed him."

Valdez was stunned and looked it.

"I had no idea," he said.

The old woman took that to mean that he was a friend of the late Heberto. "You missed the funeral," she admonished him. "It was a very sad affair. His daughter, bless her, she was hysterical with grief. Like any good daughter."

"His daughter," Valdez stammered. He had lowered his hands.

"You do not know her?"

"I knew only Heberto," he said, going with it. "We were, um, business associates."

"Ah," the old lady said, as if that explained everything. "You can pay your respects to Mercedes."

"And where might I find the poor girl?"

"At her *botánica*," the old lady said, retreating into her apartment. "On the Calle Ocho. She is a Santería *bruja*. A witch."

CHAPTER FOURTEEN

Sara had long ago decided that hospitals, like people, had personalities: Mass General, where she had served her residency, was harried, nervous, brilliant, a genius nerd with leaky pens in his pocket. Cypress Medical Center was cool, impersonal, an opinionated, air-conditioned schoolmarm with a sharp tongue.

And slow elevators.

She took the stairs, asked directions, located the surgery complex. She had expected to find a security guard blocking the door—it was that kind of place, and Miami was mad for private security. But no one blocked her way or questioned her visiting physician's pass.

Inside there was access to lockers and a central scrub room. From the scrub room you could see all four surgical theaters, separated by walls of thick plate glass. Only one was being used. She could make out Dr. Harding, a surgeon, and a surgical nurse.

Although she had no intention of contaminating anything with her touch, Sara dutifully followed the rules, scrubbing quickly and donning greens, gloves, booties, and a paper face mask.

Sara pushed through the door. The nurse's eyes registered surprise at the intrusion.

Despite being told that the victim's face had been severely damaged, Sara wasn't quite prepared for the grim reality. Bone and gristle had been exposed from the corner of the eye socket to the base of the jaw. Most of one ear had been torn away. The nose would need to be almost entirely reconstructed.

With a sense of overwhelming relief she noted that the victim's hair was red. It was not blond Kurt Palmer on the cutting table.

"Who is this?" Harding demanded. "Carter, is she one of your associates?"

Carter, the surgeon, muttered that she was not. He had his hands full cleaning the wounds, and clearly expected the chief of medicine to handle the situation.

"Dr. Sara Copley," she said, aware that the mask and cap made her hard to recognize. "From the PHD. We met the other day."

Harding blinked, his eyes hard and blue behind steel-rimmed glasses. "Don't Public Health employees know better than to break into the middle of a procedure, Dr. Copley?"

"I thought I might know this man."

"And do you?"

She shook her head.

"Then please leave the room, Doctor. You'll have to indulge your curiosity some other time."

The surgeon was about to begin suturing, working pieces of muscle tissue together right at bone level. Sara noticed the music playing in the background, a Chopin piano sonata. It seemed a strange contrast to the controlled violence of surgery.

"Can I ask you a question, Dr. Harding? Why is there no anesthesiologist present?"

The surgeon glanced sharply at her and then back to his work. Harding gripped her elbow with a gloved hand, steered her away.

"You'll have to get out," he said. "This is a private facility. You have no authority here."

It had been a long, stressful day. Sara could feel a hot blush of anger moving up from her neck to her face.

"I'm not here to write out a complaint, damn it. But I'm not leaving until you tell me why there's no anesthesiologist."

Dr. Harding responded as if lecturing a child. "It's very simple. The patient is in a vegetative coma state. He is insensitive to pain. Therefore, no anesthesia is necessary."

"Detective Valdez reported that the victim appeared to be in great pain."

"He was mistaken. I'm warning you, Dr. Copley. This is not your concern."

"You're performing major reconstructive surgery without anesthesia, of *course* I'm concerned. It's inhuman."

The door was at her back. Harding pushed her through it, pulled the door shut behind him. He yanked off his mask.

"How dare you suggest that we would subject a patient to inhuman pain? This is a unique situation here. Anesthesia might actually be dangerous."

"The man can't react," Sara said. "You can't know what he might be feeling."

"He doesn't feel a thing," Dr. Harding said. "I personally guarantee it."

It was as if he floated slightly above the table, paralyzed but acutely sensitive. His will to move was a fist-sized thing inside his mind, and the fist could not be unclenched.

No matter how hard he tried, he could not tear himself away from the source of pain, the cruel needle that burned, hot and searing, each time it pierced him. A pain even more unendurable than the tiny, gnawing teeth that had torn his flesh.

Fingers probed raw bone and nerve endings. The needle stabbed. Pain came in wave after wave, eroding the small, unnamable core of his sanity.

He was disintegrating. He was screaming inside, but no one could hear him.

PART TWO
AWAKENING

"Fear is the great tenderizer of human souls."
—EMILE VIDOC, M.D.

CHAPTER ONE

Monday, October 2

Emile Vidoc was awake in his hammock when the colonel entered his cabana an hour or so before dawn. He rarely slept deeply. The nylon hammock, designed to suspend burn victims, helped him rest and recover his strength. He zoned out, letting his mind go blank, but he never dreamed. The concept of surrendering control to a REM state was so normal, so abhorrent.

He recognized the colonel's heavy step, that distinctive bow-legged gait, and reached for the .45 Colt automatic he kept in a Velcro pouch under the hammock.

Trust the colonel? No way.

"Emile?" A voice hissed from the dark hallway. "Are you awake?"

Vidoc shifted in the hammock, aimed the .45 at the bedroom door.

"Come on in, Colonel."

A hand fumbled, the door opened.

"I have news," the colonel said. His left hand patted the wall inside the door, searching for the light switch.

"Never mind the lights," said Vidoc, who had excellent night vision. "I'm resting my eyes."

"What?"

"Speak. What news do you bring?"

"They've been found."

Vidoc twisted himself to an upright position. A sparkle of anticipation tickling his hairless scalp.

"My units?" he said softly. "My volunteers?"

"The police located the stolen van. Some junkyard near the Calle Ocho. Your, um, volunteers were nearby."

"Who told you this?"

"I have many loyal friends," he said, "in the Cuban community, in county government, in the police department. Naturally they keep me informed."

Vidoc touched his sandaled feet to the tile floor, steadied the sway of the hammock. "They were alive?" he asked.

"I think so," the colonel said. "They were taken to an area hospital. The Cypress Medical Center. One of them was badly bitten. Some animal in the junkyard, apparently."

"Alive," Vidoc said. "Ten days without care or feeding. It's remarkable."

"My concern, Emile, is the hospital. These men will be examined, tested."

Vidoc was smiling in the dark. Ten days and they were still alive. Proof positive that his method worked.

"Not to worry, Colonel. Each unit has had its fingerprints removed, which will slow down the identification process. And even if they *are* identified, all reference to my clinic has been eradicated from the VA computer files. This can't be connected to me. Or to you."

"You're sure of that?"

"Quite sure. We can proceed with the replacement units. Run the live-combat demonstration as planned."

"So we leave these men as they are? In the custody of this hospital?"

"For now," Vidoc said. "I suggest we monitor the situation."

The colonel felt for the door.

"Next time I bring a flashlight," he said.

Vidoc aimed the .45 at the small of his retreating back. All it would take, a little squeeze, turn out the colonel's light forever.

Not yet, though. Money first, then sanctuary. And finally, in the darkness that followed, whatever he liked.

CHAPTER TWO

Sara surrendered her purse and walked through the metal detector. The policewoman glanced into the purse, handed it back.

"You don't carry no gun?" she asked.

"No."

"Where you hail from, mind my askin'?"

"Boston," Sara said.

"I bet it real nice up there, huh?"

"It's okay," Sara said.

"Well, miss, I mean Doctor, you might think on it."

"Think about what?" Sara asked.

"Arming yourself. This a different world down here. Won't be no proper Bostonian gentlemens steppin' up to defend you, not in Miami. Male or female, citizen or criminal, *everybody* in sunny Florida got a gun. 'Cept a few tourist, they don't know better."

Sara forced a smile. "I'll think about it."

Cleared through Metro-Dade Police security, Sara found her way to the Missing Persons Unit office. The door was locked. She knocked. A shadow moved behind the frosted glass, and then Lee Valdez was greeting her.

"Sorry. Office won't be open to the public for another hour. I'm trying to catch up on paperwork."

Valdez was dressed casually in a crew shirt and jeans. He looked younger, almost boyish, although his eyes were bloodshot—evidence of a late night and the early morning that followed. He handed Sara a mug of coffee, indicated that she should follow him into his office. She noticed the glow of a computer screen, a desk littered with files.

"You sounded pretty upset when you called," he said.

Sara took a seat. "Maybe I overreacted. But I'm starting to think that something very strange is going on at Cypress Medical Center."

"What exactly happened?"

She described the incident in the surgery, Dr. Harding's reaction. "I got the impression he was trying to hide something," she said. "That he had his own agenda."

"Any idea what that might be?"

Sara shook her head. "He threw me out before I could get a really good look. And there's always the possibility that Harding is right about the insensitivity to pain. Maybe the humming you heard was simply an involuntary nervous reaction. Some kind of seizure."

"Maybe," Valdez said doubtfully. "You're the doctor."

Sara sighed. "Not on this case, I'm not. Two o'clock in the morning I get a call from my department supervisor, reminding me that PHD staff have no authority to intervene in a private facility."

"What did you say to that?"

"What could I say?" said Sara, frustrated. "I promised to stop bothering the great Dr. Harding. But I can't help thinking it could have been Kurt in there. And that we still don't know what drug they were exposed to."

Valdez gestured at the computer screen. "Our best lead into Surfer Dave's drug history is the doctor who wrote him prescriptions," he said. "Emile Vidoc. He's licensed in the state of Florida, all right, but I can't seem to find an address. Seems to have been deleted from the registry."

Sara frowned. "That's odd. And he's not listed in the phone book? Or any of the professional directories?"

Valdez shook his head. "There are two possibilities," he said. "Maybe he's moved to another state."

Sara waited.

"Or maybe he doesn't want to be found," Valdez said. "More coffee?"

Nando loved *Sesame Street*. Especially Ernie. Whenever Ernie came on the screen, screaming in badly dubbed Spanish, Nando would go into fits of laughter. Sometimes the laughing fits would infect his brother Jorge, who preferred cartoons and car-chase scenes, and then the two boys would scream and laugh, rolling on

the soiled carpet of their Coral Gables motel room until Luto came
by and told them to shut the fuck up.

"Shoe fuck up!" Nando would parrot. "Shoe fuck up!"

Both brothers were learning a few handy words in American
from Luto. Filthy pigs. Dirt balls. You scum. Also "hambuggerfry,"
which is what they were fed two or three times a day. The meals
arrived, soggy and cold, in Styrofoam containers. For the rest they
subsisted on crackers and cans of sweet discount soda pop, supplied
a case at a time.

"Is this the paramilitary?" little Nando kept asking. "Very
strange army. When do we learn to be soldiers? When do they give
us rifles?"

Jorge, though he was a man of fifteen, had no answers. They
had been locked in the room for days, forbidden to leave or to show
themselves. The door opened only for the delivery of food or, every
morning, for sheets and towels, which they dutifully stored in the
bureau. Fine white sheets, very valuable. Twice the doorway had
been filled by the tall, elongated figure of the man they called El
Tigre, because of his terrible white smile. Both times he had poked
and prodded them, testing their courage by sticking long, sharp
needles into their arms, taking with him bright red vials of their
blood.

Jorge assumed the blood was being given to a priest, who would
bless it or drink it, he wasn't sure, exactly. He knew, because of
what he had seen in the village, that priests did things with blood to
make soldiers strong, to appease the gods of war.

Nando thought El Tigre was drinking it himself.

"I can see the blood in his eyes," he said, convinced that El
Tigre was only part human, and a bad part at that.

"We must obey," Jorge assured him. "They are testing us.
Deciding if we are brave enough to join the army. You heard the
great colonel. Only a few strong men are required. The weak are left
behind."

Although they did not speak of it, the two brothers had a great
fear of being abandoned in the motel room. Of a day when the door
would never open, and the pictures on the tube would go black
forever. What would become of them? Would they have to eat the
mattress? Chew paper straws for nourishment? They had no clear
idea where they were, except that it was somewhere in the great
nation of Miami.

Sesame Street was not quite over when, on what was to be their final hour in the room, the colonel himself arrived to fill the doorway, bathed in sunlight.

"*Soldados!*" he cried in his wonderful, resonant voice. "*Leones de libertad!*"

He stepped into the room, choked and coughed, and then barked in English, "What a stink! Luto, put these two pigs in the shower."

"But, Colonel, the shower stinks even worse than they do."

The colonel insisted. Luto guided the boys to a clean shower stall in an adjacent unit and made them strip and stand under the water. Afterward their clothes were put in the shower separately, while Jorge and Nando stood by, naked and confused. What had they done wrong? Was this part of the training? Was this a test of courage?

The brothers were loaded into a windowless transport van, dressed in their dripping clothes. The colonel, immaculate in a snow-white *guayabera*, saw them off. "Lionhearted men of liberty! This is a great day! In a few hours you will be in Camp Libertad, training with experienced freedom fighters. Your platoon commander is Sergeant Hernandez. Do exactly as he says."

The brothers swore on the life of their mother to honor and obey Sergeant Hernandez. Colonel Calavera slid the van doors shut and threw the lock. When the vehicle was clear of the parking lot, he turned to Luto and said, "Be sure to have the room fumigated. Why is it these *campesinos* always stink of shit?"

CHAPTER THREE

Paul Hobart, the Dade County toxicologist, wore his blond hair in a neat ponytail. Under his lab coat was a T-shirt emblazoned with a picture of James Dean and the motto LIVE HARD, DIE YOUNG, BE AN ORGAN DONOR. Sara knew Hobart only slightly, but he seemed a sympathetic type, open and friendly.

"Call me Hobie," he said. "Everybody does."

"Hobie, I need a favor. Can you request test samples from a private facility?"

"Depends," he said. "What samples, what facility?"

"Blood and fluid. From Cypress Medical Center."

He shrugged. "They send work to us all the time. I don't see why it would be a problem."

Sara was relieved, and showed it. "The patient's name is David Melborn. Until yesterday he was listed as a John Doe."

Hobie nodded, wrote down the name. "Okay. Mind if I ask what your interest is?"

Sara hesitated. "I should tell you right up front this isn't a PHD case, not yet. Melborn is a friend of a friend. I'm . . . worried about him."

Hobie gave her arm a reassuring squeeze. "That's good enough," he said. "What are we looking for?"

"Neurotoxins," she said. "He may have been exposed to a designer drug—I was told there were traces of an alkaloid substance. And that's all I know."

"I'll see what I can do," Hobie promised.

Later, at her office, Sara wondered if she had done the right thing. Going behind Dr. Harding's back could be dangerous—he'd already demonstrated his willingness to complain to her superiors. And yet she felt that she *had* to know what had happened to Kurt's friend Surfer Dave.

Lee Valdez and his computer would go at it from the identification angle. She would bring her expertise to bear on the condition itself. If the drug that caused the strange sleeping coma could be isolated, maybe the symptoms could be reversed.

Dr. Richard Harding on the phone to a consulting editor he knows at the *New England Journal of Medicine:*

"Dexter? How goes the battle? Appreciate your indulgence, Dex, we've got something interesting going here. Shaping up as a unique neurological disorder, I think you people might be interested. . . . I have under my care six patients, all with identical symptoms. Victims of a drug overdose, that's my theory, some designer drug, you know these underground chemists, they're all whacked-out from trying their own recipes. . . .

"Their condition? Well, that's where it gets sexy. Casual observation leaves the impression of a vegetative coma state, with some form of paralysis that radically slows heartbeat and respiration. . . . How radical? Try thirty beats per minute, Dex. And steady, almost no variation. . . . Brain scan? I was getting to that. CAT shows no obvious damage. EEG is inconclusive, but the odd thing is that all six seem to be in a deep alpha state, as if under the influence of a hypnotic drug. Metabolic rate is extremely low. You see the charts, the blood workups, you'd almost have to conclude they're in a hibernative state—except that humans don't hibernate, right, Dexter? . . .

"No, I'm serious. Dead serious. I'm also intrigued as hell. Because, Dex old boy, last night one of my sleeping beauties needed emergency surgery—and the surgery was successfully performed *without* anesthesia . . . No, we didn't tie him to the gurney, we didn't *have* to, that's my point. *They do not react to pain*. . . . No, the spinal-nerve system is intact, no evidence of cerebral damage. . . . Yes, I *told* you this was interesting. . . . There's more, Dex, just hang on, okay? During the surgical procedure? Heartbeat, blood pressure, respiration, all remained constant. And the patient remained totally immobilized, not even a muscle twitch. . . .

"Yes, of *course* I see the possibilities. If we can isolate this mystery drug, moderate the side effects, there are patent possibilities. . . . that's right, Dex, a new nerve blocker. And yes, I'm well aware of how much revenue a new form of painkiller could generate. The pharmaceutical corporations will fall all over themselves, bidding for rights to the patent.

"First thing, Dex, I'm going to transfer these boys to our Experimental Medicine wing. I forgot to mention one thing, ha ha—all six are indigent patients. You get it? This is a perfect opportunity. No family members to raise a fuss if we put them in a controlled situation, see just how deep this pain blocker goes. . . ."

CHAPTER FOUR

On his lunch hour Lee Valdez crossed the Calle Ocho and entered the *botánica* owned by Mercedes Raimez, daughter of the late Heberto Raimez, who had been driving the sleeper van the night he died. Figuring, You want to know something about a man, go to his family.

Incense and perfume, his first impressions of the little religious store were olfactory. He paused just inside the door, waiting for his eyes to adjust to the dim light. A bell had tinkled as he crossed the threshold, and he was aware of a silky movement in the back of the shop.

"Buenos días, señor."

The voice was light and playful. A jazz flute of a voice, he thought, very sexy. A woman in a shimmery emerald-green sheath dress emerged from the shadows, regarding him from heavily made-up eyes.

"¿En qué puedo servile?" she began, initiating the polite and rather formal verbal dance of the skilled shopkeeper. Valdez smiled politely as she inquired about his health and the health of his family. Her Spanish was precise and well-spoken, but with a distinct American accent. Raised from childhood, he surmised, in Miami—as he himself had been.

Still, she dressed like a woman from the Old Country.

"You are new to this place," she said, meaning her *botánica*. The heavy makeup gave her complexion the ceramic quality of the religious statues and icons that filled her shop.

"Do I have the honor of addressing Mercedes Raimez?"

The dark eyes clicked, the retail smile froze.

"Now you have me at a loss. Because you I don't know."

The dance was over.

Valdez switched to English and introduced himself as a Metro-Dade detective. The sudden coolness in the room condensed. Even the incense smelled cold.

"How may I help you, Detective?"

The sheath dress flashed in the low light as she glided behind a glass counter, a display of plastic Baby Jesus dolls in a variety of skin tones.

"I'm investigating your father's death," he explained, and was met by a stony silence.

The woman seemed to be waiting him out, a painted Cuban Sphinx. Finally he coughed—the mingled scents were making his throat tickle—and said, "Heberto Raimez *was* your father, do I have that right?"

She cocked her head, staring at him. "My papa died of a heart attack. There is nothing to investigate."

Valdez picked up a rhinestone-encrusted crucifix. Heavy plastic dipped in gold paint. "Not his death, exactly," he said. "We're interested in what he was doing the night he died."

She snatched the crucifix from his hands.

"What happens if I tell you to get out and leave me alone?"

Valdez shrugged. "Another detective arrives. Possibly not as polite as I am. If that doesn't work, two or three redneck cops, you know the type. They'll make a fuss, they'll interview other shop-keepers on the block. They'll come to your home."

Valdez was making it all up—if Mercedes didn't cooperate, this particular line of inquiry might have to be dropped—but he sold it with well-mannered conviction. He could tell from her pained expression that the idea of boorish Anglos in her sacred religious store was simply too horrible to contemplate.

"My father was a hero," she said, after lighting a cigarette and perching herself on a stool behind the counter. "A patriot. He fought with Castro. The mountain campaign. And then later, of course, after Castro betrayed us, Papa joined the brigade."

The Bay of Pigs fiasco. Yes, just about every Cuban male of a certain age claimed to have been somehow involved in the aborted invasion of the homeland. Valdez had heard the story a thousand times from a thousand different men. According to Mercedes, her father really *had* been in the famous brigade—and taken prisoner, to boot.

"Papa never really fully recovered, I think. We in the family believe his heart troubles began at the moment Kennedy refused to provide air support."

She puffed deliberately at the cigarette, as if playing an instrument, blowing plumes through her fine nostrils. Daring Valdez to contradict her. He did not. If she wanted to believe that President Kennedy was to blame for her father's bad heart, so be it.

"I don't doubt that your father was a great patriot," he said. "Was he on a patriotic mission when he died?"

Her laughter was withering. "Papa was on his knees when he died, praying for salvation."

"Or maybe reaching for a phone," Valdez said.

"What exactly is that supposed to mean?"

"Your father went into a restaurant. He was trying to get to a phone when he collapsed. Do you know who he might have been trying to contact?"

Mercedes was scornful. "The man was sick, dying. He wanted, I am sure, an ambulance."

Valdez decided to try a slightly different tack.

"He was driving a rented van that night. Do you know anything about that, Miss Raimez?"

"Nothing. I know nothing about a rented van."

He showed her a snapshot of David Melborn. "Have you ever seen this man?"

She barely glanced. "No."

"We think he was in that van your father was driving the night he died."

"I told you. I know nothing about a van."

Valdez produced another selection of snapshots. The other, as yet unidentified, sleepers.

Mercedes was contemptuous. "What are these, dead people? Why should I know dead people?"

"They're not dead, Miss Raimez. Look again—did you ever see any of them in the company of your father?"

"I never see them period."

He put away the photos, decided he had nothing to lose, go for it. "You admit your father was political. Who was his *padrino*? Who was his boss?"

"You're the detective. Find out for yourself. Ask your Anglo bosses."

Valdez shrugged. "I can find out easily enough."

"Exactly as I said. You understand? Like my father, I am a patriotic Cuban."

Valdez leaned on the display case, showing his teeth. "And I'm not?"

"You are an American."

Coming from her lips, it was the greatest of insults. To be uninvolved with the fantasy of liberating Cuba, of making the revolution go away, that was to be less than Cuban. Less than a man. Valdez knew there was no way to reply, nothing he could say that would shake her convictions.

He took a card from his wallet and placed it on the glass.

"Call me if you change your mind."

She looked at the card without touching it.

"Lee Valdez," she said. "Valdez is a common name, but you look familiar."

"We've never met."

"No," she agreed, calmer now, "but your face . . ."

Valdez turned away.

"Wait," she said. "Enrique Valdez. The famous Santería priest. Ricky Valdez, who speaks in the tongue of *las orichas*."

He headed for the door.

"You are his brother!" she shouted after him.

Returning from his lunch break, Lee Valdez found his office under siege. A dozen or so sweaty, stressed-out citizens were waiting to file reports on loved ones who had not returned after the weekend. He knew from experience that most of the cases would be resolved without action from his unit—lovers who would slink back home, children who would eventually contact their parents.

Maybe one in twenty cases would enter the long-term file. Cases like the elderly woman who went into a Bal Harbour movie complex and was never seen again. Or the Hialeah housewife who took the dog for a walk—and only the dog returned, dragging the leash and whimpering. Or the young retarded man from Opa-Locka who seemed to have pedaled his bicycle into eternity.

Metro-Dade had hundreds of such unresolved cases on file.

Most of those who waited were polite and patient, despite their anxiety. Thanks to televised cop shows, civilians tended to be aware that there was little the police could do beyond circulating flyers, checking computer files, and, as he'd mentioned to Sara Copley, matching up unclaimed bodies.

When the afternoon rush was over, Valdez left his clerical staff in charge and retreated to the privacy of his office. Thinking about his visit to the *botánica* made the blood pound at his temples. He took two aspirins, washed them down with coffee.

Of *course* Mercedes Raimez would know his brother. Her shop sold items, candles and incense and potions, to the followers of Santería—and his little brother, Ricky, was now a very powerful *santero*, or priest, with a loyal following in the Cuban community. Little Ricky playing at magic, rolling on the floor and speaking in incomprehensible tongues.

Santería, with its animal sacrifice and spirit conjuring, had always made Lee uncomfortable, but he had figured it was strictly Ricky's business until that night when their father lay dying. Ricky had performed a Santería ceremony in the hospital room, evoking African gods that the old man, a devout Catholic, had suffered in mortal silence.

Lee had been outraged. The bitter fight with Ricky had never been resolved, and the trauma of that terrible night—the fight, his father dying—had changed his life. The old neighborhood, his brother's religion, the bittersweet Cuban heritage, all of it had seemed claustrophobic at the time.

After the funeral, estranged from his brother, Lee had moved out of Little Havana and settled in nonethnic Cherry Grove. Better to live as an American, he told himself.

Most of the time he still believed it.

When the aspirin had taken effect, he switched on the computer terminal and began to search the Dade County files for any mention of the late Heberto Raimez.

CHAPTER FIVE

"Gently now," Dr. Harding said to the orderlies. "No bumps, no bounces. And keep the gauze pads over their eyes—these patients are not to be stimulated in any way."

The six sleepers were being transferred to the new Experimental Medicine wing, where a special intensive-care facility had been set up.

Dr. Harding took a keen interest in every aspect of the transfer—he wanted nothing to go wrong. Walking beside the gurneys, he admonished his orderlies.

"Keep your voices down," he hissed. "And watch that the padding shields their eyes."

Harding needn't have bothered with the eye pads. Not one of the sleepers transferred that day so much as blinked.

In the late afternoon Sara escaped from her office, with its never-ending paperwork, and went to visit a disease-control clinic in Liberty City.

"Excuse me, please. I need to get through here," she said, working her way through the crowd outside.

As there was not adequate room inside the clinic building, many of the clients crouched on the steps, holding appointment cards issued by county social workers. Others squatted directly on the dirt under the unkempt palms. Vending carts crowded along the sidewalk, hawking grilled meats and soft drinks. A circus of the sick, the infirm, the quietly dying.

Sara was used to it now—as used to it as she would ever get—but at her first clinic visit she had been appalled by the misery.

Though there were a few chronic complainers, most of those who staggered, shuffled, or limped in for the free examination were genuinely ill. The disease-control clinic, intended to treat infectious disease, had become a clearinghouse for those afflicted with the mortal disease of poverty.

By signing a form, Dr. Copley and the other staff physicians could ensure that a client received treatment at an area hospital. The only alternative for most of the impoverished was to wait until a crisis situation occurred—internal bleeding, kidney failure, seizure, and the like—at which point their chances of being admitted via an emergency-treatment facility were somewhat improved.

For many, Sara knew, the existence of the neighborhood clinic meant the difference between life and death. She greeted the clinic team, comprised of an internist who was volunteering his time and three staff nurses who functioned virtually as doctors, doing everything short of prescribing medication.

"Plenty of customers," said Sara, surveying the crowd.

"Always plenty of customers," the internist replied with a laugh. "Dr. Copley, do me a favor? See that Haitian over there, the one with the red kerchief and the pockmarks? Talk to her. Convince her we need to inoculate her baby."

Liberty City, one of several ghetto areas in Miami, had a growing population of Haitian immigrants. Many, like the young mother the internist had pointed out, had the characteristic pockmarks of smallpox. Supposedly wiped out in the continental United States, smallpox, like tuberculosis, was again on the rise, a new and deadly import.

The Haitian poor spoke a form of Creole, and Sara knew only the French she'd learned in school, but the young mother seemed to understand when asked to follow Sara into a curtained examination booth.

Fearful, eyes downcast, she clutched her baby to her breast.

"Your name is Maria Baptiste?" Sara asked, reading from a card filled out at the reception desk. "And this is your baby boy Joseph?"

A shy nod.

When Sara made motions to examine the baby, the mother relented. Tears ran down her cheeks—she seemed to think the baby was going to be taken from her.

"Tell you what," said Sara, placing the baby back in the mother's arms. "You keep holding him, okay?"

After a lot of halting French, Sara managed to convince the mother that a smallpox inoculation would protect her baby from the same disease that had scarred the mother's face.

"Nice sales job," the internist told her later.

"I think she really wanted to do it all along."

"Hey, give yourself some credit. The lady wouldn't let *me* near the kid. Said I was a white devil. Least I *think* that's what she said."

A gaudy Florida sunset was under way when Sara finally left the clinic. The sky over the ruined ghetto buildings looked postcard perfect, as if airbrushed by some giant hand.

As she turned from the door, a man scuttled away from the entrance, keeping his back to her. She caught a glimpse of shoulder-length yellow hair.

Although dirty and unkempt, he looked hauntingly familiar.

"Kurt?" she said.

Keeping his face averted, the man ducked into an alley.

Not possible, she thought. Unless Kurt somehow knew she'd gone to work for Public Health, wanted to contact her, then lost his nerve.

"Kurt!"

She ran to the alley. The man was squatting behind an overloaded dumpster, his face in the shadows. Sara wanted it to be Kurt so much that she'd almost convinced herself—until he spoke.

"Lady, I need some juice."

"What?"

The voice was not Kurt's. And as her eyes adjusted to the shadows, the resemblance melted away.

"Juice. Methadone. I'm sick, see?"

He held up an arm scarred with needle tracks, a trembling hand. Sara realized he'd been skulking around the clinic, looking for dope.

Feeling sick herself, she led him back into the clinic and phoned around, trying to find an opening in a drug-treatment facility. And then when she finally had a bed reserved, the junkie changed his mind about treatment and ran out the door.

On the expressway at last, headed for home, Sara realized that she was on the verge of tears. Damn Kurt Palmer.

Why hadn't he given her another chance to help him?

* * *

The record search for Heberto Raimez had been a bust. The man had a few traffic violations, a small real estate holding in Coral Gables. No criminal record. No Vice investigations, no DEA sheet.

Nothing to connect him to a drug enterprise.

Valdez leaned back in his chair, rested his tired eyes. Had to be some way to establish a line of investigation on the man. Drug labs were not solo operations. If Heberto had been transporting comatose overdosed drug victims, it made sense to assume he had some connection to a criminal enterprise. And yet none of the enforcement agencies had a file on the late Heberto Raimez.

Better put it aside for now, Valdez decided, concentrate on the sleepers and work back from there.

Weapon of choice was the GRT-2000 data-retrieval system, affectionately known as GRETA. GRETA gave him access to files normally made available to law-enforcement officers, but to chase down Surfer Dave he was going to have to bend the rules. Go with his bootlegged MAC.

MAC was a military access-code modifier able to crack off-limits systems.

U.S. Army files, for instance.

He linked up with Washington, initiated a search for David Melborn, and sat back to wait. MAC turned up a score of *Melborn, David*s and then began the process of winnowing them down by race and age.

A fax machine, tied into the computer modem, supplied him with file photographs.

One turned out to be a pretty good likeness of the intense young man who'd shared a jungle with Kurt Palmer. David Vincent Melborn, a Special Forces sergeant who had seen action in Grenada and Panama, given an honorable discharge for "medical reasons."

That was another thing he had in common with Kurt Palmer—a medical discharge. Getting into the medical files turned out to be easier than the initial inquiry for Palmer had been. The request was shunted to the Veterans Administration Medical Center, Miami, Florida.

"So he's a home boy," Lee said under his breath.

Crazy thing, talking to a computer, but he couldn't help it, he got a real charge out of doing good police work. Nailing down local treatment on Surfer Dave, that was *primera* detection.

Routing through the Washington system, he got into the Miami VA files and requested "all relevant data." Selected a dump to hard-copy printout, figuring he'd be able to drop a nice fat file in Sara Copley's lap.

The printer spit for a few seconds and stopped.

Valdez, thinking that the paper feed had screwed up, discovered that Melborn's medical file took up less than a page.

This can't be all, he thought.

He tore the sheet out and saw a by-now-familiar phrase under *Reason for Discharge*: "Combat stress syndrome."

What followed was a recommendation that Melborn receive "further clinical treatment" at the VA Medical Center in Miami. And that was it. The file went blank.

If David Melborn had ever sought help at the VA hospital, there was no record of treatment. And when Valdez requested the actual evaluation paperwork for the "stress syndrome" diagnosis, he drew another blank.

NA the screen told him. Not available. An old hand at getting the runaround from cranky retrieval systems, he tried wording the request another way.

This time the refusal to cough up data was more specific: *NAFP Not Available, Files Purged.*

CHAPTER SIX

First night in Camp Libertad for Jorge and Nando. After a two-hour drive in the windowless van they had been delivered to a long open-air barracks under a rusty tin roof. The torn mosquito netting that had been draped from the eaves didn't help much.

The barracks was teeming with insects when Sergeant Hernandez came to induct them. There had been some confusion, as neither of the brothers was familiar with the concept of being sworn in. Hernandez cursed them soundly, although without any particular animosity, until they complied, one hand for the book, one for the heart.

"Repeat after me," he had recited in his rapid-fire Spanish. "I swear before God and my honor as a man that I shall obey my officer. That's me, boys. For the next couple of weeks I'm God *and* the officer."

With that the sergeant retired to his command post, an air-conditioned Winnebago.

Nando, much to his delight, had been issued camouflage fatigues, underwear, socks, and jungle boots. Jorge, less easily satisfied, complained that his boots were too large. He was issued another pair of socks.

"This means we're soldiers," Nando said excitedly, trying on his camo gear. "Guerrilla fighters. We will be heroes soon."

Not wishing to disagree, Jorge said nothing.

Under the leaky barracks roof the brothers joined more than forty other young men. Lying on their canvas cots, they fought a pitched battle with a suicide battalion of mosquitoes. Numberless swarms, bred in a thousand square miles of stagnant water. The bugs clotted the netting, slipped through in a hundred places.

The buzz of insects and tree frogs from the great swamp was at times almost deafening.

The two brothers, unused to the company of strangers, or of mosquitoes, for that matter—their mountain village was too high up to be bothered by such infestations—hid themselves under their gray sheets. They soon discovered that the hardy, glade-bred bugs were capable of biting right through the sheets.

"When do they give us weapons?" Nando hissed to his big brother. More than anything he yearned to hold a rifle in his hands. Possibly the mosquitoes would be less impudent when he was armed.

Jorge's reply was a ragged whisper. "Perhaps tomorrow," he said. "Everything will be much better tomorrow, I promise."

"Sleepy Dave, how you doin' tonight, honey?"

A night-shift nurse went down the row of beds, checking on the sleepers. Isolated now, in the new Experimental Medicine facility. A buffer zone of silence, away from the frenzy of the main hospital.

The nurse made sure that Melborn's catheter was drawing. It was—not much, to be sure, but just enough so there was no immediate danger of uremia. Dextrose in, urine out.

The nurse checked blood pressure, counted pulse.

"Heart like a clock," she muttered. "You the slowest boy I know, Dave. I'm going to take a few drops of your blood now, then I'll leave you in peace, check on these other sleepy gentlemen."

There was no reply. She hadn't expected one.

He was aware, in some far removed way, of the touch on his penis. The slight, almost playful squeeze set off a little buzz of stimulation. Triggering a chain of vague memories that came and went in sequence. Clicking on and then off like faint lights:

Water and wind and blinding sunshine. The smell of wet sand.

He remembered an uncertain, girlish smile. Shy brown eyes. Then the smile was gone, and the girl. Uneasiness.

The last memory in the chain was of dark laughter.
Laughter that opened like a fist of thorns.
And then a terrible voice, saying:
You're dead, now you belong to Vidoc. Now you will know nothing but
fear.

CHAPTER SEVEN

Tuesday morning. Sara arrived with sticky buns and coffee. The faint medicinal smell of the lab was at once familiar and welcome. Work was being done here. And Sara wanted, needed, a long, hard day of losing herself in the task at hand.

"Ah, Dr. Copley, I see you got my message."

Paul Hobart accepted the bag of rolls and coffee and dug in happily, handing her a cup. "To our health. To everybody's health."

Sara sipped the coffee out of politeness. She'd already had two cups, trying to get her head clear. Dreams of Kurt, just his voice calling to her from somewhere in the city, had unsettled her sleep.

"Weird compounds," she reminded Hobie. "That was the message you left on my machine."

"Yeah, well, to me this stuff is weird. Not only for what it is, but for the way it was formed."

He walked her over to a nook area, his own corner of the lab. Celebrity photos were tacked to a pegboard, defined by blood type. A computer screen glowed amber. Hobie ran a mouse over the desktop, bringing an arrow to bear on the display.

"We ran metabolites of the David Melborn samples through the CG," he said, meaning the gas chromatography equipment. "This display is from the spectroscan for alkaloid compounds known to affect the nervous system. Recognize this little devil?" he asked, pointing to a compound on the screen.

"$C_{11}H_{17}N_3O_8$?" she said. "Okay, you've stumped me."

He shoved his hands in the pockets of his lab coat and nodded happily. "Tetrodotoxin. Very nasty stuff. Highly toxic in small amounts, and we show *very* small amounts."

"Tetrodotoxin?" she said. "Isn't that a fish poison?"

Hobart chuckled. "Yes indeed, old tetro-d has been isolated in a few species of blowfish, and also an odd little newt. Might even be the 'eye of newt' the witches were dropping into Macbeth's cauldron."

Sara gave him a look. Eye of newt?

"Seriously," he said, "there are experts who think that Shakespeare knew a thing or two about organic toxins, at least the kinds that Elizabethan poisoners would have had access to. 'Toe of frog' can also be a powerful drug, if you happen to use a *Bufo marinus*, which is really a toad and has glands that are loaded with toxic chemicals." Hobie paused to sip his coffee. "Little hobby of mine, folk medicines. Someday I'm going to write a book. Most scientists don't like to admit it, but folk medicines are closely related to modern pharmacology."

"Like digitalis comes from foxglove."

He beamed. "Exactly."

"The tetrodotoxin in David Melborn's blood," Sara said. "Was it enough to induce paralysis?"

Hobie shrugged. "Hard to say. I'd have to know how long the stuff was in his bloodstream. It *is* a nerve toxin, however, and in Japan they actually eat the stuff."

Sara nodded. "Sushi for sex fiends."

Hobie laughed. "They call it fugu, the chef needs a special license to prepare it. The tricky thing is making sure almost all of the tetro-d is removed from the fish. There have been cases of fugu eaters being paralyzed, even dying, but the literature says the effects rarely last more than a few days."

Hobie searched a bookshelf, pulled a reference manual.

"Okay, here it is. Halstead says that in fatal cases 'the victim may become paralyzed but the mental faculties remain acute until shortly before death.' Unquote."

Sara immediately thought of the sleeper who had undergone surgery without benefit of anesthesia. Dr. Harding had run the same tests for alkaloids; he must have been aware of the tetrodotoxin.

"What are these?" she asked, pointing out other spectroscan code bars on the screen.

"Molecular structures we can't quite nail down. Alkaloids, but not easily scanned because they seem to have either broken down into subparticles—lots of unraveled carbon chains—or recombined with other alkaloid structures. Without a base sample of what your friend ingested, it's going to be tough. Maybe impossible."

"We're not even close to that," Sara said, sighing. "Any bright ideas?"

"I'll keep playing around, see what I can come up with. There are a couple of extraction procedures I haven't tried yet."

"Thanks, Hobie."

"Cheer up," he said, reaching into the bag for another sticky bun. "Maybe your sleeping beauties will wake up on their own. Stranger things have happened."

CHAPTER EIGHT

Valdez waited, the call on hold. Be a scary thing, he thought, to add up all the "hold" minutes. Probably waste a month or two out of your life, tapping your pencil and listening to Muzak.

"Detective?"

"Yes, I'm still here."

"Look, I can't find anything here—I'll put you through to our accounting department. Please hold."

He sighed. What could you do? And the Veterans Administration was not exactly your sleek, efficient organization. You want facts, data, maybe a new lead, you had to pierce a very thick bureaucratic hide.

"Accounts, Forman speaking."

"Mr. Forman, I'm Detective Lee Valdez with the Missing Persons Unit of the Metro-Dade Police. We've identified a Special Forces veteran who was referred to your hospital for clinical treatment. We're trying to run down his medical records."

"Alive or deceased?"

"Alive," Valdez said. "Special Forces Sergeant David V. Melborn, 001-38-948."

"Let me punch it up here. Hold, please."

The line went hollow. Valdez felt as if he were holding a big conch shell up to his ear, listening to an ocean of static. A minute or so later the voice came back on the line.

"Detective? I show an open file for 001-38-948."

"That means he was treated there?"

"Not necessarily. It means he checked in here at the outpatient service and they opened a file. However, the file shows no entries.

Which indicates that he never showed up for his first appointment."

"Is there any record of a follow-up?" Valdez asked.

The clerk sounded impatient. "Look, Detective, this facility treats thousands of vets each week. If one doesn't show up for an appointment, no, we don't chase him down. We're here to provide a service, not act as a guardian."

"Just one more question, please," Valdez said. "Is there a VA clinic for combat-stress syndrome?"

Big sigh. "Please hold."

This time Valdez held for six minutes, thirty-eight seconds, according to the digital clock on his desk. When the clerk came back, he sounded refreshed.

The son of a bitch has been out to get coffee, Valdez thought.

"Detective? Are you still there? There are between twenty and thirty outpatient-treatment clinics held each week. We have clinics for alcohol dependency, drug dependency, depression, social adjustment, career counseling, et cetera, et cetera. Any time there is a need or enough interest, a new clinic is formed."

"Using VA hospital staff?"

"Sometimes. Often we contract with outside physicians or psych workers or whatever. We have no current clinic for combat-stress syndrome, but I *do* show a code number. Nothing under the file, however."

"You mean the file for the combat-stress clinic is blank?"

"Well . . . yes. I suppose it is."

Valdez thanked the clerk and hung up. Blank files. He kept running into blank files. The big spooky question: Were they really blank, or had the files been erased?

And if so, why?

The prospect of wasting a few more days of his life on hold did not appeal to Lee Valdez. The only way to do it, go over there to the VA hospital. Get close enough so he could reach out and touch someone.

A huge flock of redwing blackbirds had settled into every available tree and several of the roofs in the VA hospital complex. Looked like a scene out of that Hitchcock flick, what was it? Right, *The Birds*. Nature out of control. In reality, Valdez knew there was not a hint of danger from a flock this size.

The birds blended in, they belonged.

Inside the complex, he took a place in line for the Information desk. Valdez was used to cooling his heels; there was more of that in real detective work than the car-chase stuff they showed on TV. Still, he was mildly irritated by the time he got to the desk. His shield impressed no one. Combat-stress clinic?

Try searching the bulletin boards, Detective, maybe you'll find something there. Next?

He had moved away from the desk and was trying to decide exactly what chink of the bureaucratic armor to attack next when a high-pitched voice said, "'Scuze me, you a cop?"

He turned to see a huge individual leaning on a cane.

"My name Tiny," the man said, keeping both huge hands on the cane. "Heard you at the desk there."

Tiny was well over six feet, but the impression of sheer, massive size came from arms like big country hams, fists the size of melons. Coming from a man that large, the squeaky little voice sounded comical. Valdez didn't even smile, no way. Take a sharp-shooter with an elephant gun to bring Tiny down.

"You say something about syn'rum. Combat-stress syn'rum. Thas my syn'rum, man. I got it."

"Excuse me?"

"You wanna know 'bout combat stress, jess as' Tiny. He know."

They found a park bench outside the complex because Tiny had a problem with puny chairs. They tended to explode, he explained.

"The thing about the syn'rum," he said. "It affect different mens different ways. It a nerve thing, you dig? Me, I get nervous and eat. Other mens, they might drink or get violent. Do his own thing, whatever it may be."

Valdez explained that he was following up a lead on a veteran named David Melborn. "You know him by any chance?"

"No, suh, can't sez I do," Tiny said, studying the snapshot. "He a criminal, this gentlemens?"

"Not as far as I know."

"You bein' a cop and all. And it wouldn't be no surprise, a stress-syn'rum man get into some violent situation. Some mens, not all of 'em, gets to *like* the violence, it make them feel alive. See, that why they have a clinic, help these mens."

"So you know about a clinic, Tiny?"

"'Course I do. Signed up for it, didn't I? Only went a few times, he couldn't do nuffin' for me."

"Who couldn't, Tiny?"

"Doctor run that clinic. Tells me what I got is a eatin' disorder. I already knows that. I eats 'cuz of nerves an' I gots the nerves 'cuz of the syn'rum. But the doctor, he send me to a diet workshop, say he don't want my fat butt in his clinic."

Valdez got out his notebook. "Do you remember the doctor's name?"

"Sure I 'member. Dr. Vidoc. Tall white dude with no hair."

CHAPTER NINE

Vidoc shopping at a Coral Gables mall. Wearing a long-billed fisherman's cap, polarized sunglasses, loud print shirt, chinos, boat shoes. Blending into a crowd was not one of his talents; he preferred playing a role.

Today he was an eccentric, wealthy Anglo with a hobby.

"R.C.," he said to the Cuban clerk who manned the counter at Radio Shack. "Radio control, *comprendez?*"

"Yeah, sure I *comprendez.* We got a big section, all kinds of model aircraft, boats, race cars, whatever you want."

Vidoc smiled, and was pleased to see that the clerk looked vaguely uneasy.

"Let's see a transmitter," he said. "It must be reliable, and have an effective range of a thousand yards or more."

The clerk unlocked the cabinets, showed him several transmitters and an assortment of solenoid devices that manipulated model-airplane controls. Vidoc made his selection, paid with an untraceable charge card the colonel had supplied.

"So you don't need no toy airplanes?" the clerk asked as he rang up the items.

"Not today," Vidoc said.

Next stop was a franchise store called Medical Supermarket. Aisles and aisles of wheelchairs, hospital beds, oxygen tents, bedpans. Physicians received a discount, but Vidoc didn't intend to have his real name connected with the purchase. He, or rather the colonel, would pay full price.

"You carry subcutaneous-medication pumps?" he asked.

"That's a warehouse item. Any particular manufacturer?"

"I want it simple, reliable, and lightweight. With a fifty-cc reservoir capacity."

Vidoc and the clerk went through the catalog, picked out a model. "I'll take a dozen. No, make that two dozen. Better safe than sorry."

Seeing the clerk's hesitation, Vidoc made himself smile and said, "It's for a science project."

"Whatever you say," said the clerk, taking the charge card.

Back at the cabana Vidoc laid the new equipment out on the kitchen counter. It took him only a few minutes to wire a solenoid to one of the medication pumps. He filled the pump reservoir with 50 ccs of tap water and tested the radio transmitter. When he pushed the toggle switch, the solenoid instantly activated, pushing the plunger on the medication pump. Water streamed from the needle.

So simple, he thought. And so very deadly.

Vidoc glanced at his calendar watch. In a week's time he would be overseeing the first live-combat demonstration. The designated volunteers were already in place at the training camp, receiving instruction. The serum, the radio-activated devices, everything was ready to go.

He couldn't wait.

Is this what children feel like, he wondered, waiting for Christmas?

After the first round of morning exercises the recruits were given a breakfast of black beans, hard bread, and coffee lightened with evaporated milk. Jorge and Nando ate with relish; after a week of cold hambuggerfry, the syrupy heat of the beans was good. Jorge, being the eldest, attempted to make conversation with some of the other recruits. There were certain difficulties—the dialect of his mountain village was not widely known in the lowlands, home to most of the fighters. More serious was the traditional city loathing of the ignorant mountain people.

When Jorge named his village, a boy with the tattoos of an urban gangster scoffed.

"That is not a village, it is a shit hole. A sewer."

Jorge, determined to make the best of it, merely smiled. Nando paid no attention to the exchange. His eyelids were swollen with mosquito bites, producing a sleepy look that belied his excitement.

At dawn, bellowing a kind of reveille, Sergeant Hernandez had promised that the day would bring *armas*. Nando hadn't forgotten.

Weapons. That meant they were to be issued rifles, or so Nando believed. The fantasy that had sustained him since leaving home was a picture of himself marching in step with his big brother, returning to their village dressed in uniforms, fully armed.

They would be brave guerrillas, as depicted in the glorious slide show presented by that great freedom fighter Colonel Calavera. A day would come when the colonel would flash slides of Nando on the white sheet, and boys no older than he would be envious.

Nando prodded his brother and hissed, "*Armas*, Jorge. *¡Armas!*"

His brother nodded nervously, eyeing the contemptuous lowlanders.

After the beans and coffee the new recruits ran ten kilometers, back and forth on the ruined airfield wearing backpacks loaded with chunks of limestone.

Sergeant Hernandez screamed until he was hoarse.

"Run, you bastards, run! This is only make-believe, but one day soon you will be running from real bullets. Now run! Run until your hearts stop!"

Later they were issued mock rifles made of wood.

CHAPTER TEN

Sara's first impression of the Cypress Medical Center's Experimental Medicine facility was that it smelled new. It had the freshness, the hopeful gleam, of a place where anything was still possible.

Getting a visiting physician's pass was simply a matter of presenting her Public Health Department credentials, as before. Sara breathed a sigh of relief—being barred from the surgical theater apparently didn't mean she was no longer welcome in the hospital.

The sleepers were being treated in a glass-enclosed ICU by a staff that never numbered less than three RNs for six patients, a ratio that ensured, at the very least, high-level maintenance care.

"We have standing orders to inform Dr. Harding if there's even so much as a change in heart rate," the shift supervisor said with obvious pride. "This is the most technically advanced facility in the Miami area. Your friend Mr. Melborn is getting the best of everything."

Everything included computer-driven life-monitoring equipment that could print out EEG, EKG, and metabolism updates at the touch of a button. Sara was impressed. Aware that family or even extended-family interest in a patient frequently resulted in more attentive care, she didn't bother correcting the impression that Surfer Dave was a close friend.

"So the condition is basically unchanged?" she asked.

The nurse nodded. "Yes. But something interesting has happened. Check out the cardiac graph lines."

Sara stared at the monitor screens. It was so obvious, it took her a few moments to realize what she was seeing. "Their heartbeats have synchronized."

"You can't see it on the monitor, but they're all breathing together, too."

"So they must be aware of each other, on some level," Sara said.

The nurse shrugged. "I guess. Dr. Harding says it's the, um, 'subconscious expression of the involuntary response mechanism.' Like women in the same household having the same menstrual cycle."

From close up David Melborn appeared, if anything, even more comatose. The musculature that helped define facial expression had begun to atrophy—he had the soft, lifeless look of a wax dummy that was slowly melting. Soon not even Charlene, the brown-haired surfer girl, would recognize him.

Sara bent over him. "Dave? Can you hear me?"

Nothing.

"Your name is David Melborn. You were in the army. You were a sergeant—Sergeant Melborn. Now you live in Golden Beach. You work at the Hang Tuff Surf Shop. You have a friend named Kurt Palmer."

No response.

"David? Blink your eyes if you understand, if you can hear me."

She waited. His eyes remained closed. The head RN was giving her an odd look.

"He's in a veggie coma state," she said. "They all are."

"People have been known to awake from supposedly irreversible comas," Sara reminder her.

The nurse, clearly, was unconvinced. To her, the sleepers were a lost cause. Strictly maintenance.

In the next bed was the victim who had been mauled by rats. His sutures were neat and nearly invisible—it was as fine a job of reconstructive surgery as Sara had ever seen. It made her wonder if she had misjudged Dr. Harding. Maybe he wasn't the unfeeling ogre he'd seemed in the surgery that night.

Maybe he'd been right all along—neurological dysfunction was so profound that the sleepers, brain-damaged or not, were completely cut off from their bodies.

* * *

Fragments of memory continued to unravel in the mind of the man who had been David Melbom.

Dr. Vidoc looming over him, saying, You have no will, no self, you are as nothing.

That terrible hairless face. The syringe, a teardrop of clear liquid at the end of the needle. And Vidoc's voice.

"Your personality is being unpeeled like an onion. A layer with each injection of my serum. First I peel away your name. Next your ego. Now you are disconnected from your body. You cease to exist. Even your fingerprints will cease to exist."

Faint whiff of acid. A stronger smell. Burning flesh. Pain.

"You are gone, erased. Not even a fingerprint to prove you existed. Rest now, my little nothing. Sleep. Your time will come again."

That was the promise. But something had gone wrong. The little that remained of him was fading. A photograph bleaching in the sun. Soon there would be nothing left. Fade to white.

Death.

Again.

"Dr. Copley!"

Sara was on her way out of Experimental Medicine when Dr. Harding caught up with her. She turned and waited, hating the fact that the man could make her stomach clench just by shouting her name.

He arrived out of breath. "Thought I'd missed you," he said, panting. "I wanted a chance. To apologize. For the other night. Rude of me."

It was the last thing Sara expected. Dr. Harding chuckled when he saw the expression on her face.

"I had you pegged as a troublemaker," he said. "A bureaucrat masquerading as a physician. I was wrong, and I'm man enough to say so."

"Excuse me," Sara said, "but what changed your mind?"

"I looked you up," he said. "Checked your credentials. You graduated from Tufts Medical School at the top of your class. Residency at Mass General. Highest evaluation. Career tracked for a top research position at the Lahey Clinic—and yet you settled for a low-paying job in public medicine."

The way he said *public medicine*, as if it were a loathsome infection, put Sara immediately on the defensive. At the same time she didn't want to risk offending the chief of medicine again. So she swallowed her resentment, put on a smile, and let him talk.

"Nothing wrong with being young and idealistic, Dr. Copley. But by now you must know that the most important factor in good medicine is adequate funding. Health care is a business, like it or not. We're careful to keep Cypress running in the black, and as a result our patients get the highest level of care. Our new experimental facility is a perfect example."

"I was very impressed," Sara said, fighting to keep her smile in place. Who did this pompous ass think he was talking to, a schoolgirl? A first-year med student?

"You've obviously made a decision, very early in your career, to explore opportunities in an area I would have to call socialized medicine."

Sara's smile was getting very brittle. "And you don't approve?"

Harding shrugged. "Look, I've done my stint at a nonprofit facility. I know the frustrations. Not enough staff, second-rate equipment, budget crunches. It gets very old. The best opportunities are in the private sector. We make things happen, Dr. Copley. And I must say, I think a young physician with your credentials is wasted in public medicine."

"You're entitled to your opinion," Sara said.

Harding gave her an avuncular smile. "Look, all I'm suggesting is that you keep an open mind. If you get bored or frustrated with the PHD, remember that there are other options. For instance, the new department here is going to need a take-charge epidemiologist. You'd find it a lot more challenging than taking throat swabs in some dirty little clinic."

Sara had had about enough. "Those dirty little clinics save lives."

"Of course they do. But *anyone* can take throat swabs." Harding glanced at his watch. "Well, if you'll excuse me, I've got to run. I've enjoyed our little talk, Dr. Copley. See you again."

Get used to it, she told herself on the way out of the building, there are a lot of Hardings in the world of medicine. Learn to use them.

Somehow that didn't make her feel any better.

* * *

Sara met Hobie for lunch under the big banyan tree near the courthouse complex. The banyan was a magnificent specimen that towered above adjacent palms. They dined on food purchased from the street vendors who mobbed the courthouse steps.

Sara nibbled at a salad pouch as Hobie unfolded photocopies of the latest chromatography results.

"I nailed down two more of the trace compounds. First is a white crystalline alkaloid, atropine." He reeled off the carbon-chain formula. "Mean anything to you?"

"I've heard of it. Used topically, I think. Something to do with the eyes."

"Right on. As a solution it dilates the pupils, and that's the most common pharmacological use. Atropine is one of the more powerful agents derived from belladona. But also present in several other plants."

"Belladona? That's hardly a 'designer drug.'"

"There's more," Hobie said, smoothing out the sheet of paper. "Scopolamine. Also found in several toxic plants. Sometimes used as a sedative in surgery. Has a hypnotic effect."

Surgical sedative? There had been no sign of recent surgery on any of the sleepers, Sara pointed out. Just needle tracks and the burned fingertips.

He nodded. "Keep in mind it was found in conjunction with the atropine. You've got to ask yourself, what alkaloid compound has atropine and scopolamine in roughly these proportions?" he added, shaking the photocopy.

"Come on, Hobie. You're the toxicologist, not me."

"Well, there's this plant. *Datura stramonium*. Fairly common in Cuba and Haiti. Old datura is a very popular source of toxin in certain folk medicines. And if you break it down, you'll find both those compounds in exactly those proportions."

Sara shook her head. The designer-drug theory was falling apart here. Underground narcotic labs wouldn't be messing with obscure folk medicines or the toxins found in puffer fish. It didn't make sense.

"This is pretty rare stuff," she said, indicating the lab report. "Not exactly available from your local pharmacy or chemical supplier."

"Maybe not in the Boston area," Hobie said. "But you could buy all three compounds within a few miles of here."

"What?"

"Just try your local *botánica*."

Sara was puzzled. "I thought a *botánica* was a religious store. Candles and statues and prayer beads."

Hobie was nodding. "All of that, sure, but most *botánicas* also stock items for Santería ceremonies. You know about Santería?"

"Just that it's a Cuban religion of some kind."

"Well, Santería believers conjure spirits, cast spells, and so forth. Some of the potions they use contain organic toxins. Ground-up puffer fish, for instance. And powdered datura. My point is, all the alkaloid compounds found in the sleeper blood can be purchased right there in Little Havana."

Valdez got the bureaucratic shuffle with the inquiry on Emile Vidoc, M.D. Everybody had excuses.

Like:

"He was never a staff physician at this facility, that's all I can tell you."

And:

"We hire numerous outside contracters to conduct clinics. But as you can see, Detective Valdez, we have no record of any such physician or any such clinic."

Or:

"Problems with the computer system? Sure we have problems. Any organization this size has problems, okay? Could the system be tampered with? You *know* it could, Detective. But why bother?"

Valdez returned to his office convinced that Emile Vidoc, M.D., was an important link in the sleeper case. The mere fact that a licensed doctor could not be located by any ordinary means aroused suspicion. What did he have to hide? Put that together with the fact that Vidoc had been prescribing drugs to David Melborn, and you moved beyond "suspicious behavior" and into the range of "suspect."

Somehow or other he had to get a line on the mystery doctor. Valdez decided to have Emile Vidoc, M.D., put on the computerized Fugitive List that circulated to police departments in Florida. He hated to rely on Tiny's description, but it was all he had to go on. Your basic tall white dude with no hair.

Under Special Instructions he put *Do not arrest, no warrants pending. Hold for questioning, notify this office.*

Sara Copley called just as he finished punching in the information. She started talking about blood alkaloids and Little Havana, and he had to ask her to slow down.

"You were saying something about poison?" he said.

"In Melborn's blood. I asked this toxicologist to run a sample through the lab. I was expecting traces of some exotic designer drug, right? But what he found were traces of organic neurotoxins that are available over the counter in Little Havana."

"Over the counter? Where?"

"At a *botánica*. The toxins are common ingredients in Santería potions."

It clicked instantly.

"The van driver's daughter runs a *botánica*," he said. "I interviewed her and got nowhere."

"You know anything about Santería?"

Valdez closed his eyes and sighed.

"I'm no expert. But I know someone who is."

CHAPTER ELEVEN

Going down the steps to the basement room, Valdez felt as if he were entering a pool of dread. Dread lapping his ankles, dread splashing upward, until he was drenched with the sensation. Already he could hear the drums, the chanted hysteria. There would, he assumed, be bloodletting—little brother Ricky was not one for half-measures.

He was recognized at the door. An old man, the gatekeeper, touched the brim of his porkpie hat and smiled secretly. Lee vaguely recognized him—the old man was a gourd carrier, one of Ricky's loyal parishioners.

"*Hermano del santero,*" the old man muttered. Brother of the priest.

Lee ducked through beaded curtains into an overpowering stench of guttering candles, incense, and the cheap cologne that was used to douse evil spirits from the dancers. Before he got his bearings, he was embraced by an enormously fat woman who kissed him ecstatically, shouted something in a language he did not recognize, and then flung him out of the way of the dancers.

Although the mass of writhing bodies bumped him now and then, no one else tried to embrace him, or engage him in the dance. As a nonbeliever, he was invisible.

Lee backed into a corner and watched.

There were three drummers at tonight's ceremony, all beating furiously on the two-sided *bata* drums. The intricate rhythm pattern summoned the Santería spirits. Spirits that for many years had been called by the names of Catholic saints, as a means of disguise. Ricky, to his credit, had dispensed with that. These were African *orichas* or gods, brought over by slaves who cut the sugarcane, later adopted by white Cubans, and Ricky had returned to the old names. Eleggua, god of the crossroads, Chango, god of thunder, and so on. Powerful, localized gods who could dispense favors, or cure disease, or intervene in love—all for a price set by the *santero*.

The first dancer to be seized by an *oricha* was a slender, long-limbed youth with inky-black hair. He was being ridden by Oggun, god of metals.

> *Espiritu Oggun!*
> (drumbeat)
> *Dios Oggun!*
> (drumbeat)
> *Bueno Oggun!*
> (drumbeat)
> *Oggun poderoso!*
> (drumbeat)

Brother Ricky, wearing a red satin ceremonial suit with trousers that ended at the knees, danced alone on a small raised platform. Feet and legs bare, shining with oils. His long-lashed eyes were closed. His head hung loose, a wobbling thing precariously balanced. Behind him was the altar, a collection of small statues cloaked in gauze to hide the identities of the gods.

A dancer broke away, flung himself at Ricky's feet, shouting.

"Babalu-aye! Babalu-aye!"

The chanters picked up the words, the name of a god, incorporated it into the rhythm of the drums.

"Babalu-aye! Babalu-aye!"

Lee wanted to laugh—how absurd it all was, an act, a con job—but laughter was a shard of ice stuck in his throat, melting into the dread he'd encountered descending into this smoky basement, this so-called church.

Ricky. Babalao Enrique now, a high-ranking priest, leader of a faction that was veering into the darker regions of the old religion. Bringing back the *bata* drums, once forbidden, resurrecting the practice of animal sacrifice.

"*Babalu-aye! Aye! Aye!*"

The possessed dancer, eyes rolling white, lips spraying spittle, clung to Ricky's feet. Ricky grabbed a quart bottle of cologne from the altar, sprayed it on the dancer, who released him, crying, "Enrique! Enrique!"

The old man in the porkpie hat came out of nowhere, offering Ricky a drink from a gourd. The crowd screamed, "Aye! Aye!"

Ricky grabbed the gourd, poured water over his own head. Hair gleaming, he beamed in ecstasy, rolling his eyes. Those long lashes wet with the water, maybe with tears. The old man fed him honey from a plate. Ricky lapped it with his tongue and shivered himself into a fit of dancing.

Lee knew that his brother had seen him. Ricky saw everything, tranced out or not. Lee waited, guarding his little corner, keeping himself apart. About twenty minutes later the drums suddenly stopped, the chanting ceased abruptly, and suddenly Ricky was no longer on the stage.

The fat woman appeared again, locking her arms around Lee's waist and urging him through the crowd.

"Oh, be sweet, be sweet, be sweet to your little brother," she babbled, kissing his neck, smothering him with the pongs of cologne and sweat. "Enrique has the word, Enrique speak the tongue, Enrique know the truth."

The truth was waiting behind another beaded curtain, in the small kitchen at the back of the basement. Ricky rested on a stool, leaning against a countertop while the old man toweled his hair dry. There were pots simmering on an old gas stove. The fragrance of spiced black beans played over the cooling stench of the cheap cologne. There would be food to eat before the ceremony resumed. Strength for the dancers.

In a corner was a wooden cage, in the cage a white chicken, head bobbing and weaving behind the slats.

Lee felt like gagging. It was all too much; the commingled odors, the human density, the muggy air of the crowded basement, the idea of ceremonial bloodletting.

"Hello, big brother."

Ricky took the towel in his own hands, buried his face, came up grinning. Still the handsome boy Lee remembered. The charming trickster who got all the girls.

"Is that going in the pot?" said Lee, indicating the chicken. "You and your friends having *pollo* for supper?"

Ricky grinned again. "Maybe."

"Animal sacrifice is still banned by law, you know."

The dark eyebrows made perfect semicircles on Ricky's olive-smooth forehead. "Is that what you came here to do? Bust me for killing a chicken?"

"Not my department."

"But it's okay if the Catholic priests drink the blood of Christ at every mass?"

"There's a big difference," Lee said heatedly.

This was an old, old argument. He and his brother always veered into roles firmly established in childhood. Lee knew it, couldn't help himself.

"Forget it," he said. "Do what you like. Kill the goddamn chicken. Pray to it. I really don't care."

The old man brought Ricky a cold beer, offered the same to Lee, who declined. The old man withdrew behind the curtain, leaving them alone.

"So why did you come?" Ricky asked.

"I'm on a case. That's the only reason."

Ricky laughed, shook his head. "You're on a case. You're on *my* case, right?"

Lee sighed, folding his arms as he leaned against the counter. The mess on the stove was actually starting to smell good.

"I hope not," he said. "All I want is a little information."

Ricky waited, the bottle poised at his lips.

"You know Heberto Raimez?" Lee asked.

Ricky nodded. "He's dead. Bum ticker."

"He had a daughter. Mercedes. Runs a *botánica* on the Calle Ocho."

"Sure. I know Mercedes. A beautiful woman. You should get together with her, big brother. Come back to the neighborhood, get married, settle down. She make you a good Cuban wife."

Lee ignored the taunt. "The night he died, Raimez was transporting six Anglos. They'd been injected with drugs that might have come from a *botánica*. You hear anything about that?"

"Of course not. Heberto didn't have anything to do with drugs, Lee. He was an old *político*, a patriot. I'm serious about Mercedes. You could do a lot worse."

"Ricky, I need to know who Raimez was working for."

"You marry Mercedes, maybe she'll help you remember who you are."

Lee snorted. "I know exactly who I am. I'm a cop. I'm working a case. You could help me out," he added.

Ricky studied the floor. "Maybe. I wasn't close to Heberto. He never came to me."

"But you know the daughter," Lee insisted.

He shrugged. "Some of my people frequent her *botánica*."

"Come on, Ricky. I'm surprised I didn't see her here tonight, throwing herself at your feet."

Ricky grinned and wiggled his carefully pedicured toes. "Jealous, big brother? A *santero* has special powers, you know. I can fuck all day and all night."

"Don't change the subject. Who was Raimez working for when he died? Who is his *padrino*?"

The grin faded. Ricky was suddenly sober, serious.

"I am a *santero*, a simple priest. I do not involve myself with political matters."

"Cut the crap, Ricky."

"Really. I don't know, okay? Heberto knew a lot of people."

"You could ask Mercedes," Lee urged. "You could help me out here, Ricky. Just a little."

There was the hint of a real smile, a softening. "I'll do this much, big brother. Go see Felipe."

"Felipe? Who's Felipe?"

"Trust me, you'll love him. Or her. Heberto went to Felipe for counseling and divination. Felipe was supposed to cure his bad heart—I guess maybe his medicine isn't so good, huh?" Ricky chuckled. "Anyhow, Felipe speaks through Mrs. Caberra, a *madrina*."

Ricky gave him the address. "Go tomorrow night," he advised. "Ask your questions when she's in her trance."

"How will I know her?" Lee asked.

"Can't miss her. She'll be smoking a fat cigar and speaking in a deep baritone. Felipe is the spirit of a Creole slave. He is very wise."

"Terrific," Lee said, unable to temper his sarcasm. "I want to find out about the dead, I have to *talk* to the dead."

As he left, the drums resumed at a higher pitch. He could hear the chicken screaming in panic.

CHAPTER TWELVE

There was a message on her answering machine. A young woman with a southern accent saying, "Shee-it, ah hate these thangs. What happen is that creep Hank at the Hang Tuff give me this number, toll me you-all might know where kin ah locate that jerkoff Dave worked on the beach. Who ahm after, though, is his cute fren Kurt. Maybe ah'll try again, see if a real person answer."

Sara unpacked the takeout Chinese she'd brought home and tried to eat. Found she had no appetite.

Someone who knew Kurt Palmer. Someone who was looking for him. Should she call Detective Valdez? But that would tie up the phone, and there was always the chance that the girl would ring at the same time, hear a busy signal, and never bother to try again.

Sara put the food away, tried to watch the news. Saw talking heads, smoke billowing from a shopping mall, more talking heads, but nothing really registered.

She played the message back several more times, reassuring herself that the girl had promised to try again. Well, not promised exactly.

When the phone rang, she found that her hand was remarkably steady.

"This a machine again?"

The voice was louder, there was loud rock music in the background.

"This is Sara Copley speaking. You called about Kurt?"

The Pink Kitten was a hotel lounge in the Art Deco district of Miami Beach. The hotel itself had yet to be renovated, and looked as if no amount of paint and polish would ever transform it into an architectural curiosity. It was plain and small and situated on the wrong side of the street, away from the beach. There were empty rocking chairs on the porch and the vacancy sign was lit.

The loud rock Sara had heard over the phone came from a jukebox. Two Argentinian teenagers were pushing quarters into the slot, punching combinations for heavy metal. Sara knew they were from Argentina because Liddy Anne said so. A large family of Argentinian tourists were booked into the hotel, a shopping trip to Miami.

"These people party hearty, lemme tell ya," Liddy Anne said. There was only her and a sour-looking male bartender. "Don't tip for shit, though. And tonight they're all off to see Wayne Newton or something, left us here to baby-sit."

Sara sat at a table near the bar, as far from the blaring jukebox as possible. Liddy Anne brought her a drink, something pink with a paper umbrella. "Better start you a tab, or Handsome'll bust a nut."

Handsome, Sara gathered, was the bartender. Giving her, yes, a beady eye, then studying his fingernails as he leaned against the speed rack.

"Don't mind him, honey, he's all bite, no bark."

Liddy Anne was a pretty little redhead, very petite. She wore her hair long, a pink leather skirt and matching boots. There were large rings on her fingers, big hoops in her ears. The bar was too dimly lighted to tell, but Sara suspected she had freckles. In any case she wasn't much more than the legal drinking age, despite the hardened cocktail-waitress veneer. Only a year or two separated her from the boys playing the juke.

"Let me guess," said Liddy Anne, pulling a seat up close so they could talk. "You're his wife, right?"

Sara shook her head. Stirred the little umbrella around, not tempted to try the pink whatever it was. "An old friend. After Kurt got out of the army, he stayed with me for a while," she said. "Then he left to come down here. To see his friend Dave. Is that how you met him, through Dave?"

"I guess. They come in together, into this place I was workin' up the north end of the strip. The Five Palms, you been there? No? Real nice, better than this toilet. What happened, the owner started hitting on me, he looked like Don Rickles only worse, he had these warts? So I quit. Serves me right, I guess," she said, looking around the Pink Kitten. "So you ain't found old cutey-pie Kurt, huh? Hank says Dave is in the hospital, he's maybe got something fatal."

Dave had been the talky one, she said, but it was Kurt who caught her eye. Kurt who came back alone the next night. Kurt who had dated her, "sort of."

"You're not gonna do a jealousy number on me, are you?" Liddy Anne asked. "'Cuz I really hate that. Up the Five Palms we had these two girls, tried to claw each other's eyes out over some guy? It was disgusting."

"I want to know everything you know about Kurt Palmer," Sara said. "And I promise not to get mad."

Liddy Anne nodded. "'Cuz it's not like we was engaged or nothing. But, you know . . ." She let it hang, waiting for Sara's reaction.

"You slept with him? Look, Liddy Anne, you may think this is strange, but I'm almost glad you did, okay? Because that means maybe you know something that will help us locate him."

"Us?"

"The police are looking for him, too. We're afraid he may be in trouble, just like Dave."

Liddy Anne looked suspicious. "I thought Dave was sick."

Sara told her about David Melborn. Liddy Anne was appalled. "You're sayin' he shot some weird Cuban drug in his veins? I never liked Dave much, but I never figured him for a thing like that."

"No sane person would ever knowingly inject a neurotoxin, Liddy Anne. Either these men thought they were injecting a different drug—heroin or cocaine—or else it was done *to* them."

The girl was shaking her head, stroking a spot on her thin little arms. "Stick a needle in your own body? That's disgusting. Sayin' it might be smack or coke doesn't make it any better."

"So when you knew Dave and Kurt, they weren't doing drugs?"

"No way. But I never knew Dave, really. Didn't like the way he looked at me. It's Kurt I know. He stayed with me almost a week. Well, five days."

"He moved in with you?"

Liddy Anne nodded. An older man had wandered into the lounge, and she had to get up and wait on him. The man sat there holding a straw hat in his hands until Liddy Anne returned with a beer. Then he put his hat on and drank.

"If I'm real lucky, he'll leave me a dime and a penny. The penny means I did a great job," she said, taking her seat.

"Did Kurt ever tell you what his plans were? What he intended to do in Miami?"

The girl shrugged. "You knew him, right? What I would call spacey. Real cute, but kind of dreamy. I ast if he was goin' to get a job or whatever, he said yes he was but first he had to take the cure."

"The cure?"

"Beats me. Had something to do with Dave, though. Old Dave was seein' this doctor, and he wanted Kurt to see him, too."

"Did he say what doctor? Or where?"

She shook her head. "'Course I ask him what was wrong, he give me that secret little smile of his. Then he taps his forehead, you know? Like he's got a head problem. I say, Kurt honey, there's nothing wrong with your head, you're just a little dreamy is all."

"What did he say to that?"

"He laughed. Said it was a good thing I didn't know the real Kurt." Liddy Anne rubbed her nose. "So, did *you* know the real Kurt?"

"I don't think I did, no," Sara said. "Something had changed him."

"Yeah?" That seemed to encourage Liddy Anne.

"I think Kurt *did* have some mental problems. Related to his time in the army. That's why he gravitated to Dave. They'd both been discharged from the service with something called 'combat-stress syndrome.' Did he ever mention that?"

"No. I asked him about the army, but he never wanted to say nothing. Just do that smile, you know?"

"Yes," Sara said. "I think I do."

"You don't think he's in bad shape like Dave, do you?"

"I hope not," Sara said. "What prompted you to look for him, Liddy Anne?"

She got quiet, studied her fingernails. "Well, to be real honest, my rent is overdue. And the last time I saw Kurt, he asked could he borrow a hundred dollars."

"And you gave it to him?"

"All I had was eighty, so I give him that."

"Did he say why he needed the money?"

"He and Dave were going to see this doctor. Kurt didn't know what it would cost, but he wanted to have some money with him, just in case."

"And that's the last time you saw him?"

She nodded. "Three weeks ago. When he never came back, I figured maybe he met some other girl."

Sara opened her purse, got out her checkbook.

"What's the idea?" Liddy Anne said. "I'm not sayin' you should pay for what Kurt owes me."

"But I want to."

"Forget it, honey." Liddy Anne stood up, patted Sara's shoulder. "Nice try, but I'd rather he came around himself. I'd kind of like to see that funny little smile again."

When Sara left, the two teenage boys followed her out to the porch. The way they were giggling she suspected they'd got something stronger than Coke from the bartender.

"Hey *rubia*," they called. "Hey, you got yellow hairs in the *puta*?"

They followed her for a block, taunting her. When Sara turned and raised her purse, ready to swing, they ran back to the hotel, shrieking with laughter.

CHAPTER THIRTEEN

When the knock came, Vidoc was lying naked in his hammock, reading *Troilus and Cressida*. He slipped on his robe and stepped into sandals to answer the door.

"Good evening, Colonel."

"Can I come in, Emile? Or do you have company?" he added with a leer.

"I never have company. Would you like a drink?"

"Cognac."

Vidoc poured from a snifter of the colonel's own cognac. The same bottle that had been in the cabana bar when Vidoc took up residence. He never touched the stuff. With the colonel he drank a little distilled water poured over ice cubes made from distilled water.

The colonel sniffed the cognac. He had a sly look that Vidoc didn't like. "I saw Wilson tonight," he said.

"The Company man? I thought he was at Langley."

"He's back in town. We had a cozy little meeting at the airport."

"Oh," Vidoc said, and waited. He was seated in a sling chair, very composed, his ankles crossed, having positioned lights in such a way that his own face was in slight shadow.

"We had a very interesting conversation," the colonel said.

Vidoc waited.

The colonel sighed and said, "There's a new crowd running Langley. A bunch of *maricones* who seem to think you can run a covert war without shedding blood. Without developing new techniques. They want to cut off funding. They want to stop the project."

Vidoc stiffened, forced himself to appear calm and serene. "What do we do?" he asked.

"First, don't worry about funding. We have other sources of revenue. Money is not the problem. The problem is Wilson. If he reports back to Langley . . ." The colonel let his words drift, staring into the shadow, his expression impassive. The message was clear enough.

In his patch of darkness Vidoc smiled.

"I'll handle Wilson," he said.

CHAPTER FOURTEEN

From his recliner, perched on a crumbling slab of concrete in the small yard behind his bungalow, Valdez stared into the night. Around him was the stillness of Cherry Grove. An army of wilting palms rose over the other, nearly identical bungalows on the block. Each streetlight was haloed with insects. The bug zapper was flashing bolts of purple neon; toasted moths drifted to the ground like singed snowflakes. He never heard the zapper go off without thinking of the electric chair. Maybe because he'd once heard death-row inmates referred to as "june bugs."

The Grove was an area of middle-class boxes, not a neighborhood, really. Simply a place. Suburban scene, genus Florida. And that was fine, just fine. Lee liked living here. He liked not knowing his neighbors too intimately, liked the atmosphere of casual anonymity.

He felt utterly normal here, completely American.

He sipped from a bottle of watery American beer and waited for the ethnic dread to seep out of his bones. A long, cool shower had washed away the stench of cheap cologne and incense smoke. The rest would fade in time, provided he did not return to that fetid little basement, or the *bata* drums.

Was it wrong, as Ricky believed, to want a life that was simply American, rather than the fashionably hyphenated life of Cuban- or Hispanic-American? It was not as if he ever denied his heritage; bilingualism was an advantage he had no intention of relinquishing. He would never forget who his parents were, where they had come from, what they had gone through. In his heart there would always be a place for his people.

What more was necessary?

What really troubled Lee, what caused him to finish one beer and reach for another, was the thought of facing the *madrina* Caberra. One freak Santería experience was enough, thank you.

He was heading back inside to grab one more cold, sleep-inducing beer when a night-shift homicide detective called.

"This is Paloski. In case you don't remember, you matched up a couple of stiffs for me back in July. Couple of drugstore cowboys ended up in the bay. Execution style."

"I remember."

He did, too. It had been messy, but he'd managed to get prints off the bodies, they hadn't been in the water too long.

"Why I'm calling, I've got a line on the Emile Vidoc, M.D. You put him on the Fugitive Suspect list, right?"

"That's right. Is he dead?"

Paloski chuckled. "Hey, I occasionally come across a live one, okay? Your guy happened to witness an accidental drowning out in Coral Gables, I remembered his name, that's all. There can't be too many Dr. Emile Vidocs out there."

"I'm not even sure there's one," Valdez said. He'd snaked a beer out of the refrigerator and twisted off the cap, trying to keep it quiet.

"I heard that." Paloski laughed.

"So tell me about Vidoc. This accidental drowning."

"Not much to tell. Cuban gardener slipped and fell in a swimming pool, this big estate. In there for hours before anybody noticed. Your man pulled him out, called EMS. They called us. Clean accident, autopsy showed copious amounts of chlorinated water in the lungs. You'll understand why I remembered the doc when you see him. Tall, spooky geek with no hair. I mean, not even eyebrows."

"You have an address?"

"Try the estate," Paloski suggested. "He was a guest there, staying in this fancy cottage by the pool. Owner's name is Calavera. Colonel Calavera, I didn't ask what army. I got the impression he was a big wheel in the Cuban community. Is that true?"

Valdez sighed, closed his eyes. "I'm afraid it is," he said.

CHAPTER FIFTEEN

The colonel's Coupe Deville had a trunk large enough to accommodate your average Toyota. Emile Vidoc, surveying the spacious interior, decided there was more than enough room for his purposes.

He donned dark glasses and a summer-weight Stetson and drove at a leisurely, law-abiding pace, west through the sleepy, oak-lined streets, until he intersected the Palmetto Expressway.

It was a lovely, blue-skied morning. Traffic was light. Vidoc made his image smile in the rearview mirror as the big Caddy accelerated onto the expressway. He liked the look. Shades and a Stetson, very cool and western. He drove serenely south, melding into the Dixie Highway, and eventually into the Florida Turnpike.

Vidoc was thinking about Wilson, the Company man who wanted to cancel the project. He'd invited Wilson to dinner, to discuss the situation in a civilized manner. Wilson had accepted. Now it was simply a question of what to prepare.

Vidoc wanted it to be something special.

Lee Valdez was driving slow because he had a hangover. The Alka-Seltzer had helped. His head felt like eggshell stuffed with cotton. Oddly enough a cup of Cuban coffee, quaffed like a dose of medicine, seemed to calm his nerves.

After the call from the homicide detective he'd had several more beers, he couldn't remember exactly how many. Enough to make sleep a thick black fog that had rolled up as soon as his head hit the pillow. Enough to make him decide he would never ever drink again.

The address Detective Paloski had supplied was in an exclusive area of Coral Gables, a section of large, secluded estates. An older part of the city, with quiet streets shaded by live oaks drenched in moss. Security fences, high walls crowned with broken bottles set in concrete, attack-dog moats, bullet-proof gates, remote-camera surveillance—all the accoutrements of postmodern, paranoid wealth.

"Excuse me," the security guard said in Spanish. "You must have an appointment."

Valdez aware that the rear end of his car remained dangerously exposed in the street, got out and showed the guard his Metro-Dade shield. It made little impression.

"You still need an appointment, Detective."

"Is Colonel Calavera at home?"

"We're not supposed to say."

"Do me a favor? Make a call, tell whoever's in charge that Metro-Dade detective Lee Valdez wants to ask a few questions."

The guard was apologetic. "I don't think that will do it, sir."

"Try, please. It's regarding the accidental-death investigation."

"What accidental death, sir?"

"Gardener drowned in the swimming pool, I believe."

"Oh, that."

Oh, that. Giving the impression the matter had already been settled to the satisfaction of all concerned.

"Make the call," Valdez said. Adding, "Please?"

The guard phoned the main house and then emerged to announce, "Someone will see you in a little while."

"Can you at least let me park inside the gate?" Valdez pleaded. "I'm going to get rear-ended out here."

A system for accommodating unexpected visitors had, it seemed, been worked out. The procedure involved surrendering the keys to the guard and waiting on the other side of the street until the vehicle was safely transferred into the driveway and the gate relocked. Only then was Valdez invited to return to the proximity of the guard shack.

"Some security system you've got here," he said. "You ever been to the White House?"

"The what house?"

"White House. Where the president of the United States lives. In Washington, D.C."

"Never been there."

"Well, they could learn a thing or two from this setup."

Twenty-five minutes later Colonel Calavera arrived at the gate, driving an electric golf cart with a surrey top. Valdez, sitting on his haunches—no chair had been tendered—rose stiffly to his feet.

"My apologies, Officer. I was unexpectedly detained."

The colonel, wearing a translucent white *guayabera*, chino slacks, and soft leather sandals, got out of the cart. The way the guy shook hands he could have been running for office.

"Detective Valdez," he said, showing off his perfected teeth. "There are many Valdez families. Do I know your father, by any chance? Is he in the wholesale grocery business?"

"My father is dead. He was in the shoe-repair business. If you knew him it was because he repaired your shoes."

The colonel shrugged, as if he couldn't be expected to remember a mere cobbler.

"Come on up to the main house," he said. "We'll have coffee."

Calavera steered the electric cart with manic ferocity, grinning as he pointed out various buildings on the estate. Packed into five landscaped acres were the big hacienda, a six-stall garage, a stable now used for servant quarters, an outdoor tiki bar, greenhouse, pool, pool cabanas, and a soundproofed shooting range. Live oaks towered over the security wall along the perimeter, screening the place from anything but an aerial view. The hacienda enclosed a courtyard that was studded with ornamental fruit trees. The white-tiled roof of the house looked scrubbed.

For Lee Valdez, who had grown up in a two-room apartment on Twenty-seventh Avenue, it was unreal, like a trip to Disneyworld. Epcot presents the Cuban-American millionaire. Note the Spanish-tile swimming pool, the gleaming gold Mercedes limo of a size favored by dictators of small nations. See the colonel pull strings, manipulating governments.

The political implications of attempting to beard Calavera on his own turf became apparent moments after they were seated in the courtyard. The colonel called for service on a walkie-talkie and then announced, "Naturally I checked you out, Detective. Impersonating a police officer is a classic method for breaching security. We have to be careful."

Valdez raised his eyebrows as if to say, Check me out? What does that mean? Calavera smiled indulgently. Behind him footsteps were crunching on the white gravel path. A servant, delivering from the kitchen. When the tray arrived, he lifted the cover, revealing a silver pot of coffee, cups, cream, sugar.

And the slightly damp sheets of a faxed report.

"You administrate the Missing Persons Unit, is that correct?" the colonel said, smoothing out the paper and squinting slightly as he read. "Let me see here, you reside in Cherry Grove—is it nice? I've never been there. Your father for many years operated a small shoe-repair shop on Twenty-seventh Avenue. So you see, my question about wholesale grocery was a little test, which you passed admirably." He consulted the report again, frowning, as if disappointed. "What else? Oh, you have one brother, Enrique, a well-known *santero*. You have never married, which seems curious, but there is no indication of homosexual activity. You passed the sergeants' exam on your first try, and have completed an advanced forensics course in Quantico, under the auspices of the FBI. Last year you filed for an extension on your tax return and paid at the end of ninety days. You have nearly six thousand dollars in a savings account and several up-to-date charge cards. There is more, but I think you get my point."

Valdez nodded cautiously, aware that he was not adequately prepared to interrogate a man of Calavera's position, that he might never be. "The point is you're well-informed," he said, trying to sound unconcerned.

The colonel shrugged. "Naturally I have many sources. And I am curious as to why an investigator from Missing Persons should be interested in a gardener who drowned in my pool. The body is not missing. I paid to have it buried."

Be careful what you tell this man, Valdez cautioned himself. "I don't care about the gardener," he said, playing for time, hoping to salvage something from the visit. "I'm, ah, looking for Dr. Emile Vidoc. He was here when the drowning occurred."

"Ah," the colonel said.

"I believe Dr. Vidoc is a houseguest here."

"No longer," the colonel said, spreading his hands. "He left soon after poor Carlos drowned. The death bothered him, he was no longer comfortable here."

"I see. Do you know where I can find him?"

"Unfortunately he did not leave a forwarding address."

The colonel poured coffee into two cups, passing one to Valdez.

"Please understand, Sergeant, I do not mean to be rude. Only I am a very busy man, and I assume you are also busy, so I wish to save us both valuable time. You know what I know about you—now what do you know about me?"

Valdez sipped the coffee. It was, no surprise, excellent. "You're a businessman," he said.

"Come now, you can do better than that."

Valdez shrugged. Just his luck to be hungover when a heavy-weight like Calavera wanted to play mind games.

"Colonel, I know you're an important man, obviously well-connected. You own real estate all over the county. I think you own a couple of banks."

The colonel spooned heaps of sugar into his coffee. When he smiled, Valdez was reminded of a tanned, well-fed shark.

"Business, yes," he said. "I have been most fortunate in business. But I think we should speak of patriotism. That is more important, do you agree?"

"I'm a police officer," Valdez said. "We're not supposed to be involved in politics."

"Yes, but you are a Cuban. You were born in Havana."

"I was three years old when we left. I don't remember it."

"Your father was not a cobbler in Havana. His family was quite well off, I believe. Batista had him arrested on trumped-up charges, then seized his money and his land. Surely you now about that."

Valdez nodded.

"So you know how political things work. The ones in power can do as they like."

"In Cuba," Valdez said. "This is the United States."

"Power is power," the colonel said. "The country doesn't matter. More coffee?"

When the turnpike petered out, Vidoc was in Homestead, gateway to the Everglades and chemical garden for South Florida. Crop dusters cut billowing white lines along the flat horizon of the farmlands, moving through the sky at a pace that did not seem sufficient to keep them airborne.

Vidoc kept the air conditioner on recycled air. He had a healthy respect for toxic fumes.

After a few miles he turned onto a spur road paved with white marl that made pinging noises under the fat tires, like small-caliber weapons fired at random. He passed a large agricultural complex, huge tractors and sprayers that looked as if they had been designed by NASA for work on the moon. The odor of chemical fertilizers and insecticides penetrated the imperfectly sealed atmosphere of the automobile.

Vidoc tried not to breathe too deeply. Lungs were precious.

The spur ended at an immense, tin-roofed storage building. Owned by an agricultural combine, the building served as a holding facility for toxic chemicals. Drums of nasty stuff the local landfills would no longer accept. The unwanted effluvia of chemically drenched produce. Herbicides.

Inside the building pallets of drums were racked in stacks thirty feet high. Some drums were labeled, others had been corroded to an eggshell thinness. No inventory was kept. The less paperwork available to bothersome environmental agencies, the better. No security patrol. Who would want to steal these ghastly chemicals? And who cared if they did?

Vidoc parked on a slab of steaming concrete and popped the lid of the trunk. This was not his first visit to the shed. He knew exactly where to find the phosphoric acid. Slipping on thick rubber gloves, Vidoc set to work. He was able to fit eight of the five-gallon containers in the trunk. Forty gallons. A special treat for Agent Wilson.

Vidoc adjusted the rear air shocks and began to retrace his route. Along the way he stopped at a shopping mall—there were dozens to choose from—and used cash to purchase a fourteen-inch electric chain saw equipped with a carbide-tipped chain.

It was a few extra bucks, but what the hell, a dull chain was dangerous.

"Well," the colonel said. "This has been most pleasant. I'm always happy to make another friend in the police department."

He stood up. The lecture on power politics in the Cuban community was over. It was clear that Valdez was supposed to leave.

The detective remained seated. "Excuse me, Colonel, if you could answer one question? If you're barely acquainted with Emile Vidoc, why was he living here?"

The colonel shrugged. "The man needed a place to stay, so I obliged. Now he has moved on. I heard he left the country."

Calavera was in a cheerful mood as he drove Valdez back to the gate. "All these missing people you search for. Do you ever find any?"

"A few," Valdez said. "Now and then."

The colonel laughed. "What a frustrating job," he said. "I have been all over the world, and you know one thing I learn?"

Valdez got out of the cart and waited for the gate to be opened.

"I learn," the colonel said, "how much easier it is to make people disappear than to find them."

CHAPTER SIXTEEN

"Their condition has deteriorated in the last twenty-four hours," the neurologist said. A plump little man with a pink, scrubbed-looking face, he wore double-breasted suits to minimize his paunch, a ruse that fooled no one but himself. "You saw the chemistry. The latest metabolism results?"

Dr. Harding nodded. They were standing away from the ICU station, so as not to be overheard by the nurses. As to the sleepers, well, what could they hear? "Heart and blood pressure remain fairly constant."

"Yeah, for now. You want my opinion?"

"Of course I want your opinion," Harding said, unable to keep the irritation out of his voice. "That's why I asked you to consult."

"Then take it from a neurologist. Neurotoxins often have bizarre, long-term effects. None of the alkaloids you isolated would produce these symptoms taken alone, but in combination—well, see for yourself. Basal salts are out of whack and getting worse. As you say, the heart rate is steady, but it's also so low that cells are not being properly vitiated. There's bound to be severe cardiac damage. Can't be avoided, if you look at the chemistry."

Harding shoved his hands in his coat pockets, teetered slightly on his heels. He didn't like the sound of this at all. "So what are you suggesting?"

"I'm not suggesting anything. I'm just saying the chances of long-term survival are very slight. Maybe if we'd been able to treat them directly after exposure . . ."

"It was a fluke we have them at all," Harding reminded him. "We have to make the most of whatever time we've got. Agreed?"

"Agreed."

"What's your best estimate?"

"A week, maybe less."

Harding nodded. The neurologist's assessment of the situation was pretty much in line with the consulting cardiologist's, and with his own, for that matter. Something had to be done.

"We'll need to formulate a radical treatment procedure."

"How radical?" the neurologist asked.

"Whatever it takes."

All around him the soft noise of the machines, the padded footsteps of the nurses. Poking needles, adjusting wires. Speaking to him as if he were asleep or dead. Could they not hear that he was screaming inside? Clawing to get out of this human coffin?

He was buried alive. Buried alive inside his own body.

Out! the insane part of him screamed. Let me out!

Let me out—or let me die.

Vidoc in his disposable paper jumpsuit, cleaning house. He wore a charcoal-filter respirator to avoid the disinfectant fumes. Breathing unpurified air was bad enough here, all those airborne microbes, industrial pollutants, carcinogens.

He was mopping the floor in the little kitchenette when the colonel came calling. The man had a bad habit of dropping in unannounced.

"Emile?" He opened the door, coughed at the ammonia. "*Madre de Dios*, it makes my eyes water. I tell you before, Doctor, you don't have to do this. I get you one of the maids to clean. I got one now, little girl from the Dominican Republic, she'll scrub the floor and let you fuck her, too."

Vidoc paused with the mop in his rubber-gloved hands, slowly pulled down the respirator. How was he to interpret such an offer? Was this supposed to be an indication of male bonding, the sharing of women? A test of some kind? Vidoc decided to remain impassive—the colonel, who had a habit of scratching his testicles whenever a female was near, would never understand Vidoc's indifference to the idea of sexual intercourse.

"You're meeting Wilson tonight?"

Vidoc nodded. The colonel knew very well that he was meeting Wilson tonight. "We will discuss the problem over dinner."

"He's already made up his mind," the colonel said.

"So have I."

The colonel smiled uneasily. "Be discreet, okay? Another cop came by today. Claimed it was about Carlos drowning, but really he was looking for you."

Vidoc put the mop in the bucket. "Why would he want to see me?"

The colonel shrugged. "Don't worry about the cop. He's a nobody, the son of a cobbler. I'll take care of the cop. You attend to Wilson."

He turned, paused at the door, and Vidoc understood that he was about to ask the question that had really drawn him to the cabana. "Emile? What will you do?"

Vidoc picked up the mop, began to scrub at the tiles. "I'm going to make him disappear," he said.

CHAPTER SEVENTEEN

October. In Boston they would be pulling down storm windows, raking up leaves, thinking about when to put on the snow tires. In Miami Beach it was 80 degrees at dawn, and Sara had gone swimming before leaving for work. Just a few laps in the pool after she spotted the beach glistening with jellyfish washed ashore in the weedline. Having been stung a few times, she now recognized the delicate, soap-bubblelike creatures. The inflated sails of the poisonous man-o'-war.

The beach was always an adventure. Hidden tar globules, stinging jellyfish, medical waste, you never knew. Hence the proliferation of swimming pools built right on the beach. In Miami Beach only the young and the foolish swam in the sea.

Before leaving the condo tower, Sara tried to contact Detective Valdez at his office. She wanted to tell him that Kurt Palmer was alive as of three weeks ago, that he and Surfer Dave had been on their way to seek treatment from the same doctor the day he disappeared.

"Detective Valdez is not in this morning," she was told. "Can you leave a message?"

"When will he be back?"

There was a rustle of paper. "It says here he's expected by noon."

"Ask him to return my call. It's urgent," she said.

At her office Sara decided to try his home phone. Was he sick? Taking a few hours off? She got his answering machine and decided that if he hadn't called by noon, she would go over to Metro-Dade Police Headquarters and make her report in person.

* * *

The disc jockey was wearing a hairpiece that looked a lot like a small black beret without the button on top, Sara thought.

"Come on down, folks, to the Sunnyland Mall. Shop till you drop, then drop in and see the good people at the heart-lung clinic. They're here all day to check out your ticker, take a snapshot of the old airbags, make sure you're the picture of health. And the best part—no charge, folks, this is brought to you by Dade County government, your tax dollars at work making Greater Miami a healthier, happier place to live. That's right, the service is abso-pauso-luta-tively *freeeeeee*."

A Sinatra song followed the pitch. KFOX, the Silver Fox Station, was directed at the senior market, which in radio was apparently anyone over fifty. Most of those who availed themselves of the service were considerably older than that. And not everyone appreciated the free clinic.

When Sara arrived on a routine check, a blue-haired lady, all of five feet tall, was shaking her cane at the medical technicians and shouting at the top of her evidently healthy lungs.

"X rays give you cancer! That's a fact! My husband, Morrie, got X rays and he died! So why you people coming in here, trying to give everyone cancer!"

"Ma'am, if you could please sit down? One of our staff will explain the procedure—"

"Keep your hands off me! Help! They're going to give me tumors! Call the police, somebody, I want them arrested!"

Sara felt bad about it, but there was really no choice—she let mall security escort the old woman away. It happened now and then, clients who claimed some evil force was beaming radio frequencies into their heads, or people like the old woman who were convinced that Disease Control was involved in spreading disease, rather than trying to eradicate it.

Often these beliefs had some basis in truth. Overexposure to X rays *could* cause cancer, although the chances of dying from unde- tected lung tumors was much higher. But dealing with the crazies came with the territory. To Sara's way of thinking, this was the front line of medicine, even if you had to do the fighting in an urban shopping mall.

When things were back to normal with the staff, Sara excused herself for a few minutes. She was heading for the public telephones when someone called her name.

"Lee?" she said, startled by his unexpected appearance. "I was just about to call you."

He nodded, smiled. "The message said it was urgent. Here I am."

Sara told him about Liddy Anne, and where Kurt had been going the last time she saw him. Valdez was nodding thoughtfully even before she finished, as if none of the information came as a surprise.

"It's this man Vidoc," he said. "Surfer Dave's doctor. His name keeps popping up."

He told her about his inquiry at the VA Medical Center, that despite no computer record, an eyewitness had named Vidoc as the doctor who was treating veterans for combat-stress syndrome.

"This case is starting to get scary," he said. "There's a connection with a Cuban mercenary."

"What?"

"I know, I know. It sounds pretty wild. And maybe it is, but I need to establish who the van driver was working for before I go any further. That's one reason I came out here to see you in person. I want to ask you a favor."

"Of course," said Sara, expecting him to request help from the lab, or a medical connection of some kind.

He explained that his inquiry into the source for a *botánica* toxin had resulted in an appointment with a *madrina* who claimed to be possessed by the spirit of a dead Creole slave.

"You mean she's psychic?"

"Oh sure," Valdez said. "And I'm the Prince of Darkness."

"You sound pretty skeptical."

"I hate this kind of freak show. And I don't know anything about potions or neurotoxins or magical plants. So it would be a great favor if you'd accompany me. We could have dinner first, talk over new developments in the case," he added. "I mean, if that's convenient."

Sara agreed to meet him at a restaurant in Coconut Grove.

CHAPTER EIGHTEEN

"Good evening, Doctor," Wilson said.

Vidoc forced himself to shake hands. "Glad you could make it."

The table was set with white linen napkins and thin, translucent dinnerware the color of shallow green water. On an adjacent dolly were trays covered with silver domes. He wanted Wilson to think he was making a special effort.

Soften him up for the big surprise.

"The colonel's kitchen is catering tonight," said Vidoc, playing the warm host. Wearing his paper jumpsuit though, for when things get wet. "Broiled dolphin—the fish, not the mammal—Caesar salad, saffron rice with almond flecks, and braised asparagus tips. For desert, some mango thing with flan."

"Sounds delicious."

"Would you care for a dry martini? I make an excellent dry martini."

"Sure," Wilson said, easing his bulk into a chair, "why not?"

Vidoc picked at morsels of the fish, crunched a few almonds in his strong white teeth. He kept on pouring wine for Wilson, who was a prodigious eater. Masticating heavily and making enthusiastic noises about the broiled dolphin. Disgusting, even for a normal.

Surprising him was going to be a pleasure.

"Did you know the old COS in Chile? Henderson?" Vidoc asked.

They had moved to the sitting area, where he had adjusted a zone lamp so that it would shine in Wilson's eyes.

"No, I can't say I knew Henderson," said Wilson, blinking.

"Pity," Vidoc said. "Henderson had imagination. He had style. Made G. Gordon Liddy look like a wimp."

Wilson puffed himself up. "I assume the colonel mentioned our conversation?"

Vidoc sipping his distilled ice water, nodded. "Just in passing. Said you had some questions about the project."

"Well, yes. More than a few questions, I'm afraid."

Vidoc unfolded a few of his elongated limbs, repositioning himself in the sling chair. His paper suit made soft crinkling noises.

"I was under the impression the project had already been given approval," he said.

"Provisionally," Wilson admitted. "Based on your original proposal. Now the whole thing is up for review. The environment has changed in the last few months. All this spread-of-democracy bullshit? A lot of interesting projects are on hold."

"Why is that?"

"Fucking Congress," Wilson said. "The Intelligence Oversight Subcommittee. Couple of influential fags on the committee are raising a fuss about Company policy. Demanding a major reevaluation of the charter. Ever since they caught Ollie North fibbing under oath, they've been as prickly as a porcupine on steroids."

Vidoc made himself smile. He'd heard the colonel tell the same joke, assumed it was making the rounds at Langley.

"You mean Congress has been briefed on *this* project?"

Wilson chuckled. "No way. Are you kidding? Your, um, experiment isn't taking place on foreign soil, so there is no legal requirement that we inform the committee."

Vidoc stood, stooping slightly to avoid the paddle fan. "I'm relieved to hear there has been no security leak. Would you like a cognac? The colonel has some excellent cognac."

"Sure, don't mind if I do. Just a small one though."

Wilson took the glass balloon, set it untouched on the table beside him. That smug look meant he was about to drop the hammer.

"It's this way, Doc. I'm due back in Langley tomorrow noon, to brief the SPS—that's special projects supervisor—and I'll have to tell him I think your project should be aborted."

"That's pretty drastic," Vidoc said quietly. As if he were turning down the volume inside, preparing for the worst. Let Wilson think he had scored—it would keep him docile. "What changed your mind?"

"The colonel assured us this little experiment could be carried out without any risk of exposure. We thought it might have interesting applications elsewhere. Then you lost your, um, volunteers, a screw-up in transportation, am I right? Volunteers who were supposed to be totally clean, untraceable?"

"That wasn't my fault," Vidoc said. "It was an error in transportation."

"Nobody blames you, Doc. But the fact remains, six of your guys are in a local medical center, subject to civilian inquiry. It's only a matter of time before they're all identified."

"Impossible," Vidoc said without any particular emphasis.

"Hey, the bit with the fingerprints was cute, but one of your boys has already been made. The others are sure to follow. Plus we've got a hotdog cop who's been nosing around government files."

Vidoc sat up straight.

"What?"

"The system was breached with some bogus software. Nothing new, a lot of the state and local enforcement agencies sneak access to classified records."

"Who is this cop?" Vidoc said. "What did he find in the computer files?"

"Relax. Just some schmo detective from Missing Persons, trying to clean up his caseload. Don't worry, he didn't find anything. The files were purged months ago."

Vidoc was quiet. He removed his dark glasses, folded the stems, and tucked them into a zippered pouch on his paper suit. "It doesn't matter if the original group is identified. They still can't be tied to us. None were married or had families, I made sure of that. They were all loners, losers."

"That's not it," Wilson said. He picked up the cognac glass.

"They'll begin to expire within the next week or so. Then they'll just be dead losers. Who cares?"

"Not me," said Wilson, sniffing the liquor. "The problem we have is bigger than that. The problem we have is with your project. And frankly, Doc, with you. Nothing personal, but there it is."

Vidoc made himself attentive.

"A problem with me?"

"First the project," Wilson said. "Damn useful technique, if it works."

"It will work," Vidoc said.

"Maybe. The point is, what if it does? If the side we're backing goes on a righteous rampage, there will be increased surveillance by the opposition. Remember how the shit hit the fan when our boys floated a couple of mines into that harbor in Nicaragua? Imagine the fuss if the body of one of your, um, *experiments* falls into the wrong hands?"

Vidoc was hunching forward, his chin cupped in his hand. He made himself look worried. "That's a second-stage scenario," he protested. "The original contract specified that we were to document an experimental procedure in a live-combat situation. Then all relevant data would be evaluated. Any problems with eliminating physical evidence—your 'body falling into the wrong hands'—could be dealt with at that juncture."

"Yes, well," said Wilson, spreading his hands. "You know how it is. Once a project gets off and running, it assumes a life of its own. Much harder to call a halt at that stage. Better to pull the plug now, before some human-type failure occurs a few months down the line and we have to deal with revelations concerning your, um, résumé."

"My résumé?"

"Data relevant to your career. For instance, the problem at Fort Dietz."

"I left Fort Dietz of my own accord."

Wilson shrugged, as if to say, Who are you kidding? "Let's get real, Dr. Vidoc. There were serious questions about that project, too."

"It was an approved surgical procedure. Perfectly legal."

"Maybe legal. But folks get very nervous about the idea of lobotomy."

"Psychosurgery," Vidoc corrected, very calm now. "Nothing at all like lobotomy, which is a crude procedure intended to permanently sedate an uncontrollable patient. My methods at Fort Dietz were on the cutting edge of psychosurgery. The experiment was abandoned simply because my immediate superiors seized on a few early failures. Besides, that was a completely different procedure. My new method doesn't involve major surgery."

Wilson was nodding, as if eager to get on with it. "What's done is done, but you see what I'm getting at here, Doc? The big picture we have to deal with? It's an image problem. A couple things go wrong—and we've already had a serious failure—your, um, experiment could become public knowledge. Then we get the subcommittee going nuts, demanding to know all the nasty little details. And admit it, Doc, your method *does* get ugly."

Vidoc shrugged. "War is ugly."

"You could be accused—not by me, of course, but by the media—of tampering with the natural order of things."

Vidoc sighed. "I can see you've made up your mind."

Wilson stood, finishing off the last gulp of cognac. "Doc, I'm real sorry. It was an interesting idea, but times have changed. We all have to adjust. Face it, the world just isn't ready for the Vidoc Method."

Vidoc walked him to the door. Doing his best resigned-to-failure look, all you had to do, slump the shoulders, leave the eyes downcast.

"Your expenses will be paid," Wilson said, oozing magnanimity. "And of course we always take care of our old friend the colonel."

Vidoc reached past him, unhooked the screen door. The lights from the swimming pool glowed, giving the night an amber quality. Palm fronds rustled, suggestive of rain.

"Watch out for the little bastards," he said as Wilson stepped outside.

"Huh?"

"The mosquitoes."

Vidoc reached into a pouch in his paper suit and withdrew a pump-dispenser bottle. Extending his long arm, he pumped twice, sending a mist directly into Wilson's face. Surprised, a little angry at the impertinence, Wilson opened his mouth to protest.

The potent knockout gas took hold.

Wilson fell to his knees. Right now a great heaviness would be descending down his spine, rendering his limbs useless. Vidoc knotted his fingers in Wilson's hair and dragged him back inside the cabana. The man was overweight, he ate too much.

A few moments later he remembered to lock the screen door. The mosquitoes really were a problem.

CHAPTER NINETEEN

Valdez waited for her in the bar at Monty's Stone Crab. Had to catch his breath when she came into the room. That dress, what was the color? Dahlia blue, something like that. Showed off her legs, her slim waist, although the outfit was modest by Miami standards. No plunging neckline, slits up to the crotch, nothing like that.

"Pretty dress," he said, getting up from the barstool.

"Thanks. I'm late again, sorry."

"I didn't notice." He'd been checking his watch every thirty seconds for the last fifteen minutes.

Following her from the bar to their table at the restaurant, he caught a whiff of the fragrance that lingered in her vicinity. An aura, he decided, of orange blossoms. Dizzy stuff.

Be cool, he told himself.

Monty's had the usual crowd of locals from the Grove, a mix of tourists and business types from the city. They lingered over cocktails for quite a while before they were able to order.

"Sara, I gotta be straight with you," Valdez said, shaking his head. "I may have blown the whole investigation today."

She paused with the drink at her lips.

"What?"

"I had a lead that Emile Vidoc might be in residence at this estate in Coral Gables. And like an idiot I went in there cold. Thought maybe I could snatch the guy as a material witness, really break this open. Instead, I got my head handed to me by Carlos Calavera."

"Is he the mercenary you were talking about?"

"He's that and a lot more. The colonel's pretty famous here in Miami. Helped organize the original brigade for the Bay of Pigs invasion, and he's been dealing arms or training guerrillas ever since. Makes no secret of his CIA connections—hell, that's his power base, the fact that everybody knows he's connected. For years he was making a hell of a lot of money exploiting the Contras in Nicaragua. Now that the Contras are no longer in business, his new gig is a land war in Bolivia. Different country, different ideology, but I guess that doesn't matter to a mercenary."

"But what does he have to do with the sleepers? Or this doctor who treated Dave Melborn?"

Valdez sighed, jiggled the ice in his glass. "I wish I knew. And now, because I bulled my way in there, we may never know."

"But why was it a mistake for you to check the place out?"

"I should have been better prepared. Made discreet inquires that wouldn't tip Calavera off to a police investigation. It would have been smarter to arrange for surveillance, put in a wiretrap if possible." He finished the drink, reached for a breadstick.

"I think you're being hard on yourself."

A waiter arrived with wine, uncorked the bottle, and poured. They went through the little ritual of tasting.

"You know what I think? Strictly a theory, I've got no proof, just a cop's gut feeling. Maybe Calavera is marketing some damn biowarfare weapon—this neurotoxin, whatever it is. The sleepers were guinea pigs. Either Vidoc is involved in testing this stuff on combat veterans or he was *also* exposed and the colonel has had almost all trace of him erased, right down to the VA computer files."

"So what do we do?"

"That's what's really killing me. I'm not sure there's anything we *can* do. Except concentrate on the sleepers themselves. And that, I'm afraid, is up to you and Dr. Harding."

"Mostly Dr. Harding," Sara said with a trace of bitterness.

The cold crab claws arrived. Valdez, a stone-crab aficionado, showed her how to remove the tender meat and dip it in Dijonaise sauce.

"You don't trust Harding? As a doctor, I mean?"

"Not as far as I can spit. All he cares about is the research. The possibility of patenting the toxin, turning it into some kind of business proposition."

Valdez couldn't help noticing that vehemence brightened the gray light in her eyes. After a while they dropped the shop talk and settled into the meal, consuming the rich crabmeat, polishing off the wine, but the spark remained.

Over coffee Valdez felt compelled to raise the big question. He tried to say it small, as if her answer did not concern him personally. "Sara? Can I ask you this? What happens if we locate Kurt Palmer?"

She looked away. He could see where she was chewing on her lip. Nothing major, just a nibble.

"Maybe start over," he suggested, having to clear his throat. "Give it another shot, is that what you have in mind?"

"No," she said. "I don't think so."

A double answer. Well, what did he expect? This was not a woman who gave up easily.

"You two go way back. King and queen of the prom or whatever."

Now she was laughing, shaking her head. "Is that what you think? No way. It wasn't like that, believe me. I didn't have the money for the prom."

"But the guy pays, right?"

"This is ancient history," she said. "Are you really interested? Is this part of your investigation?"

"Yeah, I'm interested," he said. "And no, it's not part of the investigation. You *know* it's not."

She hesitated, giving him a look. Was he for real, or was this a line he was trying? Valdez could feel it, that odd little tension between strangers that has to dissolve before they can become friends. It wasn't gone yet, but almost.

"It was just my mother and me," she said. "My father took off when I was three years old. All I remember of him is this face in the door, this floating mustache. And that could be from a photograph. You know how sometimes you can't tell whether you really remember something, or you're picking it up from a picture you saw?"

"Sure," he said. "It just sticks in your mind, you don't remember how it got there."

She was nodding, he had it exactly right.

"Mom was an LPN, which, in the places she had to work, was like being a slave. The bedpan brigade, and also you get to scrub the sickness up from the floors. And, Lee, she never complained, okay? But I wasn't going to have her putting in more overtime hours to buy me a prom dress I'd wear once. It just wasn't that important to me."

Valdez stirred his coffee, which was crazy because the cup was empty. "I didn't know," he said.

"Know what?"

"That you grew up poor," he said. "Like me."

Mrs. Caberra was expecting them, or rather expecting Lee Valdez. There was an awkward moment with the doorkeeper, who had introduced himself as Mrs. Caberra's son.

"Who is this woman?" he demanded in Spanish, eyeing Sara.

"My good friend," Valdez responded, keeping up a smile. "She has a great interest in your mother's wisdom. And of course I will pay double the fee."

Son of Caberra let them pass.

"What was that all about?" Sara whispered as they passed into a heavily curtained room that reeked of incense and cigar smoke.

"He wanted to know if you are my wife."

"And what did you say?"

"I said yes. I hope you don't mind."

"When in Rome," she quipped.

The Caberra home was a ten-minute drive from the restaurant, in a seedy neighborhood bisected by the Metrorail lines. It was an ordinary ranch-style house, with the garage converted into a room or salon where the great woman received her weekly audience. Rugs covered the floors and walls; thick curtains absorbed the noise of the outside world, although the vibration of passing trains was discernible. Admission was by invitation only—brother Ricky had made the arrangements—at a minimum cost of fifty dollars, collected by Mrs. Caberra's son, a man in his forties with a bad eye, many gold teeth, and breath fragrant with rum and Binaca. Sometimes the admission price was waived if a poor supplicant was deemed to have a "crisis of the spirits." As Valdez paid, keeping the transaction secret from Sara, he wondered if there was any way he could collect as a legitimate investigatory expense.

He decided, Forget it.

Dr. Copley was the only Anglo in attendance. She and Valdez sat on folding chairs, waiting for Mrs. Caberra to enter and begin.

Around them, filling another dozen or so chairs, were Santería worshipers who either knew of the *madrina* from previous encounters or had been recommended by *santeros* like Enrique. Most sought advice about health or family matters. One couple, both looking terrified, were trying to locate a daughter who had run away. A man sitting to the left of Valdez confessed that he was having troubles with his business partner, and was seeking a means to a resolution.

"Felipe has great wisdom," he said, shifting nervously in his seat. "I will put my trust in Felipe."

Sara grasped enough to ask who Felipe was. Valdez was explaining about the cigar-smoking Creole slave when Mercedes Raimez entered.

"Oh shit," Valdez muttered.

Mercedes was dressed in a floor-length black dress and mantilla, in the old style, and was elaborately coiffed and made-up , with great attention to her eyes. Her full lips gleamed blood red; jewelry glittered at her wrists and on her fingers.

She spotted Valdez immediately and started forward, as if to greet him. Upon registering the presence of Sara, she abruptly took a seat on the opposite side of the room and began to fan herself in a manner that Valdez interpreted as hostile.

"You know her?" asked Sara, keeping her voice low.

Valdez nodded miserably. Enrique, the great matchmaker, had set him up. Mercedes wouldn't have dressed so ostentatiously for the *madrina*—she had intended to impress a man. Now all that time and effort would be refocused into resentment, of himself and the beautiful blond Anglo at his side. Damn his brother.

"Old girlfriend?" Sara wanted to know.

"Hardly. She's the daughter of Heberto Raimez."

"The one who runs a *botánica*?"

Valdez nodded. Sara gripped his arm. "Oh, but that's wonderful. Maybe she'll help us."

"I doubt it."

He was saved from an explanation by the entrance of Mrs. Caberra. A large, round-shouldered woman with a smooth, infantile face, she did not appear to be significantly older than her son, who helped her into an upholstered chair in roughly the center of the room. She wore a tent-shaped gown of white lace, a white knitted shawl, a white kerchief on her graying head. Her plump feet were bare. There was a black lacquered table beside the chair, and a matching box on it.

The *madrina* murmured greetings, sliding her eyes from chair to chair, muttering an aside to her son when she spotted Sara.

Valdez heard the word *rubia*, a pejorative term that meant, roughly, blond Anglo bitch. He winced, shifting uncomfortably, but Sara seemed unaware that she'd been singled out. The son said something into his mother's ear and the old/young woman nodded, brushing him aside. He retreated to the rear of the room, smiling and nodding, as she groped for the lacquered box and took it into her voluminously draped lap.

The box contained cigars and a lighter.

Tension in the room increased as she picked out a cigar, rolled it between her pudgy fingers. Valdez stole a glance at Sara and saw that her attention was focused on the main act. Mrs. Caberra clicked the lighter. On the third click a flame appeared, and she began the business of getting the cigar alight. There was total silence from the audience. Only the clicking of the lighter, the greedy, breast-sucking noise of a cigar being brought to life, and the silent vibration of the passing trains.

Lee Valdez felt queasiness in his belly. It was going to start now, the whole creepy business.

Dull blue smoke jetted from the *madrina*'s moistened lips. Her eyelids began to flutter. Her head slumped. When her chin came up again, the infantile look had been replaced by an expression of cunning indifference. Her knees opened into a masculine posture as she hunched forward, puffing energetically on the cigar. Who were these people? her expression seemed to say. What did they want?

"Felipe!" someone cried out.

The *madrina* coughed and began to speak in a deep, rumbling voice.

"Is that Spanish?" Sara wanted to know.

Valdez listened intently before replying. "Yes. But a very strange accent. Supposed to sound Creole, I guess."

"What is she saying?"

"She says yes, she is Felipe, and why has he been called back to this place? He was very happy in the dark woods. It was only the prospect of smoking a cigar that tempted him to return. There is no tobacco in the dark woods where his spirit resides."

The *madrina*'s voice became a doglike growl, a barking of words in a tongue Valdez did not understand—gibberish invented by the *madrina*, he decided. The barking ceased, and the old woman, her gestures convincingly masculine, again demanded to know why he, Felipe, had been called from his rest.

A man in the rear of the room stood up and asked, stumbling over his words, if Felipe might suggest a solution to an unspecified personal problem—"my troubles." Felipe, glaring through a pall of cigar smoke, growled that the man had only to make a sacrifice to Oggun and the problem would be resolved. Get on with living, Felipe instructed, respect your elders and your gods, and do not worry so much. The man sat down so swiftly he nearly missed his chair.

Next up was the couple searching for their daughter. The father, trembling, asked if his little girl was alive.

The *madrina* coughed, spat loudly on the floor. "Hah! Your little girl, she is not so little now. She is in another city, far from here, living with a man. Her life is wicked. Soon she will resume contact with you."

The mother of the not-so-little girl burst into tears and was comforted by her husband, who vowed to give Felipe money for a thousand cigars the day their daughter called.

"He's very convincing," Sara whispered. "I mean *she* is."

Valdez merely grunted. The nausea had diminished, although he still felt ill at ease. Maybe it was the thick cigar smoke, or the pong of nervous sweat exuded by the anxious supplicants. He wanted to laugh in Mrs. Caberra's fat, greedy baby face. Instead, he sat quietly, avoiding eye contact, murmuring a rough translation to Sara:

"This man says he has troubles in his business. Should he trust his partner? The *madrina* tells him he is right to be suspicious, he must consult one who is expert in the law. I suppose that means a lawyer."

"Sounds reasonable," Sara observed.

Valdez had no comment. He was aware of a prickling sensation on the back of his neck. His heart was thudding. The *madrina* was looking directly at him. Staring with faint contempt.

"Where is the *descreído*?" she demanded. "Where is the nonbeliever? Show yourself!"

Valdez rubbed the back of his neck and studied the floor. Sara, aware that he was the object of Felipe's derision, gripped his left hand.

"The air is very bad here," the *madrina* growled. "Evil spirits attend us. The *descreído* must show himself. Now!"

Arms gripped Valdez from behind, jerked him to his feet.

He whirled, ready to take a swing, and discovered the *madrina*'s son hugging him.

"Please," the son whispered urgently, hot breath reeking of spiced rum, "Felipe means you. You must stand up and be blessed. It is the only way."

Valdez shook off the son but remained standing. The white-shawled *madrina* made a barking noise, then reached into the lacquered box on her lap. Drawing out an economy bottle of cologne, she removed the cap and demanded that the unbeliever reveal himself.

Pushed from behind, Valdez stumbled forward. The *madrina* shook the bottle of cologne, flinging a fine spray over his head and shoulders. He blinked, eyes stinging, and swore loudly.

The *madrina* laughed uproariously, and declared that the evil spirits had fled. Valdez backed up and slumped into his chair. The spirit of Felipe wasn't done with him, however.

"Felipe knows you are an outsider. You have turned your back on your people, on the true religion."

"I was raised in the Catholic Church," Valdez said hotly.

"Makes no difference," Felipe growled. "You must follow the true path. Only then will you achieve wisdom."

"Let's get out of here," Valdez said to Sara. "This is a setup."

"Wait!" the *madrina* demanded. "You come seeking knowledge. Ask and it shall be given."

The son, crouching behind Valdez's chair, urged him to cooperate. Valdez, trying to wipe away the cologne without much success, realized that he would be allowed to interrogate Mrs. Caberra only in her guise as Felipe. Which meant postulating his questions in an acceptable form.

"I ask after the spirit of Heberto Raimez!" he declared boldly. Fuck it, he could play their game. "Tell me what he was doing on the night he died."

From the other side of the room came an outraged gasp. Mercedes stood up and denounced him. "This man is an *descreído*!

He mocks our religion. He brings a *rubia* into this room, and evil spirits follow her. He has no right to speak to my father!"

The *madrina* very calmly puffed her cigar and asked Mercedes to be seated. Eyes flashing, she obeyed.

"I have seen Heberto Raimez," the *madrina* declared. "He is in a good place. Perhaps he does not want to be disturbed."

Having made his move, and having been doused with foul cologne to boot, Valdez wasn't about to give up so easily. "Ask Heberto who he was working for that night. Was it Colonel Calavera?"

More puffs on the cigar. The *madrina* was wreathed in smoke, as if exuding a fog. Silence prevailed for a short time, until the *madrina* growled again.

"Heberto Raimez asks why he should trust you?"

"I only want to help the men he abandoned the night he died. I want to know who hurt those men, and why."

The *madrina*'s fat hands fanned the air. She hunched forward and spit copiously between her splayed feet.

"Heberto has gone," she announced. "He will not return until you open your heart to the true religion, the religion of your brother."

Valdez folded his arms, disgusted. Ricky had set him up very nicely. A message from the underworld to obey his little brother, no less.

"We're out of here," he said to Sara.

The *madrina*, seeing that she'd lost him, began to hoot loudly, cackling and laughing. "Heberto won't speak to you! Nobody speak to you!"

Valdez ignored her, ignored the boozy son who begged him to be seated. Taking Sara by the hand, he marched out of the smoke, out of the room.

When they were clear of the house, he paused to inhale deeply, drinking in the night. There were faint stars, the sliver of a moon.

"What a waste," he said. "I just can't deal with these people."

"I was fascinated," Sara said. "She really *looked* like a man."

"Yeah, well, now I smell like a prostitute, so that makes us even, I guess."

They were almost to the car when Mercedes Raimez stormed from the house. Valdez turned and waited.

"How dare you! Son of a dog! Pig! You insult my father! You insult all of us!" In a rage she tore bracelets from her wrists and flung them to the ground.

Valdez knelt, retrieving the bracelets. When he handed them to Mercedes, she burst into tears and wailed that her father was dead, that he must be left alone.

"Please," Valdez said, taking her arm and guiding her back to the front steps of the ranch house, where she willingly sat down. "I'm sorry about your father, okay? I don't want to conjure up his spirit, or ruin his reputation, or make you miserable."

Mercedes sniffled. Her eyes, running with mascara, looked as if they were being erased. Her elaborate hairdo had come undone, and now strands clung to her tear-streaked cheeks.

"Your brother said . . ." she began.

"Never mind what my brother said, okay? I'm just a cop doing a job. Your father is dead, and God rest his soul, but the men he was transporting that night are still alive."

He indicated Sara, who remained by the car.

"That woman is a doctor. She needs to find out why these men were poisoned, and how."

Mercedes looked up, cast a baleful glance at Sara.

"So tell me," he said. "Was your father with Calavera in the brigade? Is that why he was doing a favor for the colonel, driving that van?"

To his profound surprise, Mercedes nodded.

"The colonel was a great friend to Papa. Is that what you want me to say?"

"Is it true?"

The fit of rage and grief had left her trembling. She hugged herself and said, miserably, "Of course it is true."

"One last thing, and I promise to leave you alone."

Mercedes had taken a white hankie from her sleeve and was loudly blowing her nose. "I am already alone. Nothing you do or say can make any difference."

"There's a man I need to talk to, an Anglo. Like your father, he is associated with Calavera. His name is Vidoc, Emile Vidoc."

Mercedes shook her head. The name meant nothing to her.

"He's a doctor," Valdez said. "Tall, thin, and bald. Not just bald, apparently, hairless."

Mercedes shot him a look that was icy with fear.

"Don't speak of him," she hissed. "He is a witch, a devil. He kills men, but they do not remain dead."

She then fled inside the *madrina*'s, shutting and bolting the door.

Valdez walked slowly out to the car.

"I think we're in trouble," he said.

CHAPTER TWENTY

Wilson was aware that his eyelids were being pried open. Vidoc loomed over him, a hairless skull with a perfect tan. Far above, a ceiling fan wheeled slowly. Panic was a small, frenzied bird trapped in his bowels. A bird with sharp talons.

"Hello in there," Vidoc said amiably. "Are you relaxed? Comfy? You'll find that you can blink your eyes if you want."

Wilson tried. It was true, he could blink his eyes. Nothing else functioned. He could feel sensation all the way down to the tips of his toes, but something vital had been switched off. He couldn't move, couldn't remember how to exert control over his body.

Vidoc held up an empty syringe. "Forty cc's of organic alkaloid neurotoxin. My own formula. Produces paralysis almost instantly. Reduces heartbeat, blood pressure, metabolism, but does not, I think, inhibit the pain messengers."

Wilson blinked.

Vidoc blinked back, fluttering eyelids barren of lash. His thin lips distorted into the parody of a smile. "The pain messengers, my dear fellow, are those tiny little nerves that carry sensation back to the cerebral cortex."

Wilson blinked again.

Vidoc chuckled. "You want to send me a message, right?" he said. "Let me guess. You've changed your mind about the project?"

Blink, blink.

"Yes, I do quite understand," Vidoc said soothingly. "You'd like to wake up in your motel bed and discover this is all a very bad dream." The doctor loomed closer, his breath cool and without scent. "I'll tell you a little secret, Wilson. I've never had a bad dream. I've never had a dream, period. When I sleep, which isn't often, I sleep like a machine. I put myself on hold."

Wilson's eyelids went into a spasm of blinking. Furious blinking.

"I know," Vidoc sighed. "You're telling me I can't get away with this. Respectfully, I must disagree."

Vidoc went away, as tall as a man on stilts and slightly blurred, as if seen from the bottom of a pool of clear water. Wilson watched the fan blade turning and willed himself to wake up from the paralyzing dream. He felt exquisitely vulnerable, as if his skin had been peeled away, leaving the raw nerve ends exposed. Did nightmares always have this flood of sensation?

What troubled Wilson was that he could not remember falling asleep. The last thing he recalled was stepping into the night air. Then something about a mist being sprayed into his face. A surge of anger, followed by a sensation of heaviness.

Now he remembered a needle being jabbed into his arm. Vidoc milking the fluid into his bloodstream.

The method.

The frenzied bird of fear inside him exploded into flight.

Please please please, he prayed, *wake me up.*

A soft padding sound as Vidoc returned. A kind of smile showing under the brim of the white cowboy hat. "How we doing down there, Mr. Wilson?" He moved away from the overhead fan, remaining in Wilson's peripheral vision, just barely. "Blink if you're scared, Mr. Wilson."

Wilson refused to blink.

"Tough guy, huh?" Vidoc said. "Well, I expected no less from a Company man. You've got real balls, Wilson, although not, I must say, for long."

Blink.

"There," Vidoc said, coming into full view, much closer. "I saw that! Don't be ashamed. After all, you're a normal. Unlike me. I've got a little something extra, Wilson. I can't dream like you do . . . but I *do* things you can't even dream about."

He went away again. Wilson keeping time by counting the revolutions of the fan. An odor broke his concentration. A pungent, chemical smell. Vidoc returned, humming a tune Wilson recognized as "The Teddy Bears Picnic."

"If we go out in the woods today," Vidoc crooned, "we're in for a big surprise."

Wilson couldn't help it, he blinked like a bastard.

"I'm not one of those physicians who believe in keeping the patient ignorant of his condition," Vidoc said. "I think you deserve to know exactly what is happening to you, and why. So blink if you want to know."

Wilson didn't blink. Vidoc smiled with just his teeth.

"Doctor knows best," he said. "So I'm telling. The reason you're in this terrible predicament is because you made the wrong decision regarding our little experiment. I'm *very* interested in fulfilling the terms of my contract because, frankly, I want the money. Therefore, you need to disappear before you report to the SPS—that's special projects supervisor," he added with a toneless laugh. "When this episode is concluded, I start a new life, Wilson. I enter a brave new world. Where I won't have to explain myself to normals like you. Where I won't have to pretend. Maybe I'll even learn to dream," he mused. "If so, Wilson, I'll dream a little dream of you. Promise. Cross my heart."

Wilson closed his eyes. He tried to retreat inside, closing himself into a fist, shutting down the synapses. He wanted to die now, quietly, in his own way.

Cool, dry fingertips forced his eyelids open.

"Pay attention," Vidoc said. "If my theory about the nerve messengers is correct, this is going to hurt you a lot more than it hurts me."

Wilson felt his legs being lifted. Now he was being dragged backward along the floor. Watching the ceiling go by, the top of a doorway, and now the bottom edge of a plastic curtain ruffling over his face.

Cool, wet tiles under him. He was in a shower stall.

The chemical smell was much, much stronger.

He couldn't see Vidoc. Where was Vidoc?

Without the fan to gauge time, he was lost. How long had it been? A minute? An hour?

"Boo!" Vidoc was right there at his ear. "I'll bet that made you jump inside, huh? Go on, be afraid. It's normal to be afraid. And I'll let you in on my little secret, Wilson. Fear is my addiction. I need to see it. I need to feel it coming off of you. Fear is like a wonderful smell, Wilson. I fill my lungs with you."

Now he was looming again. A tall white manshape. And there was something in his hands. New and shiny and plugged into a bright yellow extension cord.

"This is a Sears Craftsman," Vidoc explained. "I always go with Sears products because of the guarantee. It's a versatile little chain saw, very quiet, very light. Just in case you're curious—and I would be in your shoes—I'm going to start with your extremities and work up to your torso. Disposal will be via the phosphoric-acid method. Forty gallons in the bathtub. A bit smelly, but it has the advantage of clearing the drains."

He pulled the trigger, activating the chain.

It had a light, metallic rattle that reminded Wilson of an electric train set. Christmas. He was five years old. Mommy and Daddy.

The running chain was positioned above Wilson's left ankle. "Ready? If you're ready, don't say anything."

The chain slowed as it met resistance.

CHAPTER TWENTY-ONE

There was a radioactive glow in the sky, lights from the city. Sara, picking up on Valdez's mood—the man wanted to talk—suggested a walk on the beach. Keeping well out of the weedline—Sara hadn't forgotten the jellyfish—they walked for nearly a mile. North to Indian Beach Park and beyond. Valdez with his trouser cuffs rolled, Sara barefoot.

"Did I hear it right? You have a brother who's mixed up in this?"

"I hope he's not," Valdez said.

"But he's into this Santería thing?"

Valdez had his hands in his pockets, scuffing sand as they walked along the strip of beach midway between the condo towers and the sea. The air heavy with the smell of seaweed. Now and then Sara caught a whiff of the cologne the *madrina* had drenched him with—he seemed unaware that the scent still lingered.

"Ricky's a *santero*," he said. "A priest. Mercedes is a follower, so was her father. Ricky said if I wanted to find out who Heberto was working for, ask the *madrina*. What a load of crap."

"I get the impression you and your brother aren't exactly close."

His laugh was rueful, pained. "You could say that."

"What happened?"

"We had an ugly scene when my father died. Cancer, and it took a long, long time. I spent day after day in the hospital with him, trying to see that he was 'comfortable.'" He paused, cleared his throat. "You're a doctor, I guess you know that 'comfortable' is a code word for not being in pain?"

"Yes," Sara said.

"He was a tough old bird, my papa. He was also a devout

Catholic. Went to mass almost every day of his life. So of course the priests came to see him in the hospital. Gave him last rites a couple of different times. It seemed to help him. Did as much good as the morphine, I think. And then Ricky decided to get into the act. He put on a show."

"What do you mean 'show'?"

"A Santería ceremony. Summoning some god who was supposed to help Papa cross over into the spirit world, I guess. The Santería version of last rites. My father was freaked out—even with all the morphine in his blood, I could tell he was frightened. This was blasphemy. For the old man, a mortal sin. Ricky doing his dance, chanting his names."

"And you tried to stop him?"

"I *did* stop him, but not before he sacrificed a chicken. Sprayed blood all over my father's bed. We got into a fight. I mean a knock-down, drag-out fistfight. Naturally the nurses called the cops, and by the time I'd got it straightened out, Papa was gone. Died all alone while Ricky and I were duking it out in the hallway."

"I'm sorry," Sara said.

Valdez shrugged. "I've been sorry about it for three years. It doesn't get any better."

They walked in silence for a while.

"I think Kurt's dead," said Sara, surprising herself. She'd been thinking it, hadn't meant to say it. "I've had the feeling for a couple of weeks now, on and off."

Valdez halted. His face unreadable in the dark. "We can't be sure."

"No," Sara said. "We can't be sure. You think this *madrina* had something to do with it?"

He shook his head. "She's an old fraud. Hell, the advice she was giving could have been lifted from an astrology column. It's the connection with Mercedes Raimez that worries me."

"Because the neurotoxin could have come from her *botánica?*"

"That's part of it. She knew who Dr. Vidoc was, that's for sure—she said he made people die without them really dying, which is a pretty good description of what happened to the sleepers. And her father worked for the colonel, that's another connection."

"Can you have her arrested?"

"On what charge? What evidence? And even if I *could* arrest her, she'd never testify. The colonel's lawyers would make sure of that."

"How?" Sara asked.

"Scare the hell out of her, that's how. And she's already plenty scared. I thought she was going to faint when I mentioned Emile Vidoc."

Sara tugged at his arm, got him walking again. It felt better to keep moving. "You make it all sound like some crazy conspiracy," she said.

"The colonel is an old hand at conspiracies. And it's not only Mercedes Raimez he can frighten. The guy scares the hell out of me, too."

Sara tried to see his expression. Was he kidding? The way he'd taunted the *madrina* wasn't the act of a frightened man.

"Let me tell you something about the colonel," he said. "A few years ago he went on one of those radio talk shows. He was giving his usual diatribe about how any Cuban who favored normalizing relations with Castro was a traitor. He mentioned the name of a man who had gone back to Havana to visit his family—just a visit, mind you—and the next day the man he named was gunned down, execution style."

"Calavera did it?"

"No, and that's what's *really* scary. He didn't have to. All he has to do was point the finger, say 'traitor,' and one of his fanatical followers carried out the sentence."

"That's unbelievable," Sara said.

Valdez stopped. "Yes, unbelievable," he agreed. "Lots of things happen here in Miami that are unbelievable but true."

Emile Vidoc working the bathtub. It would take, he knew from experience, all night. Wearing elbow-length rubber gloves, respirator, and safety goggles misted with steam rising up from the acid.

Making Wilson vanish was slow, mindless work that allowed him to drift into reverie, the closest he ever came to dreaming.

All the infections that the sun sucks up
From bogs, fens, flats, on Prospero fall . . .

The Tempest. His one and only star turn, before he began to play the lifelong role of Emile Vidoc, M.D. That last year as a Harvard undergrad, placement in the medical school assured, he'd involved himself in a student production. The tidy little group of players tossed him a crumb—understudy to Caliban, the deformed slave who had some of Shakespeare's best lines—although it was never intended that Vidoc get a chance to speak them.

> *And then, in dreaming*
> *The clouds methought would open and show riches*
> *Ready to drop upon me, that, when I waked,*
> *I cried to dream again.*

Those went to a cunning little character actor, Joel, a literature student and sodomite who had turned down Prospero for Caliban. Joel had barely even acknowledged his understudy. Emile the freak, tall and gangly with his lank, colorless hair and his misplaced intensity—a mere pre-med student, pen in his pocket, no soul.

Vidoc, intent on sucking the marrow from Shakespeare, on learning how to don the various masks of emotion, had decided that his own presence onstage was required. Getting Joel alone proved to be tricky. The popular boy surrounded himself with fawning Thespian Club types and a few rough-trade queers from Brattle Street.

The touch, the perfect touch that still pleased Vidoc all these years later, was the role he had invented to get the role. Pure inspiration. Calling Joel late one night, putting on a sweet, faggy voice—the close approximation of a voice he'd overheard in a coffee shop—and trying to persuade dear, sweet Joel to meet him in Harvard Square Station very late, at a time when the trains ran once an hour.

Joel had kept trying to guess who it was.

Do I know you? Are you that cute sailor I met at that party in the South End? Oh tell me it's you, please, and Vidoc, reading from a script he'd prepared for the occasion, saying, *Do me on the Red Line, sweet baby Joel. I'll be wearing a pink carnation, you'll never guess where.*

What a surprise for Joel when he'd bumped into Vidoc in that deserted subway station.

Oh, Emile, it's you. Was there another boy down here, a slender boy with dark brown eyes?

His own dark eyes searching the station, finding it empty, looking puzzled and disappointed, not yet afraid.

It was the first time for Vidoc. His decision to make Joel go away had been rationally conceived. But when the moment came, he discovered a new and lovely thing: the thrill of inducing fear. It was the closest he ever came to bonding with a normal—that hot, wet thing that passed into him in the moment when Joel knew. The pleasure was like a climax, only cleaner, less messy.

For such a lively boy he died very easily, his thin, soiled neck snapping like a celery stalk. The killing was nothing. It was in the instant before that Vidoc discovered his vocation. His need.

The last train on the Red Line, thundering in from Park Street Station, blurred the evidence. Accident or victim of fag-bashing gangs from Somerville, no one ever knew.

It was a tragedy, but the play went on, with the understudy stepping in as Caliban. Young Emile speaking his lines so much like the late Joel that everyone said it was uncanny. Lines that he still retained, after all this time.

"'Let it alone, thou fool,'" he said aloud, stirring the tub, his goggles misted, "'it is but trash.'"

CHAPTER TWENTY-TWO

Hernandez woke up before dawn, as he always did. He dressed in the cramped quarters of the Winnebago, cinching the ammo belt an extra notch tighter around his waist. Wanting to look sharp for the boys, set an example.

Outside, away from the noise of the air-conditioning, he could hear the birds stirring in the great swamp. The heavy-scented mist, an odor peculiar to this place, brought back bittersweet memories.

He had been a raw recruit in this very camp, in those grand old days of the Cuban Brigade. An exciting time to be young and alive, when everyone involved in the effort believed they were about to liberate Cuba, take it back from the Marxist butcher Castro, traitor to his class.

The airstrip had been new then, and propeller-driven cargo planes had ferried in supplies all night long, by the light of incendiary flares. Was it the clarity of youth that had made the struggle seem so clean, so pure? Hernandez had fought in a dozen regional wars since then, as mercenary or adviser, had trained thousands of soldiers in this and other camps, always with the hope that he would find that exhilaration again. Guerrillas, insurgents, Contras, freedom fighters, the names changed but the nature of war remained the same.

Until now.

Hernandez knew only a little of what the Anglo doctor had planned. It seemed unnatural, in a strange way unmanly. For centuries it was accepted that a soldier would fight and die because he had been trained to do so, because he believed in his cause, whatever it might be.

This new method of Dr. Vidoc's tampered with the old order.

Hernandez hitched up his belt. Enough. His was not to reason why. He strode into the barracks just as the first bloody streaks of dawn broke over the sky. Rousing the recruits. Slapping the cots with a strip of bamboo, his fine drill sergeant's voice a bellowing reveille.

"Up, you sons of rats! Up and see the sun rise! Get your hands off your peckers and fall out!"

All around him forty recruits tumbled from the bunks, pulled on fatigues, boots, a few of them giggling because it was so like a game.

In five minutes the platoon was assembled on the old airstrip, ready to drill, ready to drop and give twenty, ready to do anything the sergeant commanded.

"You there, Fernando, your fly is open."

The boy, one of the youngest recruits, had possibilities. There was something about his crazy grin, the way he threw himself into maneuvers, heedless of consequence. Hernandez waited as Nando adjusted his fly, aware that the boy had never had pants with a zipper before.

"In a few days the guerrilla commanders will arrive to inspect this platoon," Hernandez said, strutting along the row of boys, hands clasped behind his back. "We must be ready. We must be in fighting trim. Combat readiness, gentlemen! From now on you sleep in full uniform, is that clear?"

"Yes sir Sergeant Hernandez sir."

"Fall out for grub. And for God's sake learn to tie those bootlaces!"

CHAPTER TWENTY-THREE

"**T**his could be an important event," Dr. Harding reminded his hastily assembled staff. "I've arranged to have the entire procedure recorded on video, as part of the medical record."

Harding's morning pep talk addressed the current crisis. The sleepers were all exhibiting similar drops in vital signs. Blood pressure, heartbeat, and respiration were more shallow than ever. Internal temperature was nearly four degrees below normal, on the verge of shock. Blood serum revealed acute anemic conditions, and glucose was not being metabolized at a rate sufficient to support life functions.

Death seemed imminent. Radical intervention was called for, and Dr. Harding intended to have his newly conceived procedure fully recorded for later release to the medical journals and the media, if the situation warranted.

If the patient survived.

"I want cameras covering this from every angle," he said, instructing the technicians. "All life-function displays are to be entered into the monitors for direct video recording, logged in real time. And after the procedure is concluded, I want a roving cameraman to record the impressions of the medical observers."

"Observers, sir?"

"Senior staff here at the medical center," Dr. Harding snapped. Didn't these boobs listen? "We'll make sure we have a couple of neutral observers as well, just for the sake of appearance."

Harding made a note to have his secretary call Dr. Copley and extend an invitation. One last shot at prying her away from that low-rent Public Health Department.

If she didn't see the light then, screw her.

• • •

Sara took an aspirin when she got to her office. Maybe that would clear the cobwebs. She'd tossed and turned all night, jerked awake by anxious dreams that confused Santería ceremonies with modern medicine. Chickens running headless through a hospital, a blood-spattered surgeon who turned out to be the cigar-smoking *madrina*. Crazy stuff that had stayed with her after she got up.

After swallowing the aspirin, she made herself a cup of tea and sorted through the message slips on her desk. One that jumped out was a call from Cypress Medical Center. She returned it.

"Dr. Copley? Oh yes, you're on the list. They'll be holding a seat for you. Dr. Harding expects to get under way by two this afternoon."

"Excuse me," Sara said. "What list am I on?"

"Observation of radical invasive procedure," the secretary said, obviously reading from notes.

"What's this in regard to?"

"Says here 'interventive treatment to enhance blood-serum viability and reverse decline of life functions of dormant patients.'"

Sara sorted through the medical jargon. Interventive treatment. Dormant patients. Had to be the sleepers. And just what did Dr. Harding mean by 'radical invasive procedure'?

"I'll be there," said Sara, her head clearing.

CHAPTER TWENTY-FOUR

Valdez pried the lid off the coffee cup but did not drink from it. He felt a little sick. It was more than exhaustion, lack of sleep. Something ugly was happening out there, and he didn't have a handle on it. Forget about rousting the colonel, he was so insulated with powerful government connections, a mere police detective would never get through. Better to concentrate on the phantom doctor, Emile Vidoc, and his ties to the VA.

There had to be some way to get into the records, maybe a duplicate filing system that hadn't been erased or altered. But how? His own access program, supposedly forbidden, was used by lots of lower agencies, and its reach was limited.

Valdez decided he needed expert advice, preferably from someone who wasn't adverse to tampering with government files. A master hacker. He flipped through his Rolodex, found the number.

It rang for what seemed a very long time. Valdez stopped counting, just let it keep ringing. Wake up, you lazy son of a bitch.

"Fuck you," said the man who finally answered.

"Morning, Wayne. This is Detective Lee Valdez."

There was a pause, the sound of a throat being cleared. "What's happening, Lee? It's the middle of the night."

Valdez laughed. "Your shades must be down, Wayne. The sun has been up for at least an hour."

"Like I said, the middle of the night."

"I've got a situation, I need your help."

More silence. "Uh-huh. Is this a life-or-death type of situation?"

"Could be," Valdez said. "That's why I'm calling."

In his straight life Wayne Tolson had been a senior software specialist for the IRS. When he grew bored with the rat race, he resigned his federal job and opted for the laid-back life, trading his Georgetown condo for a canal-front bungalow and a trimaran. His income as a computer-science instructor at the University of Miami was modest, enough to keep a used Subaru in tires, and he had carefully avoided tenure-track positions. A man of trenchant wit, with libertarian pretensions, he described himself to students as "that great enemy of legal society, the Bohemian hacker under the coco palms. Far worse than a mere snake in the grass."

It was Tolson who had taught the night class that turned Valdez on to the world of computers. The two had become casual friends. The detective helped crew the trimaran a few times—Tolson was far from an expert sailor—and Lee had reciprocated by introducing the hacker to trout fishing in the canals. Early morning emergency calls had not been part of the friendship until now.

Thirty minutes later Tolson arrived with coffee and doughnuts.

"Regular coffee, not that sweetened road tar you like to drink," he said.

"Wayne, I really appreciate this."

Tolson nodded. "I figure a life-or-death situation, we need honey-dipped crullers."

The morning rush was starting out front, the usual throng of civilians reporting loved ones who were missing. By some miracle none of the staff had called in sick. Valdez was able to put routine inquiries on hold and concentrate on the sleeper files.

"First tell me this," Tolson said, munching on a doughnut. "Is what we are doing legal?"

"No."

"Well, that's a relief. No joy if we can't break a few rules."

It was beautiful, what Wayne Tolson could do with a computer. He played GRETA's keyboard like an instrument, using all of his fingers and considerable body English. Activating a modem, he hooked up with his university computer system, duplicating a program he had stored there.

When the software was in GRETA's memory, he turned to Lee and said, "So you really want to fuck with the IRS?"

"Not if there's another way."

"There might be. But I don't know it."

According to Tolson, the notion that IRS computer systems

were inviolable was a myth perpetrated by the IRS. The system was routinely invaded by intelligence agencies and high-level hackers.

"You mean a hacker can alter tax records?"

Tolson shook his head. "No way. A hacker can *access* data, but he can't effect a change. Can't move so much as a decimal point. So you can't fuck with the actual records. Forget about fixing yourself a refund check."

Valdez nodded thoughtfully. "You're saying an intelligence agency can't erase IRS files?"

Tolson munched on his second cruller, gave it some thought. "At the top, maybe. Exert political pressure. Somebody very senior would have to sign off. Rarely done, I think."

Valdez smiled. "Glad to hear it. Let's see what they've got on Emile Vidoc, M.D."

"Just tax returns, or everything?"

"The IRS keeps more than tax returns?"

"It eats whatever it kills. And believe me, the big beast is data-hungry."

After entering Vidoc's Social Security number, culled from his medical license, Tolson sat back and folded his arms. "This may take a while," he said. "Pass the doughnuts."

As the printer chugged and spit, Tolson paced the office, pausing to stare intently at GRETA's screen. Valdez occupied himself tearing fanfold sheets, putting chunks of paper into manageable piles. There was considerable duplication, and it took a while to sort through all the data, assemble it into a meaningful chronology.

Taking it year by year, fragments of a picture emerged.

"Okay," Valdez said, "Emile Vidoc graduates from Harvard Medical School in 1969. Enlists immediately in the Army Medical Corps, is assigned to a MASH unit based in Saigon. Captain Vidoc, M.D."

What began as a fairly normal medical career took a few strange twists as the years went by. After the war concluded, Vidoc resigned his commission and began working as a civilian physician at the Medical Research Facility in Fort Dietz, under government contract.

"I've heard of that place," Tolson said. "The CIA was testing LSD there in the fifties. It's a spook laboratory, human guinea pigs."

Valdez grimaced. "Well, our friend was promoted to director of behavior modification, special projects. And then it looks like he screwed up somehow. He was forced to resign."

The details were vague. A panel of his colleagues concluded that "while Dr. Vidoc routinely deviated from standard medical procedures, he cannot be held responsible for resulting brain trauma to patients under his care."

"Brain trauma? What the hell was this guy *doing?*"

Valdez looked up from the printout, his expression grim. "I smell a cover-up. What pisses me off, they never even suspended his license to practice, or notified any other states. Just turned him loose."

After leaving Fort Dietz, Emile Vidoc was employed as a "special projects consultant" for an entity called Third World Resources, Inc. Over the next five years taxes were withheld from checks issued in Grenada, Guatemala, Haiti, Chile, and Paraguay.

"The guy sure got around," Valdez said. "Nasty dictatorships a specialty."

"Third World Resources?" Tolson said with a smirk.

"I know," Valdez said. "Sounds like a CIA front. Any way we can check on that?"

Tolson shook his head. "Not from here. If I was back at IRS headquarters, maybe. The Company is pretty good about covering its tracks. They've got hundreds of front corporations, a lot of them either inactive or operating legitimate businesses."

The printer had finally stopped spitting out paper. Valdez reached for the last sheet. Tolson said, "You look surprised."

"Do I? Shouldn't be. But it looks good to see it in black and white."

Emile Vidoc had, for the last five years, been employed as a consulting physician for the VA Medical Center, Miami. Paid on a per diem basis to run a variety of clinics. The most recent being a six-month program to treat combat-stress syndrome in veterans prone to outbursts of violence.

His last paycheck was issued less than a month before.

CHAPTER TWENTY-FIVE

The secret to success in all things, Dr. Richard Harding believed, was attention to the small details. The decisions he made in the next few hours could effect the reputation and potential profit curve of the Experimental Medicine facility.

All available data on the neurobiology of the sleepers had to be collected now, in the event his proposed treatment failed.

Nothing could be left to chance. If the patient expired—a very real possibility—he had Pathology standing by to take tissue samples before and after the event. Expiration would not, of course, be a total disaster, as the morphology revealed by a full autopsy might well provide invaluable data.

Not that he *wanted* the sleeper to die. Far from it. Swift recovery was the goal. But if intervention proved fatal, well, one had to be ready to salvage what one could.

In his heart he did not believe failure was possible. Not if he anticipated every possibility, down to the last detail. The technicians no doubt considered him an irritating presence as he made suggestions about light and camera placement.

So be it.

They had no way of knowing how much was at stake here. The enhanced reputation, the enormous wealth that might accrue if breakthrough was made in a new nerve-block painkiller, patented from traces found in the sleepers' blood.

"Make sure the cables are taped in place on the floor," he instructed. "We don't want anybody tripping over a cable while the camera is running, now do we?"

"We'll take care of it, Dr. Harding."

"And I want the patient miked. There's a possibility he may actually make a verbal response. If so, it must be recorded."

"You got it, Dr. Harding."

"And how about this?" Harding said, his eyeglasses glinting. "Bring some of that lab equipment in here and position it in the background. Might give an interesting visual effect."

When he walked away, intent on his many details, one of the technicians stared after him in wonder and was heard to remark, "Can you believe that shit? Now the old bastard wants to decorate the set!"

Sara was more than a little surprised by the circus atmosphere in the surgical amphitheater. Technicians and nursing staff hurried about, readying equipment in the glass-enclosed surgery. Video-cameras seemed to be covering the brightly illuminated area from every conceivable angle.

Dr. Harding was at center stage, gowned and gloved. The sleeper who had been gnawed by rats lay on a gurney, his face swathed in gauze.

Sara hurried into the surgery, pushing her way through the busy technicians.

"I got your message," she said, a little breathless.

Harding's steel-rimmed glasses glinted above his mask. "Ah, Dr. Copley. Glad you could make it."

"What's happened?" she said, indicating the sleeper.

"The situation has deteriorated," he said. "I'm intervening."

"What kind of intervention?"

He glanced away.

"You'll be fully informed as the event unfolds. The decision is entirely my own. You're not a consulting physician in this case."

He indicated that she should leave the surgery, return to the amphitheater. Sara stood her ground.

"Surgical intervention?"

"Look, young lady, I invited you here as an observer. This is a private facility, and I can readily rescind the invitation, is that clear?"

"Yes," Sara said. "Very clear."

"For your information, no surgery is planned. I will be attempting to revive the patient by intracardial drug therapy. A heart stimulant."

Sara was somewhat relieved. She'd pictured Harding cutting

open the sleeper without anesthesia, just to prove his theory about pain being entirely blocked.

"What stimulant?"

"If you must know, a form of synthetic adrenaline. Now if you'll excuse me, Dr. Copley. Kindly return to a seat in the amphitheater. Or leave the building."

Time to adopt a conciliatory tone, try to get through to him.

"Please hear me out," she said. "I've been giving a lot of thought to the situation. It might be more effective—and less dangerous—to use a dialysis machine to scrub the blood of any toxin traces that remain. Followed by transfusions. Then possibly some mild brain stimulants. Try to bring them around slowly. Avoid trauma."

Harding glared at her. "As I said, you're not a consulting physician in this case. A drastic situation calls for drastic measures. Now leave this area or suffer the consequences."

Sara turned on her heel and left.

Outside in the hallway she hurried to a bank of pay phones.

"Lee? I'm glad I caught you in. Listen, I need some help here. Maybe they'll listen to someone with a badge. . . ."

CHAPTER TWENTY-SIX

He was dimly aware of light. Far, far away, like a single star in the vastness of space.

Fingers prodded. Spasms of pain reached down from that great distance, finding him where he hid, in that small core of himself.

In addition to the jolts of pain, he became aware of a jostling activity. Motion. Hands touching. Noise. He struggled like a drowning man who wants to keep sinking, fighting his rescuers. But the pain—it had never really diminished, it was more that he had found a place where the pain could not find him. Now it returned. White-hot. Electric.

The scream was silent:

Leave me alone, let me die in peace.

Dr. Harding managed to exude a convincing personal warmth for the videocameras. He had a way of addressing himself to the lens that was direct and appealing.

"Here at the Experimental Medicine Division of Cypress Medical Center, we've been deeply involved in the search for new ways to block pain," he began. "Consequently we have been providing care for a number of charity cases with unusual neurological symptoms."

He paused to polish his steel-rimmed glasses, a gesture that focused attention on his craggy face and commanding blue eyes. Moving to the gurney, he lifted a corner of the sheet, exposing the torso of the bandaged sleeper.

"This subject, whose identity is unknown, remains in a condition of profound passivity. Heart rate, respiration, and metabolic functions indicate a state of virtual suspended animation—or as near to that condition as human physiology can sustain outside of science fiction. What caused these highly unusual symptoms to be manifested in the individual we call, for lack of a better name, Sleeper Six?"

The cameras moved in closer.

Sara, banished to a seat in the amphitheater, couldn't do anything but watch the performance. Dr. Harding's skill as an actor, if not a physician, was convincing. If she didn't know better, she'd be inclined to believe he was a dedicated do-gooder at the cutting edge of high-tech medical research.

"We have concluded that the subject engaged in chemical abuse. Apparently this poor fellow injected himself with a designer drug that had dire side effects. While this resulted, obviously, in a personal tragedy, some good may yet result."

Dr. Harding patted the sleeper, as if comforting him.

"Our research team, headed by myself along with Dr. Wheeling, a noted neurologist, and Dr. Weldon, a specialist in cardiovascular phenomena, discovered that in addition to the more obvious symptoms of partial paralysis and lowered vital signs, Sleeper Six is immune to pain."

Here it comes, Sara thought, he can't resist a demonstration.

"As you will see," he said, gently removing the gauze covering the sleeper's facial wounds, "the subject shows no response to the insertion of a surgical needle directly into nerve ganglia."

Dr. Harding held up the needle, indicating that the camera come in for a close shot. Sara, glancing at the monitors, saw the bright metallic glint of light refracting from the newly sharpened point. With a flourish Dr. Harding used his left hand to manipulate the facial wounds, exposing bone and the white clot of nerve ganglia. His right hand introduced the needle into the center of the ganglia.

He probed, twisting the needle deep into the nerve center.

Sleeper Six did not respond.

Lightning bolts of agony. His entire being was now a fusion of torment and inexpressible rage. He could see, through blurred eyelids, the glint of the needle, the glint of light on steel-rimmed eyeglasses.

"What is the explanation for this blockage of normal stimuli?" Dr. Harding said, twisting the needle. "Why does the subject not respond to pain? Our research team has isolated a unique combination of organic neurotoxins present in the blood and tissues. Exactly how these toxins block the pain messengers has not yet been determined. Much work is still to be done. But if we succeed in isolating and understanding this phenomenon, whole new vistas open up in the search for newer and safer forms of surgical anesthesia."

Sara snorted with disgust. How could he make such a wild and unsubstantiated claim in such a sincere tone of voice? It was outrageous. Beyond isolating the neurotoxins (already easily accomplished by one underpaid, county-employed toxicologist), Harding's so-called research team hadn't had time to research anything. They were collecting reams of data now, at this instant, but she doubted Dr. Harding had any real proof that a "new, nonaddictive pain killer" would ever be synthesized from the neurotoxins found in the sleepers' blood.

He sounded damn convincing, though. The videotapes were going to make one hell of a good advertising campaign, if he managed to obtain a patent. And if the sleeper expired, well, Sara assumed that could always be edited out.

"Today, sadly, we're faced with a troubling decision. Despite our best efforts the subject is failing."

Dr. Harding looked sad and troubled.

"If vital signs continue to decline, the subject will expire within days, if not hours. In consultation with my associates, I have concluded that radical intervention is the only hope of saving the subject's life."

A powerful heart stimulant, Dr. Harding explained, was to be administered through an IV already in place. He removed the plastic intravenous tubing and reattached a large syringe full of clear fluid. Then he paused dramatically and looked directly into the nearest camera.

"Our extensive research indicates that this precise dosage of synthesized adrenaline will shock the nervous system into action. By forcing the subject to regain consciousness, we hope to save his life."

Dr. Harding's hand closed on the syringe.

"Let's direct our attention to the life-function monitors," he suggested, "as we observe what happens when this powerful stimulant enters the bloodstream."

With that he squeezed the plunger.

* * *

Agony, then sudden awareness rushing like a swift current of liquid ice through his limbs.

Strength.

Rage.

Insane rage.

Sara was watching the life-function monitors when the first scream pierced the air. She jerked her eyes away from the rapidly elevated EKG just as the sleeper awakened.

The scream was a raw wail of anguish.

What happened next was so sudden and frenzied that it wasn't until later that she was able to reassemble the sequence of events and really comprehend what took place.

The sleeper's arms twitched.

Then his hands came up out of the sheets and closed on Dr. Harding's head. His fingers locked on the physician's ears in a spasm that whitened the knuckles.

A huffing noise came from Dr. Harding, as if he was trying to get his breath. His glasses fell away. The sleeper jerked upright and at the same time wrenched Harding's head around 180 degrees.

In the third row of the gallery, separated by a plate of glass, Sara clearly heard the bones snapping.

A surgical nurse, instinctively trying to intervene, was picked up and hurled through the glass divider. Still conscious, she flopped around on the floor, blood jetting from a wound on her neck.

In the amphitheater, hospital staff were prudently getting under their seats, or running from the room.

Sara ran to the wounded nurse.

There was another howl of rage, an explosion of glass as Dr. Harding's body was flung out of the surgery. Videocameras detonated against the wall and at her feet just as Sara reached the wounded nurse.

The next thing to crash through the glass was the gurney. Followed by the sleeper, who landed in a crouch and sprang to his feet.

He screamed and looked for something to kill.

Lee Valdez was surprised that no security guards stopped him at the entrance to Experimental Medicine. The desk seemed to be deserted. Did he have the right location? Was this where Sara said she'd meet him?

He heard the sound of breaking glass. And screams.

Valdez sprinted down the hallway. A nurse, eyes round with terror, passed him running in the opposite direction.

Not a good sign.

Metro-Dade detectives were required to have physical control of their weapons at all times. Lee kept his 9-mm Beretta on a clip at his waist. Without breaking stride, he grabbed the pistol, pulling it free of the clip. Only an average shot on the firing range, he had never, not once, raised the weapon to discharge it at a human being. Not much call for gun play in Missing Persons.

His body was light with fear. The fear made him run faster. He careened around a corner, nearly losing his balance on the polished tile underfoot.

The double doors to the amphitheater were open. A wild-eyed technician, trailing a length of video cable, nearly knocked him down in his hurry to get away.

The screams, more or less constant now, did not sound human. What in the name of God was happening in there?

Valdez was a few steps inside when something grabbed him by the ankle. He looked down and saw a chubby man in an expensive-looking suit, prostrate on the floor. He was wedged under his chair, hiding.

"Help me," the man whimpered in panic. "Save me."

No obvious wounds. Valdez jerked himself loose. By now he had glimpsed the devastation in the center of the amphitheater. Shattered glass, smashed equipment, blood everywhere.

Sara. She had her arms around a wounded nurse. Trying to stop blood jetting from a wound in the nurse's neck.

A few feet away a man in a torn hospital gown was jerking around in violent spasms, smashing a limp rag doll to the floor. Banging and smashing with incredible energy.

The bundle of rags was a human being, a doctor in surgical greens.

The berserk man stood up, holding the green bundle over his head, hurled it against a wall.

All of this, from the hand grabbing his ankle to the doctor's body hitting the wall, happened within five very rapid heartbeats.

Valdez, enlivened by his own rather incredible surge of adrenaline, hurtled over the seats just as the berserk patient turned his attention to Sara and the nurse she was trying to drag out of harm's way.

The first shot missed, wide to the side. Shit. He needed to get closer, much closer.

Valdez ran toward the target. He slipped in a puddle of blood and crashed to the floor, nearly losing control of the pistol as he slid very close indeed. Close enough to see the goddamn toenails on the target's bare feet.

Sara screamed, urging him to get up and run. Hands reached for him. He rolled away and came up firing.

He was less than ten feet away, but still it was amazing to see three slugs hit in a tight pattern in the center of the target's chest.

Valdez closed his eyes. He had killed a man.

Another scream.

He opened his eyes. The dead man did not seem the least bit affected by the amazingly accurate pattern of wounds in his chest. If anything, he was more enraged.

Hands slick with sweat, Valdez took careful aim and blew a hole in the target's neck.

Still he kept coming, a froth of blood on his lips and a blind, terrible madness in his eyes. That was when Valdez saw the facial wounds and for the first time knew he was shooting at the sleeper who'd been gnawed by rats.

Powerful hands closed on him, lifting him into the air. Steel fingers ripping through his clothing, into his flesh. Raising him higher, higher.

Valdez never was entirely sure how he managed to jam the gun under the sleeper's chin and blow the top of his head off.

CHAPTER TWENTY-SEVEN

The homicide detectives were pretty cheerful, considering.

"Fucking dude was a zombie, right? Good thing the bullets worked. Imagine if you'd had to take 'im out with a stake, bang it into his heart or something."

That got a laugh.

Lee Valdez was a brother cop, the interrogation a formality. Shooting a bad guy was reason to celebrate. Pizza and beer were delivered to the crowded room. Righteous shooting like this made the news, everybody wanted to be part of it.

Valdez drained a beer. Wanting to take the edge off. Forget it, he would need more than a few warm beers to shake out the jams. Who were all these people? He hardly recognized a face.

"You'll be up for a commendation," they told him. "Valor in the line of duty."

"Shit, man, you're not sorry you blew him away, are you?"

Valdez shook his head. He didn't know what he felt. Maybe nothing. Maybe something so enormous it hadn't hit him yet.

"Here, man, have a slice."

Valdez looked at the pizza, remembered that he had no appetite. Hell, he had no *stomach;* the thing had crawled away.

"You know how they're always saying 'Where's a cop when you need one?' Well, fuck those assholes. They needed a cop today, they *had* one."

"Fucking John Wayne action there. It was me, I'd'a' been scared shitless. Fucking target takes three in the chest, he's still coming?"

"Hey, Valdez? Shit, he's not going into shock, is he?"

"Back up, give him a little air."

"It's hitting him now. I remember this from combat. You do what you have to do and then later it scares you to death."

"Anybody got a trank? Hey, Valdez, you want a tranquilizer?"

He shook them off, mumbled something about having to leave now.

"Anything you want, Detective. The world is yours tonight. We'll get this typed up, tomorrow you can sign off."

Afterward he wouldn't be able to remember who was in the room. Just a blur of faces, the smell of beer and pizza and sweat. Guys clapping him on the back as though he'd hit a home run in the ninth to win a game.

Outside, alone at last, he took deep breaths until his head felt reasonably clear. On the drive back to Cypress Medical Center he didn't exceed thirty miles per hour, it was like driving in a dream.

He found Sara Copley in the trauma center, puffing nervously on a cigarette.

"I didn't know you smoked," he said.

She looked at the cigarette, seemed startled to find it in her hand. "I don't. Somebody gave me this."

"The nurse make it?"

She nodded.

"Well, that's good," Valdez said. "Come on, I'll take you home."

The only alcohol Sara had in stock, other than the dregs of a wine bottle, was an unopened quart of tequila. Valdez cracked the seal, poured her a generous shot.

"Take it slow," he advised. "This is nasty medicine."

"Really, I'm fine."

"Yeah," Valdez said. "Me, too."

They downed the shots. Sara coughed, her eyes watering. Gave him a funny little smile. They'd been there together.

"I can't explain it," Sara said. "Adrenaline doesn't turn you into a killer."

"Maybe he already was."

"Was what?"

"Turned into a killer. Before the injection woke him up. Combat-stress syndrome can result in unexpected displays of violence, right? I'd say our sleeper qualified."

Sara nodded wearily. "You know the weird thing? I feel like my head is stuffed with cotton. Is this what it feels like in a war, when the bombing stops? The shell shock?"

"You're just exhausted."

"He was going to kill me next," she said. "I felt like I couldn't move. Like I was stuck in taffy."

"But you did move," Valdez pointed out. "You helped the nurse."

Sara had done just fine. Valdez had a very clear picture of the well-dressed physician who had hidden himself under the seats. Not that he blamed the man. Fear expressed itself in different ways. Courage was simply a descriptive term for well-ordered panic. He'd been no less frightened than the unarmed doctor, but his fear made him act.

"You think the sleeper was homicidal *before* he was exposed to the neurotoxin?"

Valdez shrugged. "Maybe it was the rats drove him crazy. Or being poked with that needle. Any hot day in August we get guys go that crazy for a lot less reason."

"You know what else?" Sara said. The tequila made her tongue feel thick, anesthetized. "I think he *wanted* you to kill him. He picked you up, but he didn't throw you. It was like he was waiting for you to end it."

Valdez didn't comment. There was no way to know what had motivated the insane rage or the fateful hesitation. If Sara found comfort in the idea that he had helped put an end to the thing's suffering, that was fine. You experienced incomprehensible violence, it was natural to try and rationalize it into something that made sense.

"What are you going to do now?" she asked, walking him to the door.

"Go home and sleep like the dead," he said. "Tomorrow I'll go see a friendly judge I know, take one last look for Emile Vidoc. I want to check out that cabana."

"Be careful," Sara said.

"I'll be okay as long as I stay out of hospitals," he said.

CHAPTER TWENTY-EIGHT

The bronzed Mercedes limousine pulled to the curb in the heart of the Calle Ocho. The colonel emerged, an unlighted cigar in his teeth, and strode directly into the *botánica* owned by Mercedes Raimez.

He walked through the darkened shop, to the glow of light he saw in the back room.

"Mercedes?"

She was sitting on a stool, surrounded by plastic statues of saints, staring intently at a small television screen. She nodded at him, switched the channel. "It is on every station," she said. "They show it over and over again."

"You have something to tell me?"

"But watch this, Colonel. It is beyond belief."

He'd been watching the six o'clock news in the limo when Mercedes called. A sleeper come to life, hurling doctors through plate-glass walls, finally getting his brains splattered.

"That's Lee Valdez," Mercedes said excitedly. "See him shoot that crazy man? He's very brave, no?"

"Is that why you called me? To tell me how much you admire this man?"

He shut off the television. The room was now illuminated by the glowing saints. Low-watt bulbs inside plastic casts.

"The woman is there, too," she said, indicating the blank screen. "The *rubia*."

The colonel sighed. "I am very busy. Make your point."

Mercedes told him about Detective Valdez visiting her shop, the incident with the *madrina*. "He is asking about my father. About you. About the other one, the hairless man with the terrible eyes."

"I'm aware of this. But who is this woman you mention?"

Mercedes described Sara Copley.

"They say on television she is a doctor. Lee brings her to the *madrina*. I think it is this woman who makes him do these things. He is under her spell."

When the colonel emerged from the shop, he lighted the cigar, puffed it as he scanned the length of Calle Ocho. It was a hot night, Eighth Street was crowded. Squint so the drab Florida storefronts blurred, and it almost looked like the Old Country. The same faces, the same family names on the *farmacias* and restaurants. Valdez? The man came from nothing.

He slipped into the rear compartment, told the driver to go around the block, park by the monument to José Martí.

How much did this *paisano* Valdez know? And what of this Anglo doctor?

He punched a number on the cellular phone. "Luto? Meet me in fifteen minutes. The monument."

He sat back, puffing the cigar. Little men like Valdez were like smoke. Easily blown away.

PART THREE
THE DEVIL'S GARDEN

"I do not take pleasure from pain.
I take beauty, strength, and genius."
—EMILE VIDOC, M.D.

CHAPTER ONE

Friday, October 6

Emile Vidoc pulled off the causeway and parked the colonel's Cadillac a few feet from the waters of Biscayne Bay. At this early hour the only marine traffic was a string of barges clearing Government Cut, headed for Port of Miami. A thin haze of pastel pink smoke streamed behind the barges.

It was a perfect morning, the kind of day that made you glad to be alive.

He unfolded his long limbs from the driver's seat and sauntered to the edge of the water. Today's outfit was a tropical orange jogging suit with a matching cap. Against the pale water he had the electric presence of an incandescent exclamation point on a sheet of cloud-blue paper.

The pull-off was a favorite spot for bird lovers. A flock of merganser ducks, used to begging for handouts, paddled over to where Vidoc stood. He pulled a plastic Baggie from his sagging rear pocket and began to finger the contents. The ducks circled eagerly, quacking in anticipation.

At last his long arm whipped out. An arc of white pellets seemed to hang in the air before dropping to the water, scooped by eager beaks. In the crepuscular light the white pellets looked like stale bread crumbs.

They were human teeth, smoothed and rounded by the action of phosphoric acid. Vidoc watched the ducks peck at the sinking teeth and smiled. Inside he was refreshed, invigorated.

"Thank you, Wilson," he said.

CHAPTER TWO

Detective Valdez did have the satisfaction of flashing the search warrant at the smug security guard who'd refused him entry the first time he visited the estate. The guard hesitated, then said he'd have to wait for Colonel Calavera, who was not presently at home. Could the officers come back later in the day?

"No way. Open the gates or we bust 'em."

Officer Derrick Clancy, his black face split in a grin, was hefting a ten-pound sledge hammer that still had the price tag on the handle. The nervous guard buzzed the lock, the gate swung open, and they were in.

Valdez led the way, speeding down the long curve of the chipped-stone driveway. Clancy followed with two other officers hastily recruited for the search. Nearing the main house, Valdez veered off the driveway and continued right over the perfect turf lawn, halting with his bumper a few feet from the guest cottage. The cabana, as the colonel liked to call it.

Car doors slammed.

"Do we bust it down?" asked Clancy, indicating the cabana door.

Valdez went to the entrance, signaling that someone should cover the windows. The door proved to be unlocked. Clancy was visibly disappointed.

"Man, I was ready to rock 'n' roll," he said, dropping the hammer.

Valdez pushed the door open and stepped inside. An air conditioner was sighing. He knew instinctively that the cabana was empty. There was a pervasive odor of cleaning fluids and air freshener.

The tile floors gleamed.

Clancy was beside him, hand on his unsnapped holster. "Left it spick-and-span," he commented, his quick eyes darting around.

"'Fraid so," Valdez said.

He picked one of the patrolmen for the inside toss and instructed the other to search the grounds within a perimeter of thirty feet outside the cabana, as dictated by the limits of the warrant. *Any physical evidence, to include pharmaceutical drugs and chemicals, on premises known to have been occupied by Emile Vidoc, M.D., as of September twenty-one.*

Clancy was on his hands and knees, going through the cabinets in the small kitchen.

"Most 'a these pots and pans never even been used," he said.

"Maybe the son of a bitch sent out for pizza."

Valdez hadn't expected to find Dr. Vidoc in residence; still, he was hoping for *something*. Letters, a forwarding address. A nice, neat clue that would point him in the right direction. Hell, anything.

While the two officers went through cabinets and shelves, checking seat cushions and bins in the refrigerator, Valdez wandered through the little cottage. Actually not so little. Larger, actually, than the apartment where he'd grown up. A dining area with polished teak table and matching chairs. Nice comfy sitting area with the overhead fan. Expensive furniture, a small but more than adequate bar. Cove lighting. A fantasy bachelor pad, of the type featured in *Playboy* or *Southern Living*. The *Casablanca* look.

In the bedroom he discovered that the king-sized bed frame had been disassembled and stored in the closet. There were two new bolts in the wall at eye level. For what purpose? Did Dr. Vidoc sleep in a hammock? Or were the bolts for some sexual toy of the colonel's?

Valdez searched the bureaus.

The drawers were empty; not only empty but the liner paper stripped out and the interior rubbed with furniture polish. He knew at once that not even a fingerprint would remain. He checked under and behind the drawers. No sign that incriminating evidence had been taped there. It took a clever man to remain invisible, far too clever to leave any obvious clues. Tossing the place was something that he simply couldn't avoid, a message to the colonel.

He was inspecting the closet when Clancy appeared at the door.

"This is related to that poor dude in the junkyard?" Clancy asked. "Mr. Rat Man?"

"I think so."

"Rat Man the one you had to pop last night, right? That ugly hospital scene. What happen to make him so crazy?"

"That's what I want to ask Dr. Vidoc."

Clancy left the bedroom shaking his head. "Doctors, what a bummer. Can't never find one when you need 'em."

In the bathroom Valdez checked out the tub and separate shower stall. Both gleaming, like the recently mopped tile floors. Using a pen knife, he checked the drains for hair. Found not one strand. The copper drainpipe glowed, as if recently polished. Was that possible? What kind of fanatic had cleaned this place? The whole interior had been sterilized.

Prowling through the empty cabana, Valdez despaired of ever locating his quarry. A man who polished the insides of drainpipes wasn't going to leave a forwarding address.

"Hey, Sarge? Check this out."

Valdez hurried into the main room. Clancy was standing there with the louvered doors to the bar cabinet open. "We looking for Roy Rogers or what?"

Clancy was pointing inside the cabinet. Valdez saw a few liquor bottles; gin, vodka, an expensive cognac. And there on the top shelf, brim curved in the crisp approximation of a smile, was a white cowboy hat. Valdez removed it from the shelf and turned it over. A Stetson, size nine. It reeked of cleaning fluid.

"Size nine?" Clancy said. "Man, this dude got a big head. You get that on the warrant, doctor with a fat head?"

Valdez had the peculiar idea that the Stetson was a message of some kind. A taunt. *I'll leave nothing behind but my hat, you dumb cop.* "He's laughing at us," he said, and flipped the Stetson into a corner. Damn hat probably cost the equivalent of his take-home pay for a week. "Come on, let's get back to work. We're not going to find anything useful, but I don't want to leave here thinking we might have missed something, okay?"

"Sure, Sarge."

In the end they did find one more thing. The officer assigned to the perimeter of the cabana returned with a five-gallon container.

"This was in the dumpster out back. Mean anything?"

He held it up. A strong odor of garlic emanated from the bucket. Clancy made a face. "Ooh-ee, man, that stinks. What you got there?"

Holding the container at arm's length, his nose wrinkled, the officer read from the stencil on the lid. "Phosphoric acid. What's it good for?"

They all looked at Valdez, who shrugged. He had no idea.

"Can't be for nothing good," Clancy said. "Not with a smell like that."

CHAPTER THREE

The Experimental Medicine Unit had been cleared of all unnecessary personnel.

A nurse supervisor met with the reduced custodial-care staff.

"Revised policy," he announced, reading from a clipboard. "Following an emergency executive session, the hospital board issued the following directive: 'Regarding those vegetative coma state patients previously referred to as *sleepers:* Under no circumstances is a stimulant of any type to be administered orally or intravenously. A strict quarantine will be maintained. Staff will remain within the ICU station, monitoring said patients via electronic means whenever necessary."

The supervisor looked up. "Don't go in there unless you have to. And if you have to, request a security guard. Understood?"

"What is the procedure in the event of sudden cardiac arrest?"

The supervisor gave the nurse a sharp look. "These files are marked DNR, is that clear?"

No one argued. They'd seen what happened with adrenaline. Why take a chance with the paddles? Do Not Resuscitate seemed very reasonable, considering.

Sara reported to work as usual. Hobie, calling after he saw the news reports, had urged her to take a few days off. She declined—she didn't care to be alone, even in the sun-drenched sanctity of her apartment.

There were things she didn't want to think about. Possibilities that did not bear consideration.

"Anything I can do?" he said when she arrived.

"Sure. Find me an antidote for the neurotoxin."

Hobie rolled his eyes. "You know as well as I do that most alkaloid poisons have no antidote. The toxin has to run its course. Some victims recover, some don't."

"That sounds bleak."

"Think of it as realistic."

"They're fading, Hobie. Dying by inches."

"From what happened yesterday, I'd say that's not necessarily a bad thing."

Sara had no answer for that. Were the other sleepers as potentially violent? More important, did she dare to find out?

"I want to formulate a program of treatment," she said. "We can use computer models to generate possible antidotes, if any exist."

Hobie was dubious.

"Computer models are fine, as far as they go, but it's almost impossible to predict how a substance will actually react when introduced into the human body."

They both knew it was probably a moot point. The surviving sleepers remained the responsibility of Cypress Medical Center. There was no legal basis for enforcing any recommendations the agency might make.

"Tell you what," Hobie said. "They're sure to do an autopsy, right? I've got a friend in the Medical Examiner's Office. I'll check with him in a day or so, see if there's any data on accumulation of alkaloids in the nerve dendrites. That would give us something more to go on."

"Thanks, Hobie."

In her office Sara told the switchboard to hold any calls. This was going to be a catch-up day. Review all those neighborhood-clinic files that had piled up. The staff evaluations. Work on the budget request for the next fiscal year, all the numbing correspondence from allied county agencies.

Pushing paper, that was all she was fit for today. What she should do, check out Cypress Medical Center, make sure the level of care hadn't declined in light of the tragedy.

She couldn't do it.

The thought of going near the sleepers made her feel cold and tight and almost giddy with anxiety. The images: Dr. Harding transformed into a bloody bundle of rags; Lee Valdez with the gun under the sleeper's chin; Sara praying that he would fire and end the terrible madness.

She'd wanted that sleeper dead.

And after it had happened, after he became, like the others, a broken doll, she had felt nothing. No guilt, no remorse.

Feeling nothing. That was the scariest thing of all. And the other thought that tore at her with little rat's teeth:

What if it had been Kurt?

CHAPTER FOUR

Drill Sergeant Hernandez was beginning to be impressed. At first the ragged platoon of new recruits had been hopelessly green. City scum mixed with raw peasants, what could be worse? But over the last few days the group of petty thieves and farmers had begun to gel into something that might, just might, eventually become a fighting unit.

Of particular promise was the boy Fernando, younger brother of Jorge. Nando threw himself into the training, crawling on his belly through rough terrain, shouldering the wooden gun in drills, his teeth flashing a smile that begged for approval. The boy would do anything, he never questioned an order. Climb the barbed-wire fence? Nando charged it, clawing up the links, catapulting himself over the coil of barbs to land on the other side well ahead of the other recruits.

In hand-to-hand combat drills Nando had been fearless, standing up to men nearly twice his weight. Knock him down and he was right back up, throwing it in your face, unwilling to concede. His older brother was doing well in comparison with many of the others, but Jorge lacked Nando's fire, his guts.

Jorge would in time be a good soldier. Nando, and this was a rare thing, a beautiful thing, showed promise as a killer.

Only yesterday in fixed bayonet drill he had been so ferocious, his scream so bloodcurdling, that none of the others would drill with him. They believed that in the heat of the moment little Nando might gut them with his dull bayonet.

Hernandez had a star pupil. It made him happy.

"Hokay," he said to the assembled recruits, who stood at ease in the hot sun, "now we go to the live-ammunition drill. The object is to accustom you to the sound of gunfire, and what it is like to have bullets striking very near. In a real firefight there will be no one to tell you where it is safe to crawl and where it is not. You must rely on instinct and courage. For today, I will tell you what is safe. Obey my instructions, and you will not be hurt. Disobey me, and you may find out what it is like to be wounded, or dead."

He led them over to the obstacle course. Truck tires had been strewn over an area of waist-high saw grass. Nearby, a roll of barbed wire had been strung between stakes, just inches above the soggy ground. Next was a pool of stagnant water, the overflow from an irrigation canal. It glistened with green scum and the hot buzzing of insect wings.

"This morning each of you ran through this course. That was for exercise, and to ready you for what will happen next. Pay close attention now, and I will tell you something that may save your worthless lives."

He indicated three points in the obstacle course: the last tire, the barbed wire, the left side of the pond.

"This is where the fire will come. On the ground here." He raised an AK-47 to firing position, bracing the harness sling around his cocked elbow, and pulled the trigger.

Bullets struck near the tire, spattering mud.

"By the fence here."

He fired at a height eighteen inches above the ground, in the vicinity of the barbed wire.

"And into the water here."

He sprayed the left side of the pond.

"Is this understood?"

There were murmurs of assent. Hernandez demanded a proper response, and the recruits shouted in unison, *"Yes sir Sergeant Hernandez sir!"*

"Good. Now form up and run the course."

The sergeant was an expert marksman. In all his years of drilling recruits he had wounded only one man, who stupidly stood up at the wrong time. The wound was not serious, a bullet through the meat of the buttocks. If a recruit became confused and strayed too close to the hot spots, Hernandez was prepared to adjust his fire, although afterward the recruit would be punished.

He was not prepared, however, for the boy Nando.

Each of the men began in the tires, running with knees up. At the last tire many leaped or flung themselves high through the air so as to avoid the bullets their sergeant was calmly blazing into the muddy earth. At the fence some hugged the ground so close as they came under the barbed wire that Hernandez was not sure they even heard his shots whizzing overhead. At the pond it was almost comical. Men crawled at the edge, flopping in the mud, keeping as far away from the deadly splashes of gunfire as it was possible to do and still cross the pond.

Not Nando. He seemed to dance through the tires, anticipating where the bullets would hit. The shots missed only by inches because Hernandez couldn't adjust quick enough. Then the boy was gone, diving through the saw grass and emerging from under the barbed wire so fast that once again Hernandez didn't have time to divert his fire. He was sure he'd shot the boy in the head, but no, there he was, running like a gazelle for the pond.

By now Hernandez knew enough to wait. He didn't want to kill the boy. He would warn him away from the left side by firing early, showing him where the bullets would go. Hernandez fired, kicking up little geysers of pond scum.

Nando dived directly into the line of fire. Hernandez swore and lowered the AK-47. Now the boy had surely done it. Did he *want* to be wounded? Did he care so little for his life?

The sergeant ran to the pond, shouting for help. Just as he got there, Nando emerged laughing, covered with the green scum, unhurt.

"Fernando, in the name of God, why do you dive into the bullets?"

The boy sneezed, oblivious to the swarm of insects around his head. "Sergeant Hernandez, sir, yesterday you tell us what a good soldier must do in the heat of battle. You say he must do the unexpected."

Hernandez sighed. Nando was going to make one hell of a fighter, if he lived that long.

CHAPTER FIVE

A stuffed animal crouched atop the wooden phone booth inside the Rod and Gun Lodge in the village of Everglades City. On the walls a flat airbrushed tarpon, the bill of a saw-toothed shark, numerous heads.

The canal outside the windows was hot with sunlight, a slant of it catching motes of dust in the old lodge building. Vidoc kept his breathing shallow, aware of swamp funk, microbes, airborne larvae.

The phone rang. He slipped into the booth, pushed the creaky door shut.

"Emile?" It was the colonel's voice.

Vidoc grunted.

"Our friend paid another visit today. To the cabana."

"He found nothing," Vidoc said.

"No, of course not. What concerns me is the computer access."

"The files were . . . adjusted."

"Still, it is troubling, yes? As a precaution, I have arranged to take away his toys."

It was cool and dark in the phone booth. A mahogany box not unlike a glass-fronted coffin.

"Bring him to me," Vidoc said. "An interrogation might be interesting."

He could feel the colonel's hesitation.

"For now I will do it another way."

"As you wish," Vidoc said.

Later, in a whitewashed cabin under the great banyan tree, Vidoc screwed hooks into the walls and strung up his special hammock. He could hear the noise of fishing boats in the canal, unloading wealthy sportsmen for dinner at the lodge. The screens on the great porch rattled with the lies of fishermen.

One more night in this fetid place, and then he would begin his important work at Camp Libertad.

He lay suspended in the nylon straps and pondered love. An obsession of normals, who used it to justify mating rituals and financial obligations. Even the great Bard used it as a kind of vigorous plot propellant. The fact that the act itself almost always ended in betrayal did not seem to temper the fervor of the obsession, in Shakespearean drama or in normal life.

Love, like guilt, was alien to Emile Vidoc. He craved neither response, but lately he found a way of defining love-prompted behavior that would, he was confident, prove interesting once he took possession of Castillo, his sanctuary.

Normals spoke of loving their various gods. As near as Vidoc could determine, this love of a god was something akin to awe: the recognition of a force so powerful, so terrible, that the ordinary mind could not comprehend it.

Love was worship. And worship was fear. Therefore, love was fear.

As a way of amplifying on this interesting theme, he allowed himself to recall, in perfect detail, the circumstances under which he had first seen Castillo nestled in the mountains of Paraguay. Not just the seeing, but the understanding of what he could make happen there, of who he would become.

Vidoc is airborne, en route to a small city in the province of Toquerón. Something gleams white in the green mountains. The pilot banks the six-seater, giving Vidoc, his only passenger, a good long look. The pilot cheerfully recounts the sad tale of the unfortunate Bolivian pharmaceutical entrepreneur who had caused the estate to be constructed in such a remote locale.

"They recover only his hands, still holding very tight on the wheel of his BMW," the pilot says. "The rest of him, it vanish in the explosion."

"Who lives there now?"

"Nobody, *señor*. The governor, he has appropriated the property. He wish to sell it to another Bolivian, perhaps, but these Bolivians, they are taking their business into the Caribbean, or some of them to Switzerland."

"How much?" Vidoc asks out of idle curiosity.

"That is for the governor to say."

As it happens, Vidoc is conducting an AIT (Advanced Interrogation Techniques) seminar for the local governor and his chief of police. The chief, a grim little man with a horsehair toupee who supplies live test subjects. The governor, in contrast, a lively fellow who runs a thriving protection scheme, extracting a small and reasonable percentage from refugees who arrive with sizable assets.

His name is Hugo Kronar, he is related in some vague way to the Stroessners, and he speaks fluent Spanish with a discernible German accent.

"*Herr Doktor!* I so look forward to these seminars!"

Vidoc recognizes in Kronar a somewhat kindred spirit. This is a man with a huge and varied appetite who shares a similar contempt for normals. He takes what he wants, does what he likes, all with the frisson of confident manipulation.

Here in Paraguay, in this remote province, it is not necessary to adopt the mask. Vidoc had suspected this, but Hugo Kronar is the living proof.

"What can you show us?" Kronar asks as they assemble in the small sound-padded cell where the demonstration is to take place. "If I may be so forward, feel free to improvise. You are among friends, *Herr Doktor*."

As a consultant for Third World Resources, Vidoc is somewhat circumscribed by Company policy. The aim is to market state-of-the-art science to worthy police states—the very latest in behavior modification, interrogation techniques, and peasant control.

Still, a seminar leader has *some* leeway, and the necessity of modifying techniques to reflect local custom is understood. Consequently he begins by demonstrating how the *pilau*, a poisonous snail indigenous to the province, produces the desired effect in the test subject, one of whom expires from stress before the *pilau* touches his flesh.

The governor is vastly amused. Following the seminar he treats Vidoc to a sumptuous meal (which Vidoc will disgorge later, in the privacy of his hotel suite) and a sampling of rare wines in his private cellar.

No attempt is made to disguise the fact that the cork-lined cellar is also used to indulge certain other appetites. The governor seems to recognize that Vidoc shares an interest in radical surgery, and will not disapprove.

"But of course you are a trained physician," the governor says, showing off his instruments, "while I am simply an enthusiastic amateur."

Vidoc, viewing the blood-stained table and the limb restraints, assures the governor that his methods are remarkably professional.

"Of course, I read books on the subject," the governor says, preening. "I follow the diagrams. And I take many photographs."

Vidoc asks to see the pictures. This sharing of forbidden images cements their friendship. It is later, after an impromptu continuation of the seminar—the police chief is very accommodating about providing fresh test subjects—that the governor mentions the vacant estate.

The very next day Vidoc is whisked to Castillo. There are no roads into the area, no navigable waterways. The only access is by helicopter.

"The Bolivian wished to make a world of his own," the governor explains, taking Vidoc into the fortresslike building. "There are gardens, cattle, solar generating systems, air-purifiers, all designed to be self-sufficient. The Bolivian's desire was to retire here, untouched by outsiders. I assured him that this would be so, for a small annual fee—quite reasonable. He was, of course, a paranoid psychopath with a drug habit, and he made the mistake of returning to his home province on business."

The estate includes all the amenities that might be expected of a crazed drug lord. What appeals to Vidoc, more than all the absurd spa fixtures and circular beds, is the native Indian village.

"These people were *very* disappointed when the Bolivian did not return," the governor explains, pointing out the drab little huts, the small, feral inhabitants.

"Oh?"

"Understand, he was like a god to them. He employed many of the younger women in various capacities. It is necessary only to give them a little food, they do not seem to comprehend the idea of money. Now, without a master, they are back to eating insects and small rodents." The governor sighs in a meaningful way and adds, "Whoever buys Castillo, he owns these people. Body and soul, as the saying goes. For a man of your skills, *Herr Doktor*, this could be most interesting."

Yes, Vidoc thinks, the fortress as laboratory, stage, sanctuary. And the village a field study in fear. Yes yes.

"How much would this all cost?"

"Ah," the governor says, taking his arm. "Let us enter into discussion. I think we can find things to agree on, you and I."

In his hammock Vidoc dozed lightly, aware of sounds in the canal, birds in the banyan tree, water dripping in the shower stall. He steered his vision of Paraguay, aiming for the scream in the quaking dark.

CHAPTER SIX

Barbecue time in Cherry Grove. Charcoal smoke drifted through the neighborhood, an aroma of charred beef and tomato sauce. Valdez regretted only that he lacked an apron and a chef's hat. He was pretty sure that cooking on the outside grill was an invention of American culture. For sure it was an American pastime—way more American than apple pie. Foregoing the beef and traditional bottled sauce, he'd opted for skewered boneless chicken soaked in a marinade of olive oil, lemon, and garlic. He grilled potatoes, painting them with melted butter until each chunk was uniformly brown and crusty on the outside, hot and white within.

The vegetable course was a green salad, washed repeatedly in fresh water to remove any taint of Homestead crop chemistry. Caesar dressing courtesy of Paul Newman.

"I figured a bachelor like you would eat out of the microwave," Sara said.

"Don't own one," he said. "As a chef, I'm a pretty good fireman."

Sara laughed. The detective wore sandals, cotton shorts, and a University of Miami T-shirt. He looked almost boyish, maybe because he was relaxed and smiling, quite obviously enjoying the task of preparing a meal. Looking around the convergence of backyards, all similar variations on the same theme, she said, "It seems so nice and normal."

Valdez, hunched over his plate, nodded.

"That's why I live here."

"I was expecting something different."

"Like what?"

"I don't know. Just different."

Valdez smiled to himself. He knew what she'd been expecting. Something a lot more ethnic. Lee Valdez at home in his ethnic neighborhood, eating ethnic food, doing ethnic things. Well, he'd fooled her. Sara Copley would have to learn to expect the unexpected. Santería séances and backyard barbecues. Bullets and barbecues would be more like it, he reasoned, losing the mood.

"What's wrong?"

"Nothing," he said. "Thinking."

"About what happened?"

He nodded. "You notice it didn't make the evening news tonight? They've dropped it already."

Curiously the memory was already beginning to have the once-removed feeling of a dream. Some other person's experience. The time would come when he would have to face the anxiety he'd wrapped up and hidden away. Not now, though, not tonight.

"We searched Vidoc's place today," he said. "We got *nada*, and if the colonel wasn't pissed off before, he will be now. There's something about the guy, I can't resist yanking his chain."

Sara put down her fork. "I've been thinking about what you said the other night. This colonel and Vidoc being part of a conspiracy. Maybe we should go to the media with the idea. The *Miami Herald*. They do a lot of investigative journalism, right?"

He thought about it, shrugged.

"Not yet. All we've got is a theory based on what's missing from military files that it was illegal for me to access in the first place. I give 'em that, I could lose my job."

"We've got the sleepers," Sara said. "We've got what happened to one of them yesterday."

"A patient goes berserk and kills a doctor? That makes for nice headlines, but at the moment we can't demonstrate a legal chain of evidence that connects the colonel and Emile Vidoc to the sleepers. And until we have something that would stand up in court, we're just a couple of people with a crazy idea."

The nice thing about a dump like Cherry Grove, they had low fences. Luto didn't even have to get out of his car. He could sit right there behind the wheel in the air-conditioned Trans-Am lease job with the smoked-glass windows and the blow-your-hair-back sound system and check out the Cuban cop and his *rubia* girlfriend.

Luto adjusted the binoculars. The *rubia* had nice legs. Very nice legs. Was she blond all the way up? What a waste—sitting there eating hot dogs or some crap with a *maricón* cop in this flavorless Anglo neighborhood.

He reached out, punching in a new radio frequency. Loud salsa music filled the car. Smoky twilight was descending. Any minute now the streetlights would go on. Luto settled in. He might be here all night. The colonel's orders were to check out the cop and the bitch doctor, see what kind of connections they made. The colonel was smart that way, wanting to know an enemy before he made any irrevocable decision.

Luto, a good soldier in his way, intended to obey orders, even if it meant doing a creepy-crawl. Truth, he kind of liked the idea of a crawl.

The *rubia* got up, followed the cop into the bungalow.

When he wanted to, Luto could move like smoke. Flowing from shadow to shadow, blending into the featureless landscape. On the street he was a resident out for a stroll. Approaching the house, he was returning home. In the yard he did his blend, nothing hurried or nervous or suspicious, just a man standing on his own patch of ground a few hours after sundown.

Dried-out palm fronds crunched under his feet. Didn't matter, a noisy air conditioner was on, the little bungalow was sealed. Nothing less than a siren or gunshot would penetrate. And there would be no gunshot, no siren, not tonight.

Around the corner of the bungalow, shielded by an untamed frangipani tree, he leaned against the outside wall. The air-conditioning unit would be in the bedroom, of course. There it was, a few inches to his left, rattling and dripping. Cheap piece of shit. This Valdez lived like a pig, just as the colonel had said.

He heard other sounds, very faint. Music. Maybe the *maricón* detective was getting lucky. Luto waited, biding his time. Then he turned and looked into the bedroom window.

The mosquitoes chased them inside. Large and aggressive, the killer bugs had arrived at sunset. Lee said they were swamp skeeters, marauders from the Everglades. You could tell, he said, because they had gator teeth and buzzard wings. Laughing and swatting, Sara had followed him into the bungalow, her first look inside the place he lived.

Cream-white walls, a few framed prints by an impressionist artist she didn't recognize, tidy shelves stocked with well-thumbed books, and a collection of LPs that took up most of one wall. An AR turntable and Fischer amplifier that looked old and well-tended.

"Antiques," he said. "Everything is CDs now. Except a lot of the stuff I've got hasn't made it to CD yet."

He put on a record. A muted trumpet made itself known.

"Jazz?"

"Miles Davis, the master." He showed her an album cover so worn and scratched the image on it was obscured. "This is an old piece," he added, gesturing at the speakers. "'Flamenco Sketches,' off the *Kind of Blue* album. Bill Evans on piano. Coltrane on tenor. Cannonball Adderly on alto. Paul Chambers bass. I forget drums. No, wait a minute, James Cobb." He checked the back of the album cover for the credits. "Right. James Cobb."

A tenor sax had taken over from the muted trumpet. It was cool, moody, romantic music. Also melancholy, in a pretty way. Not at all flamenco, where had that come from?

Flamenco or not, it made her want to dance.

"Come here," she said, slipping her arm around his waist, moving to the sax.

Valdez, moving to the soft music, put his lips to her ear.

"Just keep dancing, okay? Don't stop. But I think someone is watching us."

"What?" Sara said.

Was this an excuse to tighten his arms around her? Sara was aware of his lithe, muscular body. Aware also that she hadn't been in the arms of a man since Kurt had embraced her at the airport. Months ago. Eons.

"We'll go to the left," he whispered. "Nice and slow. That's it."

They moved closer to an open door. There was no light on, but Sara could see it was his bedroom. Did he really expect her to fall for a lame routine like this?

Then he was dancing her back, away from the door. When they got to the corner of the room, almost bumping into a wall, he abruptly let her go.

"Stay right here," he hissed. "Don't move."

He crept over to the bookshelf, reached for a small leather pouch. His gun, Sara realized. He looked at her, grinned, and held his finger to his lips. A moment later he'd slipped out the front door.

Sara froze. Had he seen something in the bedroom? The idea knotted her stomach, made her knees feel strangely weak.

A moment later she heard something crash through the bushes right outside the door.

Valdez yelled.

She ran to the door, opened it, and heard a car screech away, burning rubber down the street.

Valdez was extricating himself from the bushes. "Ah shit," he said. "Almost had the bastard."

"Who was it?"

"Peeping Tom, I guess. I caught just a glimpse through the bedroom window." He came back inside, put away the gun. "Sorry if I scared you."

"You get a lot of that around here?"

He shook his head. "Not much to peep at, I'm afraid. There's another possibility, though, now that I think of it. Maybe he wasn't a peeper."

"What are you suggesting?"

"Maybe it was someone checking up on me. Or you." Seeing the look on her face, he said, "Look, I'm probably just a little paranoid, but how about if I follow you home, just to make sure?"

Sara thought that sounded like an excellent idea.

CHAPTER SEVEN

Saturday, October 7

A noisy heron greeted Vidoc at dawn. It perched on the gutter over the porch of the little cabin and squawked until he threw open the creaky screen door. The bird rode its wings to the ground, turning round in the air like a falling leaf, and began that strange mechanical heron strut.

"Fuck off, bird."

Still, it was good to be on the move. Dawn was starting to bleed into the little swamp village; he wanted to be out of here before light was full.

In the canal the charter boats were converging on the Rod and Gun Lodge. A big canopy extended from the grand old lodge building to the dock. Under it, lined up like good little scouts, each awaiting his turn, were the lodge guests. Rich white northerners spending thousands of dollars to be abused by local fishing guides.

It was an impulse that Vidoc could not fathom. As a quarry, fish were primitive wet things, hardly able to manifest fear. And why spend money on guides who openly despised you *and* your money?

Vidoc went back into the cabin, unhooked his hammock, packed it into his carryall bag. He would not, he decided, clean himself in the dingy shower. There was mold on the plastic curtains, a few stray body hairs in the drain—for the next few days he would have to rely on a ritual of antiseptic sponge baths; there was no getting around the lack of proper facilities at Camp Libertad.

He would make do.

It was seven exactly when he drove out of Everglades City. Vivaldi on the stereo. He liked the precision of the music.

* * *

The narrow access road was tough on the Cadillac. He drove slowly, a plume of marl dust rising from the rutted tracks. On either side the dense foliage of the great swamp. A glimpse, here and there, of shallow water.

There were places where the gravel had been washed away, where the swamp wanted to swallow the road.

When Vidoc arrived at the gate, he sounded the horn sharply. The guard was a black-haired, baby-faced recruit in fatigues. Vidoc started to speak, but the boy ran off, returning fifteen minutes later with Sergeant Hernandez in tow.

The sergeant offered to take the wheel for the final leg into the camp. Vidoc folded himself into the backseat. Twenty minutes later they were crossing an old airfield.

The barracks were adjacent to the airstrip. Beyond it, barely visible through the trees, an old fire tower stood like a sentinel over the camp.

"From here we have to walk," the sergeant announced.

Vidoc unzipped his black nylon bag, produced a vented pith helmet and mosquito netting. He put on the helmet, draped the netting over his face, around his shoulders.

"I need a machete," he said.

Hernandez went and found a machete, tested the blade against the ball of his thumb, and presented the machete to Vidoc without comment.

"Lead the way," Vidoc said.

The sergeant, drenched with sweat, pushed through the overgrown trail. Mostly tall saw grass and palmetto, but the saw grass could cut you. Sharp little ridges on every blade of grass.

Behind him Vidoc wielded the machete. Swish, swish. Widening the trail, cutting the saw grass back. He liked the way Hernandez moved a step faster whenever the blade snicked grass at his heels.

At last they came to the bunker. It was set in a small clearing, covered in kudzu vine. A thick-sided concrete box maybe twenty feet wide and sixty feet long.

Hernandez was panting, out of breath.

"You cut your lip," said Vidoc, interested. "I have some styptic ointment that will stop the bleeding."

"It's nothing," Hernandez said, licking the blood.

The iron door to the bunker was padlocked. Hernandez produced a black iron skeleton key. The lock, recently oiled, turned smoothly. He grunted, pushed the heavy door open. Vidoc was aware of the stink of disinfectant.

"What about power?" Vidoc said.

"Honda generator," the sergeant said. "Just push a button."

He demonstrated. A string of bare light bulbs began to glow inside the bunker. Empty in there. Bare walls, newly damp floor. The disinfectant didn't quite obscure the bitter scent of nitrate from when the bunker had been used to store ammunition for the Bay of Pigs invasion. All of that gone now.

Vidoc glided inside. He lifted the mosquito netting, peeled off his dark glasses. "It needs to be scoured. All they did was splash disinfectant around."

"I'll send some men out with wire brushes."

"Have them bring a drill," Vidoc said. "I want to hang my things."

CHAPTER EIGHT

They were waiting for Valdez when he got to work. Tall blond guy and a short black guy, a Mutt-and-Jeff team. Both with fat briefcases. The smaller black guy with an aristocratic air about him, smoking a brown Nat Sherman cigarette and looking very elegant and pleased with himself. His white partner just a little overweight, licking pastry sugar from his fingertips.

"Detective Valdez? We're from Internal Review. Lieutenants Ford and Tarsi."

Valdez put down the cardboard container of coffee he was carrying and shook hands. Lieutenant Ford was sticky. Tarsi, the black prince, had a dry, papery grip.

Valdez said, "Two louies, huh? I guess I should be honored. This regarding the discharge-of-weapon report?"

They both nodded. Nothing to catch there about whether this was routine or more serious. He thought, I wouldn't want to play poker with these two.

"They told me over at Homicide I could sign off today, get this behind me."

"Could we go into your office, Detective?"

"Hey, yeah, of course. Make yourselves at home."

Lieutenant Tarsi produced a gleaming aluminum ashtray from his briefcase, placed it on the desk, and snubbed his cigarette neatly out. Not withstanding the fact that there was already an ashtray on the desk. Valdez took it as a bad sign. Also, he wasn't too crazy about the way Ford glanced with faint distaste at the discolored carpet under his big feet. As if he took seriously the idea that the rug made the man.

They seemed to be waiting for him to speak. He obliged. "You got the paperwork?"

Tarsi nodded. "Very good, Sergeant. You seem to have filled in most of the blanks."

Mother of God, you couldn't tell if this guy was kidding or not. Did he mean the actual blanks in the report form? Or was he making a joke?

"I observed the suspect killing a man," Valdez said, lapsing into the cop jargon he'd used for the report. "I didn't feel I had any alternative response."

"Right," Ford said. He opened his briefcase. "You made that clear."

"The crazy son of a bitch was going to kill me next," Valdez said.

Both men nodded. No other reaction, just a nod. Although Valdez had never before discharged his weapon in the line of duty, or anywhere outside the firing range, he knew enough about the way the Internal Review Bureau usually handled line-of-duty shootings to feel very nervous about the Mutt-and-Jeff act.

"You guys are supposed to be on my side," Valdez said. "What's the problem here?"

The big blond lieutenant was burrowing in his briefcase. He removed a document and passed it to Tarsi, who did most of the talking.

"What you left out," he said.

"What I left out? I didn't leave anything out."

Valdez could feel his face getting red. The smart thing would be to remain cool, assess the situation. Let them do all the talking. But it wasn't easy to do the smart thing. Who were these guys to come into his office with this attitude?

"The suspect was killing people," he said, appealing for understanding. "I shot him. End of story."

"We know the end," Tarsi said, igniting a new Sherman. Very nice gold lighter. Was that a diamond on the lid? "We're interested in why you decided to leave out the beginning."

"What beginning? The incident was already in progress when I got to the scene."

Tarsi rattled the pages he'd got from his partner.

"The beginning here. Or maybe this isn't really the beginning either. Maybe we need to go back, way back."

He tossed the pages on the desk. Valdez glanced down. What was this shit? What was going on here?

"This is a request for EMS," he said, puzzled.

"We know what it is, Sergeant."

Valdez flipped through the pages. "I don't get it. I called for medical assistance, so what? That was last week, an unrelated event."

The lieutenants seemed amused. "Unrelated?" Ford said. "You expect us to believe that?"

Valdez scowled. "Maybe I should have an attorney here."

"That's your privilege."

"How about we just get this over with. How about you two cut the bullshit and tell me what the hell's going on here."

It was nice he could make them laugh. Guys who worked Internal Review didn't have a lot to laugh about.

"It starts with the EMS request," Tarsi said, blowing perfect smoke rings. "A patrolman reports an unconscious male in Little Havana, which is not unusual. But who does he call? A cop from the Missing Persons Unit. Now that *is* a little strange, wouldn't you say?"

"I thought this was about the discharge-of-weapon report."

"Oh, it is," Tarsi said. "But one thing leads to another. Like we couldn't help but wonder what this same Missing Persons Unit officer is doing a few hours later, entering a salvage yard without a warrant."

"Had a report of individuals in need of help, that's why."

Tarsi shrugged. "So you say. But what we noticed is the funny coincidence."

"Funny coincidence?"

"A Missing Persons officer responds to a patrolman's call from a Cuban grocery. Your job description is basically clerical, you don't go out on the street. Then you go into a locked salvage yard without probable cause or warrant, on the word of a known drug abuser, and bring out a number of individuals who have been seriously injured. A week later you appear in the hospital and shoot one of those individuals."

"Shoot to kill," his partner added, for emphasis.

"So I gotta call that a funny coincidence," Tarsi said. "Comment?"

"Bullshit, is my comment. Somebody upstairs reached out, told you to roast me. You didn't think up this crap on your own."

A brittle smile from the black lieutenant.

"Why would 'somebody upstairs' do that?"

"You tell me."

Tarsi smoked for a while. Enjoying his visit to Missing Persons, like maybe he would drop in more frequently. Bring his own ashtray, of course. Lieutenant Ford seemed bored. He had better things to do. Gave the impression he was already thinking deeply about lunch. Where to go, what to eat.

Valdez knew that what he should do was shut up, put in a request for a Police Association lawyer. But his collar felt tight, and he was pissed off at these two bozos. What did they know? Had they ever stood their ground, knees knocking, against a berserk killer who wouldn't go down?

"Something you find amusing?" Tarsi said, stubbing out the Sherman.

"You think I don't know what's going on?" Valdez said. "They want me off the sleeper case, right? Fine, I'm off it. Done. Satisfied now?"

"You know what he's talking about, John?"

"Haven't got a clue."

"Guys? Fuck yourselves, okay? Fuck your ashtray and your sticky fingers."

Lieutenant Tarsi stood up. It didn't make him any taller. "Are you refusing to cooperate in an Internal Review investigation?"

"Just write down whatever you want, okay, Lieutenant? Any funny coincidence that comes to mind. Next time some maniac is about to crush my head, I'll turn the gun on myself, save you all the trouble."

As they left, he heard the big blond lieutenant say, "What was that about sticky fingers?"

Valdez had the window open, airing out his office, when his unit commander came in, accompanied by two uniformed officers. Right away he knew what was going to happen.

"Lee, I don't know what the hell you did, but somebody is after your head, and there's nothing I can do about it."

After that it was almost routine. Turn in his weapon, his badge, clean his desk of personal belongings while the two uniforms watched to make sure he didn't steal any Metro-Dade property.

"This is just a suspension, Lee. Couple of weeks, a good lawyer, maybe you can straighten it out."

When he had the box full, mostly fishing tackle he'd stowed in a bottom drawer, they walked him through security and out to the bright lobby of Metro-Dade Headquarters.

"Sorry about this, Sarge," one of the uniforms said.

"I know," Valdez said. "You're just doing your job."

"Gee, Sarge."

"Look, just fuck off and leave me alone."

CHAPTER NINE

Luto sitting in his leased Trans-Am, parked in a shady spot under the palms, within sighting distance of the Opa-Locka Disease Control Clinic on Ali Baba Avenue. A dirty stucco building that had once housed a retail store. Now they had AIDS for sale in there, TB and STD, all those alphabet diseases.

He had followed the *rubia* from her Miami Beach apartment tower to this dirty place, where the smog was jellied by aircraft descending into the Opa-Locka Airport. She was in there now, treating a range of dark-skinned people.

He'd had a nice shot that morning, of the *rubia* getting out of her car, going into the clinic. The way the sun was, he had seen right through her skirt. Gave him a tingle, a few interesting ideas.

When the time came, he intended to make this one last.

Luto amused himself for an hour or so dialing 900 numbers. A man looked important using the cellular phone; he might be talking to his broker or his coke dealer. Or, as it happened, the Red-Hot Mamas of Coco Beach.

"Gimme the one call herself Nadine, she got a nice little scream."

Nadine with a voice box drenched in semen; Luto got a kick out of her, and the best part, it all went on the colonel's bill. The girl talked about playing with herself, but Luto was pretty sure she was sitting there drinking a Coke, that was the slurpy noise he heard.

After a while he got bored with the fake passion, got out of the car to have a smoke. The *rubia* probably in there for the duration, fussing over Haitian trash.

It had got freaky for a second there, the previous night, when the cop tried to snatch him by the bedroom window. But it was fun freaky. Had the cop actually *grabbed* him, Luto had a blade ready to go, cut him a new wet smile.

When the cellular tone began to beep, he merely reached inside, picked up the receiver unit. The colonel, demanding to know why he'd tied up the phone for the last hour.

"This girlfriend of mine, Nadine? She have like a medical emergency. She get something stuck in a bad place."

"Never mind. You have this other little *chica* in sight?"

Luto said he did.

"You remember the various situations we discussed?" The colonel was using the scrambled link; it made his voice sound like sheets of tin.

"Sure, I remember."

"I've taken care of the first problem. He's been neutralized."

"That's good," Luto said. He didn't really care about Valdez. What fun was there in killing a dull cop? It was too much like work.

"The other situation, it needs to have an accident. Victim of random violence."

"Random?" The way Luto thought about it, violence was never exactly random.

The colonel sighed from his hollow place. It sounded like wind in the palms. "Just make sure it can't be connected to you."

"Oh, *that* kind of random."

After the call Luto got back in the car, turned on the stereo. Get himself in the mood to rock and roll. Dance with the lady.

CHAPTER TEN

The only thing Valdez could think to do when he left Metro-Dade was go visit his father. Check in on Mama at the same time.

The cemetery was a block from Calle Ocho, blistered with white monuments and family crypts. Palms, live oaks, a few shady spots, jogging paths.

Nothing so fancy as a crypt for the Valdez family. Just a plot was hard enough to come by in Miami. The ground was bad. There were places where six feet down would find contaminated water—the graves were of necessity shallow, or above ground in the crypts.

He found the two little rectangles of engraved stone set in white gravel. The light here was white-hot, blinding, and he almost didn't see the geranium that had recently been planted between the headstones.

Ricky had made a visit, too.

Valdez raked the gravel smooth with the side of his hand, tried to get a handle on what had just happened to him.

He'd been fired.

They called it a suspension, that was bullshit. Unless his superiors decided to back him, he was finished with Metro-Dade. That Calavera was behind the Internal Affairs investigation he had no doubt.

How could he have been so stupid? He knew better. A low-ranking cop had no business messing with a heavy-duty political animal like the colonel. What had made him do it?

Partly it was because rich exiles like the colonel had always treated his father like dung. The other part had to do with Sara

Copley. Wanting to look tough and smart in her eyes. It was pride, dumb macho pride.

Now look what the colonel had done. Probably accomplished with a simple telephone call. *Valdez has offended me. Pluck him out.*

Out of habit he switched on the scanner when he returned to his car. He heard an excited voice requesting EMS at a familiar street address.

Peanut's human junkyard.

The hot sun was glinting off the ambulance when Valdez arrived at the salvage yard. Bright enough to seem like it was going to burn a hole in his Polarized sunglasses. Miami at high noon. With undead bodies surfacing every few days, it was like the city had a tunnel into hell.

"'Scuze me, sir!" Valdez shouted. "You the man who called EMS?"

Big beefy guy in a shiny aluminum hard hat, he was hard to look at, standing there with his arms folded. Behind him a battered semi and a big open trailer full of scrap metal.

"That's right. The medical boys are checkin' him out right now. There's another cop back there, too, takin' pitchers."

"'Scuze me," said Valdez, pulling out his notebook. "I got to get this all down. Name?" If he was going to impersonate an on-duty officer, he had to do it right, go by the book.

"Shit, I don't know his name. He ain't talkin', and I didn't check his wallet or nothin'."

"*Your* name, please."

"Right, what am I thinkin'? Truman Gates, I run Gates Scrap Metal, out of Homestead."

"You're here to what, pick up a load of scrap?"

"You got it. Come by here every couple a months, mostly auto parts."

"And you found this body under a vehicle?"

"Way under, like he'd been shoved in there. We popped the mag onto the car lid—picking it up with the crane, see? And there he was."

"Better show me."

They went into the salvage yard. Place looked a whole lot different in the daylight. And there were no rats—little bastards had been frightened away by all the noise of the heavy equipment. The

EMS team was kneeling around a mud-caked body. Officer Clancy was taking photographs.

"I almost didn't see him," Gates said softly, "the way he blended into the dirt."

"Hey, Sarge!" Clancy said. "I called your office, they sounded weird when I asked for you. Must be a new person on the switchboard."

"That's it," Valdez said. Decided he would tell Clancy later.

An emergency medical technician was wiping at the victim's face with a wet sponge. Caucasian, Valdez saw, and a streak of yellow hair. After cleaning him up a little, the technician eased him gently onto the gurney. Snaking an oxygen tube into his nostril.

"Not much of a pulse. He's barely there."

Something tickled in the back of Valdez's mind. He'd been carrying the photograph for weeks now. He didn't really need to see it again, but he took it out, just to be sure. The face was thinner, devoid of expression, but the resemblance was very strong.

"We can I.D. this one," he told Clancy. "Name is Kurt Palmer."

CHAPTER ELEVEN

The drive over to Cypress Medical Center was nerve-racking. Traffic was psychotic, the usual high-speed lane changers, and Sara was having trouble concentrating.

Had they really found Kurt?

She kept thinking maybe a mistake had been made. Not Kurt but some other blond-haired sleeper. All this time she'd wanted him to turn up, and now it had happened, a dream turned into a nightmare.

A security guard at the Experimental Medicine entrance thought about telling her to move the vehicle away from the entrance, then saw the look on her face and changed his mind.

"Just leave me your keys," he said.

She tossed him the keys and hurried inside.

Never noticed the black Trans-Am with the smoked-glass windows that glided into the lot behind her.

Inside the lobby she paused to take a few deep breaths, calm herself. The security guard was outside, moving her car, so she didn't have to wait for a pass.

Sara headed down the hallway, forcing herself not to run. Her sensible flats echoing as her feet hit the tiles. Thinking that only the day before yesterday people were running for their lives down this same hallway; now the place seemed eerily empty.

There was only one nurse on duty at the ICU station, separated from the surviving sleepers by a wall of a thick plate glass.

"We have a new policy," the nurse said. "Custodial care, nonintervention. The patients are in a vegetative state, we're just supposed to monitor their condition."

Meaning keep out of the room in case another of them comes awake, Sara thought. She counted five beds. Where was Kurt?

"I'm here to check out the new arrival," she said. "He's been identified as a friend of mine. They just brought him in."

The nurse looked away, flustered. "I better call one of the staff physicians," she said.

"What, have they taken him to the Trauma Center?"

The nurse shook her head, bit her lower lip.

"You better tell me what happened," said Sara, her heart sinking.

"Um, the victim was deceased when he got here."

"What?" said Sara, thinking, No, no. There's been some mistake.

"Expired in transit," the nurse said. "That's what they told me."

"Where's the body now?"

"Well . . ." The nurse hesitated.

"Look, I'm not sure if it's really my friend they found. I want to be sure, do you understand?"

The nurse told her to try the hospital morgue.

The sign on the swinging doors said STORAGE FACILITY, and so it was. Storage of hospital cadavers, awaiting autopsy or transfer to an undertaker.

It was cool inside, and Sara shivered. No one around. Well, why would there be? Nobody complained in here. Nobody rang for the nurse.

Just a dozen or so gurneys covered with white sheets.

Sara wanted to take a deep breath, slow the thudding in her chest, but the smell of phenolic disinfectant was too strong. The death smell. What she needed to do was get it over with. Turn back the sheets until she found the seventh sleeper, see if it was really Kurt.

Instead, she just stood there with her hands in her jacket pockets, saying a little prayer.

Don't let it be him.

Sara went to the nearest gurney, turned back the sheet.

An old woman with sunken eyes and skin the color of bone. Under the next sheet was a black male. Rigor mortis still in effect, giving him a leering kind of smile. After that she hurried, flipping back sheets.

Feeling angry, she didn't know why, angry at this terrible mocking silence.

He was there in the back of the morgue, waiting. Mud caked on his bare torso made the sheet sticky. Someone had washed his face. As soon as Sara touched his neck, she knew. The body was cool, room temperature. She felt for a pulse just in case, but there had been no mistake.

Kurt Palmer wasn't missing anymore; he was gone forever.

The nurse was a gift. Cute little thing in starched whites, startled brown eyes, soft brown hair in a bun under her cap. Pink lipstick as she chewed on a pencil, making notes on a clipboard.

Luto watched her for a while, savoring the moment, then stepped inside the ICU station and touched the nape of her neck.

"Ah!"

Got what he wanted, a nice little jump and squeal. He gave her a toothy grin when she turned to confront him, but he could tell she didn't like the way he smiled.

"You're not supposed to be in here," she said. "Not without a pass."

Backing up in her chair, the wheels squeaking.

"'Nother girl come in here," Luto said, hooking his foot under the chair. "Where'd she go?"

"Get out!" The nurse raised the clipboard, tried to bat away his hands.

"Jess tell me where she go, you don't get hurt."

The nurse ducked under his arm, took to her heels. He had to chase her. Feet heavy with the firepower strapped to his ankles. Salty taste of blood in his mouth where the clipboard had cut him. He reached out, snagged a starched collar. The little white cap flew off, and the nurse opened her mouth to scream.

Luto yanked her back, clamped his hand over that cute pink mouth. Forced her backward, banging her head against the floor. Not too hard, not yet—he wanted information first.

"Tell me where the lady doctor goes, okay?"

He was kneeling, holding her down, ignoring the fists beating at her legs. Somehow the girl knocked the gun right out of his ankle holster. He smacked her head down again, snatched up the gun before her fingers could close on it.

Madre de Dios, that was close.

The nurse bit him.

Luto stifled a scream, hit her with the butt of the gun, a love tap in the chin. She slumped back, still conscious, looking up at him with dazed eyes.

When he shoved the gun barrel against her teeth, the brown eyes got very big. The struggle was over now. Freeze time. Now there was that small, intense spark passing between them. Life to death, death to life. Better than anything. Better than sex.

"Tell me where the lady doctor goes," he said. "Then maybe I don't rape you."

The nurse tried to speak. He'd whacked her pretty hard in the chin, and she was having trouble moving her jaw. He lifted the gun slowly away, keeping it aimed between her eyes.

"You tell me now, okay?"

She told him. He raised the gun and slammed the butt end into her forehead, hard, felt the bone give way. He stood up, rubbing the hand she'd bitten, and thought, This is okay, this is going to be fun.

Tasting blood from the small wound, he went looking for a room marked MORGUE. Walking right by the Storage Facility, he found himself in the bottom of a stairwell, a dead end.

What was this shit? Had the little nurse been lying? Had she looked right into that big bad gun barrel and told a fib? You couldn't trust nobody these days, not even those about to die.

He turned, headed back the way he'd come.

Froze when he heard footsteps.

The echo made it hard to tell, but he was pretty sure the footsteps were not far ahead, around the next corner. He picked up the pace. This was supposed to be a hit-and-run job; he'd already been inside too long.

Came around the corner, there she was. Cute ass under that skirt, but there might not be time to really check it out now. Do her quick and disappear.

Luto dropped down, reached for the gun in his right ankle holster. The bitch must have heard him or sensed him, because she turned just as his hand closed on the gun.

He tugged, brought it up, but shit, she was running, skidding around the next corner.

* * *

Sara ran, heart pounding. A scrawny little man with blood on his lips and he wanted to kill her. Who the hell *was* he? No time. Run. Think about it later.

The first door she came to was the ICU. She slammed it behind her, locked it, and nearly tripped over the sprawled body of the nurse. An ugly, pulpy-looking dent in her forehead. Looking up with dead eyes.

Sara felt for a pulse, found none.

Footsteps in the hall.

Was there an exit through the sleeper ward? Had to be. She hit the light switch, and a shadow fell over the six beds visible through the glass.

He was close now, hesitating outside the locked door.

She slipped into the ward. Running between the sleepers, she slammed her hip into an EEG machine and fell, skidding on her open hands.

Stay down, she thought. He has a gun, stay down.

Crawling as fast as she could, the floor hard and slick under her knees, she slipped under the beds. Scooting between them. Duck and cover. One. Two. Three. End of the room. Now she had to traverse an open space. Should she get up and run or stay on her knees? Stand or crawl?

Crawl it was. Pretty dim back here, and the glass wall in the ICU would be reflecting lights from the monitors.

She headed for the rear door, praying that it would lead to an exit.

CHAPTER TWELVE

The locked door into the ICU was easy. Break the glass, flip the button. Luto came in crouching, holding the gun, a Beretta 84. Twelve rounds of 9-mm shorts ready to fire. Letting his eyes adjust to the darkness. The dead nurse giving him a look.

Peekaboo.

Nobody home. He stood up. All kinds of TV screens here, glowing with wiggly green lines. A glass wall, and beyond it another room. Quite dark. He could make out beds. Lumps on the beds. Were they alive or dead in there? Was *this* the morgue? Nothing moved.

Luto opened the door and eased inside. The darkness was a challenge. You had to relax your eyes, let it all drain in, concentrate on picking up movement. He padded softly to the first bed, eased the sheet down with the gun barrel. Dead-looking guy, all wired up. Tubes running in and out.

He placed a hand on the guy's chest, detected a slight quiver. So they weren't dead, not quite.

He walked quickly through the ward, gun hand loose at his side, ready to swivel and fire if so much as a shadow twitched. Found another door at the rear and thought, Shit, the bitch got away. Opened the door and discovered a custodian's closet. Mop and bucket, a sink, the smell of institutional soap.

No exit, sweetheart.

He turned from the closet and surveyed the six beds. Limited hiding spots here. He crouched, getting a clear line under the beds. Was that a shape down there? A human form, hugging the floor?

He padded forward, swooped low, checked it out. No. Just a

shadow, tricked his eyes. So if the *rubia* wasn't in the closet or under the beds, where was she?

Not breathing was the hard part.

Around her she was aware of the other sleepers. They shared a stillness. A waiting. A paralyzing fear of what was to come as the intruder stalked between the beds, radiating malice.

The sheet was drawn up to her chin. She'd stuck telemetry wires to the side of her cheek. Not medically correct, but it helped obscure her face. Gauze bandages were tucked over her forehead, around her hair. The plastic tube in her mouth tasted awful.

Hard to see where the man with the gun was. Didn't dare open her eyes wide, or move her head. Rely on the soft padding of his feet for location. The slippery squeak of rubber soles. Where had she seen him? Something about that face, the way he held his head. Never mind. Nothing mattered but getting in tune with the sleepers. Become one of them. Sinking, sinking deeper, entering into the stillness.

Her heart was giving her away. Surely he could hear it thumping. Loudest thing in the room.

When Dr. Harding had been killed and the raging sleeper was coming at her, it had all happened so quickly she hadn't really had time to be afraid.

This was different. Not hot fury, but cold deliberation. Matter of moments now.

He was just one bed away.

Squeak of rubber on the floor tiles.

The gauze bandage was torn away from her head. Blond hair fanning out.

"Buenas noches," he whispered, placing the gun barrel between her eyes.

Sara found that she could not move. The barrel was strangely warm, like a hot thumb pressed against her forehead. Now his other hand was sliding under the sheets. Moving snakelike down over her shoulder, between her breasts, pausing over the tight drum of her belly.

The hot steel thumb on her forehead pressed harder, pushing her head back into the pillows.

Snake fingers moved under the waistband of her skirt, fumbled at the elastic of her underpants.

Fight him. She tried to summon the will. It was no use, she could not move.

Suddenly there was light. The door was crashing open.

"Let her go! Drop it!"

Valdez.

The gun barrel raked her forehead. Sparks burned her face as he fired across the bed, toward the doorway. Rapid explosions that shattered the glass wall. Then she was sitting up, screaming.

Valdez was diving under a bed. The man with the bloody lips was crouched, arms extended, trying to find his target.

Why didn't Lee fire back?

"Run!" he was screaming. "Run!"

Just like that she was out of the bed, trailing telemetry wires, running hell-bent for the closet. More shots exploded.

Don't let him die, she thought.

In the closet she slammed into a wall. Bottles crashed to the floor. Ammonia fumes rose instantly, bringing tears to her eyes. There had to be a weapon here. Something to hit with. Hammer, stick, anything. Her hands closed on a slippery glass bottle. Ammonia, bleach, it didn't matter.

She ran back into the room, skidding on wet shoes.

Valdez was rolling under the beds. The little fucker was shooting at him. Throw? No, never hit the son of a bitch that way.

Sara screamed, charged, smashed the glass bottle over his head. An explosion of liquid soap. She fell, landing on top of him. He was moving, fighting her. Her hands found his face, tried to dig in, slipped away.

Valdez screaming, "I've got him! Sara, let go, I've got him."

The detective on his knees, shaking like a leaf, the gun in *his* hands now. A tendril of smoke exuded from the barrel, like a cigarette left in an ashtray.

Sobbing, Sara got to her feet.

What really bothered her was that the little man did not look frightened. His own gun was pointing in his face, and yet his eyes were amused.

"Who sent you, you son of a bitch?" Valdez demanded. He was having trouble catching his breath, but the gun didn't waver. Rock solid.

The little man smiled. Blood dripping from his mouth, nose,

from the gash she'd opened on his head, and still he smiled. Sara didn't like it one bit.

Something was wrong here.

Still grinning through his blood, the man reached down, lifted his left pant leg. Sara saw the second gun. Valdez saw it, too. Without hesitation he pulled the trigger.

Click. Empty.

The man's fingers were closing around the butt of the second gun. "Eat shit, *cochinos*." he whispered, never taking his eyes from Valdez. Grinning that ugly, mortal grin.

Sara reared back and kicked him hard in the side of the head. He sighed and fell over, making a wet thump on the slippery floor.

Valdez picked up the second gun. "That was beautiful," he said with admiration. "Truly beautiful."

He patted his back pockets, shook his head, and said, "Damn, they took my cuffs, too."

"What?"

"I'll tell you about it later. Let's get something to tie him up."

In the end they decided on the telemetry wires, lashing his hands and feet together behind his back. That done, they laid him on the empty bed and tied him in place with more wires. Unable to move anything but his mouth, he kept spitting and snapping his jaws until Valdez threatened to knock all his teeth out with the gun.

The two men traded insults in Spanish.

"I ask him what his name is, he tells me Luto. That's a street name. It means sadness or tragedy, which fits him."

Luto, confident that he wasn't going to die, spit again and turned his eyes to Sara.

"Pretty lady," he said. "Pretty lady feel pretty good, eh? I *like* to feel pretty lady."

Sara shivered, remembering what his hands had been doing to her just before Lee Valdez burst into the room.

"Sara?" Valdez said, taking the Beretta from his waist. "Excuse me, please, you may not want to watch this."

There was a brutally murdered nurse in the next room; at the moment Sara didn't care what happened to the man who called himself Luto. She watched as Valdez placed the gun under his twitching chin, ignoring the spittle.

It was the same spot that had finished the sleeper.

"Luto? I'll do it. I'll put out your lights, man. Unless you tell me who sent you."

His knuckles tightened on the gun. After a moment Luto coughed a few words in Spanish: *Coronel manda asesinar.*

"Colonel says kill?" Valdez responded. "That's it?"

Luto refused to say more.

"I gotta make a phone call now," Valdez said. "Then we better get out of here."

He phoned from the ICU station while Sara covered the dead nurse with a sheet. The call to the Metro-Dade Police did not go well. Valdez requested a homicide team and then was transferred to his unit commander.

The report rapidly degenerated into a shouting match.

"Hey, Captain? Just shut up and listen, okay? I got three words out of this insect. 'Colonel says kill.' That should be clear enough. This is Carlos Calavera we're talking about, okay? He's the one who put the heat on, got me suspended. So *you* figure it out. The fuck I will, Cap. Hang around while you interrogate this little shit? Wait for Calavera to hit us with something else? Forget it. I'm out of here. You arrest the colonel, *then* maybe I'll surface."

He slammed the phone down. Moments later they were out the door, into Valdez's car, slipping away from the hospital as sirens whined in the distance. They were on 95 North, cruising in a fast lane of heavy commuter traffic, before Sara's head cleared enough for her to say, "Hey, Lee? What are we doing here?"

He gave her a funny look. "We're running away."

"And you think that's a good idea?"

His smile was weary. "It's the only idea I've got, right at the moment. The colonel wants you dead, Sara. He won't stop just because Luto got caught."

CHAPTER THIRTEEN

Night fell on the great swamp. A gaudy, blood-red sky fading to burnt orange, then darkening quickly. Blink. Turn out the big light. He liked the effect, liked the way cooling vapors blurred the nightscape, softened the edges.

Vidoc left the newly scoured bunker wearing a full mosquito-intervention net, covered head to foot. Darkness did not impede his progress. He had excellent night vision, a strong sense of exactly where he wanted to go.

Outside the barracks he paused, listening.

He liked what night did to the recruits. Bright and chattering in the daylight hours, full of macho confidence in their fighting prowess, night cooled them out. Nary a peep coming from that leaky, open-sided building now that the sun had set. A few quiet whispers, like kids at camp, easily spooked by what they could not see.

Vidoc smiled behind his veil of protective netting. If only they knew. There *was* danger out here in the dark, but it was not confined to lumbering reptiles or slithering snakes or whatever simple peasant nightmares the recruits brought with them. The swamp itself held no terror. The gators were relatively placid, the snakes were not aggressive.

The danger was fear itself.

Vidoc believed that most humans experienced fear as an uncontrolled emotional state. His method, developed over a lifetime of casual experiments, recently refined and perfected, brought a new and useful dimension to the concept of fear.

Find the right balance of chemistry and instinct and you could channel the stuff like a powerful electrical current. The idea was to give fear a direction and purpose. Of course, you had to utilize a holistic approach, treat the mind as well as the body. You wanted maximum effect, you couldn't ignore the psychological aspects, or the importance of theater. Old Bill knew all about it when he made Macbeth speak of fear that made *"the heart knock at my ribs against the use of nature."*

That was the stuff. Heart-knocking, rib-thumping fear. Give 'em more than they bargained for. And in this age of high-tech warfare, even hayseed guerrillas demanded the best of special effects.

Tomorrow he would select the volunteers. The sergeant had made a preliminary list of potential candidates, based on Vidoc's criteria. This time there would be no mistakes. The demonstration would go on as scheduled. The contract would be fulfilled, and Dr. Emile Vidoc would no longer have to rely on the kindness of strangers.

He turned silently away from the barracks and returned to his bunker. The little Honda generator hummed with an insect drone. The starkly illuminated interior of the concrete bunker pleased him. It was now acceptably clean, for a field situation.

In the white glare of the lights he unpacked his bag, laying the contents out on the workbench the drill sergeant had thoughtfully supplied.

The Vidoc Field Kit, stripped to the bare essentials:

1. A box of syringes and sterile needles
2. Disposable gloves
3. A surgical kit
4. A sealed liter of synthesized neurotoxin, his own special formulation
5. Several smaller vials of various interesting compounds, mostly psychotropics and stimulants, some not yet tested
6. Twelve thumb-sized radio-control servo units, courtesy of Radio Shack
7. A transmitter and battery pack
8. Twelve subcutaneous-medication pumps, modified

Total weight of the kit was less than three kilos, with a volume of a cubic foot or less. Coupled with the volunteers, it had the destructive power of a full-scale air barrage. Psychological resonance was even greater, with the ability to demoralize a large civilian population.

The guerrilla commanders would buy it. How could they resist?

He packed the kit away, turned off the generator, and strung up his hammock in the dark.

Suspended a few feet above the concrete, his flesh exposed to the free circulation of air, Vidoc did not sleep. He imagined his eyes glowing in the night. It was a good thought, a powerful thought.

CHAPTER FOURTEEN

They had holed up in Pompano Beach, in a place called the Faro Blanco Motel, surrounded by arsenic-green carpeting and sick pink wallpaper. Valdez had picked the place because the manager wasn't fussy about checking license plates or demanding identification. You gave them cash, they gave you a key. Your basic no-tell motel.

It did have two double beds.

"This is just for tonight," Valdez said. "If you want, I'll sleep in the car, or get another room here. I couldn't get two adjoining."

"This will be fine."

"First thing, I need a shower. Then I'll call Ricky, see if he can help."

A minute later he was in the shower, steam coming out from under a poorly hung door, and Sara was perched on the edge of a creaky mattress, trying to figure out how she'd come to be in a cheap motel with a cop she didn't know all that well.

She hadn't had time to think anything through. Events seemed to be propelling her forward, making her act when she didn't feel up to it. There was no time to think about what Kurt's death meant to her, no time to let herself *feel* it, no time to find out exactly why a mercenary she'd never met would hire someone to kill her.

One thing for sure, this was no cop-paranoia thing—Luto had been a heartbeat away from shooting her. And Lee Valdez had saved her life for the second time in three days.

They'll never believe this back in Boston, she thought.

Sara lay back on the mattress and closed her eyes. The whole thing was crazy. Crazy Cubans, crazy killers—what did it have to do with her life? She had no interest in covert activities, or brothers who happened to be Santería priests, or the schemes of mercenary colonels.

Why couldn't it all just go away and leave her alone?

They were waiting for the phone to ring. It was a pay phone, some distance away from the motel. Valdez, cat nervous as he waited for his brother to call back, stalked into a Tom Thumb convenience store, returned with two Cokes and a pack of cigarettes.

Sara couldn't see the beach—it was across the street, on the other side of a wall of condos—but she could smell it, the tang of salt in the hot, muggy breeze.

Valdez hunkered down and lighted a cigarette, cupping the match against the wind. "Gave 'em up for good two years ago," he said. "If being on a hit list isn't reason to light up, I don't know what is."

When the phone rang, they both jumped. Valdez took a deep breath, picked up.

"Hey, big brother."

"I'm here, Ricky."

"I talked to a couple people, like you asked. This is serious shit, brother. I don't know exactly what you did, but the colonel is after your ass, man."

Lee cradled the phone, tapped another cigarette from the pack. Two years without nicotine and now he was chain-smoking, just like that. "All I did was nose into a few things. Now I'm ready to leave it alone."

"Yeah, well, it's not so simple. Word is you messed with a secret computer file, interfered with some project the colonel has going. Is that right?"

"Like I said, whatever shit he's cooking up, I no longer care. All I want, in return for not talking, is a guarantee of safety for Dr. Copley and myself."

Lee could hear his brother taking sips, swallowing. Ricky talked so much, he was always drinking something to keep his throat from going dry. Even as a kid.

"Listen, I'm going to work on this for you, okay? You listening?"

"I'm listening, Ricky."

"The situation right now, he wants you and your new girlfriend out of the picture."

"Meaning he wants us dead."

"Well, you know the colonel. He's excitable. He likes dramatic resolutions. I got the sense, talking to my sources, that once his temper cools, he might be satisfied just to get you thrown off the police force. You're one of the family, brother, part of the community, or anyhow that will be our argument. This Anglo doctor is the real problem. She's an unknown quantity, right? An outsider. So he wants her gone. I mean permanently gone."

Lee glanced at Sara. How much was she picking up from this side of the conversation?

"I know what you mean," he said. "Forget it."

"Hey, it's not what *I* mean, big brother. It's what *he* means. Let's keep that straight. I don't have nothing to do with the colonel or his business, okay? All I'm sayin', we play our cards exactly right, he'll take his marker off you. Year or two you might even be able to get back on the cops. But not the girl."

"I said forget it," Lee said, heated. "I'm not cutting that kind of deal."

"Well, at least think about it, okay? Oh, and guess who else I talked to?"

Lee sighed, smoke curling from his nostrils.

"I'm too tired for guessing games, Ricky."

"Mercedes. Man, I think she's got a thing for you. She tell me, Enrique, you must hide him. Keep him away from the hairless one. I say, Hairless one, who the hell is the hairless one? She goes, He's like a snake with very bad poison. That mean anything to you, brother?"

"Maybe."

"So who's this snake she's so worried about?"

"Emile Vidoc. He's associated with the colonel. By the way, did you find out where the colonel is? I tried calling the estate, talk to the son of a bitch myself, but they say he's out of town."

"Leave it alone, brother."

"I need to know where he is, Ricky. It's very important."

He could feel Ricky hesitating, mulling it over. "You're not dumb enough to go after him, are you, brother?"

"No way," Lee said with rehearsed conviction. "I told you, I want to make a deal. I just need to get in touch."

"Okay. I heard tomorrow morning he will be at Camp Libertad.

Some place they train guerrillas out in the Everglades. Does that help?"

"I don't know, Ricky. Maybe. Hey, brother, thanks, okay?"

"This a family thing, Lee. Whatever I can do, I will. But you want to live a long life, ditch the girl. Forget about her."

Valdez hung up and lighted another cigarette.

CHAPTER FIFTEEN

The colonel saw it twice, once on the six o'clock, very sketchy report and no pictures, and again with expanded coverage on the eleven. The gist of the story, according to the talking heads, was that a suspended cop and doc had fled the scene of crime. File photos of Valdez and the blond lady doctor and also a sound bit of Luto being loaded into a cruiser, the two arresting officers smiling pleasantly into the camera, being very careful not to bump Luto's bleeding head as they eased him into the rear seat.

Ignorant Marielito scum. Let himself get taken by two unarmed civilians. How was that possible? Did sheer stupidity account for it? No matter, maybe it would work better this way. Valdez and the bitch on the run, it made them look bad. Made it easier to construct a believable scenario when their bodies were recovered. Something like Despondent Cop Shoots Doc, Then Himself.

Keep it simple. Simple sold best.

"*Señor?* The lady who called is waiting."

He shut off the television monitor. "Bring her in."

Mercedes Raimez entered, dressed in formal, floor-length mourning. The colonel sighed. The woman had a theatrical flair, and she was using it to remind him that her father had died in his employ.

"It is late, *señorita*, what have you to tell me?" he asked, establishing who was in charge.

"I am thirsty, Colonel."

Letting him know his hospitality was lacking.

Calavera sighed again—it was useless to fight women, particularly a woman steeped in traditional Santería—and asked what she would like to drink. Mercedes requested a large glass of soda water on ice, with straight whiskey on the side. She waited until it was poured, then humbly thanked him, keeping her handsome brown eyes averted. She sipped the whiskey, drank from the soda glass.

Calavera sniffed a cognac and waited until she had patted her lips dry with a lace hankie.

At last she said, "I come to you with information regarding the police detective, Sergeant Valdez."

The colonel put his glass down and concentrated on not looking too eager. "Yes, Mercedes? Do you know where he is?"

She nodded. "I think he is in great danger."

"No, *where* he is. His location."

She shook her head. "His brother spoke to me. Enrique, the great *santero*."

"Yes, yes," the colonel said impatiently, "the priest. I know him slightly. He has a following."

"A great following, Colonel. He is a fine man, a visionary. Enrique speaks in the tongue of Oraca."

The colonel smiled. He was a monotheist who believed only in the god of money, but he was willing to find a use for any belief so long as it advanced his own.

"Sergeant Valdez has been in contact with his brother Enrique," Mercedes explained. "He fears that he has offended you in some way."

The colonel tossed off his cognac. Extracting information from this irritating woman was like pulling teeth from a hen. Yet she had a great many contacts in the exile community. He did not want to needlessly offend her.

"Valdez is a traitor, Mercedes. You told me that yourself. He wants to ruin your father's good name."

She shook her head vigorously. "I was mistaken. He is misguided, not a traitor. He needs to be brought back into the bosom of his family. He needs . . ." She made a helpless gesture.

Yes, the colonel thought, you think he needs a wife. That is what brings you here.

"Mercedes, listen to me carefully," he said, leaning forward. "My people will do nothing to harm Sergeant Valdez. But we must speak to him, do you understand?"

"He is not to be killed?"

"No, of course not."

He made a dismissive gesture. Preposterous, the idea that he would have a man killed.

Mercedes appeared greatly relieved.

"Oh thank you, Colonel. I could not bear to think that anything I said might have put his life in danger."

The colonel rose from his chair, strutted to her side, and rested a meaty hand upon her black-upholstered shoulder.

"Rest assured, child, he will be safe in our hands. Anything you can do to locate him, I'd be in your debt. Did, ah, did his brother Enrique say where he might be found?"

Head shake.

"I think he is not in Miami," she said. "He is hiding somewhere."

Calavera grimaced. This woman was impossible.

"Colonel, there is another thing. The bald one. The man you sent to me."

"What?" he said, momentarily confused.

"The strange Americano doctor. He bought many potions from my store. Very powerful poisons."

Vidoc, of course. He had almost forgotten that Emile had gone to her *botánica* for certain supplies. Source chemistry, he had called it. That was months ago, before the method had been tested on the first group. Before that fool Heberto had dropped dead and almost ruined the project.

"He is an evil man," Mercedes said. "If Sergeant Valdez finds him, I'm afraid of what will happen. I have dreams, Colonel, terrible dreams. They tell me Sergeant Valdez is in great danger."

The colonel rolled his eyes. This was really too much. Next thing she'd be wanting to sacrifice animals in here, spatter his expensive carpets with blood.

"Dr. Vidoc is gone, Mercedes. He left for a long European vacation. So forget about any few things he may have got from your shop. You never met the man. Is that understood?"

Mercedes was hesitant. She finished her whiskey before saying, "Of course, *Padrino*. Anything you say."

"The doctor did good work for our cause. Now it is over and done and he has left the country," the colonel said firmly, using his voice of command. "That is all you need to know. And if you hear anything of Sergeant Valdez, you must tell me. I cannot guarantee his safety unless I know where he is. Understood?"

After she left, he poured himself a generous cognac. Damn troublesome woman. He would have to keep her under surveillance. It was unlikely that Valdez would be dumb enough to contact her directly, but you never knew.

Dumb things often happened to people the colonel distrusted.

CHAPTER SIXTEEN

Sara decided the walls were exactly the color of Pepto-Bismol. She was sitting on the bed with her legs folded; Lee was in a seedy-looking armchair, smoking his way through a pack of cigarettes.

"Is it that bad?" she said. "These people must be crazy."

"Yes, it is," he said. "And yes, they are."

The call to his brother had done nothing to allay his fears, from what Sara could see. A sticky kind of dread had come back into the room with them, like something that stuck to the bottom of the feet and wouldn't scrape off. Neither of them felt like eating. The cellophane-wrapped sandwiches they'd brought back from the convenience store were untouched on the bureau.

"There must be somebody we can call," Sara suggested. "The FBI?"

Lee shook his head, sucked the cigarette until the end glowed molten red. "I go to the Bureau, they'll just turn me back over to Metro-Dade. And you'll be out here alone."

"The newspapers?"

"I've been thinking about that," he said. "They can't protect us, but I guess it wouldn't hurt to talk to the *Miami Herald*."

The reporter arrived, as promised, in a yellow Datsun. She parked in a slot at Burger King and got out, holding a notebook high in the air.

Like a white flag, Sara thought, as she watched from inside the restaurant. Lee was across the street, standing just inside the door of a McDonald's. This was, he had said wryly, a fast-food rendezvous.

The reporter, a slim woman with thick, shoulder-length auburn hair, leaned against the yellow Datsun and studied her watch. No doubt deciding she'd been led on a snipe hunt.

After a few minutes Lee signaled from the McDonald's. Sara got up, walked out into the hot night, and approached the Datsun.

"Lynn Harnett?"

The reporter jerked herself to attention.

"Um, Dr. Copley, right?"

"Leave your car here. Follow me on foot."

Lee had ordered a tray of food, secured a booth near the front, where he could watch the street.

"Relax," said the reporter, accepting a cup of coffee. "I've already been in contempt a couple of times, for not reporting a source. You mind if I take notes?"

"Go ahead."

Harnett uncapped her pen and smiled.

"You two are hot news," she said. "I appreciate the call. I should tell you right off, I'm not authorized to pay you anything. If that's a problem, we'll have to consult with my editor."

"We're not looking to get paid," said Lee, shaking his head. "We're just trying to stay alive."

They talked for nearly an hour, Lee laying out the details of his investigation, Sara handling the medical side, what she knew about the neurotoxin.

When Lee started in on the Calavera connection, the reporter grew thoughtful.

"This could be a problem," she said.

Lee sighed. "What? The colonel is pals with the publisher?"

Harnett laughed. "Not hardly. We ran a series of investigative articles on Mr. Calavera a few years ago, the Ollie North connection, smuggling arms, all of that good stuff. So now he's suing us. He can't prove malice—he can't even prove that the articles were inaccurate—but that hasn't stopped him from siccing his lawyers on us."

Lee picked up his cigarettes.

"Come on," he said to Sara, "we're wasting our time."

"Hang on," Harnett said. "I'm not saying we won't run this story. We get sued all the time, that doesn't mean we stop reporting the news. Whether it runs or not won't be my decision—that'll be up to the editors."

"So what's the problem?" Lee said.

"We'll need more than hearsay evidence. The legal department is going to demand that we make every effort to vet this story."

"The sleepers are right there," Sara said. "There's your evidence."

Harnett got up, put her notebook in her purse.

"It's great stuff, combat veterans exposed to a neurotoxin. But we can't run a story tying the Calavera organization to it without some solid proof. You're a cop, Mr. Valdez, you know how it works."

Lee watched the yellow Datsun vanish into the night, shaking his head.

"That's about what I expected."

"We'll just have to do it," Sara said.

"Do what?"

"Get some solid proof."

It didn't really hit her until she was in the shower, washing her hair. She managed to get out of the stall, wrap a towel around herself. Shivering like crazy in a steamy little room, must have been 90 in there. Still shivering as she came out of the bathroom, wet hair clinging to her face.

Lee put out his cigarette, got up from the chair.

"What's wrong?"

Sara couldn't speak, her teeth were chattering so hard. All she could do was shake her head.

Lee put his arms around her, hugged her tight.

"Easy now," he whispered. "It'll be all right. You're a doctor, you know what this is. A delayed reaction. Someone you loved died, someone else tried to kill you."

"I f-feel s-so *empty*," she said through chattering teeth.

He held her, talking softly to her in Spanish, until the shaking gradually diminished. Then he carried her to the bed, placed her on it, smoothed the wet hair from her forehead. When he started to get up from the bed, she put her arms around his neck and pulled him back down.

Sara found his mouth and kissed him hungrily.

The man called Luto lay on the thin bunk, staring at the ceiling. Head bandage like a turban. Nine detainees, four bunks, and nobody questioned his right to have a thin mattress all to himself. It was all in the attitude. It helped if you looked like a stone killer, and no question, he'd *earned* the look, unlike these stinking drunks and child molesters and public pissers who cluttered the cell.

He could do one night easy. Arraignment tomorrow morning. The colonel's lawyers were already working to reduce the charges. Murder down to manslaughter. Our client falsely detained by suspended officer who fled scene. Our client victim of brutal assault, blow to head. Improperly bound hands and feet, Your Honor, in violation of code. Request low bail.

He'd be out by eleven, noon the latest.

"Hey, pal."

Luto shifted his eyes to the left. Pudgy-faced Anglo with bad teeth and flat blue eyes standing there with an impudent look.

"You want a smoke, pal?" the Anglo drawled. Swampy accent. This was some kind of redneck gator-skinner.

Luto shrugged. Actually he did want a cigarette.

"The deal is, hep me pusswade these shithaids it share and share alike. Then we split what we takes off 'em."

"You do it."

That was how he hooked up with Lester "Bunny" Burkus, better known to numerous arresting officers as Swamp Thing.

CHAPTER SEVENTEEN

Sunday morning, Camp Libertad.

The Mercedes limousine arrived first, followed by a four-wheel-drive pickup towing an Airstream trailer. The limousine came to a stop on the airstrip while the truck continued across, circling near the drill sergeant's Winnebago like a dog preparing to lie down.

Colonel Calavera exited the big limo dressed in combat fatigues. A pair of pearl-handled pistols nestled in a gleaming holster at his waist. The idea was, impress the new recruits. Many of whom he'd signed up personally, on his last sweep through the disputed provinces.

The boys were lined up on the airstrip now, in the heat of the morning sun, standing at parade rest, and they came to attention when Hernandez barked. More or less in unison, not bad for rookies. A nice mix of peasant farmers and hooligans, representative of a typical guerrilla platoon.

"Lion-hearted men of liberty," he began, "this is a great day! You have already begun the fight that will free your great nation from the shackles of the oppressor. The villains who stole the land of your masters will pay with their lives! Their blood will irrigate the soil! Freedom will bloom like a red, red rose!"

And so on. It was a variant of the speech he'd given many times before, in many small nations, and it never failed to rouse in his own heart the strong conviction that if there was a way for money to be made out of a difficult situation, he would find it.

Luncheon followed in the Airstream. The colonel had had his fill of camp food in the last few months, and so his trailer was fully stocked with catered goodies. No rice and beans this time out.

Tinned prawns, caviar, a good pâté, smoked salmon, a nice mango chutney, marinated veal, a box of foil-wrapped Italian chocolates.

Dr. Vidoc joined him but did not partake of the repast.

"I'm fasting for the next few days," he announced, arranging his long jumpsuit-clad limbs in a canvas sling chair some distance away from the table. As far as one could decently get in a thirty-two-foot Airstream. "Fasting cleanses the system. It purges the toxins from the blood, improves muscle tone, sharpens the concentration."

"Is that a fact?" said the colonel, pouring a full glass of California white wine and contemplating a veal dish that smelled exquisitely of saffron. "We had a slight foul-up. The cop and his girlfriend got away."

Vidoc made a dismissive huffing noise, like a cat choking up a fur ball. "He can't hurt us."

"Probably not," the colonel agreed. "The pig has been taken care of, suspended. Also, he's now a suspect in a police-brutality case. I'm working on an indictment for murder, this young nurse. Maybe a jealousy angle of some kind."

"You've been busy," Vidoc said. He studied his long, carefully manicured fingers rather than see the ugliness of Calavera masticating.

The colonel mopped at his lips with a linen napkin. His fork, when it hit the plate, made a sound like fingernails on slate.

"So," he said, "is it going well? Have the volunteers been selected?"

Vidoc sat perfectly motionless in the canvas sling chair. Reminding the colonel again of a giant praying mantis, the way he cocked his inner stillness like a trigger.

"These new men are not nearly as impressive as the original seven, but they'll have to do."

"Very good," said the colonel, sipping his wine.

"Have the Bolivians agreed on a unit price?"

The colonel nodded, blinked his fat-lidded eyes. "If the method is as effective as you've promised, they will pay thirty thousand per unit, with the initial buy at one hundred units."

"Three million," Vidoc said instantly.

The colonel smiled, his teeth clotted with strings of unweaned calf meat.

"Think of it as a down payment," he said. "They'll need at

least five hundred units to overrun a province. I figure fifteen million to turn the war around. Or at least keep it going."

Of the seven recruits who had volunteered for special duty, the most impressive was the boy Fernando. This was a pleasant surprise—having seen the two brothers living like pigs in that fetid motel room, Vidoc never imagined the younger boy would have the killer instinct.

"Rattlesnake mean," the drill sergeant said, handing over his list. "This kid Nando, you want men who get off on violence, he's prime. Either he's convinced that bullets can't kill him or maybe he's crazy enough he wants to die. I can't decide. Make a hell of a good commando either way."

"Send them in one at a time. Nando first."

Nando marched into the bunker carrying his wooden parade rifle. He stood rigidly at attention. Warned that the boy's grasp of language was rudimentary, Vidoc kept it simple.

"You have done well," he said, circling his volunteer. "The sergeant says you are a brave soldier."

Nando beamed. His eyes were blinking rapidly, adjusting to the dark interior of the bunker. He seemed cleaner, less feral.

"Do you remember me, Fernando?"

"El Tigre," the boy said, nodding.

"That's right. Now take off your shirt."

The boy stripped off his fatigue shirt and stood again at attention. Small but muscular. The benefits of stoop work in the coffee fields. No doubt the improved diet and rigorous exercise here at the camp had increased his muscle weight. For maximum effect he should have another month of training, but there was no time for that.

"Lie down on the cot."

When Vidoc presented the syringe, the boy did not flinch.

CHAPTER EIGHTEEN

First stop was a shopping mall on the strip in Pompano Beach. Lee went to an automatic teller, used his cash card. Sara entered a clothing store alone—he said it was better they not be seen shopping together, a Hispanic male and an Anglo blonde, that was how they'd been paired on the television news.

In the clothing store Sara went directly to the discount racks, picked out a few pairs of pants, some tops, underwear, had the clerk pack it all into a canvas overnight bag. Ten minutes, tops, the quickest shopping trip of her life.

At a discount drugstore she bought a toothbrush and toothpaste. The boy behind the cash register squinted, as if she looked familiar, then shrugged as he took her money.

Outside, in the sun-blasted parking lot, she felt safer with her sunglasses on. Lee came out of the Sears carrying an armful of packages.

"Got it." He grinned. "One of these Super-eight jobs, supposed to work in low-light conditions. Built-in zoom, the works."

They put the new videocamera, extra battery pack, and tape cassettes in the trunk.

"What's this?" said Sara, holding up a smaller box.

"Shells for the Beretta."

"I thought we were going to shoot videotape?"

He shrugged, slammed the trunk lid.

"That's the idea," he said. "But you never know."

After driving west on the Tamiami for an hour or so, they veered off onto a haphazardly paved county road. Miles went by as it curved deeper into a place that seemed to be tall grass from horizon to horizon, bisected by the scratched line of the road.

Here and there little clots of trees stood up, as if gathered together for protection against the vastness of the sky.

She'd read about the Everglades, of course, seen a few nature films, but nothing had prepared her for the sheer size. And the emptiness.

Or what *appeared* to be emptiness.

Lots of critters out there, Lee insisted. Wildlife abounds. And yet she saw nothing but a few high-wheeling turkey buzzards. If this was the great Everglades, it seemed harmless and strangely arid. Now and then they would bump over a low concrete bridge and Sara would be aware of dark pooling water and a sudden explosion of green-mossed trees, but for the most part what she saw was a dry, grassy world.

"The water is under the saw grass," Lee explained. "They hold back a lot of it with a system of dikes and irrigation canals."

"Hold it back for what?"

Lee smiled. "Turn the tap in Miami Beach, that's the Everglades coming out of the faucet. Via Lake Okeechobee."

They were going to see an old man he knew, a Seminole guide. Lee seemed confident that whatever Colonel Calavera and his men were doing in the mind-numbing vastness of the Glades, Sam Darter would know about it. Sara didn't see how it was possible. This was no theme park, she could see that now, this was a world all to itself. How could one old Indian know everything about the place?

After a long interval on the county road they turned down a rough and narrow fire road, no more than a rutted trail, numbered rather than named. For long stretches the dense foliage blotted all but a glimmer of the sky.

They drove as if in a tunnel, neither talking much.

The small feathers were bright in his hands. Fingers stained to an ocher shade by nicotine, his thick nails yellowed. The older he got, the more his hands became like claws. Strong claws of the fishhawk or the kite. Harder now to work the feathers into lures, the cork poppers that drew trout from the murkiest depths of the irrigation canals. Not that he guided for trout much anymore—the bird-watchers booked most of his time now, on those days when he felt like working—but the lures still sold well to other guides, and to those anglers savvy enough to know that Seminole Sam's Special Number 3 Popper worked better than any store-bought lure.

A long-billed Miami Dolphins cap shaded his eyes. Sam had been to many games when his son was alive. Now he rarely went into the city, or anywhere beyond his river of grass. He had an airboat—two, actually, if you counted the one with the engine torn down—but he seldom used it these days. Birders preferred to be poled, and although that was tough on the arms and back and lingered in the small muscles of the leg, the silence was welcome. Sometimes he made the birders pole pack to the chickee, and usually they *liked* it, being made to work for the old Seminole guide. Go back to their homes up North and tell their friends they'd poled for the Indian when he was short of breath. Part of the adventure.

Sam smiled as he tied the feathers. He liked the funny birders. They were good people, underneath all those cameras and binoculars and bird charts. And didn't they love his gator holes! Out there supposed to be spotting thirty rare species of flying creature from woodstorks to hummingbirds, and they just went crazy for the gators. As part of his act Sam would say things like "that sack of shoe leather don't fly none, ma'am, ain't gonna sprout wings," and they would grin happily and click cameras at the bulls sunning on the mud banks or the juveniles gliding serenely through the black water, jaws slightly agape in hopeful anticipation of a nice juicy garfish.

He was thinking about garfish, how they like to float with their long, prehistoric snouts into the almost indiscernible currents of the Everglades, when he heard the chugging whine of an automobile engine. Mile or so off, coming from the east along the fire road.

No birders booked today. And tomorrow he would bring his lures out to the loop road, so it was unlikely that any of the other guides would trouble the long drive in. Six miles of ruts, take most of an hour each way, long way to come for a two-dollar popper.

Taking his time—he knew almost exactly where the automobile was from the way birds flew up from the live oaks along the fire road—he came down from the shade of the elevated porch and ambled over to a hardwood hammock that afforded a clear view of his chickee house, dock, and yard.

The hammock was an island of trees in the muddy grass, cool and dry under his feet. When the rains came and the river of grass flowed deep, it was truly an island. He stored his firewood here. Sometimes he came out to the hammock just to smell the cut wood.

Oak had a perfume all of its own, not as sweet or heady as cedar. A dry smell.

He stood camouflaged in the lushness of the lower branches, rolling an unlighted cigar in his mouth, waiting. Didn't recognize the automobile when it emerged from the fire road. Windshield covered with dust and tree sap, the left front tire low. It halted near the raised platform where he kept his dry goods locked in wire mesh, away from the marauding coons. The door opened and the driver emerged, stretching his arms, rubbing the back of his neck.

Sam grunted to himself, lighted up the cigar, and strolled out of the hammock. He was about halfway there when the woman got out of the car. Dark glasses, yellow hair, fair skin that was going to get fried if she didn't cover up or use sunscreen.

Now the man had spotted him and turned, hands shading his eyes. It was no accident that Sam was walking out of the sun. Kept strangers at a disadvantage, although this man was no stranger.

"Lee," he said, waving the cigar. "Hello, good morning, welcome."

Shaking hands was not a big thing with Seminoles. Lee, aware of that, merely nodded a greeting. "Sam Darter, this is Dr. Sara Copley."

"I'm feeling fine," Sam said with an expression of mock horror. "Why do you bring a doctor?"

He expected Lee and his woman to laugh, but the joke died like a sigh in the hot sun. The woman shifted nervously, glanced back at the car. The trouble with these white people, even the slightly less white ones like Lee Valdez, they didn't have a sense of humor. Their mirth was unpredictable.

Sam puffed his cigar.

"Come up to the porch. We'll drink cold drinks and you can tell me what's wrong."

Sara on the porch of this strange little house on stilts. In the yard below a clutter of rusted machine parts, corroded drums, and a narrow, muddy creek with a rickety-looking dock. Pulled into the tall grass, possibly abandoned, was a strange craft with a giant propeller mounted in the back, enclosed by a mesh cage.

An airboat—she'd seen a few zooming along beside the turnpike, tourist rides touted on billboards that blared SEE THE FLORIDA

GATOR! Sam's airboat looked to be settling deeply into vegetation, just another chunk of rusted machinery.

Sara didn't see how this sweet, gentle old man with the arthritic fingers could be of any help to them. Sam knew nothing of their situation until Lee laid it all out, because he did not have a television set and saw newspapers only on the days he drove into the town of Everglades City to pick up supplies.

"This man Calavera is a bad *hombre*, that what you say?"

"That's what we're saying," Lee said. "He sent a man to kill Sara."

"What happened?"

"What happened is she whacked him with a soap bottle, then kicked him in the head."

Sam looked at her, really looked at her, and nodded his approval. Sara, resting in the heavy shade of the porch, noticed that she was beginning to pick out more details in the sun-drenched landscape. The creek, she realized, was not simply muddy but dark, like overbrewed tea. In the thick-bladed grass at the edge was a short green heron. Now and then the bird would stab its beak into the dark water and withdraw so quickly not a ripple was disturbed. A little distance away was another of those strange tree islands that dotted the horizon. Was that where old Sam had come from when they arrived? Now she noticed the profusion of air plants that sprayed leaf and bloom from the upper branches of the trees, contributing to the impenetrability of the foliage.

It was all very . . . different. Hard to believe they were only a few hours out of Miami. Seemed more like centuries, as if they had traveled against the grain of time. Odd, very odd. And the oddest thing of all was that she felt strangely at peace here. As if she could sit in the shade of this porch forever, and never have to utter another word. Let the two men jabber. She, like the small green heron, would blend into the landscape.

"Any of the old military bases active in the Glades?" Lee asked. They were drinking strong, cold tea from sweating mason jars. "Any place the colonel might set up a mercenary training camp?"

Sam thought about it, shook his head. "No. Not in the Glades. One or two places where they land cargo planes. Crazy bush pilots, they come in on their bellies, no gear down. Unload all the dope and just abandon the aircraft."

Lee looked pained. He didn't want to admit they'd come all this way for nothing.

"Now up Big Cypress country, that's different," Sam said. "Couple prime spots up there. First is a regular base, where the National Guard trains. Big party for the boys every summer, they make enough noise to frighten away game for ten miles round."

Lee perked up, glanced at Sara, who was sitting back in an old wicker rocking chair, her hair tied up in a bun to keep it off the back of her neck.

"'Nother camp further on," Sam continued, "out that swampy way they call the Devil's Garden."

There was something about the way he named the place that focused Sara's attention. A tone of voice that implied not just a geographical location, but a way of life.

"Old airfield in there, where they brought in supplies for that Bay of Pigs things," Sam said. He leaned back in his chair and thought about it some more. He shared with Lee the capacity for maintaining a silence, waiting for the reservoir to fill before he spoke again. "U.S. Air Force hired me and my airboat to ferry generals in and out. Could have gone by chopper, but they wanted to ride, I guess. One 'a them generals tried to shoot up a gator hole with a submachine gun"—he smiled faintly at the memory—"he blowed himself right off the boat. I had to gaff 'im up out of the mud."

There was a long pause, his eyes crinkled happily around the edges. "He wasn't much pleased, that Air Force general. Never hit one gator."

Lee was up on his feet. That was it. Had to be! An old Bay of Pigs training site would be perfect for the colonel. He'd been involved in the original invasion scheme; it was likely he'd return to familiar territory.

"How do we get there?" he demanded. "Is it accessible by road or do they fly in?"

"Can I ask a question here?" Sam wanted to know. "What are your intentions, you do locate this man?"

"Well," Lee said, glancing at Sara. "What we'd like to do, we'd like to make a movie."

A considerable silence ensued. Sam just looked at them and shook his head. "Know what, Lee?" he said after a while. "Guess I always did know you was loco."

CHAPTER NINETEEN

Bunny was an interesting guy, for an Anglo. Ask him how he came by the name, he gets this funny smile on his pudgy face. Puts two fingers up on each side of his head, mocking rabbit ears, and he goes, "I'm an animal lover, I fuck bunny rabbits."

You had to love a guy with a sense of humor. A guy who saw things from the same angle as Luto. Like the point of life was extracting maximum pleasure. Also, he shared with Bunny the belief that guys who really and truly understood the pleasure principle were special. They could do special things, forget about the rules.

The other idea he and Bunny had was that nothing you ever did was wrong unless you got caught, and then the wrong part was *getting* caught.

Most people were too stupid to understand. That was yet another thing they shared, the belief that just about all other human beings were stupid and deserved whatever happened when the pleasure principle was being demonstrated.

You met a special individual like Bunny, you didn't let him go.

"This morning I get bailed," Luto told him.

Bunny wagged his rabbit ears, letting on he didn't care if Luto got bailed or not.

"Thing is, you coming with me."

"Cost you five hundred. Caught me flag grunt, an' I ain't got the cash."

"Not me. The colonel's lawyer."

"Who this colonel you keep braggin' on?" Bunny wanted to know. "Colonel Sanders? Guy who fucked all them chickens?"

"My colonel very big man in Miami," Luto said, knowing he should be indignant but flashing on an image of Colonel Sanders in the act, old goat-faced dude in a white suit mounting a chicken. "Very important. He owns Cuban newspapers, radio stations, motels."

Bunny looked interested. The icy blue in his eyes warmed up a shade. "Man, I always wanted to meet Castro, you know? Shove that big cigar right up his butt, light him off."

Luto couldn't help it, he giggled. This guy was seriously funny. "The colonel give you big reward, you do that, Bunny. He *hate* Castro. I hate Castro, too. He put me in stinking jail."

"Yeah? What'd you do?" Bunny asked.

"Nothing, man, I never do nothing."

Bunny gave him a little poke in the ribs. They both knew that Luto's idea of "nothing" was really something pretty special. Reserved for those few who understood the pleasure principle.

"I get you out, you'll help me, right?"

"What kind of help we talking here? Walk you across the street? Help you with your homework, what?"

Bunny with that bad-toothed grin, those unreal blue eyes.

"Help me find a guy," Luto said.

"Let me guess. The guy who smacked you in the head and put you inside here. Or was it really the bitch who kicked you, huh? It was the bitch, right?"

That was another thing Luto liked about Bunny. He could fill in the details. You didn't have to tell him every little thing.

Luto and Bunny on the Calle Ocho a few minutes after noon. Bunny would get this impish look and say, "I get it, man, you kidnapped me. We're in Cuba, right? Fidel's in one of these greasy little restaurants, right? No, no, that's him over there playing dominoes."

Bunny was such a cutup. The colonel's lawyer hadn't been eager to post the bail, but Luto made it clear that Bunny was not a problem, he was part of the solution.

"He a special type of person," Luto had insisted, and the lawyer, squinting that lawyer-type squint, had said he could see that Mr. Burkus was a unique individual all right.

Now here they were in the heart of Little Havana, doing these unique, individual things. Like Bunny funning with a couple of elderly tourists, a paunchy Anglo dude and his silver-haired wife. Bunny goes up to the old bitch, says, 'Scuze me, mam, you dropped this, and hands her an old scum bag he'd peeled from the gutter. Says, Way to go, Pops! and salutes the husband.

Leave 'em quakin', that was Bunny's motto. Do the unexpected. Never apologize. Share and share alike. Get it while the gettin's good.

Bunny had a lot of handy mottoes.

"Got a notion," he said, sailing down Eighth Street with his pale white gut hanging over a wide leather belt, faded Wrangler blue jeans dragging low enough so the crack of his butt showed, not that he cared, "less you an' me get us some greaser hose."

"Hose?" Luto had a good ear for American, but Bunny did things with words he'd never heard before.

"Hose. Bitches who do it for money."

"Ah," said Luto, comprehending, "*putas*. No *putas* on Calle Ocho, man. Not this time of day."

Bunny gave him a look, like who was he kidding?, but Luto didn't want to get distracted here. They had a mission.

They wandered into several *botánicas* before locating the place now owned by Mercedes Raimez. Bunny just loved the little plastic saints that crowded the shelves. Wasn't aware that you-all prayed at dolls, he drawled to one startled shopkeeper, kin I get me one a' them inflatable-type saints? The kind never say no on the first date? The shopkeeper shooing them out of the store as Luto broke up, giggles coming like hiccups.

"That smell," Bunny said, referring to the cloying odor of incense familiar to all *botánicas*, "my granny had a girdle smelled like that. Old lady smelled so bad, one time I pushed her down the stairs."

"Push *yaya* down stairs, man? You really do that?"

"Hey, like I said, she smelled really bad."

They strolled along the sidewalk, side by side, cutting a pretty wide swath on the Calle Ocho. More than a few citizens crossing the street to avoid Luto, who was well-known. Luto saying, "So what happen, man?"

"What happen when?"

"When you push Gramma down stairs, man. What happen?"

Bunny turning those pale blue eyes to him, saying, "Nothing. Except, you know, she bounced."

Something told Luto not to push the grandmother thing any further. Let Bunny have his joke and leave it go.

A bell tinkled as they entered the last *botánica*. Bunny made a playful swipe at the bell and accidentally knocked it loose. The bell hit the floor and rolled, a tinkle fading under the counter like a cat's toy lost in the dust balls. The shop was dim, and the first thing Luto noticed was the glow of a cigarette. Then a husky female voice hectoring him in rapid, precise Spanish. Who was he, what did he want? The betting shop was on the next block, go away.

"Señorita Raimez?" Luto said sweetly.

He moved forward until she had a clear look at his face. Mercedes recognized him. The expression of displeasure was replaced by caution, uncertainty.

"I know you," she said. Watching Bunny as he ran his pudgy hands over a display of altar candles, flicking the wicks as if he were shooing flies. "You work for the *padrino* sometimes."

"For the colonel, yes," Luto said. Casually he'd worked himself up close to the counter. Mercedes sat perched on a tall stool. She'd put the cigarette in a brass ashtray on the counter. Luto picked it up, took a puff, smiled. "You're a pretty lady, Mercedes."

"Ask her she got any inflatables," Bunny said. He was checking out a brown-skinned Baby Jesus, tickling under its chin.

"What do you want?" Mercedes asked. Holding herself pretty rigid on the stool, but Luto noticed that her eyes flicked at the beaded curtain behind her. Back room in there, maybe an exit to the alley.

"Colonel say you know about Valdez and the *rubia*."

She shook her head. Heels braced on the lower rung of the stool. Luto figured she was getting up the nerve to bolt.

"Come on, Mercedes. The cop and his girlfriend. You talk to the brother, right? What did he tell you?"

There, she was off the stool, slipping through the shimmering beads. Exactly the move he expected. Luto caught her inside the back room, yanked her by the hair. Heel came off one shoe, and already there were tears in her eyes.

Bunny right there. Quick on his feet when it counted. "I locked the front door," he said. "We're closed in here."

Mercedes weeping quietly. She knew about Luto, his errands for the colonel.

"Relax, Mama," he said to her in American. "We're having fun."

She closed her eyes. Mascara running. Luto knelt down, tickled the side of her face. "Peekaboo," he said. Got her to open up those big brown eyes, but he noticed she wouldn't look at Bunny. Big guy like that, she pretended he wasn't in the room.

"All you gotta do, tell me where Valdez is hiding, then we go."

She was babbling quietly. *Padrino* this, *padrino* that, finally Bunny says, "Hey, who is this *padrino* dude. I thought you worked for Colonel Sanders, the chicken man."

"She call him *padrino* it's okay. Means like godfather."

"No shit? Hey, I love it."

Bunny had found a dress hanging on a hook. A dark green spangled thing with lots of ruffles. He was holding it over his belly, modeling it, blinking his fat blue eyes. "Waddaya think, Lute? My style?"

Luto giggling. He reached up behind Mercedes, knotted his fingers in her hair, pulled tight. "Hey, Mercedes? Be nice."

When she'd cried herself dry, the serious fun started.

CHAPTER TWENTY

They unloaded the video gear and covered Lee's car with a rust-stained tarpaulin. He didn't think air surveillance was likely, certainly not from the Metro-Dade Police, but you couldn't be too careful. For all Lee knew, the colonel had access to satellite photographs. Their unauthorized computer search had triggered an alarm somewhere, hadn't it? Better to take precautions.

"They'll assume we're on the run," he said, tugging an ear of the tarp down and weighting it with a chunk of iron. "If they're serious about locating us, they'll be checking the airports, the bus and ship terminals. State cops will have the plate number by now. Metro-Dade will just go through the motions. Nobody on the force is going to be enthusiastic about bringing in a brother cop, no matter *what* kind of strings are being pulled at the top."

"So you think we're safe here?" Sara asked. Sam had given her a baseball cap to wear, and she tugged it down, drawing the shade line across her eyes.

"For now."

Sara went back to the porch while Lee helped Sam with the airboat. She couldn't believe they'd ever get it out of the weeds, let alone running. But there must have been a thin layer of water under the saw grass, because when Lee pushed, the hull skittered sideways. With the two of them glomping through the mud, the boat was soon positioned in the creek next to the dock. Sam uncoiled a hose, ran it down to the boat. Lee held the nozzle in the tank while Sam turned the pump handle atop a fifty-five-gallon drum.

Soon the smell of gasoline drifted up to the porch. Sam pumped the drum dry, moved the apparatus to another drum, pumped that dry, too. Big engine tied to that prop. Must burn a lot of fuel, if they ever managed to get it going.

Men and their noisy toys.

It started on the first try. Amazing. And it had the smooth and steady purring of a well-maintained engine. When the old Indian engaged the prop, the airboat glided away, heading purposefully off through the sea of grass, over water she could not see, had not even suspected was there. Lee stood at the dock with his hands on his hips, watching until his friend was a speck on the horizon.

The effortless launching of the boat was the first indication that things were not quite what they seemed at the Sam Darter homestead.

Sara would discover that the chickee was surprisingly functional, though lacking indoor plumbing and electricity. A compact little stove and refrigerator ran off propane tanks periodically trucked in. The interior was lighted by a combination of kerosene and propane lanterns, several of which came on at the flick of a switch, just like the real thing. She had to keep reminding herself that it *was* the real thing—just a different version. After all, her own grandmother, a Vermont farm girl, had grown up under conditions not so very different—although it was true, Gramma hadn't lived in a house on stilts.

Lee came back up to the porch, sat down beside her.

"How long will it take him?" she asked.

"Be back tomorrow morning."

"Maybe we should have gone along for the ride."

Lee shook his head. "Sam said no. Indian guide alone in an airboat won't attract much attention. Part of the landscape, really. He can check it out in daylight. If the camp is being used, I'll go up under cover of darkness, get situated."

"*You'll* go up? You mean *we'll* go up."

"We'll discuss that later."

Sara let it go. They would indeed discuss it later. Lee, making peace, went inside and emerged with two small miracles. Cold bottles of beer.

"You probably hate it here, out in the middle of nowhere."

Sara held the sweating bottle against her forehead.

"I think I like it," she said, looking around, trying to spot the little green heron. "How did you get to know Sam?"

"His son, Tommy."

"I didn't know he had a son."

"Doesn't anymore. Tommy got himself in trouble with a posse of Jamaican drug runners up in Opa-Locka. He was a pilot, and they killed him."

"Oh," Sara said. What else could you say to news like that?

"For quite a while he was just missing. Sam would drive into the city once a week, check with me at the office. Got so it broke my heart to see him come in the door. Finally I was able to match up some remains with a dental chart. Helped him with the paperwork so he could collect the body."

"So he feels he owes you a favor?"

Lee shook his head. "We're just friends. I used to fish with him. Now a couple times a year we visit. Just sit here on the porch and visit."

"And nobody knows we're here?"

He stared out at the creek, the island of trees, the river of grass beyond. "How could they?" he said.

The first time she heard the sound Sara thought a truck with a broken muffler had pulled into the yard below. Then she heard it again and she thought, That's not a motor sound. No way.

Lee was smiling at her. "Bull gator," he said. "Makes quite a racket, huh?"

The roar filled the twilight. Not so much loud as taking up space, defining territory.

"I never heard anything like it," she said. "Is he, um, close?"

"Not too far," Lee said. "Don't worry, they don't climb steps."

They'd made a simple dinner out of canned goods. Three-bean salad, tinned salmon. Lettuce would have been nice, but Sam didn't have any lettuce. The cold salmon salad was fine, more than enough. Neither of them much hungry. Lee popped the lid on a can marked FLOUR and produced Oreo cookies for dessert. "Served only in the finest Seminole restaurants," he said.

Oreos and beer. Sara found the combination interesting. Everything was a new experience out here in the wilderness. The chickee, old Sam, the sound effects, and now the way Lee was looking at her. She hadn't realized it until last night, but for months part of her had been closed off, dead.

Now the yearning was alive again, ready to be ignited.

"What's going to happen to us?" she said.

Lee stared out through the screening.

"We'll be okay. Get something solid for the newspaper, maybe they'll break this wide open."

"Not that," she said. "Us."

Lee nodded. He knew what she was really talking about.

"Tell you the truth, I don't know what scares me more. Being on a hit list or falling in love with you."

"Maybe you better think about it."

He grinned. "I'm thinking."

They kissed, Lee's hands riding light on her hips.

"We better clear the table, wash up."

Lee worked the pump handle while she scraped and washed the dishes. After the dishes were put away, they went out to the porch again and he smoked a cigarette and stared off into the lingering twilight, in the direction Sam had taken.

"What's the colonel doing out there, Lee?"

"Wish I knew," he said.

She slipped her arms around his slim waist. Rested her chin on his shoulder. It was kind of neat, making love to a man who was almost exactly her size.

"Not much to do out here at night," he said.

"Oh, I don't know about that," she said, slipping her hands inside his shirt. "We'll think of something."

This time they made love hastily, eager to be unclothed, to touch and probe. Afterward they lay slightly apart, not quite touching.

Sara was aware of his heat. She could feel him thinking.

"Lee?"

His hand slipped into hers, traced a shape on her palm.

"I was thinking about my brother, Ricky," he said. "When we were little, sometimes we would camp out on the roof of the apartment building. Tell each other scary stories. Then run inside where it was safe."

"You don't really hate him, do you?"

He brought her hand up to his lips, kissed her fingers.

"Right now I don't feel like I could hate anybody. We get back, maybe I'll take you to see him. Not one of his crazy ceremonies, I'm not ready for that. Just dinner. A family dinner. Then maybe I'll show you the *real* Calle Ocho."

"I'd like that."

Sara settled her head against the bare flesh of his chest. She could feel his heart, steady and strong. His fingers stroked gently through her hair. When the gator roared in the night, neither of them reacted.

CHAPTER TWENTY-ONE

Night birds screeching in the swamp. So it must be night. Hard to tell, for the darkness lingers here in the concrete cavern.

Sensations: The can't move, the can't speak, the closing in. The fear that has begun to uncoil, poised like a rattlesnake ready to strike.

A soft nimbus of light approaches, glowing behind a thin green curtain. The snake of fear shivers. The pale tiger is returning to the lair.

Vidoc in the bunker, checking on his volunteers, holding his lantern aloft. Seven cots separated by cheap curtains. Your back-to-the-basics clinic. Another selling point to the guerrillas—no modern facilities required. The units can be manufactured anywhere. Cave, root cellar, peasant hut, it didn't matter. Supplied with the Vidoc Field Kit, anyone with rudimentary medical training can make it happen. Nurse, medic, local witch doctor. Anyone.

Of course, it helped to have a certain bedside manner.

Vidoc opened a curtain, looked in on the boy Fernando. Lying there rigidly immobile on the cot. At this stage he was still able to move his eyes a little. Look how they followed the lantern.

Vidoc settled himself on a canvas camp stool, placed the lantern on the floor beside the cot. Whether or not the boy understood his formal Spanish was almost beside the point. The right tone would suffice.

The idea here was to create a thrum of fear so deeply felt that it resonated through the psyche.

"Let me tell you what will happen," Vidoc said. "You have been injected with a neurotoxin, a poison. Do you understand poison? This poison makes it impossible for you to move. And yet you can hear, see, feel. The injections will continue over the next thirty-six hours. At each stage another layer will be unpeeled. Already you have lost the ability to act for yourself. Next to go will be your very identity."

Vidoc withdrew a syringe from his field kit. He drew the cold needle across the boy's brow. The point left a line in his flesh but did not draw blood.

"First I peel away your flesh," he said. "Then your muscle, then your bones. All of you will be stripped away."

He prepared the syringe, drawing the clear fluid of his base solution into the cylinder. Squeezing a glistening drop from the point of the needle, he held it up to the underglow of the lantern.

"Here we go," he said, and eased the needle into the boy's vein. Heartbeat was slowing gradually, metabolism was chilling out.

"Going, going, gone," he said, pressing the plunger home.

With the nervous system shorted out, mind and body became truly separate, vulnerable to all kinds of interactive stimuli. At this stage simple isolation would produce the desired effect. Leave a man alone in the dark for a few days, totally paralyzed, and the personality will unravel like a badly tied knot.

Of course, a little interaction helped.

"Nando is gone, extinguished," Vidoc said, as if explaining to a small child. "Nothing of him remains. From that nothing we will make a unit. A killing machine. And to make sure that the boy called Nando has been completely eradicated, we're going to remove his fingerprints."

The bottle of acid was not part of the field kit. Print eradication was no longer necessary—who cared what happened to a few anonymous peasant boys? No, taking fingerprints was his own variation on the theme. A personal touch.

"This is phosphoric acid," he said, holding up the bottle. "You'll notice it smells rather like strong garlic. Very handy stuff. In weak solution it gives a tang to soda pop. At this strength it does a very adequate job of dissolving human flesh. Give me your hand, I'll demonstrate."

Vidoc unfolded the boy's limp fingers. He lifted the dropper from the bottle.

"You'll feel an astonishing rush of pain. Truly astonishing."

He squeezed the dropper. A clear, viscous fluid emerged,

oozing over the exposed fingertip. After a moment bubbles rose through the fluid, and the flesh underneath began to blur.

"The sharp odor, stronger than the stink of garlic, is your skin burning away," Vidoc explained pleasantly. "Now nothing whatever remains of you. Nothing but the pain and the anger."

He applied drops of acid to all ten digits. Wisps of vapor rose like smoke from the boy's fingertips. Vidoc raised the lantern, checked out the unit's open eyes. Looking pretty empty in there. That was good. To make a good unit, you had to start with nothing and build from there. Fill in the blank.

Wind the killing spring.

"I'll be back," he whispered, and slipped through the curtains to the next cot.

There were lights on in the Winnebago. The Airstream was dark, but the air-conditioning unit was rattling away, so it was safe to assume the trailer was occupied.

Sam kept his distance. He remembered the camp as it had been in the old days. The airfield was new then; a couple of thousand eager exiles had been camped in tents along its edge. Convinced they could take back their homeland by an act of crazy courage. Now all that remained was a leaky barracks building.

Only one guard was posted outside the barracks, and he had no awareness, could not read the night shapes well enough to know that someone was out there. Be a simple thing to slip up behind, slit his throat. If a man wanted to do such a thing, which Sam didn't. But he could have. And that meant the men who ran this place did not feel threatened. Did not expect or fear any nocturnal visitors.

In the darkness Sam smiled. Maybe this wasn't going to be so hard after all.

CHAPTER TWENTY-TWO

Luto and Bunny on the two-lane Tamiami Trail. Breaking eighty in the Trans-Am. Luto driving. Bunny saying that was okay, he never drove wheels he wasn't stealing. What was the fun in that? Lights came at them, an air horn sounded. Wa-ooooooo! Big tractor rig, heading east to Miami, didn't like the way Luto was crowding the center line.

"Fucking trucks!" Luto said.

He screamed out the window as the headlights flashed by.

Bunny waited until he'd settled down. Crazy little Cuban had a way of bouncing around in the seat, very excitable, you didn't want him to let go the wheel.

"You sure you know where this place is?" he said.

"Told you, man, I been there."

"Yeah, but can you find it again?" Bunny having a little fun here, getting under Luto's skin.

"Watch me, man."

Luto stepping on the gas, pushing the Trans-Am up to ninety-five. What was that Chuck Berry song about the car going ninety-five? Bunny bounced in his seat, shoving his weight against the door. Boom, boom, making the car rock.

"Hey, what you doin', man?"

"Rockin' and rollin' from side to side," Bunny said. "You ever hear that tune?"

Luto didn't think he had.

CHAPTER TWENTY-THREE

Monday, October 9

Sara woke up to the smell of coffee. Aware of Lee in the small kitchen area, making breakfast sounds. Thin, pale light filtered in through the uncurtained windows. Barely dawn.

She sat up, put her hands around the mug of coffee as he knelt down.

"Better get dressed," Lee suggested. "Sam will be back in a few minutes."

How did he knew that? Then she heard it, a background noise becoming more distinct. The airboat. She didn't try to mask her disappointment.

"Yeah, I know," Lee sighed. "Reality intrudes. Why can't it stay the way it is? Just you and me. That what you're thinking?"

"That's what I'm thinking."

Sara pulled on a pair of jeans and a long-sleeved blouse, took her mug of coffee out to the porch. Below in the creek the airboat was gliding up to the dock. She waved. Sam lifted his hand in greeting. In the dim light of dawn she couldn't read anything in his expression.

The smell of cooking bacon wafted onto the porch. By the time Sam climbed the steps, cap in hand, Lee was bringing out a huge platter of scrambled eggs, grits, and thick, salty bacon. Sara, not usually a big eater in the morning, dug right in, loading her plate.

"Coffee?"

"Please."

Just beyond the screened porch the swamp was coming to life, birds screaming and bickering in the hardwood hammock and along the creek. Good morning, Everglades, not a place for late sleeping.

"Now you're off the force," Sam observed, "you can open that restaurant. Lee's Grill. Or was it the Valdez Grill, keep it simple."

Lee grimaced. He sipped coffee, pushed his food around the plate, waiting for Sam to finish eating so he could report. Finally the old man patted his lips with the back of his hand and leaned back in his chair. Black hair without a trace of gray in contrast to the finely detailed map of wrinkles on his face. The sun was rising at his back, hot and blood red, which made his expression more impenetrable than ever.

"Place ain't what it used to be," he said. "Lot of the old buildings been torn down. Airfield is all growed over. All they got now, one barracks with a tin roof an' open sides, little bit of wispy mosquito netting. Thirty or so men in the barracks. Quite a few no more than boys. Looks like a boot camp."

"Guerrilla training?"

Sam shrugged. "Could be, I guess."

"Calavera?"

"Now I didn't knock on the door, but there *was* this very plush Airstream parked there. And a gold Coupe Deville an' also this gold-colored limousine, a Mercedes, I believe it was. All of 'em with Dade County plates."

Lee turned eagerly to Sara. "He's there. Got to be him."

"This other fella you mention," Sam said. "The tall man with no hair. Didn't see him, least not in the barracks."

Sam finished his coffee, returned the cup to the table with a delicate move.

"Not a big army up there," he said. "Not a real army at all. Stay undercover, keep your head down, I think you'll be okay."

Sara had expected an argument from Sam when he heard she was coming along. To the contrary, he seemed to think it was a good idea.

"Can't leave the lady here unattended," he commented. Then, after a longish pause: "Never know who might stumble in."

Sara immediately flashed on Luto. Who, Lee was convinced, would soon be out on bail. Could he track them this far? It didn't seem possible. But why chance it? She shuddered at an image of the scrawny little killer clawing his way through the screens, pressing a gun to her head, running his intrusive hands over her body.

"We better gas up," said Lee, rising from the table.

* * *

"What we're doing out here," said Sam, handing her a pair of binoculars, "we're bird-watching, okay?"

The idea was, they'd be Audubon types who'd hired Seminole Sam to guide them. Nothing more natural than for birders to be up in the Big Cypress, using long-range lenses and video equipment.

The old man had set up an itinerary, checking out nesting areas along the way.

A few miles or so from the chickee he shut off the engine. The prop made a whooshing noise, then slowed to a stop. The relative silence was stunning. Into the quiet came the small, bright sounds of the great swamp: birds, bugs, the soft lap of water.

Sam got out his fiberglass pole, began pushing the airboat. They had crossed a wide area of grass he called the "prairie" and were approaching a thick cluster of cypress trees. Shrouded with moss, vine, and strangler fig, the trees seemed to be caught in the throes of an ancient struggle, as if tearing themselves free of the clinging earth.

"Swamp area here," Sam announced, his breath coming deep and regular as he pushed the pole.

Lee explained that they were crossing from the Glades into the Big Cypress Swamp.

Sara gathered that it was not, as she had pictured, one vase steaming swamp, but numerous swamps separated by "prairie" and pine slash and willow clusters or "heads," quite a varied landscape. Unlike the Everglades, the Big Cypress was not a designated park but only a preserve, afforded some protection from further development. The ambiguous status made the wilderness useful for quasi-legal or covert activity. Mercenary training on abandoned military camps, smuggling operations, game poaching, and the like.

The boat picked up speed. Not because Sam was pushing harder, but because the water was suddenly deeper, less choked with saw grass. Sara ducked under a looming branch, felt the eerie brush of damp moss trailing over her back.

They were entering a kind of lagoon enclosed by the thick cypress, barely open to the sky.

"Lettuce lake," Sam announced. "Should be ibis in here, maybe a wood stork."

The "lettuce" he referred to was a lilylike plant that seemed to cover every inch of the water, forming the illusion of a flat green meadow. Looked as if you could get out and walk. Until you saw the deep black water under the leaves.

A white object swooped very near. Sara instinctively ducked.

"Yup," Sam said. "Ibis."

The large white birds sat perched like huge feathered ornaments on a mossy Christmas tree. Long, impudently curved beaks, wing tips dipped in black, the ibis had an ancient stillness that was interrupted only in that instant when they launched into flight, gliding low over the water and rising to unhurried wingbeats to claim another perch. The birds did not seem very disturbed by the intrusion of human visitors.

"Used to me," Sam said. "See that stump, where it's broke off? Red shoulder hawk."

Sara had to squint and concentrate before she could discern the hawk blending into the stump. Lee touched her and said, "Beautiful in here, huh?"

"In an eerie way, yes."

There was a steamy, primeval quality to the place that made her think they had somehow crossed to the other side of history. This was the soup where life began, where the first creature dared to crawl from the slime and sun itself on that very stump where the bold hawk glared with one glittering eye, the other hooded in a timeless wink.

"Know what?" said Sara, glancing around the quiet lagoon. "I sort of expected to see alligators."

Both men laughed.

"What?" she said. "What?"

Sam looked at Lee and Lee nodded. Then Sam cupped his hands around his mouth. A deep, clicking roar emerged from his throat. It was a fair approximation of the bull gator they'd heard the night before. The leaves seemed to quiver.

Most remarkable, several logs were loosened from the mudbank and slipped into the water.

Wait a second, logs?

"Alligators," Sara said, feeling embarrassed.

How had she missed them? Now that they were moving, she could see four, ten, more than a dozen. At the same time a glistening stump began to glide, cutting a wake through the layer of water lettuce within spitting distance of the boat. The stump was a snout, and there were others.

They were *surrounded* by gators.

"Is it dangerous?" she said. "What if you fell in?"

Sam shrugged. "Those gators used to eating garfish or turtle or snail. You a pretty big package. Better if you stay in the boat, though."

No problem. New rules to live by. Stay in the boat, do not swim, restrain the impulse to trail fingers over the side, probing the dark mirror under the leaves.

"We push on through here," said Sam, hefting the pole. "Keep to cover. Had plenty of rain this season, so there's water most of the way. Come a time, though, we have to get out and walk."

Oh boy, Sara thought, what fun.

Old Sam had a rhythm, a way of poling the boat mile after mile that did not seem to exhaust his energy. Maybe it was the way he breathed. Opening his mouth, inhaling deep and slow. Then expelling air through his nose as the pole plunged into the water, found bottom, propelled them forward.

Lee offered to help, but Sam shook his head. He was fine.

"If we had a canoe, we could all paddle," Sara suggested.

Lee nodded. "Yeah, but if we have to get away quick, we'll be glad of the airboat. Right, Sam?"

Sam nodded, pushed on the pole. The sun was high overhead, bleeding through the foliage. Sara was starting to be able to see things. Small shy birds that blended into leaf and branch. Water snakes that moved so effortlessly they were almost invisible. Air plants that were not, as Sam had explained, part of the tree, but independent cascades of leaf and blossom.

She now knew to look for alligator flag, a leafy water lily that often marked a solution hole—a deep depression in the limestone carved out by the weak acid of decaying vegetation, frequently occupied by one or more gators.

"They back strong," Sam said when a half-dozen of the lumbering beasts plodded into the water and became, just like that, graceful creatures. "Time back, I had me only a few secret locations, show off them gators. Places the poachers couldn't get to."

"What happened?"

"Stop killin' 'em, they come back strong."

"Simple as that?"

Sam nodded.

It was clear to Sara that Lee shared Sam's reverence for the backcountry. The worry lines had eased from around his eyes, and though it was almost oppressively hot and muggy, he seemed infused with energy. His newly formed optimism was catching. They would find the camp, tape the colonel in action—whatever mercenary operation he was preparing—and go public. It was comforting to believe that nobody, not even the colonel, would dare to harm them once the truth was known.

A plaintive wail split the air, echoed among the cypress trees.

Sara was instantly alert. The cry was almost, but not quite, human.

"Limpkin bird," Sam said.

Sara breathed again.

"Hey, relax," Lee said in a low voice, hands kneading the stiffness from her shoulders. "We're safe here. Sam'll keep us safe."

Still, she wondered. A cry half-human. It made you think.

CHAPTER TWENTY-FOUR

Bunny was sound asleep on the hood of the Trans-Am as the hot ball of the sun edged over the bulrushes. He was snoring like a chain saw, almost as loud as the damned birds.

He'd climbed out there when they came to the end of yet another dead-end road, unable to find the right path into the fucking colonel's fucking camp, and he'd announced, very firmly, Lute honey, shut it off, we waitin' for sunrise.

Luto had slept in the backseat, the keys in his pocket. Not that he didn't trust Bunny. The man had, after all, been raised in Everglades City, he knew the big swamp. And it *had* been getting sort of spooky, driving down long rutted roads into the black heart of nowhere. Luto fighting that panicky feeling, agreeing that yes, it would be a very bad idea to run out of gas in this particular part of the world.

"We get hungry, I'll hoot up a gator," Bunny had offered before falling asleep on the warm hood. "Or we can skin out a snake. Say it taste like chicken, which is a lie. Snake taste like snake."

Luto believed him. No way was he eating snake. See a snake, you kill it quick, chop off the head, maybe use it as a charm. Forget eating the damn thing. Might grow the head back, eat you from inside the belly.

"Hey, Bunny?"

The snore choked off. The big man groaned, turned on his side, aimed those flat blue eyes through the bug-spattered windshield.

"Lute honey, what's for breakfast?"

Luto had been saving a Snickers bar in the glove compartment.

It was soft with the heat, but Bunny peeled the wrapper and slurped at it like an ice-cream cone. Chocolate sticking to his bad teeth. He had a crafty look.

"You think that bitch tell us true?"

"You hear her, man. She talk to Valdez's brother Enrique. And he tell her he's afraid his crazy brother is going after the colonel, *mano a mano*. So we go there and wait, maybe they come right to us. The colonel, he give us a lotta money, we do the cop and the girl."

"Know what I think?" said Bunny, licking his plump fingers. "All you greasers are crazy."

"Hey, man."

"Easy, Lute honey." Bunny closed his eyes as he sucked up the last of the melted Snickers bar. Mmmm good. "I *like* crazy. It my favorite thing in all the world."

Vidoc's outfit for today was baggy camouflage fatigues, camouflage hat, mirrored shades, combat boots. An appropriate costume, he decided, for a hot morning in the last real swamp wilderness in North America.

The colonel, decked out in full uniform, was here to see the volunteers.

"'Morning, Emile."

Vidoc pushed open the bunker door. The colonel stepped inside, squinting in the relative dark. Vidoc pulled aside the curtain, and the colonel impassively examined the seven cots, the seven bodies. He did not recognize the boy Fernando, had indeed forgotten that such a thing existed.

"I've been told the Bolivian commandos arrive later today," Vidoc said.

"Are you ready?"

"Of course. But I would like to begin with a teaser, if you agree."

"Teaser? I don't understand."

"For the commandos. A little surprise, soon as they get here. It will help set the tone."

"Oh?" The colonel slipped his thumbs in the belt of his holster, wiggled to loosen up. "What exactly did you have in mind?"

Light on the green curtain. Not a lantern this time. Shaft of daylight sneaking in through a slit in the bunker wall.

Concentrate. Find the name.

Small boy in a mountain village. In the fields picking coffee beans, they called him something. What was it? Who was that boy?

Trapped. All that is left of the boy in the field are random thoughts inside a husk. An awareness of pain. Hot pain, lingering in the fingertips. Who was the boy? What was his name?

Long silhouette on the green curtain. Him.

Fear.

Fear is the name.

The colonel, busy with his own preparations—the commandos would expect a welcoming meal—left Vidoc hovering at the head of the seventh cot.

He unzipped his field kit.

"We're going to have a busy day," he announced, in English. Wanting the boy to hear the tone but not the substance.

Vidoc settled onto the camp stool. He drew clear fluid into a syringe, slipped it into the soft spot on the inside of Nando's arm.

Found the vein, plunged it home.

"We're pushing the edge," he said softly, observing a red drop climb back into the cylinder. Evidence that blood pressure wasn't totally flat. "We're going for it. Make you into a unit in record time, if your heart doesn't stop."

He withdrew the needle. "But you've got a nice strong heart," he said soothingly. Soothing himself. "Right? Heart of a soldier, a born commando. Wouldn't dream of stopping. You'll be fine. You'll be . . . perfect."

This was by no means a certainty. Vidoc had never used so much of the neurotoxin in so short a time. This unit was positively *drenched* with the stuff. Couple more days and it would expire from liver and kidney failure, even if the cardiovascular system didn't collapse. But of course it didn't have a few more days. Hours was more like it. Vidoc used a stethoscope and satisfied himself that the boy's heart would last as long as required.

"You'll be the tease," he said, nodding to himself. "Get their attention. The commandos are going to *love* you."

From his field kit he removed a subcutaneous-medication pump. It was a simple procedure to wire the little package to the radio-control device. Neat and simple.

Vidoc believed that genius was, by definition, a profound

understanding of simplicity. Peel away all the complications, strip off the badly glued veneer of so-called morality, under it all, untouched, was the naked force of pure genius. The creation-destruction cycle, the snake god eating its own tail.

Tap into that cycle, and you were elevated to the next stage of evolution. The way Shakespeare turned the language inside out. The way Einstein turned the universe around. The way Emile Vidoc was retooling the human psyche.

All you had to do, make a man empty, then fill him with rage. It was simple, perfect, and as brand-new as the idea of bending light. Any fool could make a better mousetrap. That was mere plodding invention. It took genius to trap a man in the perfect killing machine: his own body.

Vidoc showed the medication pump to the boy who could not remember his own name.

"What is going to happen, we'll make a small slit in the epidermal layer over your diaphragm. Minor operation. Very little training required. Normally, of course, a local anesthetic would be used."

Vidoc worked his long fingers into a pair of rubber gloves and said, "But we don't need any anesthetic, do we?"

The gloves were not intended to protect the unit. What did the unit care about infection, about anything? The gloves were to protect *him*.

The Trans-Am limped into Camp Libertad with an overheated engine, broken shocks, a busted muffler. Steam shooting out from under the hood. Luto parked near the colonel's flawless limo, like maybe the proximity would be healing.

Bunny got out and stretched, his T-shirt riding up over his belly.

"Hey, Lute?" he exclaimed, taking in the ragged barracks. "Whyn't you say so? We come to the Boy Scout Jamboree, get our own little merit badges."

Luto frowned at him. This was serious business. Fun was fun, but the colonel didn't have much of a sense of humor. And mostly he didn't like Anglos. In particular he didn't like redneck swamp crackers like Bunny. Luto would have to explain that they needed Bunny, but he wasn't quite sure how to do it.

Explain about the pleasure principle and Bunny being a special person? Tell the colonel that Bunny was from Everglades City, he knew the backcountry? How useful it was to have Bunny around when you wanted to make someone talk? Or afterward, when it was time for fun?

Where to begin?

Colonel was in the barracks, talking to the drill sergeant. He looked over, saw Luto waving, and stormed right through the mosquito netting. Got his cap knocked off, didn't seem to notice or care.

Luto saw the look, started backing up quick.

"Colonel? Hey, Colonel!" Luto flinched. He couldn't help it.

It started like a roundhouse punch. At the last possible instant Calavera opened his hand and slapped Luto hard enough to open one of the cuts on his face.

"¡Tonto perro! ¡Estúpido!"

Bunny stopped in midyawn. What was going on here? Crazy greaser in a spiffy uniform, shouting dog words in Spanish. Giving old Lute a pretty good whack in the kisser. Look at the little dude, he was bleeding.

Bunny came over, scratching under his arm, and bumped the greaser with his belly. Calavera jerked around, stared at him, shocked. His hand poised for another slap but not moving.

"Hey, you the colonel? We been all night on the road, looking for this fucking dump, okay?"

The colonel's hand dropped to his holster. Cupping the pearl handle of the revolver at his hip. Bunny saw the move and grinned. Dab of chocolate on his teeth.

"Hey, Colonel? You gonna shoot me or what? Do I get a last request? 'Cause I would surely appreciate a meal before we take out this cop who's probably over there in the bushes somewhere, putting his sights on your fat fucking neck."

The colonel let his hand slip away from the pistol. He turned to the cowering Luto and said, "Who's this?"

After introductions were made, they went into the shade of the barracks. Hernandez had the recruits drilling out on the hot airfield. Both Luto and Bunny liked the idea of being undercover, watching all the activity without having to lift a finger.

"You're not supposed to come out here," the colonel said to Luto. "You know that. You've just been bailed out, had your face on the news. Maybe somebody followed you."

"Nobody follow," Luto said.

"Anybody tail us, they dizzy motherfuckers by now," said Bunny, chomping noisily on a banana he'd found under a cot. "Hey General? The important thing, we'll cover your ass, take care of this cop you don't like."

"You say Valdez is coming here? How do you know this?"

That line of inquiry made Luto a little nervous. Right away Bunny picked up on the fact that the extensive fun they'd had with the lady in the *botánica* was not sanctioned, exactly.

"Mercedes say Enrique worried his brother will come here looking for you," Luto said, not meeting the colonel's eyes.

"Tell you what I want," said the colonel, folding his arms in a way that emphasized his gold-braid epaulets. "I want this *puerco* Valdez brought to me. Alive, you understand? He must be interrogated."

"Hey, General?" Bunny said. "We could integrate the man for you."

"Not necessary. Bring him alive. And the woman, if she is with him. We must interrogate her also."

Bunny grinned, dropped the banana peel onto the dirt floor, and hitched up his drooping pants. "Hey, that could be tough. Lady try to kick me in the head, I'd have to react."

"Alive," the colonel emphasized.

CHAPTER TWENTY-FIVE

At noon they stopped to rest and drink water from the wet canteens. Lee had packed food, but the heat spoiled Sara's appetite. Now she could see the advantage of a big breakfast—carry you through the rest of the day. Sam nibbled on what looked like a chunk of soft wood. Dried venison, Lee said, best thing in this heat, but she noticed he didn't eat any.

"This as far as we take the boat," Sam announced, chewing very slowly with his back teeth.

Sara looked around. This place, deep under cypress cover, appeared no different from any other region of the swamp. Except the mosquitoes seemed to be getting more active. Maybe that's why the locals called it the Devil's Garden. She had doused her pants, blouse, and cap with a strong repellent, and that had worked for a while. Now the little bastards were becoming bold, biting right through her blouse material. Was it her imagination, or were these mosquitoes a bigger and sturdier variety?

She noticed that old Sam didn't even bother to swat them away. Lee, not nearly so stoic, cursed and slapped.

"I always forget how bad they get," he complained.

After a brief rest they unloaded their gear. Lee and Sam nudged the airboat onto a tuft of mud, and Sara helped them cover it with moss and liana vine, shading any metal surface that might catch the light.

"Follow me," said Sam, hefting a machete and a hunting rifle. "Soft spots in the mud."

Sara kept right behind him as they slogged through wet prairie grass, covering a hundred yards or so to a big hardwood hammock.

She didn't sink deep, but the mud seemed unusually sticky, sucking at her feet. Was there quicksand nearby? She didn't voice the question. She didn't want to know.

Lee, lugging the video case, slapped and swatted and cursed himself for a fool.

"What a stupid idea," he growled. "Should have hopped on a plane for Boston, got the hell away. They have mosquitoes in Boston?"

"No way," said Sara, lying cheerfully.

The hammock rose a few feet above the wet prairie. Sara scrambled up the side, yanking her feet free from the clinging mud. Linking hands with Sam, she and the Seminole pulled Lee up. He came too quickly, tripped, and sprawled on his back, laughing.

"Really. I should have my head examined. What are we *doing* here?"

"Nerves in the stomach," Sam explained to Sara. "He'll be fine, come the time."

They ducked under the broad leaves and into the silence of the hammock. Almost immediately there was relief from the mosquitoes. The ground underfoot, composed of decayed vegetation and a thick top layer of leaves, was relatively dry. There was a pleasant, mossy odor, a cleanness in the air.

Sara looked up. Glimpsed through gaps in the hardwood canopy, the majestic royal palms looked like paper parasols jutting up from a giant tropical cocktail. It was quiet and peaceful and profoundly green, the kind of forest setting Sara had seen only in storybooks.

"This way," Sam said.

He led them to a newly built lean-to, wove from palm fronds. It was so perfectly camouflaged Sara didn't see it until she almost bumped her head. Inside, neatly arranged, were five gallon cans of water, a Primus stove, tinned food, a flashlight, an ammunition locker, a deer rifle wrapped in cloth.

Lee nodded his approval. Getting the colonel on tape might take a few days. If so, this would be the base of operations.

"How far to the camp?"

"Hour or so," Sam said. "Go through the pine flatwoods. They catch us, I'll say we're taking pictures of bobcat. There's a den nearby."

"They won't catch us," said Lee, hefting the camera.

Sara said, "Wait a minute. Bobcat?"

They trudged for thirty minutes without incident. Sara was only now and then aware of sky overhead, or water nearby. There was something hypnotic about the sameness of the vegetation here. She gave herself up to the rhythm, concentrated on keeping pace.

A hand closed on her shoulder, stopping her in midstep.

"Not there," Sam said.

Sara looked down. What was the matter? Underfoot a hard limestone surface, honeycombed with very small holes, none large enough to catch her foot.

"Might be a solution hole under that."

He tapped with the rifle butt. There was a distinct, hollow sound.

"Top layer sometimes the last to dissolve," he explained.

Sara backed carefully away. They were in a thick stand of small, stunted pine trees. The hollow limestone ran through like a fracture, she could see that now, a zigzag where the trees did not grow. A natural path to follow, and therefore doubly dangerous.

"Getting close now," he cautioned. "Best go real slow."

Although there was no trail—at least none discernible to Sara—Sam seemed to know exactly where he was going. Whether his familiarity with the area was from years before, when he'd hired out to the Bay of Pigs invasion force, or more recently acquired, she had no idea. Sam didn't say. Fairly taciturn by nature, out here in the backcountry he was more so. Conversation, like water, was rationed.

The last hundred yards were slow and uncomfortable.

Up ahead, light streaming in through the slash pine. At the edge of the stand a barrier of bushes that provided concealment.

They crouched, crawled, spoke not a word.

Sam showed them a place in the bushes that afforded a protected view. At first Sara didn't see anything unusual. A wet prairie area much like the several they'd already crossed. Beyond it, another island of trees.

Then something moved in the area just in front of the trees. Small, toylike figures—men in camouflage uniforms. Sam handed her the binoculars, showed her how to cup her hands around the front of the barrels to prevent sunlight from glinting in the lenses.

With the binoculars it all became clear. The tin-roofed building. A few vehicles, including the gold Cadillac and the limo Sam had mentioned. A trailer—the distinctive Airstream. Near it a Winnebago recreation vehicle.

The soldiers were marching back and forth. Now they dropped down, out of sight behind the intervening prairie grass, then popping back up and sprinting for a short distance. Back and forth. Back and forth. Some sort of drill.

The loudest thing in the bushes was the whirr of Lee's videocamera. He let her look through the viewfinder. The telephoto lens was even more powerful than the binoculars. She could see faces glistening with sweat. The dark young faces of the drilling soldiers. My God, they were so *young*. Boys.

Rising heat blurred the air, and the soldiers became distorted, creatures in a fun-house mirror.

"The airfield," Lee whispered. "Can't see it, but it's there."

She gladly relinquished the camera. And discovered that her heart was beating very hard indeed. A good solid thump against her chest.

The soldiers had guns. Of *course* they had guns.

Lee taped for twenty minutes, then turned off the camera. He had several blank cassettes in the carry case, but the battery was only good for a few hours. Best to conserve. He had a nice shot of Calavera emerging from the Airstream, walking out to confer with the drill sergeant. Flapping his big mouth at the troops. Waving his arms. And that was just about it.

So far they'd established that the colonel was training mercenaries. Big deal. Take this to the *Miami Herald* reporter and she would say yes, nice pictures, but so what? Half the guerrilla factions in Latin America train up here, with tacit approval of the government. And the colonel made no secret of his involvement, and was not, probably, breaking any laws.

Something more was needed. For instance, evidence of chemical-warfare activity—the sleeper neurotoxin—that *was* against the law.

"Where's Dr. Vidoc?" he whispered to Sara. "Why doesn't he show? Why doesn't he *do* something?"

After the first hour they settled into a routine. One person keeping watch, ready to bring up the camera at a moment's notice if things got interesting. The other two resting in a little thick-leaved area that reminded Sara of a nest. Although she noticed that Sam never really rested. He was quiet, nearly motionless, but he radiated a calm awareness that convinced her nothing could penetrate their cover without him knowing.

Like Lee, she came to believe that Sam Darter would keep them safe.

CHAPTER TWENTY-SIX

Luto had a surprise in the trunk of the Trans-Am. The way he popped the lid, like he was listening for a drumroll, Bunny almost expected to see the *botánica* lady wrapped up, maybe a little ribbon on top. Snuck her out of the back room when he wasn't looking. But there was no package in the trunk, just a greasy gray blanket.

"Hey, that's nice," Bunny said. "You can keep it, Lute, I've already got a blanket."

Luto giggled, whipped away the blanket to reveal a cache of weapons. Just unpacked from the case and gleaming with Cosmoline. Quite a selection, too. Bunny recognized an Uzi, the Jew machine gun. Also a Russian-made Kalashnikov, and your basic Chink AK-47. What was this? Yes indeed, a Beretta 9-mm pistol, just like the cops used. Awright!

He said, "Hey, Lute? What's a matter, no American guns?"

He could feel it under his skin. Cool metal something making a small lump not far from his heart.

He no longer cared about remembering his own name, or the new pain where the lump of metal had been slipped under his skin.

All he cared about was getting out.

He was trapped inside a thin layer of bone, and he wanted out. Out of his head, out of his body.

Away from the eyes that made him see things he couldn't understand. Away from ears that made him hear the sound of his own flesh being cut open. Away from the heart that kept beating, though he willed it to stop.

More than anything, he wanted to die. Finally and completely die.

* * *

Vidoc made his rounds. Gliding from one little curtained area to the next. Administering booster shots of neurotoxin. Pausing to check blood pressure, dilation of the pupils.

"Can you blink your eyes? Anybody home in there? No?"

It was a tremendous responsibility, being a physician. Making sure all seven units survived long enough to be useful. More and more he was convinced that correlating body weight to dosage was not as crucial as he'd first thought. None of the units, and the largest was an overweight specimen of just under two hundred pounds, had shown resistance to even the smallest dose of the neurotoxin. Probably a standard dose, graded on the high side, would suffice for any volunteer, regardless of size.

Vidoc loathed the uncleanness of the bunker, but the primitive conditions were similar to what the guerrillas encountered in the field. Getting back to the basics wasn't really a bad thing.

The pioneer surgeons had made do with tree saws, barber knives, catgut stitches, whatever was near to hand. This was before anesthesia became such an obsession. Hard to imagine now, but once upon a time the hypodermic syringe was a major technological breakthrough. Enabled the physician to inject directly into the bloodstream, dispense with the midwife's crude method of applying a poultice or rubbing ground-up leaves directly into the wound. Opened up a whole new science. The big drug companies had done a superb job of propaganda, convincing the public that so-called pharmaceuticals were created from scratch, conjured up in a sterile test tube. No mention of the dirty root aspirin was derived from, or the range of alkaloids taken from the plants that grubby little witch doctors had been using to the same effect for centuries.

You couldn't say ignorance was bliss, exactly. Ignorance, like pain and fear, was useful.

"Can you hear me in there? Good. Know this: You are dead. And it's going to get worse. Much worse."

After the last booster shot Vidoc undressed and climbed into his hammock. An interval of rest. He wanted to be fully alert for the little demonstration he'd planned to welcome the commandos.

He lay suspended a few inches above the moist concrete, musing on the possibilities. The initial contract was for one hundred units. The colonel hinted that it might be upped to five hundred. No problem there, he had enough neurotoxin for a thousand. Insulin pumps in quantity might be tricky—try one of the French exporters, they'd sell to anybody. The radio-control devices were easy to come by, available at any hobby shop.

A hundred units at thirty thousand per, an even split with the colonel. One-and-a-half million, minimum. It was enough to get started in Paraguay. Five hundred units would buy him a lease on Castillo, new life, a world of his own. He dozed. It was better than counting sheep.

Bunny liked the feel of the AK-47. Also the Beretta nine-mil pistol, which he tucked under his belly. Shit, just like Che fucking Guava, whatever his name was. Did Lute have any hand grenades? Bunny just kidding, but the Lute took it seriously, went to ask the drill sergeant. No, no hand grenades. Used to have grenades until the previous batch of recruits got a little excited, forgot how to count. Baboom, no more grenades for the rookies. So sorry, man.

"How about rocket launchers?"

Luto started to trot off, ask about rocket launchers, but Bunny called him back.

"Hey, I've got a bad back, fucking rocket launchers must be heavy as a bitch, huh?"

The Lute nodding seriously. Yes, man, very heavy. Bunny thought, I better not ask for a tank, this greaser'll run out and get me one.

What he really wanted, his old standby, a deer rifle: 30.06 with the soft tips. Bunny was pretty sure he could get off a killing shot from two, maybe three, hundred yards, he had a deer rifle with the right kind of scope. No deer rifle in the camp. Machine guns and rocket launchers, but no deer rifle.

'Course, these boys weren't being trained to shoot whitetail.

"So," said Bunny, hitching up his pants where the nine mil weighed him down, "what's the plan?"

Luto shrugged. With him it was sort of an elaborate gesture, like a long shiver that started around his ankles. "Find the target."

"Hey, Lute? I know that much. We trip over this cop, we're supposed to bring him back so Colonel Sanders can stick toothpicks under his fingernails or something. And this girl who kicked you in the head."

Luto had this sneaky look. "We get her, maybe we lose her on the way."

"Hey, it happens. You find a woman, and then you lose her."

"She definitely lost, man."

"Back to the plan, Lute honey. You got one?"

It was pretty obvious that Lute was relying on him to develop a plan. Bunny was the swamp expert. Luto seemed to think all a swamp expert like Bunny had to do, reach into the puckerbrush, yank out the rabbit.

"Yeah, well, let's jess say *fuck* the plan idea, okay?" Bunny decided. "What we'll do, take a little stroll around the area, see what's out there. Least we can do, shoot us a whitetail, show these boys what fresh venison taste like."

"Got to find this cop, man."

"Lute? Relax. He's out there, I'll find him."

"And the *rubia*. The girl."

Bunny smiled, patted Luto on the back.

"Hey, you really like this bitch, huh? Gonna marry her? Tell you what, I'll be best man."

They followed a new trail out from the airfield because, well, it was there. Up ahead, overgrown with vines, a spooky old bunker. Perfect place for the greaser cop to hide, he ever got this close.

What Bunny figured, no cop would really be dumb enough to come in alone with a platoon of armed guys marching around. So forget it, the cop would never show. He would play the game, though, get himself in good with the colonel, maybe something interesting would develop there. Plus it was kind of neat, strolling through the Big Cypress with enough firepower to turn whitetail into hamburger right on the spot.

Bunny walked right up to the bunker, looked into the slit. Dark in there, couldn't make out nothing. Wait a minute, he could almost see something.

Cold steel at the back of his neck.

Bunny turned around, all set to tell the Lute to quit fucking around, and found himself looking up at a tall guy with no hair at all. Not even eyelashes. The cold steel was a pistol, a big old forty-five. And oh, look at this.

The guy was naked, just a pair of sandals. And shit, not even a pubic hair down there.

"More volunteers?" Vidoc said.

CHAPTER TWENTY-SEVEN

The chopper came in and circled for a landing in the dog hours of the late afternoon. Hernandez had returned his troops to the imperfect shade of the barracks, where he issued bivouac equipment that would be used on pre-dawn maneuvers planned for the following day. The recruits were at ease, chatting amiably among themselves, arguing about who would carry the heavy tent packs and what they might expect in the war games. Colonel Calavera was resting in the Airstream, secure in the belief that the guerrilla commanders would not arrive before sunset, due to the usual air-traffic delays.

He emerged from his trailer just as the chopper sat down, kicking up a cloud of marl dust from the decayed landing strip.

Three men disembarked. The helicopter increased revs and lifted off almost immediately. Touch and go.

Brushing dust from his gold braid, the colonel greeted the Bolivians. He was disappointed to find them in civilian dress; the recruits were expecting an inspection by war generals. Would not the snappy paramilitary uniforms have been more appropriate, rather than the slacks and shirts of visiting businessmen?

"But we *are* businessmen. And what do we care what these *paisanos* think?" the senior commander scoffed. "I understand they are expendable. You have brought them here to demonstrate a new weapons system, is that not correct?"

The colonel bared his teeth in a smile.

"Yes, yes, but keep this quiet please. These men believed they are being trained to join you in the battle for the homeland. They have been told that tomorrow's demonstration is just a routine war game."

"Ah," the Bolivian commander said. "Now I see. This is to be like a play. We must all pretend."

The colonel coughed into his fist, clearing his throat of marl dust. "Come inside while my sergeant readies the platoon for inspection. We'll have drinks and *tapas*, and you must tell me how it goes."

The Bolivians were puzzled. "How what goes?"

"The battle, *compadre*, the war."

"Oh, that."

Bunny was very impressed with the doctor.

"Think about it," he said to Luto. "No hair at all and naked as the day he was born. If he *was* born. Critter like that, maybe crawl out from under a wet rock."

"Best thing," Luto advised, "we keep away from him. What I heard, he can kill with just his eyes."

They were on an old, overgrown trail a few hundred yards beyond Vidoc's bunker, Bunny leading the way, no destination in mind. He paused, jerked up his pants.

"Hey, Lute? If he can kill with his eyes, why the forty-five?"

Luto did his shrug. "What I heard, man."

"Mmmm. Maybe he's got death rays, huh?" Bunny grinning. He got a real kick out of the Lute, all these crazy greaser stories. "What I want to know, what the fuck's he got in that bunker?"

"I think we keep away."

"Could be money. He gets naked, sleeps with all the colonel's money. You say the colonel is loaded right?"

"He's a very rich man," Luto cautiously agreed. "Forget about it, okay?"

"Yeah? Forget about what?"

"Whatever you thinkin', man."

A long pause for Bunny, his eyes flatter and bluer than ever. "Lute? Are you sayin' you're a mind reader?"

Luto shifted uncomfortably. It was right about then they heard the helicopter approaching. Bunny broke from the trail and headed for the edge of the slash pines, where they could have a view of the old airfield.

"What's this action?" he said, raising his voice to carry over the throb of the chopper blades.

Luto didn't know. The colonel didn't confide his plans. Three visitors in casual dress, they could be bankers.

"Bankers, Lute? More like bank *robbers*."

Luto was a little unclear on the concept, banking and robbing being closely connected, to his way of thinking. Whoever these three new stooges were, they were being treated with a lot of respect. Bunny had it in mind that the colonel might be running a smuggling operation, these were his South American contacts. If that was true, then his idea of money being stored in the bunker might not be so farfetched.

All these nice new guns, unlimited ammo, the possibility of cash for the taking, it made you think.

"Hey, Lute?"

But Luto was gone. No, wait a minute, the little fucker was right over there, crouched in the bushes. Bunny drew the Beretta from his pants, put a bead on the middle of Luto's back. Right about *there* between those scrawny shoulder blades. Take the heart right out of him, better than surgery.

Not yet, though. Save it for later. Plenty of fun left in Luto.

"What's the deal here?"

Luto spoke without taking the binoculars from his eyes. "Saw something move."

"Yeah? Where?"

"Way over there, man. In the pine woods. Behind those little fan palms."

Bunny took the binoculars and looked for himself.

"You recognize the man?"

Luto shook his head. "He pop up too fast."

"Could be one of the soldiers. You know, running off. AWOL."

But the Lute was insistent. He'd seen somebody way over there, hiding in the fan palms. Bunny squinted through the binoculars until his eyes felt like hard-boiled eggs, and every now and then he *almost* saw something. A certain dark quality to the palm fronds. Could be turning over in the breeze. But hey, there was no breeze, the chopper had flown off, leaving the air heavy and dead.

Raccoons, maybe.

"Tell you what," he finally said, handing the heavy binoculars back to Luto. "We go check it out."

"I *saw* somebody, man."

"Lute honey? Calm the fuck down. I said we'll do it, okay?"

Only problem, how to get over there without getting hip-deep in swamp muck. Bunny had a thing about getting his feet wet. Get his feet wet and he got really, really pissed off.

Hernandez had issued the fresh-from-the-crate AK-47s to each recruit. Only six rounds in each clip, just enough for a salute, because he didn't want these boys spraying the bushes. He had the recruits resting at ease on the airfield, ready to present arms for the guerrilla commanders, when Dr. Vidoc materialized out of the underbrush.

"Sergeant? A moment of your time."

Vidoc wearing a ventilated pith helmet to protect his head from the sun, a white lab jacket with a stethoscope hanging from the pocket. He smiled benignly as he conferred with the drill sergeant. The kindly physician, an act he'd borrowed from Marcus Welby, M.D.

"I want to transfer one of the volunteers to the barracks. Could you please detail a couple of your men to carry the stretcher?"

"Doctor, we're about to review the troops. Can't it wait?"

"'Fraid not, Sarge." In a lower voice, stripped of affectation. "It's been cleared with the colonel."

"Oh," Hernandez said. "I see."

He ordered two of the stronger boys to accompany the doctor.

"Gracias," Vidoc said loudly, pretending deference. "Mission of mercy. A sick comrade."

In his hurry to tape the sudden arrival of foreign visitors, Lee had stood up with the camera on his shoulder. Sam had yanked him down in no time, catching the camera as it fell. Now the chopper was up again, flattening the saw grass, making the air feel heavy.

"Sorry!" Lee had said. "Stupid move!"

Nobody disagreed.

Sara crawled to where the fan palms opened, checked out the camp. All the activity seemed to be focused on the men who had landed. Lee had only been visible for a second, who could have noticed?

Sam wasn't happy. "We should go, come back tomorrow in a different place."

Lee wouldn't hear of it. "Whatever these bastards have planned, it's going down now. We've got to get it on tape. That's why we're *here*. Besides, they haven't been keeping watch, you said so yourself."

It wasn't the old man's way to argue. "Be dark pretty soon," he said, and concentrated on checking over his hunting rifle.

Sara happened to be running the camera when the tall, thin man with the pith helmet and the white jacket appeared in the viewfinder.

"Lee," she said in a low voice.

Instantly he was at her side. She kept the tape running, the white jacket in the center of the viewfinder. "Describe Emile Vidoc."

"Supposed to be tall, thin, and bald. Not just bald, totally hairless."

She panned to the left, following the white jacket until it disappeared into the dense foliage, followed by two soldiers. When he was out of sight, she took her finger off the trigger and said, "Got a guy that might fit the description. Tall and thin. Wearing a pith helmet, so I'm not sure about the hair."

Lee was frantically searching with the binoculars. "I can't see him."

"Gone now," said Sara, handing him the camera. "Here. Check it out on playback. You think it was really him?"

Lee rewound the tape, saw, in the black-and-white viewfinder, a tiny image of Emile Vidoc.

"The hat," he said. "I happen to know he likes hats."

CHAPTER TWENTY-EIGHT

The swamp ate Bunny's boot. Crossing a few yards of prairie grass that looked to be reasonably dry, he encountered a soft spot and sank right up to his knees.

"I fucking *hate* this!"

Bunny did the twist, a redneck Chubby Checker version, heaving his butt around, trying to wrench himself free.

Luto, light enough so he didn't sink into the mud, wanted to say something funny, but the look Bunny gave him, he decided to save it for another time.

Instead, he grabbed Bunny's pants, tried to yank him out by tugging.

The pants came down. Big hairy white butt staring Luto in the face. Bunny making this strangled noise, like he was choking. A plop! as the Beretta fell into the wet grass. Bunny tipped sideways and fell, landing with the AK-47 under him. He grabbed at his pants, yanking them up. His face looked dangerously red, like maybe he was going to explode or something.

Luto dragged him free of the clinging mud. Noticed right away that one of Bunny's feet was bare. The fucking boot. The swamp ate it.

"The nine mil," Bunny panted.

Luto went back and retrieved the Beretta. Tried to wipe it dry on his shirt and succeeded in smearing mud all over himself.

"You dirty little fuck," Bunny said, struggling to his feet. "Gimme that thing."

He jammed the pistol into his soggy waist, wrenched the AK-47 shoulder harness around.

"Take off the other boot," he demanded.

Luto didn't understand.

"This fuckin' boot here," Bunny said in a strangled voice. "Yank it. I can't walk on just one boot."

It wasn't the first time Bunny had gone barefoot in the swamp, and he didn't feel good about it, either. The way he figured, to even things out, he would have to kill somebody pretty soon.

The colonel and his visitors finished their drinks and left the trailer.

"When do you start these war games?"

"Soon," the colonel said, closing the door behind him. "The main demonstration is planned for tomorrow morning, but this evening, who knows, perhaps there will be a preview of things to come."

The inspection of the troops was cursory. A stroll along the ranks as the boys snapped to attention. A little too eager, too ready to impress. But still, they *looked* like a guerrilla platoon, and that was the point, was it not?

While the commanders went through the motions, the colonel sidled over to Hernandez and inquired as to Vidoc's whereabouts. Just as the drill sergeant was framing a reply, the doctor himself emerged from the trail, hacking rather halfheartedly at the overgrowth with a machete.

Two soldiers lugging a stretcher emerged from the trail. Seeing their fellow recruits at attention, the stretcher-bearers paused.

Vidoc, his expression a mask of kindliness, left the machete on the foot of the stretcher.

"Excuse the interruption, Colonel. We're taking one of your men back to the barracks."

"Oh? What happened to him, Doctor?"

Vidoc glanced at the boy on the stretcher, covered up to his chin, and shook his head.

"Bitten by a small animal, possibly a raccoon. I'm afraid he's had an allergic reaction."

"I see. Well, take him on through."

As the unconscious boy on the stretcher was borne toward his fellow recruits, Dr. Vidoc slipped his hand into the pocket of his white jacket.

The invalid was about halfway through the assembled recruits when an inhuman screech erupted from the stretcher, and then Nando threw off the cover and leaped to his feet.

He screamed again and picked up the machete. Foam bubbling from his lips, eyes rolling white, he whirled, slashing with the machete.

Arms, legs, head, all jerking violently, as if he were being savagely pulled by wires.

The boys of the platoon scrambled away in high panic.

Screams.

Blood on the blade.

A boy tripped over his spit-polished boots and fell. The blade flashed. More blood, a *lot* more blood.

Nando dropped the machete, tore at the dead recruit's eyes with his bare hands. In seconds the dead boy's face was torn to shreds.

Nando grabbed a partially severed arm, yanked it free, began to beat the body with the severed limb.

Blood everywhere. A storm of blood.

In the panic of the killing frenzy none of the recruits had the presence of mind to fire their weapons. They had been trained to shoot an imagined enemy. This was one of their own. Boys were whimpering, crawling away on their hands and knees, crying for their mothers.

Colonel Calavera strode purposefully through the carnage, a pistol in each hand. From ten feet away he emptied both pistols into Nando's writhing back.

Nando stood up and screamed. He hurled the severed arm and charged, blood pouring from his open mouth.

Sergeant Hernandez, seeing what was about to happen, wrestled an AK-47 from a recruit who was paralyzed with terror. As the colonel ran by, Hernandez stood his ground and fired six high-powered slugs into Nando's chest.

With his heart exploded and his spine severed, the boy ran a few more stuttering steps, then toppled like a small, stunted tree. He sprawled, twitching, at the feet of the blood-spattered colonel.

"Madre de Dios," the colonel whispered. He hoped there was so much blood on his uniform that no one noticed the small accident he'd had in his pants.

• • •

First thing the Lute did was shinny himself up a palm tree. Bunny had to admire the way he slithered, like one of those native boys in the beer commercials. Or was it Come to Jamaica? Whatever, Lute had the moves.

"They're shooting!" he called from his high perch.

"Hey, no shit, I can hear that much. The point is, *who* they shooting?"

A few more shots went off. No echoes here, the sound vanished utterly. Luto came back down the palm tree, a look of puzzlement making him appear, to Bunny, dumber than ever. Like he'd been whacked upside the head with a big, soft hammer.

"Some little dude with a machete, man. He went nuts, they blew him away."

Luto's view had been somewhat obscured by the confusion of the panicked platoon. It was hard to be sure about what exactly he'd seen. Did the boy with the machete really hack off an *arm*, use it like a club? Tell Bunny a thing like that, and he would get that look, like who are you kidding?

"Really ugly scene, man," said Luto, using a phrase he'd picked up at a punk disco. "They shoot this dude eight, ten times before he go down."

Bunny, standing there in his bare feet with his muddy jeans rolled up, was in no mood to hear a lot of inflated greaser bullshit.

"We'll go back, check it out. Any raccoons in the pine woods, they'll be gone by now."

"Man, I *saw* somebody. Had something shiny in his hands."

"Lute? Did he have little dark circles around his eyes? A big bushy tail?"

It was right about then that both of them heard a woman screaming.

CHAPTER TWENTY-NINE

"**S**ara! *Stop*."

She froze, registering the tone of urgent horror as Lee spoke her name.

They had been pushing hard. With that incredible, violent scene on tape—no doubt about it, they had witnessed another berserk sleeper—there was no point in hanging around. Use all the confusion at the camp as cover to get the hell out of there. Sara, who could move faster than old Sam, had been jogging ahead, pushing her way through the thick undergrowth. Fighting a panicked impulse to *run*. Run out of the swamp, out of Florida, just keep running until she got to a place where men did not dress up in silly camouflage uniforms and kill each other with their bare hands.

Now Lee was right behind her.

"*Don't move*. Sam, what do we do?"

That was when she felt it. A presence on her back. Not much weight, no mass to speak of, but it was moving. Slipping along her shoulder. Without shifting her head, she swiveled her eyes to the side. Nothing. And then it came sliding into view, tongue flicking: the small, beautiful, deadly head of a coral snake.

Sara screamed. At exactly that moment Sam's gnarled hand brushed the snake from her shoulder.

"Where is it?" she asked, still frozen.

"Slipped away," Sam said. "You scared it pretty good."

"*I* scared it."

"Don't see too many of them coral snakes," Sam said. "Pretty shy critters."

Lee embraced her.

"Come on, folks," Sam said.

Now they followed *him*.

Sara could see, and now truly appreciate, the way Sam Darter moved through the dense growth. Finding his way, hardly touching a branch, just slipping through. None of the startled, hurried motions that disturbed the balance of life. A dozing coral snake, for instance.

Lee, his arms wrapped tight around the precious video case, kept within touching distance, as if wanting to be reassured that Sara was really right there beside him. He was pumped up, experiencing his own adrenaline rush.

"We get back to the chickee, we'll head to the nearest phone. You know anybody with the Collier County Sheriff's Department, Sam?"

"One or two."

"Great. We'll tell 'em a couple of men have been killed at the camp. They'll have to check it out. You can be sure the colonel won't make a report on his own. Sheriff can demand an autopsy, and then we'll have our link to the other sleepers. Plus we've got it all on tape. That reporter from the *Herald* is going to go nuts when she sees this stuff."

Lee was right. The long shot had paid off. So why did Sara feel sick about it? She had to keep reminding herself that the violence would have happened whether or not they were there to record it.

She still didn't understand what she had seen. Assuming the boy on the stretcher had been treated with the neurotoxin, how had he been stimulated into rage? The man in the pith helmet—Dr. Vidoc—had been yards away when it happened. Some sort of delayed reaction? An accident? What?

It grew dim in the pine slash. Spots of sky visible overhead, but down here it was getting hard to see. The dark form of Sam blending in, holding branches back as they passed through. Was this the way they came? Or was he taking a quicker route back to the airboat?

The ground was starting to slope down. They were heading to water level. Her nerves were badly frayed, and in the twilight every branch looked like a coral snake.

Hurry, she silently urged, hurry. Can't stand much more of this place.

There was a crashing noise in the underbrush. Something large in there, moving fast. Her heart went into her mouth.

"Lee!"

* * *

Not many wild boars left in the big swamp now, maybe a few domestic pigs gone wild, but not like the old days. Bunny had been too young to be part of the hunt, he was just a snot-nosed kid tagging along, but he remembered how it was done. You had to split up. Spook the boar, making him charge in the other direction, where the main party of hunters waited to cut him down.

Tracking boar was tough, the bastards were so low to the ground you had to get down on all fours, check it out from there. See things like the boar saw them.

Think boar-mean, boar-crazy.

This was different. Two or three people in there, working their way back to the water. Big surprise was the way Luto had melted away right after they heard the scream. Not a word between them, no need to explain about a flanking maneuver. Just do it.

Bunny's feet hurt like a bastard. Funny thing was, he hardly minded. Up until that girl's scream broke the air, it was all a joke, fucking around in the swamp. Now they had some playmates.

They might be armed, and that was another reason to quit screwing around and get serious. Bunny, thinking on that, decided he wasn't going to take anyone alive unless it was convenient. Make an exception for the girl. He wanted to make her scream again.

The Lute was over there, just out of sight. Man, the little dude moved like smoke. Fine, let him circle around. They were close enough now so he could hear voices. Make a move now, before it got too dark.

Bunny stepped on a sharp root. It pierced the bottom of his foot. He jerked back, fell down, tearing branches as he went. Making one hell of a racket. Well, that would spook 'em toward Luto, let's hope the little shit was ready.

He heard a woman shout, then a man. Shit, they were a lot closer than he thought. Sitting on his butt, he scrambled backward, trying to straighten out the shoulder harness on the AK-47.

Shoot up every tree in the swamp, it came to that.

The Lute was screaming in that shrill greaser voice:

"Come out or I kill you right now!"

Well, this was interesting.

Bunny got up, found the Lute with his pistol jammed up against the chin of a fellow greaser. On the ground was a leather camera case.

Luto was so excited he was practically dancing the guy around the little clearing.

"Hey, Lute," Bunny said. "Is that the cop?"

"Is him, man. The girl nearby. Maybe one more."

Bunny checked out the darkening woods. Couldn't see fuck-all. He decided it was great the Lute had grabbed one, but now it was time to take over the show.

"Listen up!" Bunny shouted. "This is one crazy mother here. He'll kill your friend for sure. Only way to save him, come on out. Oh yeah, and keep your hands up."

Just like they always said in the movies. Made a better target, with the belly exposed.

"I kill him!" Luto insisted.

The cop looking like he was made of stone, not reacting.

The way he said *keel heem*, Bunny loved it. Little dude got excited, thought he was back in Cuba.

"Okay, folks, this is the situation!" Bunny shouted. "Got a hot Chink weapon here! AK-47. Fires slugs big enough to cut down any of the punk trees you're hiding behind. So we'll do a five count. I get to zero, I start chopping wood!"

The greaser cop started to struggle. Luto had him pinned pretty good, but Bunny thought it might be helpful if he smashed a rifle butt in the cop's gut.

Wham! Ooh yes, now he was pliable. Let the air out of his tires.

"Four!" Bunny shouted. "Hey, is this guy your friend or what?"

Over there, was that something moving? Bunny was ready to open up, fuck the count.

"Three!"

What Bunny really hoped to see, an Amazon woman. Titties hanging out and a little grass skirt. Little grass panties under the skirt. Ooh-ee, playtime.

"Two," he shouted. "You really want me to shoot up the environment, ruin all the nice trees?"

There! He was running. He, not a she. Damn, no Amazon.

Bunny fired. The guy was moving faster than he thought, clipped a tree behind him, it came crashing down, blocking the line of fire. Bunny ran forward, shooting as he went. Damn near lost his balance, there was some kick from the AK-47, a real muscle gun.

The runner was heading for open ground. Dumb mother, why do that? Squeeze the trigger, it was amazing how fast it fired. Bunny squeezing off short bursts, but shit, it didn't take long to empty that big banana clip.

He dropped the rifle, went for the Beretta. Guy lumbering just ahead there, heading for water. Fucking drown himself in the swamp.

Bunny stopped, took aim, fired off the whole pistol clip.

Hit the bastard, yes.

Guy turned as he was hit, and Bunny saw the face. Seminole face. Black hair and those hard, hard eyes.

Then he fell headlong into the swamp water. Bunny ran up to the edge, ready to club the mother back under if he surfaced.

The black water was thrashing with tails.

Gator hole.

"Hey, Lute?" Bunny called. "Know what's for supper? You'll never guess, man, Indian stew."

Behind him a bull gator roared.

PART FOUR
VIDOC'S METHOD

"We're talking about fugue-state fear, gentlemen."
—EMILE VIDOC, M.D.

CHAPTER ONE

Midnight in the bunker. The Honda generator chugged, powering the string of lights. The doctor paced with his hands clasped behind his back, his elongated shadow thrown in sharp relief on a thin green curtain that discreetly shielded his little clinic from the view of his audience.

"So we ask ourselves this question, gentlemen. What is the biggest problem that faces a guerrilla commander?"

Vidoc lecturing to the Bolivians. More a sales pitch than a lecture. His attire was casual. Chinos with a rope belt, translucent white *guayabera* shirt, his Birkenstock sandals, and a souvenir cap courtesy of Metro-Dade Homicide, a gift from the detective who investigated the accidental drowning of Carlos the gardener.

"Logistics? Acquiring weapons?" asked Vidoc, then shook his head. "Deciding strategy? Raising money?" Two more head shakes.

The doctor had a bounce in his step. The guerrilla commanders had been impressed with the teaser. Shock effect on the recruits was profound. Amazing to see armed and otherwise disciplined troops fleeing from one small man with a machete. But was it an effect that could be repeated and safely controlled, as the doctor promised?

"Biggest problem," Vidoc continued, "is the combat soldier. How long does it take to recruit each man, train him, engage him in a useful action? How much does it cost? Not just in time and effort, but in actual dollars expended?"

Vidoc let the question hang for a moment. "As you already know, gentlemen, the ballpark figure, including rations, weapons, and payoffs to drug lords in the disputed territory, is in excess of fifty thousand dollars per man, per year."

The Bolivians nodded in agreement. Actually the doctor's estimate was a low-ball figure because it did not include their rather considerable rake-off as regional commanders, or the generous percentage that a prudent man culls for administrative overhead. For every dollar in funds collected, less than a dime made it back to the jungle.

"And how many," Vidoc said, "how many of these fifty-grand guerrillas are actually effective in a combat situation? How many will be engaged in a decisive military action? One out of ten? Less?"

The three Bolivians shrugged. Such figures are hard to come by. How do you define "effective in combat"? Was it actual combat or reported engagements? The truth or the figures developed by the propaganda units?

"So," Vidoc said, ticking off the numbers on his long, supple fingers. "I make it roughly two million dollars to keep an average platoon in the field for a year, not counting indirect expenses. And what do you get for the money? A lot of complaining. Desertions. The continual problem of how to keep up morale. Am I right?"

There were nods. Maintaining a guerrilla force in the field was an expensive pain in the ass, no doubt about it, but a necessary evil if funding for the war was to continue. They listened patiently to Vidoc's spiel, having been adequately wined and dined by the colonel, who was elsewhere at the moment, interrogating a new prisoner.

"I have a solution, gentlemen. It is simple, foolproof, cost-effective."

Strolling to the far end of the curtain, Vidoc drew it slowly back, revealing a row of seven cots, the last conspicuously empty. Room for one more, now that the Nando unit had been expended.

"I give you, gentlemen, the disposable combat soldier."

He strolled among the cots, lifting up limp hands, letting them drop. See how complaisant these units are? How easy to handle?

"You saw the first unit in action earlier. Armed with just a machete, for safety's sake. Imagine if he, or several like him, had been equipped with *real* firepower.

"Actually," the doctor continued, flashing a quirky smile, "you don't have to imagine it. In less than five hours you'll be able to see it with your own eyes."

Vidoc had them gather around a small galvanized-metal table on wheels. He unzipped his black nylon bag and withdrew a roll of black felt.

"It's all here, gentlemen. A method that can turn this war around."

He unrolled the felt, revealing an array of hypodermic syringes, disposable needles, a sealed liter bottle of clear fluid.

"Using my method, you can take an ordinary peasant farmer and turn him into an efficient killing machine in less than three days. It's a two-step process that starts with this," he said, indicating the liter bottle. "The Vidoc neurotoxin, administered intravenously. Tell the volunteer he's being inoculated, nothing could be simpler. Moments after the neurotoxin enters his bloodstream, he is virtually paralyzed. A useful side effect is that metabolism is drastically reduced. Assuming the unit will be activated within, say, a week or so, it need not even be fed.

"For best results, keep isolated in a dark place, away from outside stimulation. The personality erodes rather rapidly, usually in less than seventy-two hours."

He indicated the motionless occupants of the cots.

"But what use are these boys, Doctor?" said the senior commander. "They seem dead, almost. The boy you brought to the airfield was full of fire and rage."

Vidoc nodded. He'd already anticipated this complaint.

"You'll recall I said this was a two-stage process. Stage One is, as you see, creating the empty unit. Stage Two is activation."

"Activation?"

Vidoc reached into his black bag, removed a small, molded plastic box about the size of a cigarette pack. He passed the box to the commander, who turned it over to his two associates.

All three looked expectantly at the doctor. What the hell is this little contraption?

"A medication pump," he said. "Slipped just under the skin of each unit. Activated by a simple radio device."

"But what does it do?"

"It injects, instantly, a very powerful combination of drugs into the unit. Naturally I'll keep the exact formulation to myself, but I can tell you that it contains synthetic adrenaline, ouabain, which is a heart stimulant, and several drugs known to produce a state of psychopathic rage."

"Ahhh," one of the Bolivians said in sudden understanding, "like angel dust."

"Something like it," Vidoc agreed. "Only much more intense."

"But in this chemical rage, how do you know your 'units' will kill only the enemy?"

"You don't," Vidoc replied. "Think of it this way: putting these units into a target area is like sending in a time bomb. All you can be sure of is that when activated they will cause immense destruction. We're talking about fugue-state fear, gentlemen. Panicked populations."

Nods all around. The Bolivians were well-acquainted with the effectiveness of terrorist attacks. They would, it was agreed, arrive at a decision regarding a contract for services following his demonstration.

"The old fire tower will serve as an observation platform," said Vidoc, showing them to the bunker door. "Four A.M. sharp. We'll watch the fun, then clean up and have breakfast."

The three commanders headed back to the barracks area.

When they were some distance down the trail, out of earshot of the bunker, one of them said, "Do we all understand that this man is *loco*? Completely crazy?"

His two associates nodded. Yes, the American doctor was a dangerous sociopath. But it was well-known that such men have their uses. The secret to running an effective guerrilla campaign was to acknowledge that war is an act of willful insanity. Accept the premise and then act upon it. Embrace the tiger.

"I wonder what the colonel has planned for breakfast?"

This prompted some discussion. It was hoped that beans would not be part of the meal.

Jorge lay in a fetal position on his cot with his hands clamped over his ears. Hearing again and again the scream of his little brother Fernando who did not know he was dead. His back riddled with the colonel's bullets—the great colonel who had come to their village with his slide show, colorful images of honor and glory projected on a white sheet that had rippled with the breeze coming down from the mountains.

This same man had murdered Nando, not even waiting for him to turn, but shooting him in the back like a coward, like a thief.

What the colonel said afterward was a lie.

Fernando had not been bitten by a rabid animal—Jorge had gone over every inch of his brother's mutilated corpse. Other than the bullets that killed him, the only marks on his body were the angry bites of a hypodermic needle.

There could be only one explanation.

The colonel and the doctor had conspired to kill Fernando. But why had they done this thing? Little Nando had proved himself to be an exemplary soldier, the best of all the new recruits. Sergeant Hernandez had said so. Now the sergeant would not talk about Fernando or the brutal violence of his death. Jorge had begged him for the truth—what had made his little brother go *loco*?

Do not ask, Hernandez had said, turning away, not meeting his eyes, *we will speak no more of this*.

That was all. It was as if Nando had never existed. As if the sergeant hadn't been forced to blow the heart out of his bravest recruit.

Nando and the boy he had killed with the machete were dumped in a hole in the swamp—Jorge himself was on the burial detail. Not a word was said over the dead. They had been consigned to the evil spirits of the swamp without a prayer. Hidden away like shameful garbage.

Now Jorge was being shunned by the others as they prepared for the war games. As if he might infect them with the disease that had made his brother rage and die.

Jorge decided that someone must pay for his shame, his anger, his terrible loss. Who would it be?

The colonel? The sergeant? The doctor?

This was a decision of honor. It would require some thought. His name was being called by the platoon leader, but Jorge did not hear. His hands remained clamped over his ears, sealing out the scream.

Lee feigned unconsciousness.

It didn't always work. Sometimes they waited until he passed out to come at him again, finding some new, untested region of his body. He was aware that he was being transported on a litter, feet tightly manacled and wrists bound in copper wire.

The colonel was nearby, directing the brutes who were carrying the litter. Two men in camouflage fatigues. More than that he did not know.

Did they have Sara? What had happened to Sam Darter?

He could think of these questions, but he was too exhausted to even try imagining the answers. He'd give up hope several hours before, when the colonel began applying the jumper cables. Extracting what little information Lee had gleaned from the computer files and, finally, whatever else he could invent to please the colonel.

That his death would be quick, this was all the hope he could muster.

"Through there," the colonel ordered. "Dump him on the cot." Harsh lights, a change in the way sound carried. He was being taken inside a place with thick, hard walls.

A new voice spoke. In English. "You're done with him?"

Then he was dropped from the litter onto a canvas cot, and the explosion of pain carried him into the darkness.

When he came to again, the harsh lights were dimmed. A tall figure held a kerosene lantern. What was that story about the Greek who searched for truth, holding a lantern aloft? Is that what this man wanted, the truth?

"Well, hello there," the manshape said. "I thought you'd gone sleepy-bye."

Lee croaked a word. It was difficult to speak because of what they'd done to his mouth.

"What's that?"

Lee repeated his question, speaking a name.

"Correct," the man said. "Emile Vidoc at your service. And you're the clever police detective. Or maybe not quite so clever, eh?"

Lee thrashed, but it was useless. Even if he hadn't been strapped to the cot, his strength was gone. He was so weak it was an effort to remain awake.

Vidoc hung the lantern from an iron hook in the ceiling and settled himself on a folding camp stool. He showed his strong white teeth in the approximation of a smile.

Lee, who thought he'd already experienced the worst at the hands of the colonel, knew at once that the worst was just about to begin.

"The colonel tells me you were quite the little chatterbox," Vidoc said. "Worried about your girlfriend? Let me put your mind at ease."

The doctor leaned closer, chin cupped in the convex of his interlaced fingers.

"She was raped," he said. "Repeatedly raped and then killed by that nasty little specimen who caught you."

"Sara dead?"

"Was that her name?" Vidoc chuckled. "But you must be in terrible pain. That crude technique with the jumper cables and the auto generator, right? Here, let me help."

He held up the syringe and squeezed a single, clear drop from the point of the needle.

CHAPTER TWO

Luto had to go back alone. Bunny was pissed about something, upset because the colonel wouldn't let him play with the cop. Also, his feet hurt. Well, that was okay. This was a thing best enjoyed by himself, when he could give his imagination free rein, not having to worry about Bunny having fun, too.

He was not spooked by the darkness or the slithering sounds of the great swamp. It was in darkness that he became truly alive.

A shadow within a shadow. The darkness *behind* the darkness.

He followed the path of broken branches to the place where he'd snatched the cop Valdez. Trees down where Bunny had blazed away after the fleeing Seminole. The girl was here, somewhere nearby, hiding. He could feel that truth like a taste on his tongue. Like blood in his mouth.

"Rubia!" he shouted into the darkness. Making the air quiver. "I am come back to find you!"

In one hand was the Beretta model 84, and in the other his weapon of choice, a blade he had carved himself. Cut from ordinary steel and honed on a grinding wheel, the handle wrapped in black tape. Basic, functional. The blade was whetted; it had already kissed Mercedes Raimez good-bye. When he was done with her, the *rubia* would get a similar kiss.

His shouts died as suddenly as the gunshots had, absorbed by the swamp.

The idea that the bitch who had humiliated him might be nearby, within striking distance, made him . . . crazy. Bright images danced behind his eyes. He was fractured with urgency. His need was an emptiness that could only be filled by her pain.

"*Rubia?* You must come to me. Your boyfriend, that *maricón*, already the colonel has made him cry like a girl. He has confessed to his crimes, do you hear me? He blames everything on you."

He listened. Tree frogs, the distant buzz of insects. He could feel her presence, that haughty *rubia* musk she exuded. There.

He lunged, came up with a fistful of pine needles.

"*Rubia?* Know what happens next? They take your boyfriend to see the doctor." Luto thought about what that meant and laughed. Did she know how clever he was being? Did she understand his little joke? "That doctor, he's going to empty your boyfriend's head, you hear me? Going to scramble his brains. So you come out, do like I say, maybe I let you both run away."

He lunged. Nothing. Twigs.

She could smell him. A distinct odor of sweat and hair tonic. Maybe twenty feet away. Radiating malice that made her feel out of breath, as if her heart might trip-hammer right out of her chest. And this time there would be no Lee Valdez to come to the rescue, no Sam Darter to brush away danger.

If only she had a weapon.

Sara knew she would not hesitate to pull the trigger and keep on firing until the gun was empty and the dark insinuation of his voice was gone forever.

But she had no weapon.

Sam had broken cover without warning, distracting Luto and his loud-mouthed crony, drawing fire away from her. She had crept away in the opposite direction, crawling through the underbrush in a blind panic. Certain that the bullets would find her, too. Had Sam taken the rifle with him? Did he drop it as he ran? Made no difference now. Sam Darter was dead, and the rifle was gone, swallowed by the nearly impenetrable blackness of the swamp.

Might be able to find that rifle in the daylight, but Luto was right here, now. Make a sound, one little noise, and he would find her.

Sara decided that when he made his grab, she would go for his eyes, do as much damage as she could. She flexed her fingers, waiting, wishing her nails were longer.

Keeping still. Waiting.

She could hear him panting, the little wheezing sounds in the back of his throat, as he moved closer.

* * *

Luto was pissed off. More than pissed off. He was so mad that his urge to play with the *rubia* was replaced by an even more urgent need to kill her quickly.

Blow the bitch away.

She was running a game on him here, leading him through the puckerbrush as if she had a ring through his nose. Making small sounds that drew him on into the darkness, deeper into places where vines tangled around his ankles and he felt the passing caress of phantom reptiles.

Silence for a while. Stillness.

Then, when he had just about decided it was all in his head, that he hadn't sensed her moving there, a twig snapped.

Yes.

He could hear her breathing. Rapid and frightened. The bitch was hyperventilating! A startled movement—more twigs snapping. He followed, trusting his ears, his instincts, the talent that had made him a supreme prowler of the dark, a shadow among shadows.

There. He sensed the shape of her. The *heat* of her.

He aimed, fired.

A crash, a cry of pain, and now he could *see* movement, not just feel it, and he fired again and again.

She fell at his feet, spraying blood.

Luto dropped to the ground and reached out and discovered that he had killed a small deer. A white-tailed fawn. This made him so angry, so bitterly disappointed, that he stabbed the dead fawn with his home-made knife. Stabbed until his arm grew tired, until he was empty again.

He had come close enough for her to smell his hot anger, and then he had turned away.

A minute or so passed.

He shouted that word again—*rubia*—and she knew he really was headed away from her hiding place and not lingering near, trying to trick her into making a move.

She waited until he shouted again—quite distant now, fading— and then resumed her crawl.

Sara was trying to head downhill. Not that the slope to the water was a hill exactly. More like a gradual incline, hard to detect. Her idea was to find the edge of the swamp water and follow it around until she came to the place where they had hidden the airboat.

Wherever *that* was.

She had no idea how to start or drive the boat. Figure that out when she found it. If she found it. Not *if*, she decided, scudding along on her knees, trying to gauge the slope with her hands, but *when*. Had to be when. Had to find the boat and get away and find help and come back and get Lee before . . . she could not bear to think of what came after the before part.

The neurotoxin.

Don't think about it. Just crawl. Find water. Keep going.

Her hand slipped into something wet and warm. Mud. Then she realized with a start that she was already up to her elbows in the swamp. Hadn't even felt the first touch of water. God, what was *wrong* with her, were her senses failing? Had she been dreaming as she crawled?

There was a slapping sound, very close, drops splashed into her eyes.

Something large moved in the water.

Sara decided that she wasn't going to be frightened of the goddamn alligators. She had given all her fear to Luto. Fear was all used up on the human factor, there was nothing left for gators or snakes or the numerous, nameless slithering things.

Until it grabbed her.

Then she was afraid.

Claws dragging her down into the water and hot breath in her face and a hissing.

Not claws, she realized, fighting to hold back, to cling to the bank, but *hands*. Not a hissing, but a human *Sshhhhhh!*

More hot breath in her face and a barely audible voice:

". . . quiet . . . must be quiet."

Sam!

She collapsed into his arms. He groaned in pain, and then *she* was holding *him*. He was slimy with mud and swamp, slippery with eel grass, bleeding from a bullet wound that had torn apart his pant leg at the knee.

". . . can't . . . walk."

Sara discovered that she could see, just a little. Patch of open sky here at the water's edge, and faint, misty stars. The wound gaped; shattered fragments of bone poked through the flesh. Sam had to be in agony.

". . . boat," he muttered. ". . . get to boat."

"Yes, yes," she whispered. "Get to the boat. Which way do we go?"

It was no good trying to carry him, he was too heavy for her to manage. The only option was to drag him backward through the knee-deep water, moving quickly so that her feet didn't get trapped in the muck. Sam helped some—he had surprising strength in his upper torso and arms. An indication that the old man hadn't lost a dangerous quantity of blood. Yet.

Don't let him die on me, she told herself, struggling to maneuver Sam without increasing his agony. She slogged backward in the black shallows, eyes stinging with sweat, moving to a very simple mantra:

Don't let him die don't let him die don't let him die

She meant Lee.

CHAPTER THREE

This is like that terrifying moment before sleep when you drop into free-fall, except that no matter how hard you try, you can't startle yourself awake.

You keep on falling.

And your eyes are open. You see a lantern, the shapes it makes on the concrete ceiling, the ruffled edge of a green curtain. You see him, *the terrible* him. *You are aware of his probing touch, of the needle he has milked into your veins.*

You keep on falling. It gets worse.

The newest unit had broken out in a cold sweat. Vidoc patted him with a sponge, neatening up. Housekeeping.

"No," he said, waggling his index finger where the unit could see him, "you're not dreaming. And yes, you *are* paralyzed. Specifically, the electrochemistry of the nerve ganglia has been disrupted by the presence of alkaloid toxins. Result: You are conscious but incapable of exerting will. It must be *very* frustrating."

Vidoc put away the sponge and rinsed his hands in a disinfectant soap solution. In the first stage the neurotoxin produced a peculiar form of perspiration, more like machine oil than sweat. The body fighting the poison. Soon the body would give up the fight, metabolism would drop, and the unit would start to undergo personality disintegration. That's when the method got really interesting, because there were so many different ways to unravel the ego.

This particular unit had fascinating possibilities. He

was . . . different from the others. The volunteers from the old combat-stress clinic had all been prone to episodic violence long before the neurotoxin took them into psychosis. And the recent peasant volunteers, well, they were somewhat limited, prey to native superstitions and therefore rather easily terrified out of their wits.

This one, a career policeman with no documented psychiatric problems, was a new type, a real challenge.

First rule: Find a weakness and exploit it.

"The colonel tells me you have an interest in computers," Vidoc said. "Is that true? Blink if it's true."

Lee blinked.

"See what I mean about no control? You didn't want to blink, you absolutely refused to give me the satisfaction, but your involuntary nervous system responded. You've been cut out of the circuit. You are an intruder in this organism. A bit of jellied software up there in the skull. All we have to do, to make this unit functional, is erase the 'you' part. Shut off the power for an instant, and 'you' will cease to exist. All I have to do," Vidoc said softly, leaning down so that the great moon of his face filled Lee's area of vision, "is press this button."

He placed his thumb on Lee's forehead and pressed.

"Click, good-bye." He made a laughing sound. "Just kidding. No button. I *could* do a quick lobo—all you need is a bit of wire and a soft touch, you can go in right through the eye socket, not even damage the eye itself. The perfect prefrontal lobotomy is stirred, not shaken, by the way. But even the wire method is primitive. The right mix of psychotropic drugs will give the same result. Neat, clean . . . and you can dance to it."

He moved away, out of the unit's field of vision. Let him think about it for a while. Meantime, there were promises to keep.

When the colonel suggested that Bunny have his cut-up feet attended to by the doctor, Bunny had said, "Hey, Colonel? Thanks but no thanks."

He'd seen enough of the doc, skittering around in that creepy bunker like a spider in a concrete web. Looking for "volunteers," which is apparently how you went into his clinic, under your own power. Funny how they never left that way, though.

Whatever that hairless geek had going in there, Bunny figured he would keep clear. This was not playing out like a normal-type drug deal. Not that the greaser element ever did anything in a normal way. Take the Lute, charging back into the swamp with his head all twisted, like a junkie who needed a fix, didn't care *what* he had to do, he wanted that girl in a bad way.

Dude goes nuts like that, time to pull the ripcord, find a safe place to land. Bunny figured the best thing, check out the area, take an inventory. Had to be something of value here, even if the colonel didn't leave a lot of cash just lying around.

He limped across the airfield to the Lute's muscle car, found a not-too-dirty cotton shirt in the backseat, and tore it into strips. Wrapped the strips around his feet and eased them into the oversized combat boots he'd lifted from the barracks.

Get back to Miami, first thing he'd do, get a pair of Tony Lama snakeskin boots. Well, maybe not Miami. All things considered, it might be better to move up the coast, check out the Lauderdale scene. Kids on the beach so dumb they'd believe any damn thing you told 'em. Excuse me? I'm scouting for the wet T-shirt syndicate, if you'll just step this way, miss.

Girls nobody would miss for days, weeks. What did it matter if you didn't get exactly the one you wanted?

Bunny opened the trunk, helped himself to another Beretta. Fuck those Chink assault weapons. Too heavy, too much kick, too much like work. He stuffed a couple of extra clips in his pants pocket and hitched up the waist of his jeans.

When he heard gunshots in the distance, Bunny cocked an ear and thought, Hey, Lute? It was nice knowing you, pal.

The bunker. All but one of the cots was empty now, the units delivered to a hiding place along the trail, ready for activation.

Vidoc's outfit for the war game consisted of camouflage gear, a combat helmet, infrared goggles. This was a night, he reasoned, that begged for blending in.

"I've really enjoyed talking to you," he said to the last remaining unit. "I'm a little pressed for time, or we'd be acid-blurring your fingertips right about now."

He paused, adjusting the chin strap on the helmet.

"The colonel tells me you were a fingerprint expert, so I'm

sure you'll find the procedure interesting when we *do* get around to it."

Vidoc searched through his field kit, locating a black nylon shaving kit. Inside the shaving kit was an army-issue Colt .45 automatic.

He emptied the magazine, shaved a little lead from each of the bullets with a scalpel, carved a neat "X" into each blunted slug.

"Of course, you can buy factory-made expand-on-impact slugs right in Miami," he said, glancing at the inert unit. "I prefer the personal touch."

He loaded the magazine, approached the cot. He pried open the unit's mouth. "You'll find the gag reflex greatly muted," he said, using the .45 like a tongue depressor. Making sure the throat passage was clear. It would be a shame to lose a unit to simple congestion. "You're thinking this old forty-five is an antique, but for me it has sentimental value."

Vidoc removed the weapon from the unit's mouth and carefully wiped it with a sterile rag. He checked the time, decided he had a few more minutes. This was a very special evening; he wanted to indulge himself. The unit made a convenient, mute witness.

"You'd never guess how this all started," he said. "I happened to glance at an old *Reader's Digest* article about the origins of the Colt model Nineteen-eleven. Old Faithful, they called it. Did you know the forty-five-caliber automatic first came into wide use in the Philippines? They had this problem with stressed-out natives. Your suicidal native would sometimes grab a machete and hack away in a frenzy until somebody managed to kill him. Old Filipino tradition. A truly berserk male can continue to kill when riddled with small-caliber bullets. So if you wanted to drop those hackers in one shot, you needed the big forty-five, blow his head off or sever his spine."

He clipped a lanyard to the handle of the .45, partially zipped the shaving kit neatly around the weapon, and looped the lanyard around his neck. Better than a holster. No need to draw. Simply grab and squeeze.

"Amazing what a source of inspiration *Reader's Digest* can be, huh? I read about the Philippine berserkers and I thought, This could be useful. Find a convenient way to induce psychotic rage and *voilà*, you have invented the disposable guerrilla. New solution to an old problem. Of course, years of research were required to develop a viable method. So the VA gets some credit for funding my clinic—dim little normals, they had no idea I was perfecting ways to stimulate violence, not cure it. Then there was the problem of marketing the product—the colonel was a big help there. It's all worked out very neatly."

Vidoc paused. It was so unlike him to acknowledge the help of others. Was this being sentimental? Or was sentimental the one that involved the tender shedding of tears? Mimicking the more subtle emotional displays was so distracting that mostly he didn't bother anymore. What a relief it would be when he could drop all the masks, be his terrifying self.

"I do have one regret, though. Wouldn't it be a hoot if *Reader's Digest* printed an 'Our Men at Arms' anecdote about the Vidoc Method? Wouldn't that be . . . perfect?"

Before leaving, he blew out the lantern. It was so much nicer in the dark.

In the barracks the drill sergeant Hernandez took a last look at the assembled recruits. After the long days of drilling and training they had become, not a veteran fighting unit, exactly, but a platoon of eager young men with the potential to evolve into effective guerrillas. They had seen two of their own number die violently and discovered the secret thrill of having survived. They were ready for blooding.

It would be, Hernandez thought with a twinge of regret, a very thorough blooding.

"At my signal you will move out and take your positions. Remember that we are simulating a night patrol. Keep formation. Be vigilant."

He ordered them to attention, had them call off names as he consulted his checklist. When the last announced himself, Hernandez frowned and went back over the list.

"Jorge! Count off!"

Silence. Hernandez walked down the line, looking for the missing recruit. Not present. Had Jorge deserted out of grief for his little brother? But where would he go? Had he any idea how vast this swamp was, how dangerous at night?

"I said attention!"

The fidgeting ceased. Hernandez glanced at his watch. No time to mount a search for the deserter.

"Move out!"

The recruits filed from the lighted barracks one by one and were instantly eclipsed by the night, like paratroopers stepping through an airplane door.

CHAPTER FOUR

In the first semester of the first year of medical school, all students were required to dissect a cadaver. More than a few students fled the cloying stench of the formaldehyde or balked at flaying the flesh from the bones. Sara bore it stoically, as something she had to get through, but she had known even then that her interest was in the science of medicine, not the wielding of scalpels.

All her training was in the detection and prevention of disease. Not patching up gunshot victims. But if she didn't do something to help Sam Darter, he was going to drift into shock.

At the airboat he'd had enough strength to haul himself over the side and then had passed out, briefly, when his knee came in contact with the seat. She had almost convinced herself that the wound wasn't that bad, that with no major blood vessels damaged the old man could function on some level. Now it was obvious that the least bump would send him off. No way he could tolerate a boat ride in that condition, or be clearheaded enough to guide her.

When he revived, she said, "I'm going to the lean-to. Get a flashlight, and some clean water, see if we can fix you up."

His hand gripped her arm. "Deer rifle," he said. "Bring it."

"I think you dropped that rifle, Sam. Way back there."

His head shook. "'Nother rifle," he reminded her. "In the lean-to. Go quick."

She was surprised at her own endurance. Dragging the old man had required all of her strength, and yet she did not feel exhausted or weak. Her mind was focused on a single goal: getting Lee out of the camp. Everything else was simply a task to be accomplished along the way.

She did not allow herself to consider the possibility that he might, like Kurt, be beyond saving, that he might already be dead. Or worse than dead.

Keep moving. Keep doing. A phrase came to mind, an echo of her Don't-let-him-die mantra: *Keep the faith, baby.* Well, she would keep the faith. She would keep on moving and doing, whatever it took.

After hours of being keenly attuned to the subtle nuances of the darkness, her night vision had improved. She found her way through the dense hardwood hammock, located the little palm-frond shelter Sam had built there. Inside, on her hands and knees, she scrambled around, locating the Primus stove, the water can, the ammunition locker. Flashlight, where was the damn flashlight?

Her hands closed on a cool metal cylinder. Found the switch. Clicked it on. And saw a spider as big as her fist squatting on the ammo locker. Thick furry legs.

Six hours ago she would have screamed her head off. Now she calmly pushed the spider off the ammo locker with the butt end of the flashlight. The hell with furry bugs, where was the rifle?

She found it wrapped in a piece of canvas, stowed under a palm frond. Get moving, Sara, she thought, gathering up the deer rifle. She almost tripped over the locker box and remembered that yes, a weapon is useless without ammunition.

Opening the locker, she discovered, along with boxes of cartridges, a first-aid kit. And not just any home-safety kit, but a U.S. Army Field Medic's Kit, complete with antibiotics and pain-killers. This was a major find, and it gladdened her heart.

Sam would have his weapon; she would have hers.

Laden with the rifle, medical kit, flashlight, water, and as many boxes of cartridges as she could stuff in her pockets, Sara threaded her way through the hardwoods to the open area of wet saw grass. The night sky had become overcast; horizon and sky were a blurred shadow. The blades of tall grass seemed to glow, faintly phosphorescent. Was that exhaustion, her eyes playing tricks, or another indication that the swamp was alive, an entity unto itself?

In the cypress, sitting up in the concealed boat, Sam seemed more alert. He took the rifle and cartridges eagerly.

"Get me up on this seat," he said. "I can still heft the pole."

She cracked open the medic's kit. "First we're going to patch you up."

"No time."

"Sam, please listen to the doctor. If you won't let me clean out that wound, you could go into septic shock. I want you clearheaded enough to either drive this boat or tell me how. Get me to the nearest telephone, that's all I ask."

She cupped the flashlight, letting a little of the light spill into his face. His skin tone was sallow, and his eyes were deep in their sockets. Every year showed, and a few more he'd picked up in the last few hours.

"Go ahead," he said.

He lay back on the seat while she cut away a patch of his trousers, using shears from the medic's kit. When she doused the wound with clean water, he groaned once, and from then on, through the entire procedure, emitted not a sound.

Holding the flashlight in her teeth, Sara probed the entrance wound, removing bone slivers from the muscle tissue. The femur was fractured but not shattered. The slug had entered just above the knee, exiting through the sinewy muscles of the upper thigh. Sara discovered, to her horror, a grapefruit-sized chunk of fatty tissue missing there, as if gouged away by a steel claw. No wonder Sam had passed out. There was no way to close the wound. The best she could do was clean it with antiseptic fluid, then wind on a tight elastic bandage that kept the knee immobile.

"Take these," she instructed, handing him an antibiotic capsule and a Percodan. He didn't want to take the Percodan. She insisted. "There's more chance you'll pass out from the pain than from the painkiller."

He swallowed the pill.

"Okay, hand me up the pole."

"I'll pole," Sara said, hefting the long fiberglass pole. "You guide."

CHAPTER FIVE

Crack! and the faint belly-rumble of distant thunder. Ooo-ee, a storm moving in from the west.

Bunny knew all about the violent electrical displays in the Big Cypress. Lightning that would eat you alive. Rain squalls that sucked all the air from the sky. You wanted to be inside when it happened.

As a child, he remembered, inside was almost as bad as outside, the way the roof leaked and the water came flooding over the dirt floors. Most folks call it thunder and lightning; in the Burkus household the phenomenon was a mud storm. Fall out of the crowded bed and splat! you woke up with a mouthful of wet dirt. Complain about it and whoever was playing Daddy that night would grab the back of your little neck and smear your face into the stuff:

Eat a peck afore you dies, har har.

Gramma liked a man with a sense of humor. You had to laugh through the tears, that's what Gramma liked to say. Before the stairs interfered. After that she quit talking, got very, very quiet.

Bunny checking out the transportation. The Lute's car was a piece of shit. There was the Winnebago, but oh boy, what a pain to drive. No acceleration if a situation developed. The fancy limo would attract too much attention. Best bet was the Cadillac, fit right into the Lauderdale scene he had in mind. Bunny was checking under the seats for a spare set of keys when Luto returned.

"How the *pee-hez, amigo?*"

Bunny bumped his head backing out of the Caddy.

"*Pee-hez?* What the fuck are you saying, Lute?"

That bump on his head made him cross.

"Feet," Luto said, pointing. "Your feet okay now?"

Checking out the Lute in the light spilling from the Cadillac. He was covered with blood. The little dude had blood on his *ears*, that's how spattered he was.

"Hey, Lute? You have a date with your girlfriend or what?"

"No man, this a *ciervo*."

"*Oh-hair-bo*, huh? What the fuck is that, Lute?"

Luto had to think. He didn't have the word for *deer*.

"Same as Bambi," he said finally.

"You aced Bambi, huh? So I guess you didn't get the girl."

Luto spat. "She out there, man."

"Know what, Lute honey? You're out there, too."

The little dude was puzzled. "No, man, I come back."

"Have it your way." Bunny eased the door closed. The light went off. "Where's the colonel keep his keys?" he said. "I'll bet he keeps 'em in his pocket, right?"

Luto looked at the Caddy, then at Bunny, and made the connection.

"You gone steal this?"

"If I can find the keys. I don't do that hot-wire shit. The way you have to crawl under the dash? You can throw your back out. This guy I met up in Raiford, professional car thief, he had to have a disc removed. That's a thing in your spine like a Lifesaver."

Luto couldn't believe it.

"This the colonel's car, man. You can't steal this car."

"Oh?"

The way he said it, just Oh?, should have warned Luto. But he was still pumped up with the chase and the deer kill and the terrible frustration of not getting what he wanted, and he wasn't being careful with Bunny.

"Lute honey? I want to show you something. You're gonna love it."

Luto followed him to the Trans-Am, eager to have Bunny distracted from the very bad idea of stealing one of the colonel's motor vehicles.

Bunny popped the lid on the Trans-Am trunk.

"Take a look, man."

Luto looked into the dark trunk. What was in there? Didn't seem to be nothing new, just the cache of weapons.

Bunny shot him in the back of the head, *ping ping*, twice, and shoved the body inside. He closed the lid and said, "Hey Lute? It was fun."

A problem solved. Next up, the keys. And maybe find an umbrella.

Jorge tripped over the sleeper.

Earlier he had been watching from behind a cover of dense palmettos when the Anglo doctor emerged from the bunker with a man-sized sack over his shoulders, carried like a yoke.

The doctor was very strong, but the way he moved, taking care to keep himself in balance, Jorge knew the sack was quite heavy.

The doctor had marched off along the trail, in the direction of the fire tower. Jorge stayed where he was. Though armed, he was afraid of shooting the doctor. What if he did not die? It seemed a distinct possibility.

And Jorge was curious about the sacks.

He had watched as Vidoc made six trips, each time with a sack balanced on his shoulders, his long, powerful legs splayed for balance. Jorge realized soon enough that each sack contained a body. Was El Tigre disposing of men he had killed?

When the doctor returned to the bunker and did not emerge, Jorge moved off along the trail to the fire tower. That's when he tripped over the sleeper. The doctor had artfully camouflaged the body with palmetto fronds.

There were, Jorge soon discovered, five other bodies similarly hidden at intervals along the trail.

Using a Bic lighter for illumination, he recognized the recruits who, like Nando, had been assigned to the volunteer patrol, a great honor. He recognized also that the recruits were not exactly dead. Their eyes responded to the cigarette lighter. Shallow breath warmed his hand as he cupped it over their mouths.

Dead but not dead. Like Nando on the stretcher. This was very strange. Even more strange was the fact that each had an AK-47 taped to his hands.

It began to rain. The coolness cleared a small corner of his mind. He selected the smallest of the sleepers, a boy no bigger than Nando, and hoisted the body onto his back.

Jorge had no plan, no purpose, no particular destination. His need to avenge the death of his little brother was formless. Shooting the great Colonel Calavera would not be enough. The colonel had to be made to understand the depths of his betrayal before he died. He had to suffer, as Nando had undoubtedly suffered.

Jorge trudged through the dripping palmettos until he emerged at the airfield. Kerosene lanterns still glowed in the barracks, although he could see the place was empty. So they were gone, off on their great mission.

His eyes, blurred by the pouring rain, took in the drill sergeant's Winnebago and the Airstream trailer.

He gravitated to the Airstream. This was where the colonel lived, where he had entertained the guerrilla commanders. A big silver box. Grander than anything Jorge had ever seen in his village, more luxurious by far than the fetid motel room where he and Nando stayed when they first arrived in the great nation of Miami.

Jorge placed his burden gently on the steps of the trailer. Dead but not dead, a ghastly reminder of what had been done to his brother. He tried the door.

Locked.

Each recruit had been issued a knife. Jorge used his to force the lock. Inside, the sheer air-conditioned *dryness* was a shock. There were muted cove lights on, illuminating glistening Formica surfaces. A closely woven carpet underfoot, softer than the jungle floor. A strong sense, to Jorge, of extravagant, taunting luxury.

He hauled the sleeper up the steps and inside, propping him against a wall. A puddle formed under the inert body. Dark eyes staring straight ahead, face devoid of expression.

Dead but not dead.

"Colonel?" he said, gripping the knife. "Come out and see."

He crept the length of the trailer, as if drawn forward by the knife. The knife was his compass, it led to the heart of betrayal. Jorge's wet boots made a squishy noise on the carpet. He followed the knife through the dinette area, where the bottles of liquor were doubled by elegant reflections in the highly polished counter. Through the railway kitchen, with its complexity of plumbing and cabinets, each glistening knob a mystery.

Did the colonel own so much that he needed all of this to contain his wealth? It was unfathomable, more than the mind could contain.

Jorge pushed open the door to the toilet stall and saw himself in the mirror. The knife seemed to grow out of his fingertips. He looked away—there was something forbidden and sinful about a mirror.

The bedroom door slid into a pocket in the wall. It took him a while to figure that out. By then he knew the colonel was not inside, although the cool, starched smell of him lingered on the elevated, satin-covered mattress that filled the room. Each wall was a mirror, creating an illusion of vastness that made Jorge feel that the air was being drawn out of his lungs.

Before leaving, he carried the sleeper into the bedroom and placed him gently on the great mattress. A kind of throne, he thought. And now there was an infinity of boys who were dead but not dead, uncountable eyes that stared straight ahead.

A gift for the colonel.

CHAPTER SIX

The morphine-based painkiller did funny things to Sam's hearing. Everything was either strangely muted or made more acute, as if misfocused. Night birds, all of which he could normally identify by call alone, blurred into a background static of chirping. The distant thunder sounded phony, more like a sheet of tin than the real thing. The fiberglass push pole, as handled by the young woman, had a new sound altogether, more brittle and ringing than when he used it.

Strangest of all was the bullet wound in his leg. It sang to him. The pain had been converted to an expression of sound. Was this the Percodan or a trick of his own mind, a means of diverting away the unbearable? The singing was very unpleasant—a grating, sawing kind of noise, nagging at him like an old woman at a tribal dance. But he could stand it, and the singing of the pain left him clear-eyed.

Yes, his eyes were fine. He could see the subtle change in the air that signaled the oncoming rain. And when the sky opened and the inundation began, he was able to discern the shape of the camp in the blurry distance, and tell Sara which way to pole.

"There!" He pointed. "There!"

Behind him, perched on the higher seat in front of the prop cage, Sara coughed and sputtered. The sudden downpour had caught her by surprise. She struggled to keep a grip on the slippery pole.

Remarkable endurance for a white woman, he thought. Earlier he had discussed the options with her: whether to crank up the noisy airboat engine and make a ten-mile run south, hoping to intersect with the highway, or pole the boat directly to the camp in relative silence, under cover of darkness.

The nearest telephone, Sam had reminded her, was at the camp. He had noted the cellular antennas on the gold Cadillac and the limousine the first time he reconnoitered the place, and knew a man so important as the colonel would never be far from a telephone.

"If you can sneak up on the car, I'll cover you," he offered. "You make the call, then I'll crank up the airboat and we'll fly out of here."

He had no intention of leaving the camp without recovering Lee Valdez, alive or dead, but he wanted Sara to have the option. She might not be able to pilot the airboat all the way to the Tamiami Trail, but he was reasonably sure she could get far enough away to be out of rifle range, at least until daylight. By which time the Collier County sheriffs would be sniffing around. Assuming, of course, that Sara got through on the cellular phone.

If not, he had another diversion in mind that involved conserving gasoline now and using it later, all at once.

And so they poled through the cascading rain, a crippled old man and a young woman who had never fired a gun, each with the same secret determination.

"Is it far?" Sara asked, not for the first time.

"Almost there," he said, the deer rifle slick and ready in his gnarled hands.

The boat had nearly flooded with the downpour. They had both bailed, Sara with a fury that surprised herself more than it did Sam, who was no longer surprised by anything she did. Drag him through the swamp, patch him up, pole the boat—she would have made a fine Seminole, he thought, even though she had the yellow hair that was supposed to be a sign of treachery. His people had no legends about the white gods—they had been chased south into the river of grass by an army of blond butchers who were anything but godlike.

Sam's people, though nearly exterminated, had never formally surrendered, had never signed the bundle of lies the white devils called a treaty. He was thinking about that, how purely stubborn he was, when the boat jolted, almost made him pass out.

They had come ashore behind a clump of pines, not far from the airfield.

"Sam!" Sara whispered urgently. "Are you okay?"

He took a deep breath, nodded. The rain was starting to lessen. The thunder was now very distant, moving off to the east.

"I need to get up a ways."

Sara locked her hands around his chest, dragged him out of the boat and through the clump of pines. Once or twice the pain fogged his mind, but he never relinquished his grip on the deer rifle.

"Here," he finally said.

She helped him brace up against a tree trunk.

"I can't see the car!" she said in a sudden panic.

"It's there," Sam said. "See, to the right of the camper?"

Sara squinted, made out the boxy shape of the camper, a silhouette against the light from the barracks building. And yes, there, blending into the background, was the long, squat shape of the Cadillac.

"Promise me you come back right after," Sam said in a warning tone. He was sighting the rifle, picking out targets in the dark.

Sara nodded, ran into the darkness. A few moments later she returned.

"Sam, where is this place? How do I tell them how to get here?"

He thought about it. "Tell 'em the old airfield in the Devil's Garden," he said. "There's only the one. And be sure to tell 'em Lee is a cop. That should help. Them sheriffs'll move fast to help a cop."

"Should I mention your name?"

He laughed.

"Why not? Maybe they'll come out here to arrest me."

Sara crouched by the silver Airstream, waiting as the rain lessened. She needed to see. The barracks building appeared to be deserted, just rows of empty cots and a few forlorn piles of soiled clothing. Torn mosquito netting, soaked with the rain, fluttered down the eaves of the tin roof.

She'd been concentrating on the idea of finding Lee inside the barracks. But the place was empty. Where had all the young soldiers gone? Had they taken Lee with them to some other place even deeper into the swamp?

Pay attention, girl. You're here to make a phone call, remember?

First things first. She crept along beside the trailer, aware that the rain had almost stopped. Made it easier for her to see and also to *be* seen.

Careful now.

She edged around the back corner of the trailer. There it was, looking polished by the rain, no more than a hundred feet away. The gold-colored Cadillac, picking up a glow from the barrack lanterns. No doubt it would be locked.

She felt around on the wet ground, searching for a rock, something hard, anything, and found a chock propped under the rear wheel of the Airstream. She tugged hard at the cord, yanked it free.

Perfect. Do it now, quit stalling. The old man has you covered, or thinks he does.

Sara ran in a crouch to the big car, tried the door handle. It opened. Beautiful! But now the interior light was on. Damn! She dived into the front seat, hooked the door shut with her foot, and sighed as the light went out.

Getting spooked. There was nobody there to see the light blink on and off. Nobody but Sam, who would know she had made it this far.

Bunny taking his ease in the Airstream. The roof drummed with the rain, but it was nice and dry, and the colonel was thoughtful about keeping beer in the cooler. Had left the door unlocked, too. Neighborly man, the colonel.

First thing, he'd eased off the boots, rewrapped the bandages around his cut-up feet. Beretta right there at hand.

Bunny lay back on a little built-in divan within easy reach of the bar. Very comfy. It was tempting to snooze off, just let events unfold around him. Check out all the plush installments in the trailer later, when his feet had stopped throbbing. Save his strength. The colonel had to return eventually, no doubt leading the troops, hut two, and when that happened, Bunny intended to take him aside, borrow the keys.

Put the colonel in with Luto, that might work.

'Scuse me, Colonel, you better scope this out. See what your boy been hidin' in his Trans-Am? Go ahead, check under that blanket. Ping ping. *Hey, Colonel? It was fun.*

He no longer cared what kind of scam Dr. Geek was running. Some military thing, not dope or money laundering, therefore no cash opportunity. All he wanted now, transportation. The Trans-Am was shot; bad shocks and a busted muffler, it was low on gas, and the big negative, it was the kind of vehicle that cops liked to pull over on sight. Got to go with the Mister Businessman sedan, the big Caddy, perfect for blending in.

He ran options in his head.

'Scuze me, Colonel, you mind if I run out for a pack of butts? And, oh, can I borrow the car?

The nonviolent approach rarely worked. Go with the trunk option.

Bunny closed his eyes and was at the point of nodding off when the Airstream shifted slightly. He froze. At the back, somebody fucking around the rear end.

He rolled over on the divan, lifted the shade with his pinky, and felt a big, wide Bunny Burkus grin splitting his face.

Luto's bitch. Had to be. Shortage of rain-drenched blondes in this part of the world. There she was, making her move. Ooh, look at her sprint across open ground for the Caddy. Come back to find her boyfriend. Did she think he was in the car or what?

Too late for Mr. Boyfriend, sweetie. Not too late for Mr. Bunny.

He sat up, eased his feet back into the wet boots.

Outside the rain had decided to stop. Nice new feel to the air. You could still smell the swamp, but it smelled good, familiar. Kind of a wet, grassy odor.

Bunny felt right at home.

It was important to get close up on her. He wasn't fit for a chase. It turned out to be no problem. She was hunched over, just the top of her head showing. Seemed very occupied, as if she *had* found her boyfriend in there after all.

He limped over, yanked the door open. She looked up, saw the Beretta, and froze.

"Hi, sugar, I doan believe we met."

The cellular phone in her hand was making questioning noises. Bunny hung it up. First things first.

CHAPTER SEVEN

The guerrilla commanders were waiting in the fire tower. Colonel Calavera had supplied coffee, sweet pastries, and the necessary infrared gear. Communication with Sergeant Hernandez was via walkie-talkie.

"More rain coming," the senior commander observed as sheet lightning lighted up along the flat horizon.

"That's good," the colonel said.

"Why good?"

The colonel wiped his lips with a paper napkin and made a mental note not to eat any more pastries. The sugar made his teeth hurt. "What happens during the rainy season, eh? The troops bog down. Half run away and return to their villages. Same with the opposition troops. For three months the conflict is in limbo. Much valuable time is lost, and then when the rainy season ends, you're right back where you started, no ground gained."

"How will this be different? Can your doctor stop the rain?"

The Bolivians chuckled. Was this weather talk a joke?

"No, not stop the rain," he said. "But these units, the bad weather will not affect their determination to kill. They will not complain about mud or mosquitoes, and they will not run away. What they *will* do is alter the rules of engagement in your favor. From now on the war need not be seasonal."

The guerrillas nodded thoughtfully; maybe he had a point.

The colonel smiled to himself. This was pure extemporaneous salesmanship—he'd never given any thought to the effect of sleeper units on the traditional rainy-season lull.

The nice thing about Vidoc's method, it was so new and

different almost any argument could be made. There were, as yet, no negative reports to contend with.

The tower shuddered. Someone was ascending the ladder. The colonel lifted the trapdoor. At first he did not see the doctor climbing the rungs. Wearing gear that made him blend into the wet night.

Not for the first time the colonel thought that a sales pitch would be a whole lot easier if Emile would just keep out of sight.

"Greetings," said Vidoc, emerging through the opening.

He stood up, towering over the Bolivians. His helmet grazed the framework of the tower roof, exaggerating his height. He turned to the colonel.

"Where's Hernandez?"

"Marching them through a loop. They're at the edge of the swamp now, he'll bring them back to the trail that passes right below us."

"Excellent." Vidoc peered through a nightscope set up on a tripod. "Hey, what a view we've got."

Lightning jumped between clouds, followed several seconds later by the detonation of thunder. The three Bolivians stirred uneasily. There was some discussion about the fact that the tower was higher than any of the trees in the vicinity.

"Not to worry," Vidoc said. "We're grounded."

"What does this mean, 'grounded'?"

Glancing at the nervous, twitching faces, Vidoc smiled.

"Means we're perfectly safe. Every eventuality has been anticipated," he said.

They did not look reassured. Controlled war games were one thing, the force of nature quite a different matter.

"Trust me," Vidoc said.

The rain slowed the platoon to a halt. Hernandez barked orders, urging them to keep moving, but it was no use. They could not see, he could not see, the heavy rain was blinding. Also, he sensed that many of the boys were almost frozen by fear of the lightning. He knew from counting the interval of seconds between flash and explosion that the heart of the storm was some miles away, but they could not be made to understand.

"Keep moving!" he screamed. "This is an order!" His voice was hoarse with shouting. Shouting at the recruits. Shouting into the walkie-talkie to make himself understood in the command post.

Holding the walkie-talkie close to his ear, he heard the colonel burbling in the wet speaker: "Shoot one as an example, Sergeant. Show them what it is to disobey an order."

"Yes, sir!" he answered. But he himself disobeyed. He was not about to shoot one of his own men. Not yet. There would be killing enough when the rain began to abate.

The taste of the gun lingered. Why hadn't Vidoc pulled the trigger? The ultimate cruelty, not to pull that trigger.

Then, for a time wind blew through the bunker, stirring the unseen curtains. Cloth whipping at him like the panicked wings of invisible birds. He wanted to move. He screamed to move.

Nothing.

He was, as Vidoc had said, an intruder in his own body. Locked in the prison of his skull. What was it the doctor had said?—a bit of jellied software . . .

Not even that.

Lee tried to relax that part of him that clung to consciousness. Let me fly away from here, he thought. Let me be erased. Let me cease to exist.

CHAPTER EIGHT

The dark-fright thing was a puzzle. Why did a relative lack of light produce such a strong reaction in the normal psyche? It was irrational. And yet the data were clear, from Shakespeare to Jung: the standard emotional response to darkness was fear. Vidoc knew this from personal experience. Interrogate a prisoner at noon and he would spit in your face. Delay the interrogation until an hour before dawn and the same man would beg to confess.

Emotional response could not be quantified, it simply had to be used. It was no accident that Hernandez was marching the platoon through an unknown area of the swamp at this dismal hour. Superstitious peasant boys would have their nerves nicely frayed by now. Wouldn't take more than a bold raccoon to spook 'em.

The best way to wow his Bolivian guests, Vidoc had decided, was to go for the sound and fury. Do it with theatrical flair. The units, when activated, would produce sheer terror and confusion. Vidoc anticipated seeing as many recruits hit by friendly fire as by sleeper units.

They'd panic, start blasting away at each other in the dark.

He believed the three Bolivians, safe in the observation tower, would be prey to the same irrational fears. The more terrifying the display, the more they would want to control the phenomenon. Which in this case meant agreeing to a contract price. *Owning* the thing that generated fear.

"Rain stopped," the colonel said. Sitting there sipping his coffee, letting Vidoc run the show.

On cue, the walkie-talkie sputtered.

"Coming up to the mark," Hernandez said.

"Roger that," Vidoc replied, and put away the walkie-talkie. He turned, displaying the Radio Shack signal activator with a flourish. "Gentlemen, who wants the honor?"

When no one seemed eager to volunteer, he pressed the button himself. Almost immediately he heard a scream in the distance.

Bunny decided to take her back to the Airstream. Easy to control her in there, and also he didn't want to miss the colonel's return. Who knows, maybe he could trade seconds on the girl for the keys to the Caddy.

Hey, Colonel? Use it or lose it.

"Go slow," he said to the girl. "My feets are sore."

Sara couldn't comprehend his thick swamp drawl. *Go slow* sounded something like "coleslaw," but there was no doubt of his intentions. He had one strong hand firmly knotted into her hair, the other held a gun to her head. He gripped her close enough so that she was aware of a damp, mouselike odor, as if he had just emerged from a nest.

"Your boyfriend is as good as dead," came out *yabofren goodis daid* but she knew what that meant, too.

Sara was aware of Sam Darter propped up in the clump of pines. Couldn't actually see him—the iron grip made her eyes water—it was a matter of *feeling* the watchful presence of the old man. Right now this pudgy monster was so close to her there could be no clear shot. Not in the dark on an overcast night, no matter *how* sharp the Seminole eyes.

She tried tripping. Didn't work. The man who called himself Bunny was onto her, and he was strong enough to keep her upright with just the one hand.

"Try that again, I'll do you here."

That was clear enough. She was beginning to understand the soft-mouth drawl, the way his words blurred together.

He was pushing her toward the Airstream. She knew absolutely that she would not come out of the trailer alive.

Take your shot, Sam.

Sara did the only thing she could think of, she stepped on his feet. Bunny yipped loudly, and she felt the spasm of pain pass through him. His grip tightened, however, and now he was hugging her from behind, the gun jammed under her chin. He lurched her forward, within reach of the trailer door.

A flurry of gunshots in the distance, going off like a string of firecrackers.

That made him pause. Not to worry, just the greaser boys out playing in the swamp. Shooting up whitetail.

Suddenly holes of light appeared in the wall of the trailer. Sara felt the bee sting of metal sparks on her face. She heard Bunny grunt in surprise. The detonation of the gunshots came in the next heartbeat.

Rapid-fire shooting from inside the trailer, stitching fist-sized holes in the aluminum walls. Above the roar of the chattering AK-47 was another, even more terrifying sound.

A screaming she had heard once before, when the berserk sleeper had exploded from the operating table at the medical center.

The firing stopped. There was a pause into which silence dropped, heavy and ominous. Then a loud booming as something exploded against the walls.

Hurling itself in a rage that rocked the trailer. Trying to escape.

Bunny shoved her forward and ran. Released, Sara fell to the ground. She tasted mud and rain and the electric bitterness of fear.

Vidoc went to the tower rail and pitched an infrared parachute flare out into the night. In the chaos of smoke and fire, it was important to maintain visibility. The viewing equipment could only do so much.

"Over there to the left," he said.

Below, one of the activated units had charged the main body of the platoon. Having emptied the assault weapon, the unit hurled itself at fleeing recruits and speared them with the short gun barrel.

"You know," Vidoc said wistfully. "I never thought of bayonets."

A fist thumped against the trapdoor. A man screamed.

"Shoot it!" the Bolivians urged.

All three guerrilla commanders were crouched at the edge of the tower platform, not really paying as close attention to the demonstration as Vidoc would have liked.

Colonel Calavera, recognizing a prearranged signal, lifted the trapdoor. Sergeant Hernandez scrambled up into the tower and lay limp on the deck, gasping.

The sergeant appeared to be weeping.

Probably stress, Vidoc concluded, or exhaustion from running up the ladder. He pitched out another flare. This time the parachute hung up in a cypress branch, providing excellent illumination for the scene below. He had counted five activated units at the start, all blazing away or engaged in physical combat. This was good. He had expected to lose one or two to immediate cardiac failure, an unfortunate risk of the stimulant.

Of the five, one misfired almost immediately. After expending most of a magazine directly into a half-dozen recruits, it turned the weapon around and blew off the top of its own head.

"A dud," Vidoc explained. "You have to expect a few duds."

He was curious to observe that the units did not seem to focus their chemically induced rage on each other—at least not while other targets remained available. Had a bonding of some sort occurred, a mutual darkness? Or did they simply recognize themselves in the frenzied images of the others and shy away from the physical mirror?

A small point, but worth further research.

As the flare began to fizzle, he saw another unit go down, cut in half by a recruit who had, it appeared, played dead until he could rake his assault rifle. Soon enough the recruit was dead for real, seized from behind by a unit who impaled the boy on a broken branch.

Vidoc was checking his watch—a mere seventeen minutes since activation, and near total annihilation of the platoon had resulted— when one of the guerrillas backed hurriedly away from the rail and swore.

"One of those *things* is attacking the tower. *Do* something."

Vidoc leaned out over the rail and looked down. No need for night-vision goggles at this range. A unit had become fixated on the base of the tower and was throwing itself against one of the steel legs. The vibrations were actually discernible on the platform.

Ker-angggggg. The platform seemed to ring with the vibration.

"For God's sake, turn it off!"

Vidoc shook his head, amused.

"That's not how the method works, gentlemen. The unit is like a grenade. We already pulled the pin. What it is doing now, in a sense, is exploding."

Ker-angggggg.

"Make it stop!"

My, what bugged-out eyes, Vidoc thought. The Bolivians were on the verge of panic. Fully briefed on the method, they *must* know that even a fully energized unit was not capable of uprooting an anchored, stressed-steel structure that had withstood numerous tropical storms.

And yet they feared.

Imagine what the ignorant recruits had thought. How civilian peasants would react.

Kerr-angggggggg.

"Emile, enough is enough!"

That was the colonel. He'd spilled coffee all over himself. Vidoc, acknowledging that the clients were now sufficiently convinced, opened the trapdoor.

He palmed the .45 on its handy lanyard and stripped away the nylon cover. The continuing vibration threw his aim off. His first four shots missed. Finally he managed a head shot on the rampaging unit. It went down in a spray of blood and brains.

Behind him the guerrillas applauded weakly.

Sam was not at all sure the Sheriff's Department would send up a chopper at this hour, with thunderstorms in the area. Possibly the Highway Patrol, if alerted, would do so—troopers tended to the big gesture, when given the opportunity.

He had to assume Sara had got through on the cellular phone. Otherwise his gesture was wasted. The ground was too drenched to sustain a major conflagration; the best he could do was put up a signal that might be seen from the air. A beacon to the old airfield if any law-enforcement officers cared to drop in.

From his place in the pines he had a clear shot at the airboat. A damn sight clearer than he'd had of Sara's assailant. He'd been a heartbeat away from risking a shot, sick because missing would mean the end of her, one way or the other, when gunshots and screams seemed to come from all directions at once.

Couldn't trust his ears—maybe he'd been hearing imaginary echoes. His eyes, well, they were still sharp enough. He'd seen the white swamper running away like an ungainly hippo. The last he'd glimpsed of Sara, she was diving under the trailer where the shots had erupted.

Typical of that girl, to head for trouble. Might be alive, might not.

Sam fingered open a box of cartridges and started the business of piercing the fuel tanks. Nearly forty gallons remained. He fired steadily, pausing to reload. Took longer than he expected—damp air keeping the fumes down—but when it lit off with a satisfying *wump!*, the explosion carried partway into the pines, a warm kiss in the face.

He crawled away with the trees snap-crackling behind him and turned to see a huge ball of flame burning hot and white, as bright as noon.

The trailer had ceased rocking. Whatever was inside, it had stopped slamming itself against the walls. Resting or dead—Sara didn't care to find out.

The barrage of wild gunfire in the distance had also stopped. All she could hear now were the intermittent screams of the wounded piercing the air. Then she heard a single gunshot, and there was one less scream.

It happened again.

She stopped counting after that second time and covered her ears. Didn't help, she could still hear those single, deliberate gunshots. Putting them out of their misery or cold-blooded murder, the result was the same. No more screaming.

When the boat exploded, her first thought was that the camp was under artillery attack. Her reaction: good, destroy this godforsaken place. The explosion was like a powerful strobe-flash, illuminating the camp area.

Sara saw him then. A tall wraith, dressed in camouflage.

Dr. Vidoc. Maybe forty yards away, just emerging from a stand of thick palmettos. He had looked up when the flash went off, and his eyes glowed as white as the fire. Now he stood there in the clearing, watching the flames jump. No expression on his face. Sara saw the gun in his hand. Had he been responsible for those deliberate shots that ended the screaming?

There was something about the way he stood there, calmly watching the billowing flames, that made fear uncoil inside her. She knew something of his terrible strength then, in the way he carried himself. But when he turned and sauntered down another trail, she forced herself to get out from under the trailer and follow him.

After Luto and Bunny, how bad could he be?

CHAPTER NINE

The colonel had in mind a very stiff drink. Nothing as flippant as cognac, more like straight whiskey.

Strange, he hadn't given any consideration to the wounded. There was bound to be wounded, but he simply hadn't thought about it. Of course, the doctor was right—you couldn't have survivors blabbing wild stories, not here on U.S. soil. And in any case no provision had been made to treat the wounded. So the simplest solution really was the best. Still.

He made a vow that from now on he would not involve himself so directly with any of Emile Vidoc's projects. Manipulate the money and take his cut, fine, but leave the wet part to somebody else.

Two impressions as he came up to the Airstream: the fire roiling in the pines and the bullet holes in the trailer walls. Was there some connection?

It took only a moment for the anger to seep through his exhaustion. Some son of a bitch had shot up his custom Airstream! Had a recruit escaped and taken his revenge in this childish way?

The colonel pictured his expensive liquor bottles shot to pieces. Now he was *really* pissed. So pissed it didn't really register that the bullet holes were extruded from *inside* the trailer.

The door was off its hinges. It fell away at his touch.

Colonel Calavera stepped into the ruined interior. The destruction was so profound he felt a constriction of anguish in his chest. The bar area was not simply destroyed, it was pulverized. Kitchen cabinets had been torn down and smashed to kindling. Canned goods lay flattened, with contents obscenely spewed. Plumbing fixtures were ripped out, twisted. The blond teak wall-paneling was fractured in dozens of places, as if crushed *outward*. Had some kind of *explosion* taken place in here?

Shell casings were everywhere—the colonel confirmed that the weapon was an AK-47 assault rifle, further evidence that the destruction had been done by a recruit. *A filthy peasant boy*.

The colonel fumed. He could feel the fit of temper making his ears red. He had drawn one of his pearl-handled pistols. If he found the culprit, he intended to carry out a summary execution.

Blow the dirty boy away.

The bedroom door had been smashed through, as if kicked from inside. He had to raise his leg to get over the shards of teak panel without getting stung by the splinters. Every mirror in the bedroom had been shattered. The room now looked small and hopelessly confused, a jumble of mattress stuffing and broken glass. The destruction here was the most severe—the gunfire had done so much damage that portions of the wall were peeled inward, ready to roll up like a sardine can.

Colonel Calavera was standing there with his hands on his holstered hips, his feet wide apart in the rubble, when a bloody hand shot up out of the glass and grabbed him by the *cojones*.

The hand was strong, crushing strong. The colonel's knees buckled. He went down.

Making a *huh-huh-huh-huh* sound because that's all that would come out.

He had the presence of mind to hold the pistol between his open legs and pull the trigger. More glass shattered. He saw a skull under the glass. No, not a skull, a face wearing a mask of blood. A face that was dead but not dead.

The fist squeezed tighter, pain beyond pain, and then tore away the crotch of his uniform pants. His scrotum was inside. As the colonel opened his mouth to scream that he was no longer a man, another hand emerged from the pile of broken glass.

The hand clubbed him down, sought his mouth, and forced itself inside.

Fingers tearing at the softness of his tongue. The fist sinking deeper, into his throat, blocking his lungs. Some small part of his mind knew that it would not take long to suffocate.

Quickly, he thought, quickly.

CHAPTER TEN

Alerted by the Ochopee lookout tower, the Oasis Ranger Station put up a helicopter to confirm a lightning fire in the forty-four quadrant.

Prior to 1989, park policy was to let natural fires burn themselves out. That was before a sizable part of the Everglades went up in flames, polluting four counties with a Los Angeles–type smog. Now the Forest Service tended to take a more careful look, ready to react if the situation warranted intervention. The idea, avoid another repetition of the Great Smoke-out, which adversely affected not only actual wildlife, but the Miami tourist trade as well.

The fire was clearly visible from two thousand feet, range four miles. It looked hotter than your average lightning fire, which typically would smolder for several hours before bursting into flames. The spotter pilot radioed confirmation.

"Seems to be confined to an area adjacent to the old Bay of Pigs airfield. With the water level this high I doubt she'll go far."

Dawn was just now breaking, a thin, blood-orange line that made the horizon look airbrushed. The pilot, veering to circle the affected area, changed his mind about the probable lightning strike.

"Firebird to base," he said. "Source appears to be remains of a small aircraft. A flameout. Dollar says we got us another pot roast."

The backcountry was dotted with the wreckage of planes that had gone down tail-heavy with bales of marijuana. If the wreck flamed out, you had a pot roast.

The ranger-station radio operator was a minute or so getting back to him. "No bet, Firebird. We've just now got action reported in that sector. Monitor Seventy-two and be ready to set down and assist. You're cleared for loaner by the Highway Patrol, if needed."

The pilot switched to the police channel. He'd already spotted several vehicles approaching the airfield at high speed. Sheriff's Department and the Highway Patrol playing bumper tag on an unpaved access road.

My, my, he thought, *can't nobody resist a fire.*

Vidoc in the bunker, packing. He knew it was only a matter of time before some agency or other arrived to investigate the fire. He'd already appeared on one police report, linked with Calavera, and he thought it best not to be on the premises when the colonel presented his explanation. His presence might complicate a cover-up.

Besides it was time to leave, the work was done: From here on it was up to the Bolivians. If they backed off, well, there was always the opposition. Or another war elsewhere.

He added several items to his field kit, including the remainder of the neurotoxin and an assortment of psychotropic elixirs. He secured the field kit in his duffel bag and then began a methodical search of the bunker to make sure that no trace of himself was left behind.

What to do with the unused unit? There was only one prudent option, of course. Shut the damn thing off.

He reloaded the .45, went to the cot, looked down at Lee Valdez.

"Hello in there," he said. "You must be terribly disappointed. You've been expecting an acid burn, and now I have to break my promise. *Adios.*"

Vidoc was lining up a head shot that would keep his boots clear of the spatter when he heard the bunker door creak open. His finger relaxed on the trigger.

A visitor, he thought, how interesting, and slipped behind a curtain.

In the faint light he could just make out the form of the intruder. Female. This was a puzzle until he remembered that the unit had been accompanied by a woman.

She had come for her mate! Remarkable. And what a surprise she was about to get.

Vidoc was curious: What emotional response would this female display? Grief? Rage? Anger? Or would it be . . . yes, if he was a betting man, he would put his money on that old standby *fear*. Only possible response. She had, he now recalled, already interfaced with a mistakenly activated unit, one of his original seven. So upon finding her mate in a similar condition, she could not but recoil in fear.

What a shame there hadn't been time to install a medication pump and radio activator. Then he could *really* surprise her.

Well, he would just have to think of something else.

The deputy found the boy hiding behind a palmetto. Well, not hiding exactly, but on his knees with his head bowed, as if in prayer. No obvious weapons, although he was dressed in camouflage fatigues.

"Come on out of there."

The deputy was in the classic Weaver stance with his wrist braced and weapon leveled. A little thing he picked up on television. County boys didn't much hold with it, they were fire from the hip or, better yet, use the pump shotgun. Old-timers felt it was too easy to miss with that peashooter, you're better off, spray the area.

The boy offered no resistance. Just a kid, and a frightened one at that. The deputy, whose Spanish began and ended with taco, asked to see identification. Forget it, the boy didn't understand, surely *had* no identification, being an obvious illegal, right off the banana boat.

The boy got pretty excited when the deputy, himself less than a month on the job, flashed the Collier County Sheriff badge. Jabbering away and pointing. Getting agitated when the deputy couldn't read his mind, figure out what he wanted to communicate.

Wouldn't do no good to read his mind, the deputy reflected, less he thinks in American, and that is doubtful.

"Okay, jess hang on there, son," the deputy said. He had maybe five years on Jorge and could as easily have raised the *Titanic* as a mustache. "You sayin' there's something over that way?"

The deputy pointed, and Jorge got more excited. Yes, yes, yes, he nodded.

"Okay, we gone take a walk down that path and check her out."

Vigorous shaking of the head. The boy was obviously freaked at the idea of walking down that path. The deputy sighed—crazy kid, it was like trying to guess what a dog wanted, the way he barked and pawed the ground.

"*¡Muerto!*" the boy said, feigning death. "*¡Muerto, muerto!*"

The deputy stared at him, puzzled. Looked at the rolled-up eyes, the slack jaw.

"Well shit, Pablo, are you tellin' me there's a dead man in there and you're afraid to show me? Is that it?"

"*Muerto,*" Jorge insisted.

The deputy got out his hand restraint. Jorge did not resist as he was cuffed to a palmetto tree. He could have ripped free easily enough; that was not the point. The deputy wanted him to stay in one place while he checked out this *muerto* bullshit.

Mist rising out of the swamp. Foliage along the path heavy with last night's rain. The deputy walked sideways, the keys on his belt jingling as he twisted to avoid a drenching from the ferns.

Sniffing as he walked because he'd been told the dead had a distinctive smell. What was it supposed to be, overripe melons?

This was going to be the first dead person he ever encountered in the line of duty, and he wasn't the least afraid. If anything he was curious. Might have been a different feeling altogether if it were dark out. As it was, the slant of morning sunlight put a sparkle in the mist, made the green leaves shine.

He was just coming into the clearing, focusing on the concrete bunker—thinking, jeez, maybe *muerto* means bunker, is *that* what he meant?—when the woman screamed.

It was more than a scream. It was a keening, a shrill resonance of mourning and sorrow that seemed to touch him at the throat, as if he himself were screaming.

He sprinted over the wet ground, fumbling at his holster flap. He wasn't afraid. The message he got from the scream was an unspeakable sadness of grief, not a threat type of scream.

At the door to the bunker he paused with his hand on the grip of the sidearm, leaving it in the holster.

"Ma'am," he called into the bunker. "County Sheriff's Department. Can I help?"

Inside he could hear sobbing.

"Ma'am? What's wrong?"

He shoved the heavy door open enough to slip inside. Dark in here, he couldn't see much. Peculiar musty odor, but not, as he'd anticipated, the stench of rotting melons. He blinked, letting his eyes adjust, and saw a woman kneeling at a cot. Her arms thrown around whoever was on the cot. He could see where she was crying silently now.

"Ma'am?"

Something moved right beside him, a shape that seemed to emerge from the wall.

The startled deputy had a peripheral glimpse of a long arm sheathed in camouflage. Simultaneous was the *pssssst-pssssst* of a nonaerosol spray pump. His hand tightened on the pistol grip, but it was too late.

Wet, cloying mist in his face, and then he was falling as a hand wrenched the keys from his belt.

Bunny on the dirt road. Hobbling along in no particular hurry now that he had decided fuck it, he wasn't going back into the puckerbrush, not ever. For a time he'd ducked off the road and hidden himself each time a vehicle approached. Three, four cruisers raising plumes of dust, wheels slamming over the ruts. Few minutes back, as he lay concealed, an ambulance went by, closely followed by a fire truck. Overhead the whip-whip-whine of a helicopter.

Quite a party going on at the camp. Pin the tail on some other sucker, Bunny was just a guy who'd got lost in the Big Cypress. Look at his poor feet, he'd been walking for hours.

He'd ditched the guns and the spare magazines and scoured his hands with dirt because he knew about the skin test that can prove you've fired a gun recently.

His defense, if some cop rousted him: Give 'im a bad toothy grin, play drunk and stupid. *Who me? I don't know nuffin' bout no greaser shoot-out.* Might work. Somehow he had to distance himself from the contents of the Trans-Am trunk. Cops, dumb as they were, might connect the fact he and the Lute had been cellmates. Or they might not; it was a continuing source of amazement to Bunny, how much he could get away with.

Bunny hobbling as the sun comes up. Turkey buzzards screeching at him from the trees. He stopped to make himself a crutch from a broken branch. The idea, he could use it as a club if necessary. He comforted himself with visions of Fort Lauderdale Beach. Girls dumber than coconuts and a long way from home.

He heard the vehicle coming up from behind but did not turn. From the sound of that big mill, had to be a cruiser. Sheriff heading back to the highway.

Bunny exaggerated the limp. He was ready for a ride, even from a cop.

Sure enough, a deputy's car. Big gold star on the trunk. It halted a few yards ahead. Bunny expected the deputy to get out, give him one of those steely deputy looks, like to bore a hole right through him.

Instead, the passenger door swung open.

Bunny limped up to the cruiser, got inside. Had the door pulled shut before he realized the man under the deputy hat was Dr. Vidoc.

"You should get those feet looked at," the doctor said, accelerating.

"I'm a quick healer," Bunny replied. "Hey, this a nice vehicle, did you hot-wire it or what?"

Vidoc gave him a look.

"Keys are better," he said.

Bunny nodded happily. A man after his own heart. You never knew, this could be the start of a beautiful friendship.

EPILOGUE

"Ere a man hath power to say 'Behold!'
The jaws of darkness do devour it up."
—SHAKESPEARE

CHAPTER ONE

The old man was sitting up in bed, his attention focused on the window, the sky beyond, the world outside.

"All those birds," he said. "How do they live in the city?"

"How are you today, Sam?" Sara said.

His eyes crinkled in a smile.

"Yesterday they say, 'We'll take your leg,' today they say, 'You keep your leg.' So today is better."

His hand reached out, touched her.

"Have you seen him?" he said.

"I'm going there now."

"Don't be fooled by the outside, Sara." He clenched a fist, held it over his heart. "A man lives in here."

In the street below, a truck backfired, and a million redwing blackbirds took flight.

When she entered the dialysis unit, Paul Hobart was waiting. There was something in his expression that made her ask what had gone wrong.

"Two more of the original sleepers expired early this morning, shortly after they were put on the dialysis machine." He jiggled a rack of vials. "Let's hope we're not too late for the others."

"We *can't* be," she said. "Not allowed."

The four surviving sleepers remained in the unit. Other than dialysis to scrub the blood, no intervention had yet been attempted. The example of Dr. Harding's shock therapy was a vivid reminder of what could go wrong.

The extent of nerve damage, whether permanent or reversible, was still being actively debated. How exactly did the neurotoxin block impulses? What precipitated the drop in metabolic functions? Did the toxin itself produce a pathological state, or was that entirely a result of the powerful psychotropic drugs Dr. Vidoc had used to "activate" the sleepers?

If treated, would the sleepers awaken in killing rage, minds still in thrall of the neurotoxin?

Over the next few weeks forensic examination of remains taken from Camp Libertad might yield a few answers. Those sleepers who had survived did not have a few weeks, or even a few days.

Hobie, working from toxicology data and an extensive knowledge of folk medicines, had come up with a "treatment of last resort," a combination of nerve and cerebral stimulants that might, according to the computer model, renew the delicate bond between mind and limb.

"Some of this stuff is based on folklore," he admitted. "Field reports from anthropologists, not physicians. So the line we medical scientists like to draw between psychology and physiology gets pretty blurred."

"What are you saying, Hobie?"

He glanced at the unresponsive forms of the sleepers and sighed.

"I'm saying I just don't know what will happen. My instincts tell me this formulation will help. I've got no hard proof to back it up."

"If it works, you'll have proof."

"Yes," he said, "if."

The last sleeper to be admitted to the unit was Lee Valdez. Although he appeared to be as catatonic as the others, Sara could not bring herself to admit that he was not really there, behind the expressionless mask. Could he really have become so completely . . . *missing* in less than forty-eight hours?

Was his mind so damaged that he would never again know what it was to be human?

"Hobie, could you give me a minute?"

"Of course."

He signaled the nurses, who found business elsewhere in the ward, leaving Sara alone with her patient. The privacy didn't really matter. She was beyond caring what the staff thought of her conduct.

She raised his limp right hand to her lips, kissing the delicate area of his palm.

Could he feel anything? Did he know she was there?

"Darling," she whispered. "In a few minutes we're going to administer an experimental drug. There's a good chance it will help, but part of it is up to you. You have to *want* to come back. You have to want it as much as I do. And I'm going to be right here with you, no matter what happens."

She looked up, nodded to Hobie. Now or never.

Between them they had agreed that the stimulant blend would be diluted into the dextrose drip and then introduced gradually into the bloodstream. No sudden shocks. Using a syringe, Hobie drew 10 cc's from the phial and added it to the drip bag. Sara adjusted the drip feed.

Now all they could do was wait. The staff, she noticed, maintained a discreet distance. There was an armed security guard present who kept eyeing the sleepers suspiciously, as if he expected to have to open fire at any minute.

Hobie took a chair and stared at the floor, rigid with tension. He couldn't bear to watch. What if the stimulant blend failed?

What if it worked too well?

Five minutes went by, then ten. As time passed, Sara ceased glancing at her watch and concentrated on Lee's face. The daunting blankness. As a child, alone in her room, she had sometimes stared at the patterns in the wallpaper until new shapes began to emerge, until the *wanting* to see became almost real. Was this happening now? Was she imagining that a sense of *him* was being slowly infused into the expressionless mask?

Even when his hand reached up and touched her lips, she wasn't sure it was really happening. She didn't know it for real until his eyes turned to her and he spoke her name. That was all he could manage right then. It was enough.

CHAPTER TWO

Thirty thousand feet and not a bump in the sky.

The flight attendant had seen all kinds, so Seven-A wasn't a total surprise. Wearing an obvious toupee and reading a marked-up paperback edition of *A Midsummer Night's Dream*, he was, she assumed, a professor or possibly a theater type. The hairlessness must be from chemotherapy. Destination Buenos Aires, for some medical procedure not available in the States, she decided. Sick like that, hair burned off by drugs, it was no wonder he had such a strange presence, as if each phrase or gesture was long-rehearsed.

She got a bottle of Perrier from the galley, and a glass. No ice, he'd said, he didn't trust the ice. Whatever that meant. She started back, remembering to smile.

"Here we are," she said, presenting the tray.

"Has the cup been sterilized?"

"Yes, sir. They come sealed in plastic."

He prodded the cup with his finger.

"Do you read Shakespeare?" he asked.

"In high school. Was *Hamlet* the one with the witches?"

"*Macbeth*," he said. "Common mistake. I find that Old Bill has very accurate depictions of human emotional response. Tell me how you react to this: 'Ere a man hath power to say, "Behold!" the jaws of darkness do devour it up: So quick bright things come to confusion.'"

The attendant smiled.

"I'll have to think about it."

"Do so," he urged. "And bear in mind that you're a 'quick bright thing.'"

Someone coming up behind her, breathing through his nose. Seven-B, the window seat. Right. Fleshy in a new suit, with bad teeth and violent blue eyes that made her feel like checking to see her blouse was buttoned.

Seven-A said, "This is my associate, Dr. Brigham. He'd like a beer."

Bunny grinned. He'd always wanted to play doctor.